DARING DECEPTION . . .

"Please," she protested, "you don't understand. I am your w—"

Robert's lips cut off her words. Desperate now to free herself, Lili brought up her knee into his stomach.

"So you wish to fight, do you?" Robert asked, his voice strangely triumphant. "Good. There's not much pleasure in taking a limp doll to bed."

His words infuriated her, and when he covered her lips again, she bit him.

"Little vixen," he murmured. "You think to deceive me with those soft limpid brown eyes. But I know you for what you are—a biting wild thing that has never known a man's hand."

His voice was hoarse with desire. "And I shall take great pleasure in taming you this night. . . ."

JASMINE MOON

Frances Patton Statham

A FAWCETT GOLD MEDAL BOOK • NEW YORK

JASMINE MOON

© 1978 Frances Patton Statham

Published by Fawcett Gold Medal Books, a unit of CBS
Publications, the Consumer Publishing Division of CBS Inc.

ISBN 0–449–13988–3

Printed in the United States of America

10   9   8   7   6   5   4   3   2   1

JASMINE MOON

CHAPTER

1

"YOU will either marry Robert Tabor or return to the convent in New Orleans."

Eulalie's face turned 'pale and she moved a step nearer the man who had spoken, her hands held out in a subconscious beseeching.

"There must be . . . some mistake," she said in a quivering voice. "Papa Ravenal would never force me to marry someone I do not even know."

For a moment the man's stern face softened. "I am sorry, but the terms of your stepfather's will are clear."

Then the man assumed his former harshness as he continued in an admonishing tone, "You forget that Robert Tabor was his heir long before he met your mother. Since you are actually no blood relation of his, you should be pleased that he wanted to provide for his stepdaughter, as well."

"And he has not . . . provided for me, if I refuse to marry this man?"

"No, Miss Boisfeulet," the solicitor answered. "If you dare to oppose his last wish, then there is no place for you except the convent. You cannot remain here alone."

The deep-brown velvet eyes of the girl hinted of tears,

but she brushed her hand across her face, as if to deny this unwanted display of emotion.

The solicitor waited impatiently while Eulalie stared out the window of the salon. In the silence, she struggled with the sudden decision thrust upon her.

Outside, the September sun was merciless, projecting its fiery rays upon the recently drenched land. Heat steamed from the saturated earth in visible hot vapors to permeate the seldom-used drawing room of the beautiful old Carolina plantation house.

Unmindful of the vista of stately magnolias before her, Eulalie fleetingly brushed her finger across the stained strip of wood separating the leaded panes of glass. She was conscious only of the heat and the problem that had so suddenly spoiled her day.

Finally she turned and spoke. "And how does Monsieur Tabor feel about marrying someone he has never seen?"

"Robert Tabor is prepared to go through with the wedding. He has already signed the document for the proxy marriage."

"Proxy marriage?" Eulalie repeated. "Do you mean . . . "

"He wishes the marriage to take place as soon as possible. But he plans to stay in Paris for a while longer."

At the surprised look in her eyes, the solicitor hastened to assure her. "Even though there will be a stand-in for him, the marriage ceremony will be legal. All you need do, Miss Boisfeulet, is to sign the document also, and then the ceremony will be arranged, making you mistress of Midgard Plantation."

She could say nothing. Eulalie felt numb, unable to protest. He had said she had a choice, but it was not true. Who would willingly choose to be shut away from the world forever?

Her silence was taken for acquiescence, and the short, stout man led her to the writing table and handed her the quill with which to sign the official-looking parchment.

She watched as if another hand were forming the letters of her name—Eulalie Boisfeulet. When the last letter was written, the solicitor smiled and said, "I believe you have chosen the wiser course, my dear. And now that you have agreed, we can set into action the instructions Robert has given."

The solicitor, impatient to get back to Charleston before the mosquitoes began their late-afternoon bombardment, picked up the parchment and hurried from the room. It was unhealthy for the young girl to remain on the low-country plantation during the malaria season, but Robert had given no instructions for her to be moved into town. He shrugged as he climbed into his phaeton. The business of the proxy marriage would be best disposed of as soon as possible.

Long after the man had gone, Eulalie remained in the salon. She sat, unmoving, in the blue velvet chair and stared at the low needlepoint-cushioned footstool that stood to the right of the hearth—the gift she had worked on so industriously the year before for Papa Ravenal.

How proud she had been when she had finally embroidered her initials and the date on the red-and-blue circular design—E.B. 1808. It had taken many hours, but she had finished it in time for Christmas. And Papa Ravenal had been so pleased with it. But now he would never use it again to ease his gout.

Back and forth she traced the neat stitches with her eyes, until darkness crept into the room and the design became blurred in the shadows—shadows that leaped onto the walls and magnified the massive furniture of the salon.

"Maman, what shall I do?" her frightened voice finally whispered through the room, but the dark silence mocked her words. There was no one to hear, no one to give answer. And it was already too late. She had placed her name on the marriage document beside that of Robert Tabor.

At the head of the stairs she stood, while Feena adjusted the train of her ivory satin Empire wedding gown. Luckily, the heirloom veil of Alençon lace hid the stubborn jut of her chin and the angry flash emanating from her dark brown eyes.

Eulalie's mind whirled in remembered agitation at the words spoken to her on that fatal September afternoon.

And she was no more reconciled now to marrying Robert Tabor than she had been on that first day.

Robert Tabor. She recoiled at his name. A smuggler—a pirate. That's what Papa Ravenal had called him because he had flaunted the Embargo Act, taking the rice and cotton to trade in the forbidden foreign markets. Yet, all the time, Papa was planning for her to marry him. That's what he had meant when he had told her that he had changed his will to provide for her. Eulalie was even grateful at the time for his generosity, but now . . .

"They're waiting for you, mamselle," Feena whispered.

Eulalie looked down at the foot of the stairs, where the solicitor stood in his formal afternoon coat and tight-fitting breeches.

The servant's words prompted Eulalie reluctantly into motion. She started down the steps, and when she had reached the final tread, the man held out his plump hand to claim her.

"My dear, you are lovely. A pity that your bridegroom cannot see you as you are now."

"Merci, monsieur," she murmured, suddenly ashamed of her animosity. After all, it was not the solicitor's fault that the wedding was taking place, nor that Robert Tabor had not felt the marriage of sufficient importance to return in time for it.

On down the hall they walked, until they reached the doors of the salon. Two men, standing near the fireplace banked with magnolia leaves and yellow jasmine, looked up as the girl approached.

The parish priest in his white ecclesiastical robe remained where he was, but the tall, dark-haired stranger took his place beside Eulalie. And the ceremony began.

Not looking at the stranger, Eulalie said her vows in a whisper. The deep voice of the man answered her, usurping the words that Robert Tabor should have been saying. Only when the heavy gold ring was slipped onto her finger did Eulalie look up to catch the fleeting, wistful expression in the man's eyes.

" . . . by the powers invested in me, I now declare that Robert Lyle Tabor and Eulalie Boisfeulet are husband and wife. Whom God hath joined together . . . "

Many miles away from the Carolina plantation, Robert removed the white, graceful arms encircling his neck, and climbed out of bed.

"Why do you have to hurry, *mon cher?*" the woman protested. "Eet is still early."

The man deftly avoided the tapered hands that reached out toward him to draw him back into bed. Shaking his head at the red-haired beauty, he said, "You should not be so greedy, my love. Have I not spent the entire afternoon with you?"

Robert glanced quickly at the clock as he began to dress. Six-thirty. Hector would have been waiting for him for some time. Robert was not happy, remembering his reason for meeting his cousin—to celebrate his proxy marriage. Calculating the exact time at Midgard, Robert realized it was early afternoon and he was already a married man.

"Would you like to be the first to congratulate me, Babette?" he queried, the dryness in his voice unmistakable. "I was married a half-hour ago."

At his announcement, she shuttered the long, dark lashes of her sloe eyes and in an uncertain voice asked, "Theese marriage—eet will change things between us, *non?*"

A wicked grin lit up the man's handsome face, while his tawny eyes traveled insolently over the white, smooth skin that was only partially hidden by the blue silk sheets.

"Not until I decide to return home," he replied.

"And when will that be, Robert?" she purred like a contented cat, opening her eyes wide and stretching.

"When Paris no longer amuses me," he answered, leaning over to kiss her lightly on her lips.

She laughed and put her arms around him, drawing him close to her, but once again he escaped her embrace.

Resigned to his departure, she sighed and lay back on the pillows, to drink in the magnificent view of the man before he was encased in shirt, breeches and coat. His golden hair surrounded his well-shaped brow like a crown, and as she watched the muscular, strong, demanding body, she trembled in remembered ecstasy.

"Tomorrow?" she asked in a questioning tone, when he had finished dressing.

He nodded and, closing the door behind him, disappeared.

For a moment she listened to the vanishing steps, and then she sat up, holding her wrist one way and then the other. Watching the emerald bracelet, its dark green fires glittering under the lights, she smiled.

Robert left the house and stepped out upon the pavement, where a carriage waited. The two black horses pawed nervously and snorted, while the driver struggled to keep them under control.

As Robert climbed into the carriage, the white-haired man seated inside said to him, "You're late."

The young man jovially countered, "Love is not always guided by the clock, Hector." Then his face lost its pleasantness. "Only marriage," he added. "And I suppose by this time I have already been saddled with Uncle Ravenal's scrawny stepdaughter."

Hector frowned at his words and made ready to reply, but the sudden lurch of the carriage stopped the conversation. The horses' hooves struck upon the cobblestones as the carriage swung around the corner of the Rue de la Victoire. Then, righting itself, the vehicle slowed to a reasonable pace and soon came to a stop before the dimly lit café.

"Ah, Monsieur Tabor—what a pleasant surprise."

The owner of the café, wiping his hands on the apron that concealed part of his tremendous bulk, greeted the two well-dressed men and led them through the noisy crowd until they came to a table away from the steadily rising hum of excited voices.

With the tail of his apron the owner deftly wiped off the two wooden chairs and then hovered to take their orders.

"Why is everyone so excited, Adolphe?" Robert asked.

The man looked over his shoulder and in a lowered voice replied, "Have you not heard, monsieur, that the Emperor Napoleon is divorcing his Josephine, because she cannot produce an heir?"

"So it is true—the rumor I heard yesterday," Robert mused.

"*Oui*, monsieur." And then Adolphe leaned closer to impart another bit of information. "They say he has already selected another wife, the young Archduchess Marie Louise of Austria."

Hector, suddenly interested, asked, "Isn't she the niece of Marie Antoinette?"

"Grandniece," the owner corrected. "And the marriage is to take place by proxy in Vienna, the same way her *grand' tante,* Marie Antoinette, married the Dauphin."

Robert frowned and became silent while Hector, sensing Robert's withdrawal, questioned Adolphe concerning the menu.

When the food and wine had been selected and the man had left, Hector said, "You seem to be in royal company, Robert—to be married by proxy."

"But unlike Napoleon, Hector, *I* did not choose my bride," Robert said with a bitter twist to his mouth.

Hector quickly changed the subject and soon the food appeared—the thick, succulent sausages, Camembert cheese and fresh bread. When the first bottle of wine was gone, Robert ordered more.

There was an awkwardness between them. And so, steeped in their own silence, Hector watched and listened to the uproar about them while Robert, having lost all interest in the animated crowd, appeared oblivious to everything except the empty glass in his giant hands.

Gazing at the glass, his tawny eyes suddenly took on a fierce and flashing glow, and his square jaw assumed a belligerent, clamped position that indicated his annoyance.

"By God, she shall pay for this!" Robert blurted out.

Surprised at the sudden outburst, Hector looked at his handsome, spoiled cousin, who at that moment resembled some young Jupiter ready to hurl a thunderbolt at the cause of his displeasure.

"I suppose you mean your wife, Robert," the older man said above the conversation at the other end of the café. "But that is no attitude to have. It was your uncle's decision. The poor girl probably had even less to say about this marriage than you. And remember, you had a choice."

"A choice?" he snorted. "With my pockets empty and my ship and cargo confiscated by the British? No, Hector, there was no choice but to marry this . . . this stepdaughter of his, if I ever wanted to see my inheritance."

"Yes, so you decided," Hector reminded him in a dry tone. "And it is far too late to back out now."

"But God, how it rankles! Me—Robert Lyle Tabor—being forced into marriage with someone I've never even seen."

Still scowling, Robert looked up to gain the attention of the café owner, and when he had done so, he motioned for another bottle of wine.

"Don't you think you've had enough for one night, Robert?" Hector asked.

Robert ignored the question and when the new bottle appeared, he filled his glass full of the golden, bubbling liquid.

Suddenly, Robert's frown disappeared. His eyes narrowed and then a smile spread across his face—a smile far more deadly than any frown that had ever knitted his brow.

Holding the glass high, Robert said, "Well, little Eulalie Boisfeulet Tabor, when I have finished with you, I think you will regret the day that you persuaded Uncle Ravenal to change his will."

And with one gulp, Robert downed the liquid.

Hector was alarmed at the coldness in Robert's voice. He hoped the young bride had some measure of beauty—enough to take Robert's mind off his anger, and also off his *chère amie,* whom he would be forced to leave behind when he quit Paris to go home to Carolina.

"Are you ready now, Robert?" Hector asked, anxious to separate Robert from the bottle of wine he was consuming.

"No. Go ahead," he urged. "I'm going to stay awhile."

Long after Hector had left the café, Robert sat and brooded over events of his last voyage—the events that had made it necessary to accept the terms of his uncle's will.

Examining each detail, each minute action, Robert was back again, hiding in the darkness at the mouth of St. Mary's River. He could feel the endless blackness enveloping him, could smell the saltwater marshland in his nostrils, while the boat rocked gently from side to side, waiting. . . .

"They're late," he said to his companion. "I wonder what's keeping them this time?"

The swarthy, muscular seaman beside him was slow in answering. Finally he spoke in an economy of sound.

"Maybe they had to hole up on Ossabaw or Sapelo Isle for a while because of the storm. Maybe they're scairt of thunder and lightnin'. But they'll be here soon, Robert, now the storm's over. Matthew ain't let you down yet."

The man spat his tobacco juice into the deep black waters of the deserted cove.

"Well, he'd better get here before the sun comes up," Robert replied. "Otherwise, they might as well turn around and go home."

"You expectin' this to be a dangerous trip, Robert?"

"No more so than usual, Muley," he muttered while the softly lapping waters cradled the boat.

Robert listened while he continued watching from the mouth of the river for some sign of life. He slapped at a mosquito buzzing about his head but missed. The humidity clung to him, and no breeze stirred on the June night to ease the suffocating heat that straddled the coastal boundary between Georgia and Spanish Florida.

"Heard the British tars stopped another ship last week," Muley commented. "Took off five seamen, claimin' they was deserters from His Majesty's ships. One was old Lonnie Spinks, whose ma spawned him on Sullivan's Island. All they had to do was listen to 'im talk. Anybody with half a brain could tell he wasn't no limey."

"That's just it," Robert growled. "They don't care. You would think we were still their colonies and that the War for Independence had never been fought."

"The British ain't the only ones actin' high and mighty. Them Frenchies is pretty bad, too."

The noise of the katydids scraping their wings together in an eerie Jew's-harp twang came to an abrupt halt. A lone bullfrog croaked his contentment and was silent, leaving the senses with the sweet-sour smell of the swamp drifting through the air.

Then a new sound replaced the night voices. It was a whisper of movement upon the waters coupled with a creaking of poles methodically working their way through the shallow parts of the marshes.

Robert laid his hand on the seaman's arm. They both lifted their heads in the direction of the sound. Instantly alert, they waited and watched while the sound gradually grew louder.

Casually, Robert whistled the first line of the slave song peculiar to his uncle's plantation. "Tremblin' woman and a tremblin' man . . ." He listened for the next line. The answer floated over the water, sweet and pure. "God gwine hol' you wid a tremblin' han'." And Robert relaxed.

The log rafts came into sight, carrying their cargo— bulky bales of cotton and wooden barrels of rice, smuggled through the string of golden isles dotting the coast. In the shadow of Amelia Island, the bastion of pirates and privateers, Robert's ship lay safely anchored, waiting for this last portion of cargo.

"One raft lost to de wedduh, Robert," Matthew stated apologetically. " 'E dere, near Sapelo. Waves lick 'um up."

"Anybody drowned, Matthew?" Robert questioned.

The Gullah shook his head. "No suh. Ah done tell Claudius fuh de two-time 'e lucky, knowed how to swim."

"And my uncle? How is he?" Robert asked.

"Low wid de fever," Matthew replied. "She—she talk say Miss Eulalie's nursin' 'e real good, but him be bad sick. When yoonah come home, Mr. Robert?" Matthew asked.

Robert gritted his teeth and replied with an edge to his voice, "Uncle Ravenal made it clear he doesn't wish to see me until I have given up my *lawless ways.*"

There was no more conversation. Robert was pressed for time.

With the cargo taken aboard ship, the men turned their rafts northward and disappeared.

Shortly before dawn, the *Carolana*, flying a Portuguese flag, set sail from Amelia Island and headed toward the open sea.

Robert stood on the quarterdeck, his eyes searching the sparkling blue waters for some sign of a British frigate. The element of danger in running the British blockade heightened his pleasure—that and the knowledge of the tremendous profits that would be his when he delivered his cargo to Napoleon's door.

They had been out for three days when the shout of "Sail ho!" came from the lookout.

Robert, in the captain's cabin, grabbed his breeches, slid them on and stormed toward the deck. Muley stood at the rail peering through the telescope at the approaching vessels.

"How many do you make out, Mr. Mulineer?" Robert asked his first mate.

"Three, as well as I can tell, sir."

"British?"

"Can't see their colors, but stands to reason they be British, sir."

Muley assumed a formal, professional air with his captain. He handed the telescope to Robert, who then examined the minute dots upon the new horizon.

By midday, the wind had died to a gentle whisper, and the sails had been wet down to hold the waning breeze. But the other vessels were now becoming larger.

"The sweeps, Mr. Mulineer."

But fate was against Robert and his crew. Within two hours, the fleetest of the British frigates had fired a volley to leeward for the *Carolana* to heave to.

He could have fought off one vessel, and if he had had only himself to think about, he would still have resisted, even though it was madness to consider taking on all three, with their carronades in position. The *Carolana* would have been blasted out of the water.

As darkness enclosed the sea, Robert and Muley were

in irons, and the *Carolana,* with its cargo, was a British prize, manned by a British crew heading for England.

So Sir George Cockburn, the man Robert had eluded time and again, had finally trapped him, adding the *Carolana* to the five hundred ships already confiscated.

Robert shuddered, remembering those dark days and his anger as he remained in the brig of his own ship on half-rations. And then he laughed.

He would give a tankard of rum to have seen Sir George's face when he discovered Robert had escaped that first night his ship lay anchored in the Liverpool harbor. He hoped the man who had helped him had not been found out—the American seaman who had been impressed by the British.

He was only sorry that Muley had been forced to stay behind.

"I can't swim, Robert, curse the luck! But don't let me stop ya," he had whispered. "Get out while ya got the chance."

Robert became aware once more of the now almost deserted café. His hands tightened on the glass he held, while his lips curled in bitterness.

He had lost his ship, his first mate, his cargo and his profits—and in their place, he had gained an unwanted wife, waiting for him to return to Carolina.

CHAPTER

2

CAROLINA! How different from New Orleans and her beloved bayou country, thought Eulalie, as she hurried past the plantation fields on her way to the big house.

Feena would scold her as usual for being late, but Eulalie did not care. She jerked her dress caught on the fence rail and heard the rip that freed it. Oh well, what was one more scolding?

"*Mon Dieu! Je suis* . . . No, I must try to think in English," she corrected herself.

But it was so easy to lapse into her native language, forgetting she no longer lived in the Vieux Carré.

"I am a Carolinan now," she said with distaste. "I am no longer French. I must remember."

She slipped into the house from the side piazza and ran up the stairs to the warm bath awaiting her. With the help of Marcey, she quickly bathed and put on her undergarments and was waiting in front of the dressing table when Feena walked into the room.

Moving her head to the side, Eulalie protested the vigorous brushing of her wavy black hair into some semblance of order.

"Mamselle Lili, there's no need to frown and toss your

head at me. With your brand-new husband due to arrive any minute, it's only proper that you start behaving like a married lady."

"But Feena, I don't see why I have to get dressed up *every* afternoon and sit in the salon with my hands folded. It's so boring. I'd much rather be helping in the nursery."

"If your *maman*—God rest her soul—ever found out you spent your time taking care of black babies, she'd leave her grave to strike me dead for allowing it."

"Hush, Feena. You know as well as I that I'm doing a lot of good. The babies are much healthier since I've been supervising. You remember last fall when half the babies died of dysentery—well, we haven't lost but two this year."

"Even so," the woman said begrudgingly, "it's not suitable for the mistress of a fine plantation. Monsieur Robert will put a stop to it when he gets home."

"A pox on Robert Tabor!" Eulalie said heatedly.

The sound of the carriage drawing up the circular driveway to Midgard Plantation halted the reprimand on Feena's lips.

"Hurry, Mamselle Lili. That must be Monsieur Robert now."

"How do you know, Feena? You've never seen him either."

Eulalie took her time. She could hear the front door open and close, and a man's deep voice talking with Bradley, the old butler.

She smoothed the ruffle on her russet-colored silk dress. Although she had acted with bravado in front of Feena, who had been her nurse from the day she was born, inwardly she trembled as she slowly descended the stairs.

What would he be like, this husband of hers? And how old? She knew so little about him.

Eulalie, making no noise with her soft kid slippers, walked down the hall. The man stood with his back to the door that opened into the salon.

"Monsieur Tabor," she said, her voice little more than a whisper.

The white-haired man turned and stood looking at the vulnerable young girl who shyly approached him.

Surprised to see the look of pity in the man's eyes, she hesitated. He was far older than she had expected.

"I am Eulalie," she said, holding out her hand to him.

"And I am your cousin, Hector," he replied, taking the small hand in his and holding it to his lips.

Eulalie exhaled a sigh of relief. Not her husband, after all. She gave him a warm, friendly smile that showed her even white teeth and the impish dimple in her right cheek.

"You must forgive me. For a moment, I thought you were my husband, Robert."

"I left your husband in Paris a month ago. He should arrive in Charleston about ten days from now, if the weather is good."

"Is that why you came—to give his message to me?"

He paused, trying to frame a suitable answer. How could he tell this exquisite and fragile little beauty that her husband had sent no message at all to her? If there were some gentle way to warn her about Robert . . . but would a warning make matters worse?

"Eulalie . . ." He struggled with the words and as he struggled, perception darkened her brown velvet eyes.

"He sent no message, I see," she said in a flat, disappointed little voice. "Well, what can I expect? What man would be happy to have a wife forced on him?"

She gazed at Hector, and the eyes that had been velvet-soft turned into shimmering satin with the unshed tears.

"His is not the only disappointment, Cousin Hector. You see, I was not happy either with the terms of my stepfather's will. Perhaps if my *maman* had remained alive . . ."

She brushed away a tear that had escaped.

"Did you know I would have had to go back to the convent if I had refused to marry him?"

"I did not know," he answered quietly.

"Is he . . . is he very angry?"

There were few words to console her. "Yes, he is angry, little Eulalie. But once he sees you, his heart cannot help but soften."

Much, much later that night, Eulalie, still unable to sleep, tossed in her bed. She did not blame Robert Tabor for being angry. He had been Papa Ravenal's heir for so long. Who would have guessed that Papa would fall in love in his old age and marry? And that it would be to her own *maman?* Or that after she had died, he would be so stubborn as to force Eulalie into marriage with his heir, Robert Tabor?

Eulalie, with the romantic ideals of a proud Creole beauty, could not imagine a marriage without love. She was used to the fiery temperaments of men who claimed a girl by routing a rival suitor in a duel. She could not reconcile herself to a cold husband who did not want her.

How many times as she was growing up did Feena say to her, "Your husband will have to be a giant of a man, *ma petite,* with a strong sword arm, to win you. And you," the woman would add, grinning, "will find much pleasure in the marriage bed with such a fine one."

All her life, Eulalie had looked forward to the day when she would be sixteen—when she would wear a beautiful white dress and sit in a box at the Théâtre d'Orléans, to be presented to society. Young men would come to the box at intermission, to be introduced, and then her parents would take her out to a late supper. The invitations to the balls would begin and she would be surrounded by suitors.

But her dream had remained a dream, never to be realized. Her father had died. Her *maman* had remarried and left New Orleans.

Eulalie had not been presented to society. She had never had a duel fought over her. Like a piece of property, she had been handed from one man to another, from her stepfather to a husband who had married her for the inheritance—nothing else.

Oh, why did Papa Ravenal have to come to New Orleans and fall in love with her *maman?* And why had he changed his will so that she would have to marry Robert Tabor, or go back to the convent to live?

Her husband did not want her. It was plain from Hector's visit. What was she to do? In ten days, the man would arrive at Midgard.

"Feena, you must help me." Her voice was not loud, but somehow she felt that Feena had heard her.

The evening after Hector's visit, Eulalie sat at the edge of the garden and listened to the sounds around her.

In the darkness, there was something sinister about Midgard Plantation, surrounded by Emma's Bog on the east and south and cut off by the river on the west. Only at the back on higher, firm ground were the solid pinelands.

Eulalie remembered how afraid she had been of the shadowy darkness and the mist of the bog when she had first traveled up Biffers Road toward the plantation at dusk the year before, when she had left the convent.

Papa Ravenal, seeing her fright, had begun to explain the legend of Midgard and how his grandfather had named his plantation for a Scandinavian myth. Eulalie, fascinated by the story, had forgotten for a while to be afraid.

"The solid land or earth, called Midgard," Papa Ravenal explained, "was formed, so the story goes, from the eyebrows of the giant Ymir, in the middle of an abyss. It was joined to heaven by a bridge called Bifröst. That's what we're on now, this small piece of solid ground through the bog."

Eulalie gazed out the carriage. The road, little wider than the carriage, was bound on both sides by black water, teased by trailing wisps of Spanish moss brushing back and forth from the low-hanging branches of the cypress trees. A large white bird stood on one foot not far from the road.

"The land, according to the legend," Papa Ravenal continued, "was surrounded by the giant's blood and sweat. His teeth made the cliffs, his bones the hills, and his hair became the trees and thickets. . . .

"But the words," Papa Ravenal said, chuckling, "were too hard for the blacks servants to say, so Ymir's Bog disintegrated over the years to Emma's Bog, and the Bifröst Road became Biffers Road. Luckily, Midgard was easier to say, so the plantation itself has kept its true name."

The uneasiness left Eulalie immediately when she saw the house. Coming from the darkness of Biffers Road, she was not prepared for the sudden clearing, for the breathtaking illumination of sunlight on the sandy-clay low-country brick mansion. It was as if a square had been cut from the darkness to let the light shine in.

And once inside the house, Eulalie found pleasure in exploring, going through the great hall into the dining room on the right, and then finding her way into the library and the salon, or drawing room as Papa Ravenal called it, on the left. But once the sunlight had disappeared, she found her relief had gone, replaced with the same sense of dread she had felt earlier.

The beating of the drums brought Eulalie back to the present. The sounds grew wilder in the October night, with the frenzy of drumbeats accompanied by dancing and shouts.

Eulalie frowned. Feena was up to her old voodoo tricks again. But could anyone really blame her, with such fertile territory for her love potions, her amulets and spells?

The blacks at Midgard were fearful and superstitious. They had a special name for all the spirits roaming at night, and one could never get them near the family graveyard after the sun had gone down. Feena made charms for them, so that they would not be carried away by the Hiddle-diddle-dee, or the Plateye, or the Buffler, the most feared of all the night spirits.

Was it any wonder she had become a queen among them?

Eulalie could not forget how angry her *maman* had been that evening when she found Feena with the rooster's blood spattering her dress.

She had tended to ignore the charms and fetishes, but the voodoo ritual was too serious to ignore. Because of it, there was even a law against the importation of slaves from Martinique, where voodoo was strongest.

"If I ever catch you again, Feena, I will sell you," Maman had threatened.

For a while, Feena had been very careful. But after Maman had died of the fever, and Papa Ravenal took sick too, the drums started again. The overseer, crippled and old, was powerless to stop it; for Moses, the black driver, now ran the plantation, and everyone knew that he was Feena's man.

Eulalie sighed. The plantation needed a strong master.

The drumbeats stopped and then the night was quiet. Eulalie, feeling some weird power in the air, shivered.

She looked up to see Feena approaching her, and she drew back, suddenly afraid of this black woman whom she had known all her life.

"Leave the big house, Eulalie Boisfeulet," the woman said in a trancelike voice, "before your husband comes. Hide in the little house beyond the river landing, and there your husband will learn to love you. But take heed of danger. It walks behind you. . . . "

Those words, spoken in the sinister darkness, put her to flight. Eulalie ran all the way back to her bedroom, and throwing herself upon the bed, she cried herself to sleep.

It was a beautiful morning when Eulalie awoke. The sun shone through the green-tinted leaves of the magnolia tree that shaded the east wing of the house. The strangeness of the night had vanished, and she smiled at Feena, who was standing at the foot of her bed, as usual, with the hot chocolate and brioche that she loved for breakfast.

Eulalie laughed when she thought of how frightened she had been the night before. What mumbo-jumbo it had all been! As if any spell could be cast over her or her husband by Feena! It was all nonsense. . . .

But the more she thought of the little house, the more excited she became. And a plan took shape in her mind.

If she pretended to be away when her husband arrived, but actually stayed in the little house, then she would have an opportunity to observe Robert Tabor without being observed herself. She could see what manner of man he was before she had to deal with him as her reluctant husband.

Papa Ravenal had built the house as a studio for Maman, so that she could be alone to paint. Robert Tabor would not know of its existence. And it was secluded enough that it was unlikely he would stumble upon it.

"Feena," she called excitedly, "come quickly. We are moving to the river house, but no one else is to know."

For the next several days, Eulalie and Feena were in a whirlwind of activity, making the house habitable again. No one bothered them while they surreptitiously transferred food and bedding, washed the windows and polished the old furniture.

The small white house built to catch the breeze from the river had been a favorite hiding place of Eulalie's. But that was before her *maman* had died. She had avoided it for months now, because the memories were too painful. But as she and Feena worked, airing it out, washing the windows and getting everything in readiness, she felt a peace and contentment, almost as if her *maman* were in the room, seated at her easel and painting one of the landscapes she loved to do.

The easel, left in the corner with an almost-finished canvas upon it, was put away in a closet. But Eulalie could not dismiss the beautiful lush colors upon the canvas. It was a part of her *maman* that she would not relegate to a cupboard. Instead, she hung it upon the wall, where the late-afternoon sun shone through the window, giving the painting a vibrant chiaroscuro effect. It was a remembrance of the plantation house, seen in its sudden illumination when Eulalie first came from the blackness of Emma's Bog. So her *maman* had been affected by it too—enough to capture it upon canvas.

How Papa Ravenal must have loved Maman, Eulalie thought, to have built such a perfect studio for her. Yet, he had never trespassed, never tried to claim that part of her *maman* that was kept separate from the big house.

Two rooms and a breezeway that connected the free-standing kitchen with the rest of the house—a little jewel of a house, with its small porch just large enough for one rocking chair, in marked contrast to the elegance of the plantation house.

For the first time since her *maman's* death, Eulalie felt a flutter of happiness. Tired from the afternoon's work,

Eulalie stretched out upon the soft feather bed. Her eyes closed and in a few minutes, she was asleep.

"Mamselle Lili," the voice sounded in her ear. "It's almost dark. Time to be getting back to the big house."

Feena stood over Eulalie, waiting for her to wake. At first, the girl did not remember where she was. And then she recognized the bedroom of the river house.

With an unexplained sense of sadness, Eulalie sat up, put on her soft slippers that had dropped to the floor in her sleep, and walked back to the plantation house with Feena.

Two days before Robert Tabor was due, by Eulalie's calculations, she dressed in her traveling outfit and had her portmanteau carried downstairs.

She had it all figured out. She would hide the carriage in the pinelands until time to return, set the horse loose in the pastureland above the swamp, and then wait until she got up the courage to return to the big house as its mistress.

Taking the letter she had written to her husband, Eulalie went downstairs to face the old butler. She had to convince Bradley, the butler, that she was actually leaving. Eulalie knew that the proud house servant did not speak to the field hands, so if someone came across the hidden carriage, the news would not filter back to the house.

Eulalie, explaining that her ailing cousin, Marianne, had asked for her, handed the white-haired old man the note and said, "Bradley, if you do not hear from me to the contrary, I will be back in two weeks."

"Yes'm, Miss Eulalie. Ah hopes yo' cousin gits better—and Ah'll tell Mr. Robert when 'e comes."

CHAPTER

3

THE old familiar pride and excitement of coming into Charleston touched Robert Tabor as the ship rounded the point and swept into the harbor.

The ship dropped anchor with a creaking screech and shudder, and Robert leaned over the side to watch the approaching dinghy that would take him the rest of the way to land. He was impatient to leave the ship.

Five years—and the sounds, sights and smells were the same . . . the drawling voices giving out orders, the powerful muscles of the workers glistening in the autumn sunshine, and the smell of sweat, burlap and cotton, mingled with the rank odor of fish lying too long in the sun. To many, that odor was offensive, but to Robert Tabor, it stirred the remembrance of happy days.

I have stayed away too long, he thought guiltily.

Hiring a carriage, he soon left the wharf to make his way to the Planter's Hotel. His eyes were hungry for the sights of Charleston and for his own plantation. But there was much for him to do before he could set his eyes on Midgard. From the letter he had received from his factor, he knew that he would have to find a new overseer, for he had been told that old Luke Hinson was on his last legs, unable to work. And that was just one of the many problems that faced him.

The carriage came to a stop and he stepped down onto the brick sidewalk in front of the hotel. As he made for the door, his progress was halted by a shout.

"Robert Tabor! As I live and breathe—the prodigal returns home!"

Robert turned in the direction of the voice.

"Arthur Metcalfe, my old friend! How goes it with you?"

Robert's face showed the delight of seeing a former colleague, and soon they were grasping hands and slapping each other on the back.

"Come, you must have a drink with me, Robert, and catch me up on all the latest news."

"I'm encrusted with salt spray," Robert protested. "One drink only, and then I must make myself more presentable. I feel as if I have been pickled in brine for the past month."

"All right, Robert—you may have your way as to that, for I well remember the feeling. But we will meet for dinner; I insist. One cannot catch up with five years' news on just one drink."

It was over an hour later that Robert and Arthur sat down to dinner together in the dining room of the hotel. They both demolished the she-crab soup and the Charleston paella, that peculiar combination of rice and seafood unlike anything that Robert had eaten abroad. And then, at leisure, they talked over the rare Madeira until the candles on the table had burned low.

"So you are the heir, are you not, Robert?" Arthur asked jovially.

"Yes, Arthur. Uncle Ravenal had always planned to leave Midgard to me."

"But after your uncle died, what happened to the young girl living there? Did she go back to her relatives in New Orleans?"

"No, Arthur. I understand she is still at the plantation. Her people went back to France, so she has no relatives that I know of left in this country."

"Then is she your responsibility?"

"More or less," Robert commented dryly.

"It might be interesting, especially if she is a great beauty, as her mother was reported to be."

"That doesn't concern me," he said, anxious to close that topic of conversation before Arthur found out that he had married her, sight unseen. "What I'm more concerned about is finding a good overseer. Luke Hinson will have to be pensioned off. He hasn't been able to work for the past six months, and heaven knows how the plantation has been run."

"Well, you might be in luck. You remember Alistair Ashe, don't you?"

"Gregory Ashe's younger brother?"

"Yes, that's the one. I heard Gregory had ordered him off his plantation. He was getting a little too cozy with his wife. A pity, really, because Alistair knows more about the workings of a plantation than his older brother. He has no money at all, and he would probably jump at the chance to be your overseer. The only drawback to Alistair is his arrogance, but I suppose you could overlook that, if he proves to be good help."

"Where did you last see him?"

"At the Exchange, yesterday. I'm sure he's still in town."

Three days later, Robert was on his way to Midgard Plantation. Everything had gone well. He had hired Alistair Ashe, who was staying in Charleston for another week to get his affairs in order before beginning work; he had also seen his factor and gotten a good report of the last crops of cotton and rice sold, with the money lodged in the account at the bank. All in all, he was in good temper.

He felt magnanimous enough even to forgive his wife a little bit. Perhaps he would not be so hard on her after all. It might even turn out to be pleasant having a woman to tend to his needs.

It was in this mood that he rode through the avenue of magnolias, turning into the circular driveway, to stop at the wisteria-vined piazza at the front of the white-columned mansion.

"Welcome home, Mr. Robert!" The old butler grinned wide, showing the gaps in his teeth. "Ah've got yo' fav'rite brandy waitin' in the parlor."

As Bradley poured the brandy, Robert asked in a casual manner, "Is my . . . wife here, Bradley?"

"No suh, Mr. Robert. She done had to go 'way. But she lef' this note for you." He went to the silver tray on the lowboy and brought back the sealed note to Robert.

He took the note in his hand and stared at it with a frown. Then he broke the seal and read:

> Monsieur Robert,
> My cousin, Marianne, is ill and has asked for me. I will be sorry not to greet you at your homecoming. I will be back in two weeks.
>   Your obedient wife,
>   Eulalie

He crushed the note in his hand. "Cousin, indeed!"

She had run away, too scared to face him. And written lies to cover it up.

All desire to forgive was gone. She had forced him into marriage and then insulted him by deliberately being away when he arrived. If she had any sense at all, she would stay away. No one ever snubbed Robert Tabor!

He strode furiously out of the house, called for his horse and rode at galloping speed over the acres of land that he now claimed for his own.

Eulalie spent another night in the river house with Feena.

She would have to be more careful, for she had almost been seen that day by Robert Tabor. She had been on her way back to the river house from the nursery, where the fever had started again.

The news had spread quickly, even to the nursery, that the new master was home, so she wasted no time in seeking her hiding place.

How was she to know that he would be riding toward

her with the speed of one of the furies? If he had not jumped the fence and veered to the left, she would have been discovered.

As he went by, she was able to get only a glimpse of his face, but that glimpse was enough. He was a devil . . . and she was his bride!

In the early light of morning, Eulalie dressed carefully for her work in the nursery. She put on one of her plain calico dresses, with a clean white apron. She tied up her hair in a *tignon,* as she had done many times when helping the sisters at the convent tend the sick, not caring that her dress was no finer than the girls' who worked in the big house, nor that the *tignon* was a symbol of the "women of color" in New Orleans. She was tired of the silks and laces that she had worn every afternoon in the salon while she waited for her husband to return home.

Her husband—was there any possibility of his discovering her today? It was doubtful that he would even come close to the nursery, especially with the danger of the fever, and in her plain dress, he would not give her a second glance. No, she was safe. Even her suntanned skin would protect her. How many times her *maman* had admonished, "Do not forget your parasol, Eulalie. You don't want to be mistaken for a *café-au-lait.*"

Out of the yard she walked, to squeeze through the maze of yew hedge and honeysuckle vines that hid the house from view, on past the cottonwood trees near the river's edge to the winding, sandy path that crisscrossed the trails to the fields beyond, and on to the cabins, and finally to the nursery where all the babies were looked after while their mothers were at work.

Jetta and Tassy were good workers and had learned quickly from her instructions. But it was easy for them to lapse into the old ways, if she were not around. And she was uneasy about the baby, Cassius, who had been so hot to the touch the day before.

It was much later in the day that Eulalie finally lulled Cassius to sleep with a French lullaby. She covered him carefully, and as she straightened and turned toward the door, she saw Robert Tabor staring at her. Her heart gave a leap.

"M—monsieur," she stammered. "The fever . . . it is not safe for you here."

He acted as if he had not heard her. He stepped closer, never taking his eyes from her.

"What is your name?"

"Lili, monsieur—I am called Lili." She shivered, realizing she had almost given herself away. Now unable to meet his eyes, she stared down at the dirt floor.

He put his hand under her chin to lift her head and look into her face.

The color swept over her cheeks when, with his other hand, he removed the *tignon* to let her long black hair escape to her waist.

"And did I inherit you too, Lili?" he inquired.

The question startled her. Did he think she was a slave, like the others? But, of course. She was dressed like the others.

"*Oui,* monsieur," she answered quickly in an embarrassed small voice, careful to disguise the relief she felt in not being found out.

He stood for a moment, the silence binding them together, before he turned and left the wooden cabin.

After the initial fright had subsided, Eulalie became angry. What right had Robert Tabor to inspect her as if she were on the auction block? She was incensed with the indignity. And she knew his careful inspection would make it easy for him to recognize her when she took her rightful place as mistress of the house.

Eulalie slipped out of the cabin and made her way back to the river house. She was indignant with each step. She must be more careful.

Robert ate supper alone. He could not get his mind off the beautiful slavegirl, Lili. She must have come from New Orleans with his wife, Robert decided, since she spoke French. A pity that one so lovely had Negro blood. But judging from her skin, it couldn't be much.

He gazed at the mocking empty place at the other end of the table, where his wife should have been sitting. Remembering the letter, he was overwhelmed with anger.

Abruptly, he got up from the table and walked out to the piazza.

Twilight hung in the air. This was what he had missed —the lingering day, filled with the sweet smell of jasmine struggling to keep its grasp on the land in defiance of the approaching darkness. In other parts of the world, there had been no stubborn twilight. The days had easily given up their claims to the dark nights without protest.

The land was beautiful—*his* land now—with its deep stippled shadows against the lush green of the fertile earth. Robert stepped off the piazza and began walking toward the fields. The field hands were finished for the day, and the cotton fields, with part of the crop still to be picked, were turning brown. When the last white bolls were stripped from the stalks, the plants would be plowed under to make way for the next crop to be planted in early spring.

A sudden movement of color caught his eye. Robert stood up, with the broken stalk in his hand, and watched. He knew at once it was the slavegirl, Lili. She disappeared into a clump of greenery, and as Robert stood in the field, he gazed in the direction of the disappearing figure and absentmindedly pulled the ripe cotton from its seed.

The next day, Robert deliberately went to the slave nursery, but it was Tassy who met him at the door. He peered inside and saw the *tignon* lying in the rocking chair—the piece of cloth that Lili had worn the day before over her long, wavy hair. The chair gave one last sway before coming to a stop. It was almost as if someone had vacated it hurriedly—almost as if the one who had been in it had been given warning and had fled.

Robert frowned as he left the cabin. With long strides, he walked past the fields toward the river.

Again at supper, Robert ate alone in silence. The small black boy working the long fan of turkey feathers that swept back and forth above the table to keep the flies from the food was the only other human being in the room. Robert had dismissed Bradley, and now he sat finishing his glass of wine while the fan moved slower and slower.

Finally, Robert stood, flexing his powerful muscles against the boredom of a long night. It was early—still twilight—and he was restless. His long inspection of the plantation had not tired him, and there was almost nothing for him to do except read.

His trunks had been unpacked for him, with the exception of the smallest one, which contained some of the books that he had recently acquired. He had tried to replace the ones that had been left in the captain's cabin of the *Carolana*. With nothing else to do, Robert decided to unpack the books and put them in the library with the others.

Climbing the stairs, he entered the master bedroom, where the locked trunk waited at the foot of one of the massive beds.

As he neared the trunk, a peculiar scent assailed him. It was pungent and nauseous. Strange that he had not noticed it before supper. He leaner over the bed, where the odor was strongest, and pulled back the covering. He felt amid the mattress and pillows until his fingers closed around an object, a small pouch sewed across the end so that the contents could not escape. At once he realized what he was holding. He stared at it in revulsion, knowing that it probably contained cat's eyes, cemetery dirt, and other assorted potions too vile to think about. With an angry oath, he flung it through the open window.

"Voodoo!"

Robert had never known Midgard Plantation to be plagued with it. It must be some new slave, he thought, and he bounded angrily down the steps, determined to seek out the culprit.

But it was not the slave he wished to punish. It was his wife, Eulalie Boisfeulet. One hand around her scrawny neck and she would learn who was master. She would never defy him again.

On his way to the slave cabins, he felt his intense fury gradually subside. It was replaced by a voice softly whispering, "Lili, monsieur. I am called Lili."

God, he needed a woman, a woman like Lili, soft and desirable.

Before he realized it, his feet were on the path to the river.

From the moment he had seen her, he had desired her. And her efforts to elude him had made her all the more desirable. She had not known that he had followed her that afternoon, as she carefully made her way from the nursery to the river. The swinging of her skirts was tantalizing, and it was hard for him not to become known to her.

She was so small, but the soft brown eyes, at one moment resembling the velvet pansies in the garden, in another moment had changed to a seductive flame.

The harvest moon cast a golden glow upon the landscape as Robert drew closer to the river house. He sensed an urgency in the air, an awareness that the night was alive with the wild, romantic courtship of the forest.

It was the autumn mating season that the Indians called the Season of the Mad Moon.

Suddenly, Robert remembered another autumn when he had watched a beautiful young doe, pursued by a love-struck stag, pausing to glance back with her dark, limpid eyes full of allure and promise. She loped playfully on, until the stag followed her into a love bower scented with wild jasmine.

And now the doe had returned as the beautiful Lili, and he, Robert Tabor, was the bewitched stag, following her to her *bocage* of green.

He wanted her. By the time he had reached the little house, he could think of nothing but his desire for her. He did not think of the strangeness of her freedom to come and go as she pleased, or her inhabiting the river house alone. Nothing was on his mind but his desire to taste the wild honey of her lips and feel the smooth flesh under his hands.

Robert was unaware of the woman, Feena, who watched his progress from her hiding place in the thickness of the honeysuckle vines. She smiled to herself, quietly left the maze and slipped into the kitchen, separated from the main structure of the little house. There the black woman took her place on the cot in the corner of the room, satisfied that the charm had worked.

Robert walked onto the porch and with a few more steps, he had pushed open the door.

Eulalie, dressed for bed in her long white nightgown, turned to face the sound. Seeing the man, she shrank back, causing the lighted lamp in her hand to flicker from the sudden movement.

"Monsieur Tabor," she cried in alarm. "What are you doing in my house?"

"*Your* house, Lili? Tell me—how can you own something on *my* plantation?"

"I . . . I do not own it, monsieur," she said in a confused voice. "It is yours, as is everything else, but it was given to my . . . *maman* to use when she was alive."

"Was she a . . . favorite of my uncle's?"

"Yes, monsieur."

"And you reaped the benefits too, I see," he added sarcastically.

At the look on her face, he said, "Do not worry. I can be as generous as my uncle, where you are concerned."

When there was no response, he continued, "I am supposed to have a wife—but she has seen fit to leave when she knew I was coming. She is probably a cold, ugly hag, anyway. So you will help me pass the time while she is away. You will like that, will you not?"

"N-no, monsieur," the small voice choked in reply, as she backed farther away from him.

He laughed a cold, hard laugh. "Come here, Lili."

But Eulalie remained where she was.

Suddenly Robert stepped toward her, taking the lamp from her trembling hands and setting it on the nearby table. And then she was caught in his embrace.

She struggled to free herself, but it was no use. Robert would not let her go.

"Are you a virgin, Lili?" he asked in a soft voice.

Speechless, she could only nod, while staring at his boots, once highly polished but now covered with a veneer of dust from the fields.

His hand moved to her cheek and stroked the long silken strands of black hair from her face.

"Then I shall be gentle with you tonight—but only for

tonight; for I swear you were made to be loved passionately."

At his alarming words, Eulalie turned from him, ready to flee, but he caught her from behind, locking his arms around her waist. Bending over, he moved his lips against the vulnerable nape of her neck.

"No," she protested, jerking her head to the side to avoid his sensuous lips.

He laughed and loosened his hold on her. Eulalie ducked under his arms and began to run. She got only as far as the bedroom door before he stopped her.

"So you think you can escape me," Robert said.

"Please," Eulalie responded with trembling lips. "Let me go."

"No, Lili. I have made up my mind. Tonight you will be mine."

His frown devastated her; his arms crushed her to him. With a frightened cry, she struggled against him as he carried her to the bed. She immediately sat up, looking for escape, but his stern voice forbade further action.

Cowering, she watched in the semi-darkness while he removed the snowy white shirt to reveal his massive bare chest covered with golden hair.

Eulalie had never seen a white man's chest before—only the slaves working in the fields, their black bodies glistening with sweat. Unable to help herself, she stared, mesmerized by his nakedness, his body seeming twice as large in the shadow on the distant wall.

But Robert had not finished undressing. He began to shed his close-fitting fawn-colored breeches, and Eulalie, her dark doe eyes growing wider, quickly looked away, too embarrassed to continue looking.

The steady blush covered her face. Her body felt hot but her teeth chattered with fright. And she sat with her hands covering her eyes, afraid to move, yet fearing what Robert had in store for her.

At the feel of his hands on her arm, Eulalie jumped. As if taking pity on her, Robert held her gently against him and soothed her with his caressing words.

"I won't hurt you, Lili," he promised. "I only want to

love you. Don't struggle," he whispered. "Just lie still in my arms until you get used to a man holding you."

Used to a man holding her, with only the thin material of her gown separating her from his naked body? No, she would never get used to it. Warily, she lay in his arms and waited for him to continue his assault. But nothing happened.

Her body slowly relaxed, and Robert's warm breath against her neck was even and unintimidating. Maybe he was going to sleep and nothing more would happen.

Tired from the long day spent in the nursery, Eulalie closed her eyes and listened to the katydids scraping their wings together outside the window. The bed was soft and familiar and comfortable. As the yellow beams of the harvest moon slanted into the bedroom, touching the edge of the window sill, Eulalie, lulled by the river sounds, drifted into a light sleep.

The gentle caressing was soothing, in rhythm to her breathing, and Eulalie burrowed her head against the softness of the pillow. But the tempo of the caressing changed, becoming more demanding, and all at once, Eulalie awoke.

Robert. Robert's hands were moving over her body. Her muscles tightened and she reached for the giant hands to take them from her breasts. They were undeterred in their advance.

"No," Eulalie whispered. The buttons of her gown were loosened one by one. As the gown left her body, she clung in vain to the white material. But it was deftly removed from her fingers and thrown from the bed.

Now not even the thin material separated her flesh from his. "Please," she protested again, "you don't understand. I am your w—"

Robert's lips cut off her words. Eulalie shivered; her breasts strained against his hairy chest, and her legs were enmeshed with his, while his mouth sought the sweetness of her own.

Dejectedly, Eulalie realized her confession would do no good. As a husband, did he not have the right to do what he was doing? No, she would not give him the satisfaction of knowing that she was his hated wife. Her fate, if possible, might be even worse. Far better for him not to know.

Desperate now to free herself, Eulalie instinctively brought up her knee into his stomach. Robert swore and thrust his knee between her thighs, pinning her down.

"So you wish to fight, do you?" Robert asked, his voice strangely triumphant. "Good. There is not much pleasure in taking a limp doll to bed."

His words infuriated her, and when he covered her lips again, she bit him. His hands suddenly tightened, his body pressing heavily upon hers so that her breathing was shallow. The salty taste of blood spread upon her tongue while his lips remained on hers.

"Little vixen," he murmured, lifting his head to stare down at her. "You think to deceive me with those soft limpid brown pools for eyes. But I know you for what you are—a biting wild thing that has never known a man's hand."

His voice was hoarse with desire. "And I shall take great pleasure in taming you this night. . . ."

CHAPTER
4

*E*ULALIE awoke the next morning, the alien arms still enfolding her. Seeing her demure white gown on the floor, she was overwhelmed by a sudden rush of shame. And she removed Robert's arm from across her breasts.

She was now Robert's wife, but he did not know it. And now it would take even more courage to tell him, especially after . . .

Eulalie stared at the golden-haired giant, still asleep, his naked chest showing above the wedding-ring quilt that partially covered him.

So this was what it was like to be the paramour of the master of the plantation. Her body felt bruised and sore—and desecrated.

She hated him. Yes, hated him! He had thrust himself upon her, giving her no time to get used to him, to trust him. He had not cared for the feelings of a mere slave. His only thought was to satisfy his own lust.

Fear, pride, hate and resentment mixed together to flow in her veins, poisoning her mind and body against this man who had desired her and taken her without thought as to *her* wishes.

No wonder cruel masters were afraid to eat at their

own tables, fearing crushed glass in their food. More than one had slowly bled to death at the hands of his house servants.

Although it would be a sin to wish Robert the same fate, Eulalie nevertheless wished there were some way to make him sorry for his actions.

If she were more knowledgeable in the ways women had of making men lovesick, she would take great pleasure in getting Robert to fall in love with her and then spitting in his eye.

Sighing, Eulalie realized the impossibility of doing that and moved to the side of the bed. As she slung her feet over the side, strong arms reached out for her.

"Not yet, Lili. Come back to bed."

She glared at him, her dark eyes smoldering. "Monsieur, there are . . . things one must take care of in the morning."

He laughed and let her go. "Just so you come back."

Eulalie, glad to escape him, covered herself with the gown and hurriedly grabbed a dress and chemise from the wardrobe. She disappeared from the room.

Silently she let herself out the door and headed for the sheltered cove of the river a short distance from the river house. She had no intention of returning anytime soon. Let Robert wait and wonder where she had gone. His patience would not last long. And then he would leave the river house.

Eulalie stepped out of the dress and, with her chemise covering her, waded into the cool water. No one else ever came here, for it was Eulalie's own hiding place, one of the many small inlets that fanned from the Ashley River.

She sat on the bottom of the shallow pool, her hands skimming across the water in a wide sweep. Her dark wavy hair surrounded her.

Feena would fuss at her for getting her hair wet, but she did not care. She wanted to wash clean everything that Robert had touched.

A water spider crawled on the water beside her, its body glistening in the morning sun. She was still and quiet until it went away.

Thinking of Feena, Eulalie frowned. Why had the

woman not come to her aid instead of leaving her to Robert's mercy during the night? But then, Eulalie already knew the answer. Robert Tabor was master of Midgard. His word was law. He would have dismissed Feena with a snap of his fingers and she would have had no recourse but to obey.

Feena could not solve her mistress's problems. It was up to Eulalie to find a way out, to escape from Robert. But she knew she couldn't get far on the small amount of money she had stashed away. It would not even pay for one night in Charleston, much less passage back to New Orleans. Why had she not chosen the convent instead of marriage to Robert Tabor?

"So this is where you thought to hide."

Robert stood on the bank, his amused glance taking in Eulalie's dress hanging on a bush near the water.

At her disconcerted look and obvious displeasure at seeing him, Robert laughed and said, "Am I intruding? Do you also claim this cove for your own, Lili?"

"The cove is yours, monsieur. I am merely enjoying it, if you have no objection." The water covered her to the neck and Eulalie was still, not daring to move while Robert stared at her.

He disappeared behind the bush, and Eulalie, thinking he had gone, lay on her back and, buoyed by the water, stared up at the blue sky.

At the sudden splash near her, Eulalie lost her balance and sank into the water. She sputtered as her head came up again. Robert was beside her.

"You do not mind if I join you?" he asked.

"It is a little too late, monsieur, is it not?" she asked, shaking the water from her hair.

"Meaning that you *do* mind, Lili?"

"It did not matter to you last night. Why should you even bother to ask today?"

His amused look vanished. And his voice, deadly in its softness, rebuked her. "I think, Lili, that you have had too much freedom far too long. You seem to have forgotten that you are my slave. I trust you will remember it, and answer accordingly."

Eulalie lowered her eyes and shivered with a sudden

coldness. "I am . . . sorry, monsieur. I did not intend to be . . . disrespectful."

His hand went under her chin and when he forced her to look at him, he was smiling again. "You are young, Lili, and impetuous in your speech. Now that you understand, let us enjoy the water."

Her eyes, moist with tears, still looked at the man beside her, and she was afraid.

"Why did you not come back?" Robert asked.

"I . . . I needed to take a bath, monsieur." Still shaking, Eulalie nervously swallowed and said, "I am very cold. If I have your permission, I would like to leave the water and . . . and get dressed."

"You have my permission," he said and abruptly left her side to swim across the pool.

Conscious of the wet chemise that clung to her body, she waded from the water and retrieved her dress from the sweetshrub bush. With trembling, cold fingers, Eulalie slipped the dress over her head and ran all the way to the river house.

"You will take your death of cold, mam'selle, if you are not more careful," Feena scolded her, helping Eulalie out of her wet clothes.

"At least if I am dead, I will not have to suffer Robert Tabor's advances."

"But he is your husband, *ma petite,* even if he does not know it yet." Feena's eyes narrowed. "You did not tell him last night, did you, mamselle?"

"I . . . I tried to, but he . . . he . . . "

"I understand," Feena interrupted, toweling the girl's hair dry. "But it is better for him not to know for a while longer. Let him learn to love you, first."

"But what if I don't *want* him to love me?"

"Then it will be much harder for you, *ma petite.* No woman wishes for her husband to hate her. Marriage is hard enough without that."

"But I do not know how to go about getting him to love me."

"He was pleased with you last night, was he not?"

"Feena, you are embarrassing me. I don't want to discuss it."

For the rest of the day, Eulalie thought of what Feena had said. Her mind was not on the babies in the nursery, even though she took care of them with Tassy's help.

Since she had left him at the cove, Robert had not sought her out. But she was nervous, wondering if he would suddenly appear again that evening. And worrying what she should do if he did.

The mothers on their way home from work claimed their babies and, with the nursery empty and Tassy gone, there was nothing for Eulalie to do but to walk back to the river house. There was no other place to hide from her husband.

His steps alerted her, and Eulalie, already in bed, listened for the door to open. The words in the book blurred before her eyes. And the lamp flickered at the draft from the opening door.

Seeing Eulalie sitting in bed, reading, Robert looked at her strangely. Then it dawned on her. Slaves were not supposed to know how to read. She quickly shut the book and dropped it to the floor.

At her action, he grinned. "Do not stop reading on my account. Or were you admiring the pictures?"

His teasing did not sit well with her. But she took the easy way out and meekly nodded.

"Where did you get it, Lili?" Robert asked, wondering if she regularly took books from the library without asking.

"It is mi—It is yours, monsieur," she answered.

At her quick reversal, Robert walked to the other side of the bed. "I see you are learning to be truthful, Lili," he said, picking up the book and opening to the frontispiece. *Genevieve Boisfeulet.*

So Lili had found it in the river house, more than likely. Her late mistress's book. He flipped through the first several pages, and his eyebrows lifted in surprise. He stared at Lili and back at the book in his hands. There were no pictures and the book was in Latin.

Robert sat on the bed, staring at the slave girl with a questioning look, and Eulalie shrank against the pillows in fright at the intensity of his bold, tawny eyes. Seeing her reaction to him, he became aware of his stare and his look softened.

At his touch, she winced in pain. The bruise on her shoulder had become more discolored during the day— the place where Robert had subdued her with his hands.

Hearing the small moan, Robert loosened her gown and bared her shoulder to his view. He frowned while his fingers delicately traced the bruised area. Then he swiftly put the gown back in place.

"You should not have struggled so hard against me last night, Lili. You see, you will only get hurt. And I do not like to hurt you."

Her eyes were disbelieving at his words, but her lips made no reply.

"I think we should erase what happened between us. Let me be gentle with you, Lili, and love you the way I had planned. And then I think you will begin to enjoy it— my making love to you."

"No, I shall never enjoy it," Eulalie declared, shaking her head at the man hovering over her.

Her retort brought amusement to his face. "You are still a virgin in mind, Lili, if not in body. And that presents a challenge."

His voice, sounding softly against her breast, asked, "Which is it to be, Lili? Another struggle where you can only get hurt again? Or a willingness to let me teach you about love?"

"I . . . I do not wish to be hurt," Eulalie said, a trace of fear not completely hidden.

"Then do not protest, Lili."

The lamp burned on the bedside table, and in its glow, Robert, in no haste, began the removal of her gown. Eulalie, still unused to the touch of a man's hands, shut her eyes and a tremor passed through her body, but she did not protest.

His mouth moved over her smooth skin, teasing one breast and then the other, and Eulalie tensed, her hands clenched to her sides.

"Relax, Lili," he ordered.

She fluttered open her eyelids at his command, but her hands remained tightly clenched.

"Put your arms around me," he instructed, taking the small fists and unlocking her fingers.

She did as she was told, and Eulalie felt his lips brush hers. Time and again his lips teased hers with their softness. But Eulalie felt nothing but revulsion.

Did every married woman have to suffer the same thing each night with a demanding husband? Eulalie wondered. If they did, no wonder so many wives went into a decline. Loved to death by their husbands. She could see it now on some staid matron's tombstone in the cemetery. At the thought, Eulalie giggled, and Robert abruptly stopped his lovemaking to look quizzically at her.

"Something amuses you, Lili?"

He was not pleased at her behavior, and Eulalie, frightened now that he might think she was laughing at him and retaliate, hurriedly explained with a serious demeanor.

"I was only wondering, monsieur, if it were possible to be . . . to be loved to death."

Robert, startled at her question, inquired, "And do you think *you* are in danger of being loved to death?"

"I hope not. I should like to live to a ripe old age."

Robert sat up and brushed his hand through his tousled hair, his ardor considerably dampened. "Then I suggest you not make fun of a man, Lili, when you are in bed with him."

He jerked the wedding-ring quilt aside and left the bed to walk into the other room. And Eulalie, unconscious of what she had done, reached for her gown to hide her nakedness.

The oil burned out of the lamp and the room plunged into darkness. But Robert did not return.

For two days, Eulalie did not see Robert. She had displeased him. And to her, that idea seemed even more frightening than his attentions.

Should she tell him who she was? Eulalie quickly decided against it. She was a coward, afraid to tell him. She had seen his temper, scarcely controlled, when he had walked away from her. And she still did not know what she had done to cause it. How much worse it would be for her if he discovered, in his present mood, her enormous subterfuge—of hiding from her husband.

Reasoning with herself, first one way and then the other, Eulalie finally gave up making any decision. Looking for the bamboo poles, she pushed the dilemma out of her mind and, with the box of crickets in her hands and the poles, she headed for the river.

The long low cypress log was half submerged in the water. Eulalie flung the line over the water after she had attached the cricket to the hook. With luck, she and Feena would have fish for supper.

The old cork moved across the surface of the water and then plunged out of sight. With a jerk, Eulalie brought the line out of water. Hanging at the end of it was a medium-sized perch, flipping back and forth in protest at being caught. Feena came upon Eulalie just then and the woman, seeing Eulalie's aversion to handling the fish, removed it from the hook and placed it in the small basket that had been lowered into the water.

The black woman took up the other pole and settled down by Eulalie. Watching the unhappy girl, Feena said, "Monsieur Robert is very grumpy, according to Moses. Do you know the cause, *ma petite?*"

"No, Feena. I think I have made him mad, but I do not know for sure."

Feena nodded. "That is probably so. And if you have, mamselle, you must do something about it."

"But what? What can I do, Feena?"

"We will think of something, *ma petite*. Do not worry."

Feena did not tell the girl what she had done the day before—to slip the love potion into Robert's table wine. Neither he nor Bradley, the butler, had been any wiser at her action. Feena smiled in satisfaction, remembering how Robert had drained the glass while she peeked through the window of the dining room to make certain that he drank it.

Silently Feena and Eulalie sat on the bank until they had caught four river perch in the waters next to the old cypress log. As Eulalie flung her line once again toward the log, a shadow loomed over the water. Eulalie turned and stared into the topaz eyes of Robert, her husband.

Feena, seeing the man, drew up the basket of fish from the water. "I will take these, *ma petite,* and get them ready for cooking." She hurried from the bank, leaving Eulalie and Robert together.

"Good afternoon, monsieur," Eulalie said, determined not to show her fear of the man.

"Good afternoon, Lili," he responded. "I see you have found another old haunt of mine."

"You used to fish here?" she asked in surprise.

"Yes, when I was a boy. And quite profitably too. There is something about a half-submerged log that attracts the fish."

"That is so," Eulalie agreed. "Would you . . . would you care to use Feena's pole and try your luck again, Monsieur Robert?"

A boyish grin covered his face as he picked up the long bamboo pole lying on the bank. "And what are you using for bait?"

"Crickets, monsieur—in the box over there." Eulalie pointed in its direction and Robert walked to the box, retrieving one to use. Soon his line was parallel to Eulalie's line, and in the late afternoon, a peaceful silence crept over the landscape.

Robert was lucky, catching the largest fish of the afternoon, but Eulalie did not mind, seeing the good mood mellowing the too-stern face of her husband.

Sitting beside the girl in her rough calico dress, Robert was aware of Lili's beauty and her complete lack of coquetry. She was an enigma—tantalizing, a child one minute, a woman the next. As he gazed at her, paying no attention to the bamboo pole in his hands, he wondered what his haughty wife looked like.

His eyes narrowed in distaste, thinking of her. Eulalie Boisfeulet. Even the name sounded haughty. Feeling the angry lump in his throat, Robert deliberately pushed her out of his thoughts and concentrated on the moving fish headed toward his line.

Eulalie stood up, holding onto the pole and waiting for the cork to go under. Already nervous at Robert's attention, she jerked much too hard. The line sailed high into the air, with the small fish, dangling for a moment overhead, dropping off and plopping again into the river. But the momentum of the jerk continued, until the now-empty line and hook landed in Eulalie's hair.

Startled, she put up her hand in a defensive gesture, merely succeeding in feeling the sharp point of the hook in her hand. As Eulalie cried out, Robert was immediately beside her.

"Hold still, Lili. You will make it worse."

She froze and waited while Robert patiently untangled the line and removed the hook.

"Let me see your hand, Lili," Robert ordered. And she meekly held out the hand, with the puncture evident. Lifting her hand to his mouth, Robert drew blood and then spat it out upon the bank.

Her serious brown eyes did not leave his face. Her hand remained in Robert's for some time. She had no will of her own, no wish to remove her hand from his larger one. She was like a puppet, waiting for her master's instructions, conscious only of his eyes gazing into hers. Her sudden intake of breath broke the spell and she snatched her hand from him. Gone was the tender look from Robert's topaz eyes.

"Hooks are dangerous, Lili," he scolded. "You will need to be more careful."

"I am sorry, monsieur. I am not always this . . . careless."

"You probably will not get into trouble with it," he assured her, "since it has bled. But come, the sun is almost down. Time to get back."

He took the bamboo poles and wrapped the lines around them, sticking the sharp edge of the metal barbs into each cork. It was difficult keeping up with him, but he did not seem to notice. He walked slightly ahead, with both poles in his hands and carrying the large fish by its gills.

As they came to the river house, the aroma of fish wafted from the kitchen where Feena was fixing supper.

Robert laid the poles on the porch, and Eulalie, uncertain whether to go inside or not, waited for Robert to leave. But he remained where he was, his eyes still watching Eulalie.

"There is something about the aroma of fish when one

is hungry." A tinge of nostalgia was evident in the man's voice.

With her eyes still on his face, she said, "Would you like Feena to cook yours also?"

Robert glanced down at his catch in his hands, and he smiled. "Yes, that would be nice," he replied and walked with Eulalie toward the breezeway and the kitchen.

CHAPTER

5

*F*ROM the moment on the river bank, through the intimate supper in the front parlor of the river house, Eulalie felt caught up in an illusion. She could not seem to separate fantasy from reality.

She should have been afraid of Robert, the man whose very existence had terrified her from the instant she had said those vows, promising to honor and obey him—a shadowy figure that she could put no face to.

Now his face was real. His hands were real. And yet her terror had suddenly abated.

"You are very beautiful," he whispered in her ear, holding her close to him.

It was late in the evening and she sat quietly in his lap, as if it were the most natural thing for her to do. His kisses had given her a vaguely pleasurable sensation, and when he stopped, Eulalie was disappointed.

She climbed from his lap, and Robert did not restrain her. Eulalie went into the bedroom and took up the hairbrush to remove the tangles his lovemaking had caused in her long hair.

It hung down below her waist, the long silken strands that covered her shoulders. Her mother had had the same kind of hair—luxurious and thick, with no trace of gray in its velvet blackness. And Eulalie, seeing her own hair in the mirror, recalled how embarrassed she had been that day when she passed the open door of the master bedroom and saw her *maman* and Papa Ravenal together, the man brushing the long cascading tresses in sensuous motions of the brush. There had been something pagan about the ritual, and it had disturbed her.

With a silent tread, Robert came into the bedroom. His giant hand reached out to take the brush Eulalie held in her hands, and the mirror reflected the same sensuous, pagan movements of a man revealing his desire for a woman.

Her scalp tingled with each caressing stroke. And her eyes, looking into the mirror, saw only Robert and the tender look that held her.

It was more than her body could stand. She rose and took the brush from him. "Thank you, monsieur," Eulalie said, laying the brush upon the table.

His hand reached for hers and brought it to his lips. Robert turned it upward and kissed the palm of her hand. And then he stopped to stare at the small wound.

"A sacrilege to mar such perfection," he said, with a scowl on his handsome face.

"It will heal soon," she responded, hardly aware of what she said.

Confused at her contradictory emotions, Eulalie did not protest when Robert carried her to the bed. It was as if it had been destined—this attraction between them that had grown stronger as the day had grown older.

Now it could not be denied. The feeling demanded expiation, a washing away of the hurt of the previous days.

She was Robert's wife, greatly desired. And somehow it was a miracle. Eulalie, lying in his arms, forgot her former fear and responded to his kisses.

"Lili," he whispered with a groan. "Lili."

It was different this time. His gentleness guided her, bringing her to the edge of rapture, and she moaned at her awakening. She could feel the rapid beat of Robert's heart answering her own, could hear his loving words in her ear. Her world contained only Robert, bringing her body to its first fulfillment.

In exquisite pleasure, Robert tensed and the world exploded. His voice cried out and then he slowly relaxed, his massive chest slowing in its movement as his breathing returned to normal.

"Robert," she whispered, forgetting that a slave girl would not dare call her master by his name.

But was he not her master, after all? Her lord and master, whom she had promised to obey, as a dutiful wife?

"You are more than I ever dreamed or hoped for," Robert murmured, his head against her breast.

His soft, even breathing brought peace to her. Everything would be all right now. She could tell him the truth. Eulalie went to sleep, her face still flushed from the night of love.

When Eulalie, feeling the sun upon her face, opened her eyes, she saw Robert staring at her. His look was arrogant and possessive, and a smile greeted her.

She returned his smile and snuggled against him, aware of the warmth of his body. He laughed at her action. "You see, Lili," he teased, "I told you that you were made to be loved. And I am glad you have finally recognized it."

There was now no need to hide in the river house. She was anxious to return to the big house, where she could preside at Robert's table, where she could wear the beautiful silks and laces hanging in her wardrobe, where she could begin to take her place as mistress of Midgard.

Eulalie, looking up at Robert with her dark-brown eyes in a serious mood, did not know how to begin to tell him the news.

"Monsieur," she said, her voice unsure, "what if you awoke this morning to . . . to find your wife at your side instead of me? What would you do, monsieur?"

With a harsh laugh, Robert replied, "I would promptly strangle her and then throw myself on the mercy of my peers."

"You would do that?" the small voice croaked. "Strangle your wife?"

"She thought to deceive me, Lili—leaving the note for me and then running away. Would it not serve her right?"

"But perhaps she—"

"I do not wish to discuss her, Lili. Do not bring up her name again in my presence."

Frightened at the hostility in his voice, Eulalie was silent. So it was going to be harder than she had thought. And when she confessed, he would not easily forgive her.

A subdued Eulalie faced the day less sure of her destiny and even more afraid of the man who could so suddenly unleash his anger against anyone who thwarted him.

Robert's new overseer arrived and he became occupied during the days, but when the nights came, Robert returned to the river house and Lili. Conscious of his effect upon her, he now initiated her into such an ecstasy of passion that each morning she awoke ashamed of her wanton behavior.

The days passed too quickly, each day growing harder on Eulalie with the knowledge that she would have to confess to Robert that she was his wife and not his slave-girl. She could imagine his intense anger and disdain, a cruel foundation for any marriage. But she must tell him the truth. Eulalie could not put it off any longer, for it was time for Robert's wife, Eulalie Boisfeulet Tabor, to return home.

I will pack and go to the big house tomorrow, she decided. But she trembled at the thought.

For the first time in his life, Robert Tabor was baffled at his intense feelings for a woman—this light-skinned Lili. It was almost as if she had cast a spell over him. He could not eat or sleep for thinking of her.

Because he had not known he was capable of such strong feelings, he had consented to be married to a stranger. At the time, he had thought that one woman was much like another, and that it mattered little, his choice of a wife, if married he must be. His sole resentment was at being forced into this marriage.

Trying to separate his responsibilities from his desires, Robert paced back and forth in the library.

As master of Midgard Plantation, he realized this liaison with Lili was not worthy of him. He had taken advantage of her, and her protestations had meant nothing to him. Oh, many plantation owners took their pleasure with their female slaves, yet he knew it was wrong.

The proud Eulalie Boisfeulet, his wife, would be coming home in a few days. And he knew he must beget an heir to leave the land to. But already, Lili was a wedge between them.

A strange affair, the two slaves living apart from the others. The woman, Feena, watching over Lili in the river house so carefully—almost like a mother hovering over her own child.

Could it be that Feena, of mixed blood and light-skinned herself, might possibly be Lili's mother, with the father some white man? That would account for the woman's possessiveness and her care of the young girl. But then, Robert remembered what Lili had said on that first night. Her mother had been a favorite of Papa Ravenal's. Perhaps Lili had been lying about that. He had no way of knowing.

But thank God, the girl had not been sired by his uncle. Robert, still not satisfied about Lili and her origins, continued pacing back and forth. The sudden movement on the stairs caught his attention. Feena! What was she doing in the house?

Robert left the library and, silently climbing the carpeted stairs, followed in the direction that Feena had gone.

"So you are the one responsible."

Feena looked up with fright in her eyes. "Monsieur Tabor!"

She quickly slipped her hand under the pillow to retrieve the object from the bed, but he grabbed her hand and twisted the object from her.

"I will not allow your evil fetishes and rituals either in my house or on my land, Feena. You already know my orders and the penalty for disobeying—to be punished and locked up. Why did you do it, Feena?"

"It was for . . . Miss Lili, monsieur," she answered in a whisper.

Later, Robert sat in the semi-darkness of the library

and waited for his overseer. His hands covered his face and his body showed the strain of his agonized decision.

"You wanted to see me, Robert?"

He glanced up at the young man and answered in slow, measured tones.

"Yes. There is something I want you to do tomorrow. There is a girl named Lili . . . "

The morning sun played upon the blue-and-white wedding-ring quilt that lay at the foot of the feather bed.

Eulalie stretched and opened her eyes, watching the bright, swift movements of light.

It was late, far later than she usually slept, for the sun was already high in the sky. She jumped out of bed and hurriedly dressed, taking little time to brush her hair.

"Feena?" the girl called. "Feena, where are you?"

There was no answer.

Eulalie walked through the breezeway toward the kitchen. But the black woman was not in the kitchen. And the hearth was cold.

She frowned. It was not like Feena to leave her to get her own breakfast.

Glancing toward the cot in the corner where the woman usually slept, Eulalie saw that the cover was unrumpled. Had Feena not spent the night in the river house?

Well, it did not matter now. It was time for Eulalie to go back to the plantation house. There was no need to recover the carriage from the pinelands or to take her portmanteau with her. That could be carried back later, after she had confessed to Robert who she was. There was now no necessity for making it appear that she had been away.

Eulalie sighed and closed the door to the river house.

She was walking through the maze of yew hedge and honeysuckle when she saw him.

"Lili?" the voice called and she looked up at the tall, blond man who blocked her path.

It was his eyes that alarmed her—those colorless eyes with black pinpoints that seemed to stab her heart. She was instantly afraid of him and she stepped out of his way, determined to leave the green sanctuary that had become a menacing, hidden screen.

"Just a moment, my haughty little wench," he said, reaching out one long arm to stop her.

"Take your h-hands off me," Eulalie sputtered.

The pinpointed eyes narrowed and his fingers closed painfully over her wrist. She writhed under his firm grasp and her voice lashed out at him, "Monsieur Tabor will be quite angry if you do not release me at once."

The brown eyes belied her fright with their sparks of fury.

He laughed, and still gripping her wrist, replied, "I am here at Monsieur Tabor's request." His voice was mocking and his face showed his enjoyment of the scene.

"And who are you, for Monsieur Tabor to send you?" she asked, puzzled at his reply.

"The new overseer, Alistair Ashe. And we both had better obey his orders. You're to come with me."

Eulalie still lagged behind, although the overseer had begun walking out of the maze toward the waiting carriage. He gave her arm a sudden jerk, bringing her beside him.

"Where are we going?" Eulalie asked, seeing the carriage.

"I am to take you to your . . . master," he answered. He lifted her into the carriage and Eulalie, still not trusting him, watched as he slapped the matched horses with the reins and commanded them to move.

They crossed the sandy road separating the fields where the workers in the distance were picking the last of the cotton. But instead of heading to the house, the man turned toward Biffers Road.

"But we are going away from the house," Eulalie protested. "Why?"

The overseer kept his eyes on the road. "Mr. Tabor went into Charleston. We are to meet him there."

Eulalie absorbed the information in silence, but with each creak of the wheel, she knew something was wrong.

Robert, on horseback, stayed hidden in the thick grove of trees. He watched the progress of the carriage until it wound out of sight down Biffers Road.

Anger was at war with his pain as he suddenly left the copse and galloped back to the house. He stumbled blindly into the drawing room and reached for the brandy. With shaking hands he poured the liquid into a glass, swirling it in his hands before he partook. In one huge gulp he downed the burning liquid, and in a violent display of frustration, Robert threw his empty glass against the hearth, splintering the heirloom crystal into a thousand tiny fragments. But the decanter he kept intact, taking it upstairs to the master bedroom, where he remained for the rest of the day.

The thickness of the trees and the vegetation overhead in Emma's Bog cut out the sunlight, and Eulalie felt the sinister forces as the carriage trespassed the darkness of the narrow road.

The God A'mighty bird, hidden in the dense thickness of the bog, gave its unearthly shriek and then noisily flapped its wings to fly from the darkness.

Eulalie's unease turned into fright. She didn't believe in the superstitions concerning the bird. But she *had* heard that terrible, raucous shriek the night her *maman* died, and also on the day her pony broke his leg and had to be shot. Bradley and Feena had nodded their heads solemnly. The bird always forecast disaster, they had said. It was accepted by everyone on Midgard Plantation, except for herself. She did not believe it. And yet . . .

Robert had never sent for her to come to the big house, and it was even more unlikely that he would send for her to meet him in Charleston. It was then, under the spell of the frightening sound of the bird, that Eulalie realized the overseer was lying. Alistair Ashe was taking her *away* from Robert, not to him, as he had avowed.

But why? She had no way of knowing the reason. She only knew that she must get out of the carriage. She must not allow this man to take her from the plantation before she could tell Robert the truth—that she was his wife, and not a slave.

Intent on staying in the wet ruts of the narrow road, Alistair Ashe slowed the carriage. And when he did so,

Eulalie jumped from the rolling vehicle and landed in the ditch where the black waters verged the road.

Ignoring the shout from the overseer, Eulalie scrambled to her feet and, gathering her wet skirts about her, began to run as the carriage came to an abrupt halt.

She heard the muttered oath, the thud of boots hitting the dirt, but she kept running, not pausing to look back.

The hand reached out and shoved her toward the ground. As she lost her balance, Eulalie screamed, "Robert!"

She hit the ground and the breath was knocked from her. As if that were not punishment enough, the weight of the man was also upon her. She was suffocating, with her face in the dirt.

Miraculously, her face was lifted from the sand—her body twisted under his, her arms pinned under by his strong arms, but she was facing upward. When she opened her eyes, she met the cruel stare of those clouded eyes and heard the sneering voice.

"Do you think Robert Tabor will save you? When he is the one who has given orders to sell you?"

No, it was not true. Robert would never be so cruel as to sell her. Eulalie gasped for breath. Her lungs hurt for lack of oxygen and from the weight of the overseer, who made no attempt to free her.

One hand reached out and stroked the sand from her face.

"God, you're beautiful," he said. "I cannot imagine why Robert is so senseless as to get rid of you."

He traced the curve of her cheek, and with his finger he outlined the voluptuous shape of her lower lip. Suddenly, Eulalie opened her mouth and bit hard on his finger.

Alistair Ashe jerked his hand away.

"You're going to be sorry you did that," he snarled.

"Please," Eulalie said. "Take me back to Robert. There has been a mistake. I am not a sl—"

He stopped her words with his lips, pressing down on her mouth with a bruising, hard force.

The sound of a cow's bell came from the bog, and then a voice calling to the cow that had evidently strayed into the snake-infested water. "Come heah, you daughter ob Beelzebub," the irritated voice sounded.

At the intrusion, the overseer lifted his head to listen. Eulalie opened her mouth to call for help, but she was not fast enough. He clamped his hand over her lips before the sound could escape.

The errant cow splashed into view and the scowling overseer, frustrated in his punishment, hastily set Eulalie on her feet and, still holding his hand firmly over her mouth, swept her to the carriage.

The sudden blow on her chin stifled any further attempt to cry for help, and her consciousness faded into the darkness of the bog.

"She needed a little persuasion to come," the overseer's voice said, cutting through Eulalie's dazed mind. "Robert Tabor wants her sold as quickly as possible."

She was standing in the pillared marble arcade on Meeting Street.

Rough, callused fingers caught at her face and then ran knowingly over her body. Rapidly ascertaining her attributes, the man removed his hand and, as if she were not even there, he said to Alistair Ashe, "He'd get much more for 'er if he'd wait till we advertised. Won't be much of a crowd today. And it takes a crowd to run up the prices."

"Don't think it's the money he's after," the overseer replied. "Better do as he says and put her on the block this afternoon."

The auctioneer nodded and summoned his helper.

The leather thong attached to Eulalie's wrists was transferred from the overseer to the auctioneer's man, who began dragging her with him.

"No," Eulalie protested, her mind beginning to clear from the confusion caused by the blow. "Please, there has been a mistake. I must see Monsieur Tabor."

Eulalie's plea was ignored and, using all her strength, she resisted the man who had her in tow, kicking at his shins. But her strength was ineffective. He merely laughed at the show of spirit and continued to drag her to the block, where she was locked into the chain that held the slaves—black, glistening pearls on a giant necklace with an occasional mulatto to give variety to the chain.

Alistair Ashe disappeared and Eulalie was left at the slave market, to be displayed publicly and to be sold to the highest bidder.

The crowd began to gather and there was a sudden murmur in the marketplace at the sight of the dark-eyed girl with hair down to her waist.

Humiliated at the harsh treatment, Eulalie did not lift her eyes from the ground, did not look at the girl chained next to her.

"Put your head up, girl," the auctioneer said, prodding Eulalie in the back with the handle of his long whip, "and show some spirit. They'll think you're sickening for somethin'. And God knows I don't need any such rumor in *my* business."

Immediately, Eulalie's head went up, and her eyes met the blue, inquisitive eyes of a stranger standing to the side of the platform. He had the appearance of an outdoorsman, rougher-looking than the plantation owners who sat and waited for the auction to begin, seemingly paying no attention to the slaves. She watched in horror as the man approached, walking all the way around her, surveying her from every angle. Eulalie had seen many like him in New Orleans—woodsmen and trappers who traveled annually up the Mississippi in search of a fortune in furs and trading.

In shame, her head drooped again, but it was lifted upward, and her mouth rudely opened by the man to survey the state of her teeth. Then his hands, touching her body, pushed her dress off one shoulder. Suddenly, the auctioneer's whip was thrust between Eulalie and the man.

"You may look all ya want, mister, but I can't have ya undress the wench in public. Now if ya want to inspect 'er in one of the private cells with my man lookin' on, you're welcome to do it before the biddin' gets underway."

"Zat weel not be *necessaire,* monsieur. I have seen more zan enough."

The auctioneer moved on, and the man still standing in front of Eulalie asked, "What are you called?"

In a faltering voice, she replied, "Lili, monsieur."

He smiled at her answer. "So you speak French," he said, more to himself than to Eulalie. Jauntily he walked back to the chairs and took his seat on the end, and his eyes did not stray from her while the auction began.

The bidding was lethargic, with most of the slaves sold for a low price. One elderly woman, with no bid offered for her, was removed and whisked back to her cell to await the next auction.

Finally there was only one on the platform who had not been sold—Eulalie.

"Gentlemen, you see before you a prime piece of delectable female flesh," the auctioneer began in his practiced, oily voice, "the likes of which have never been auctioned before. Notice the smooth skin, the white teeth, and the perfect formation of her body. Unfortunately, the planter who owned her is at death's door, or else he would never have consented for her to be sold. She speaks both English and French, and would be a suitable . . . house-slave for any strong, red-blooded male."

There was a snicker in the audience at his insinuation.

"Five hundred dollars," the male voice on the end called out.

"Gentlemen," the auctioneer cautioned in mock horror, "you dare to begin the biddin' with such a paltry sum?"

"One thousand," another voice from the back called.

"I have a pitiful bid of one thousand dollars," the auctioneer acknowledged.

"Fifteen hundred," the same man on the end said hurriedly.

The auctioneer relaxed, and with a satisfied gleam in his eye, he said nothing, but walked toward Eulalie, bringing her closer to the edge of the platform. Slowly he turned her to the left and to the right, giving the men a chance to observe her well.

"Look alive, girl," he hissed in her ear, while his grip tightened on her arm.

The dark-brown eyes glared at him with a look of hatred, and Eulalie twisted her arm out of his grasp and stepped back, daring the auctioneer to lay his hand on her again. The chain around her ankle rattled at her sudden movement.

The auctioneer merely chuckled and turned to the crowd. "Untamed in spirit—a little spitfire to warm the coldest of nights. Gentlemen, let us proceed with the biddin'."

So the afternoon was not to be a disaster after all. But he was in no hurry to draw the bidding to conclusion. He could see the interested looks of even the oldest planters and overseers there, and the auctioneer knew the whetting of their appetites would push the purchase price up, especially with the trapper on the end not concealing his impatience at the way things were going.

"Two thousand," the tall man in the back bid, and almost before the words were uttered, another voice countered, "Three thousand."

The auctioneer looked toward the trapper on the end, and with relish, saw the angry red flush spreading over his face.

"I have three thousand," the auctioneer said. "Do I hear more?"

"Thirty-five hundred," the trapper said, his voice now snarling.

"Thirty-five hundred. Who'll make it four thousand for this healthy, spirited piece of goods?"

There was a momentary silence. And then a man seated in the front row offered casually, "Four thousand."

So, a new bidder to frustrate the two main bidders. Concealing his satisfaction, the auctioneer stood with legs spread apart. He glanced at the audience and back to Eulalie before he took several steps to the side.

Nodding his head, he repeated the last bid. "Four thousand. I now have four thousand."

"Six thousand dollars," the French-accented voice called out. The man stood up and gazed over the crowd, fiercely challenging anyone to bid against him.

A slight murmur and then again, with no one taking up the challenge to outbid the exorbitant sum mentioned by the trapper, the other bidders shook their heads and many toward the back got up to leave.

The auctioneer was content to wind it up. Far more than the skilled artisan the week before; far more than the driver the day before. He repeated the bid. "Six thousand dollars, once." The auctioneer paused. "Six thousand dollars, twice. Sold for six thousand dollars."

Immediately the trapper came toward the girl to claim her, but was stopped by the auctioneer, who guided the man into his office to complete the transaction.

The bill of sale in his hands represented a large portion of the trapper's fur money from the previous year. But the girl would be worth it; for he was not one to spend the winter alone. And another fortune in furs awaited him up the Mississippi.

The auctioneer unlocked the chain around Eulalie's ankle and handed the desolate dark-eyed girl to her new master—Jacques Binet, trapper.

The next few days passed slowly for Robert, even though he worked from sunup to sundown. But the evenings were the hardest for him. He was determined to put Lili and the river house out of his mind, but the memory of those love-filled nights returned to gnaw at him, and he ached for the touch of the beautiful slave whom he would never see again.

The plantation was settling down to order and discipline, where there had been little before. Alistair Ashe, his overseer, had managed well.

Thinking about the plantation and the workers, Robert suddenly remembered Feena. "Surely she has learned her lesson," he said aloud. "I will give orders for her release."

Later that afternoon, Robert left the house to take a look at the rice fields. The rotten flood gates were being replaced, but the dark clouds, suggesting an impending storm, worried him. It would be disaster if a sudden storm came up before the repairs were completed.

He stepped off the piazza and headed toward the stables for his horse. Feena stood in front of him, barring the way.

"Monsieur Robert, where is Miss Lili? I have looked everywhere for her."

He saw the anguished look on her face, and for some reason he felt ashamed. Then he became angry, with a desire to hurt as he was hurting.

"Some other master will be enjoying her charms to-night, Feena. She was taken into Charleston three days ago, to be sold."

An incredulous look came into the woman's eyes. She stared at him as if he were a monster. She was barely able to speak.

"You have . . . *sold* Mamselle Lili?"

"Yes, Feena. Now perhaps this will put a stop to the spells and voodoo you both have been so busy with."

Feena began to wail and to beat her breasts with her fists.

"Stop it, Feena!" Robert shouted. "Do you want to be punished again?"

She began to speak in a combination of French and English so rapidly that he was able to catch only a few words, but he knew she was heaping curse after curse upon his head.

"Mamselle Eulalie . . . *ma petite* Lili—your wife—you sold your own wife . . . "

Robert's face turned white and he reached out to steady himself by grasping the hitching post. The implication of her words struck his very soul.

"My wife, Eulalie—Lili—they are the same?" His eyes widened at the thought and he demanded in a dread, rasping whisper, "Is Lili my wife?"

"*Oui,* monsieur. You have sold your own wife."

The spirit had gone out of the woman and she sank to the ground, to rock back and forth and moan in her own private hell.

Robert Tabor became a wild man, setting out on the road to town, pushing his horse at such a fast gallop that neither he nor the horse could maintain the speed for long. He had taken no time to change clothes. His only thoughts were on Lili and the cruelty with which he had betrayed her.

Could she ever forgive him? He remembered the soft, liquid, frightened eyes. God! Had the thought of being married to him terrified her so that she had had to hide from him? She had tried to tell him something that first night, but he had not listened. And his insufferable arrogance—to think that she might have had anything to do with any love spells that the woman Feena had cast over him.

It began to rain, but Robert was past caring at any discomfort he might feel. He thought only of Lili. His heart cried out in jealousy and despair. She was too beautiful to be purchased as an ordinary slave. Some man would have bought her to be his mistress. Lili with another man; Lili, perhaps at that moment, subjected to the desires of a cruel master . . . it was more than he could stand.

Robert reached the slave arcade and, seeing the auctioneer, walked toward him in a purposeful stride.

"What can I do for ya, Mr. Tabor?" the man greeted him. "We got some fine workers due to go on sale in a few minutes—hefty field hands, some mulattos suitable for the house, and even a brickmason—"

Robert held up his hand to silence the man, who stood with legs spread out in an arrogant stance before the dejected group chained to one another.

"There was a . . . slavegirl that my overseer brought to you to be sold three days ago."

"Oh, yes. A real little spitfire, and beautiful too. Kept insistin' that it was all a mistake, but I knew better since I had the papers you signed."

Robert winced but continued in his quiet voice, "I have . . . changed my mind and wish to have her back."

"I'm sorry, Mr. Tabor. But that's impossible. She was sold that very afternoon, just like you requested. I have your money in the office."

Robert's heart was heavy at the man's words. Forcing his voice to remain steady, he asked, "Who bought her and where can I find him?"

"Now I can tell ya one but not t'other. It was a French trapper that bought her. Couldn't believe his luck. But as to where he took her, I have no idea. One thing for sure," he said, laughing crudely, "it couldn't be very far that first night, judgin' from the way he was lookin' at her—only to the nearest bed."

The pain in Robert's eyes intensified as he asked, "And the man's name?"

"Just a minute. I'll look it up for ya."

Robert followed him into his office and waited while the auctioneer took down a ledger from the shelf.

Thumbing through the pages, he came to a halt, as his eyes traveled down the list of transactions.

"Here it is—slavegirl, called Lili—sold to Jacques Binet. That was the man's name—Jacques Binet, trapper."

Robert turned to leave. "Wait, Mr. Tabor. Don't you want your money from the sale?"

But Robert did not stop.

Much later that night, Robert returned to Midgard Plantation, his shoulders drooping with fatigue and failure.

He had searched throughout the town but the trapper had vanished. He had left Charleston, with Lili beside him.

Three days—three days headstart—and it would be even more days lost before Robert could gather supplies and hire a guide to track them down.

Why had Alistair Ashe not listened to her when she had protested? And why had he not reported this to him?

He knew he could not have Alistair Ashe as his overseer a day longer than was necessary. Robert would never be able to look at him again without seeing Lili being dragged to the slave market. And for her sake, no one must know; for if it ever became known after he found her and brought her home, she would be destroyed.

He would give Ashe two months' wages and send him away. He never wanted to see him again.

CHAPTER

6

SEVERAL hours' distance from Midgard Plantation, Hector sat in his own library, his body tense and his eyes staring vacantly out the window.

His right arm began to ache and he moved it back and forth to restore the circulation, while opening and closing his hand at the same time. Consciously, he relaxed the tense muscles of his neck and softened the hard, fierce lines of his face, which had tightened as he remembered the vulnerable young girl that was now wife to Robert Lyle Tabor.

I am getting old, he thought, to be worrying like this. Still, there was an oppressiveness that had enveloped him like a pale gray shroud for the past week. And try as he might, he could not shake it off. It clung to him like an unwanted companion, silent but constantly chafing.

He had too little to do, too little to keep his mind and body occupied. That was why he had time to worry over Robert and his new bride.

Sometimes, Hector regretted that he had not married again, that he had no sons to teach to ride or shoot. And he was almost sorry that his overseer was so capable, running the plantation with an expert hand. Hector felt superfluous. If he disappeared, no one would miss him. The plantation would be run the same way with or without him.

He stretched his big frame and ran his hands through the thick mane of white hair.

Had Robert become reconciled to having a wife? Had his anger abated when he had seen the exquisite creature that his Uncle Ravenal had chosen for him?

The names of Robert and Eulalie flitted in and out of his mind, and he again felt that aura of uneasiness at the recalling of Robert's intense anger, and the young Eulalie's trusting brown eyes—eyes like those of a young doe unaware of the hunter who stood at the edge of the forest, waiting. . . .

Disgusted with himself, Hector got up from his chair. He would ride over to Midgard to see for himself what was happening. Then his mind could rest from its undue worry.

The knock at the door surprised him. He was not expecting anyone. He listened to the voices in the hallway, and suddenly the heavy oak library door pushed open, and in front of him stood Robert.

"Robert, my boy! What a pleasant—"

The greeting froze and Hector, losing his smile, stared at the haunted and devastated look on Robert's face.

Something was wrong. Hector, feeling the emotional atmosphere of the room, disguised his own unease and, with an effort to remain calm, said, "Is anything the matter, Robert?"

That was the wrong thing to say. Hector silently cursed himself as he saw the young man before him fighting for control.

"But come and warm yourself, first. It has gotten unusually chilly for so early in the year. I fear we will have a hard winter."

Robert turned his back to Hector and walked to the fire.

"Banks," Hector called to the servant hovering at the door, "bring us some brandy. I'm sure we could both do with some."

Hector kept talking, giving Robert time to get hold of

himself until at last they sat opposite each other, with their snifters of brandy in hand. Hector dismissed the servant with a nod of his head and waited for him to close the door to the library.

"And now, Robert, tell me what has happened."

"Hector, I have been in agony this past week." Robert's voice was low and strangely hoarse.

"How so, Robert?"

"I—I don't know where to begin."

"Does it concern your wife?" he asked, feeling the uneasiness at full thrust.

"Yes—and when you hear what I have done, you will never speak to me again."

"I doubt that, Robert. I know you have a terrible temper, but I cannot think you have done something so offensive that it cannot be remedied."

"Hector," Robert moaned in anguish, "I have breathed death and destruction on everything around me. From the moment I set foot on land, things have gone wrong. The slave babies at Midgard are dying of the fever, two of my slaves have run away, I've made an enemy of my overseer, and, worst of all, I have destroyed my wife."

The older man was afraid at Robert's words. "You say you have . . . destroyed your wife? What do you mean, Robert?"

In short, painful gasps, he answered, "Eulalie was evidently frightened to be married to me. And heaven knows, she had cause. When I got to Midgard, there was a note from her, saying she had gone to care for a cousin, but you and I both know she has no cousin.

"Because she had nowhere else to go, she hid on the plantation, but I thought she had deserted me. And I was determined to make somebody pay for her insult.

"There was a young slavegirl, Lili, or what I *thought* was a light-skinned slave. And she was so beautiful. I see that I was a fool to be taken in, believing Eulalie to be a slave."

Hector interrupted, puzzled at how this could have happened. "But I don't understand. You mistook Eulalie for a slave? Was she hiding in one of the slave cabins?"

"No. She was staying in the river house, but I first saw

her in the nursery cabin. She was dressed no better than the others and was taking care of the slave babies. But I was still a fool not to have guessed who she was."

Robert's mouth twisted in a sneer. "You know how the Charleston belles have always prided themselves on their white skin, never going into the sun without a parasol. It did not occur to me that my wife would be so unsophisticated that she would allow her skin to be darkened by the sun. I thought she would be like the rest of those females, concerned only with their looks."

Robert could not be rushed. He was determined to tell the entire story and to take the blame for everything that had happened. Hector sat, listening and occasionally taking a swallow of the brandy he held in his hands. But he felt sick in the pit of his stomach, knowing that Robert was not alone in the blame. By visiting Midgard and trying to warn Eulalie about Robert, he too was guilty. If he had not frightened her about Robert, Eulalie would not have hidden from her new husband.

"I looked all over Charleston for her," Robert continued. "The only clue I have is a conversation overheard by another trapper. The man who . . . bought her—this Jacques Binet—is supposed to be headed for the fur-trading territory of the west."

"And are you going to search for her, Robert?" Hector asked.

"Yes, of course—even though I know she's now the mistress of another man. She can never be my wife again, Hector. But I will bring her home and see to it that she is always cared for and protected."

The white-haired man flinched at this pronouncement. The damnable Tabor pride. Robert had more than his share of it, and that pride would ensure his unhappiness as long as he and his wife, Eulalie, lived.

"But it was not Eulalie's fault, Robert. I will have to confess that I visited Midgard a few days after I returned from Paris. If I had not tried to warn her what to expect when you came home, Eulalie would not have taken fright and hidden from you."

A surprised look came into Robert's eyes, but then he refuted Hector's guilt.

"But you were not the one who gave orders for her to be sold, Hector. I alone am guilty of that."

Both men stared at each other and shared the anguish.

"Will you be leaving soon?"

"Yes," Robert replied. "As soon as my Catawba Indian guide arrives. If I am to travel in Sioux territory, it will be safer to have a relative of the Sioux with me."

Suddenly making a decision, Hector said, "Robert, I'm coming with you."

The two men checked into the Planter's Hotel and for several days were busy gathering supplies for the trip west. Running Wolf, the Catawba, had come and was waiting for Robert's signal to depart.

Hector sat in the hotel room and stared at the now familiar map spread out on the table. He waited, and in the moments of idleness, Hector was besieged by numbing thoughts.

They were set to go northwest to St. Louis, capital of the Louisiana northern district. Someone would certainly have news of Jacques Binet there—at the gateway to the west. But what if the other trapper had been mistaken? Suppose Jacques Binet had gone directly north into Canada instead?

If they did not find Eulalie before cold, icy weather set in, they would be forced to wait until the spring thaw before resuming their search.

Would they ever find her? The task seemed almost insurmountable as Hector thought of the dangers that Eulalie would face in the vast, alien wilderness—hostile Indians, wild animals, the flooding river and the man, Jacques Binet. She was no match for any of them.

The sound of boots on the stairs mercifully interrupted his paralyzing thoughts.

Robert walked into the room and tossed a packet onto the empty chair.

"Good news, Hector," Robert announced in a relieved voice. "I just spoke with the shipping clerk for the *Jasmine Star*. Jacques Binet and a girl fitting Eulalie's description booked passage to New Orleans last Friday. According to

73

the clerk, the man was to meet his friends in New Orleans and take a boat north up the Mississippi."

A smile cut across the sadness of Hector's face.

"That *is* good news, Robert. At least now we know in which direction to start."

Robert went to the map on the table and studied it anew. "It is a tedious business, going past the English Turn. And with a little luck, the *Star* will have gotten caught on a sandbar. That would slow them down."

Robert's eyes narrowed while he still studied the map. "It's almost a straight course, due west, from Charleston to Arkansas Post, where the Arkansas River flows into the Mississippi. A much shorter route than the one we had planned to take—and a chance to catch up with them sooner than we expected."

Hector leaned over the table and his eyes followed Robert's finger as he traced the line from Charleston to the mouth of the Arkansas.

The next morning, in the early hours of predawn, three men stood in a silent tableau before Brown's Livery Stables. They were an incongruous group, those men— yet each one had the same determination stamped on his features.

The most exotic of the three was the proud, tall Catawba Indian, dressed in his deerskin pants and jacket, moccasins, and a blue feather in the long, single plait of his glistening black hair. His head was slightly elongated from an ancient Catawba custom of binding the heads of their infants. From a branch of the dreaded Sioux, this Catawba was one of the fast-dwindling warlike tribe that hunted game and enemies up and down the length of the sprawling Catawba River.

Hector and Robert resembled father and son, with the same body build, the same proud stance. The only major difference, besides Hector's white hair, was the gentler set of features belonging to the older man; for the planes of Robert's face were sharp and hard.

At that moment in the dim light from the lantern hanging at the side of the stables, the younger man could have been mistaken for a statue of stone. Only the occasional spark from the smoky topaz eyes gave evidence that he was flesh and blood.

Then the still, silent picture was blurred—the scene coming alive with moving figures of horse and man and swaying lanterns.

"Looks like you won't need another thing, Mr. Tabor, between here and Arkansas. Them pack horses is loaded to the ears. . . . Reckon your Indian friend knows where he's goin'. Don't s'pose he's leadin' you into ambush with some of his Sioux kin," the stables owner joked in a mild, laughing voice.

The Indian turned his head in the man's direction but gave no indication he had heard the joking words.

Robert smiled, held up his hand in farewell and then disappeared from the alley in a burst of impatient energy.

On through the day they rode, with no mishap except the stumbling of one of the pack horses. Beyond the vast fields of the low-country plantations they traveled, across land that Robert was familiar with, where as a boy he had hunted wild turkey and deer. It had been some years, but although there were now a few scattered cabins and some signs of cultivation by pioneers who had moved out from the town of Charleston, it was still a remarkably unspoiled territory.

They traveled until the sun had gone down. Finally the three stopped and made camp, putting the horses in a makeshift corral and starting a fire to cook their supper.

As Robert, Hector and Running Wolf sat around the campfire, sipping strong, black coffee that permeated the wilderness with its odor, Hector rubbed his full stomach and sighed. "I'm glad you finally decided to stop for the night, Robert. If we keep up this pace, we will be to the Mississippi in no time at all."

"Are you complaining, Hector?" Robert asked.

"Not for myself," he said hurriedly. "I was only thinking about the horses." His eyes twinkled and he winked at the silent Indian. Hector deliberately kept up a patter of light conversation, knowing what must be going through

Robert's mind. The trapper would be stopping for the night also, and it was Eulalie who would be warming his bed.

Robert was aware of the older man's efforts and he tried to answer in like vein, but his voice was as heavy as the thoughts that trod upon his mind.

They stopped talking and prepared to bed down for the night.

Running Wolf, apart from the other two men, took the Shawnee scalp from his belt and gave it its nightly grooming before placing it carefully under the deerskin jacket at his side. And lying down with his head to the east, to ward off the bad spirits, he went to sleep.

Robert expected to get little sleep, but he went through the motions of moving his saddle to the lean-to, wrapped the rough wool blanket about him and eased his body down to the fresh pine boughs that covered the ground.

Resting his head on the saddle, Robert reviewed the events of the past day. He and Hector would travel many miles before reaching the Mississippi, from Georgia to Alabama and on through the Mississippi Territory. Although the first day had gone well, he was not tenderfoot enough to believe that the rest of the journey would be so easy. Trouble would come, of that he was sure.

He closed his eyes and, once again, unbidden, the image of Eulalie came to haunt him. Her mystical deep-brown eyes gazed at him, not in an accusing manner, but in fright and wariness. Then they widened with hurt and shame, and Robert clenched his fists in an attitude of despair and frustration.

His thoughts would not rest. Robert finally pressed his hands over his eyes to stop the specter of Jacques Binet taking Eulalie into his arms and loving her.

Sleep eluded him for a long time.

CHAPTER

7

A BIRD chirping in the tree above him caused Robert to stir. He listened to the other sounds around him, the neighing of horses, the flutter of dry leaves caught in the gentle breeze and the scampering of small animals hurrying through the woods. The place where Running Wolf had lain was empty, but Hector snored peacefully on.

Aware of the gradual change on the horizon, Robert watched the sun approach, showing itself cautiously and then stopping. A sudden glint, red-gold on a rock, and then darkness again blotted out the light.

He stretched his long frame and was content to lie still for a few minutes longer. Off and on a vestige of light appeared until, in a spurt of boldness, the sun burst into golden shafts, touching everything with its blinding light.

Robert blinked and turned his head. He arose, folded the blanket and moved his saddle to the makeshift corral.

By this time, Hector called, "Robert, are you awake?"

"Over here, by the fire. Breakfast is nearly ready."

Hector, stiff from sleeping on the ground, limped to the fire, and after the men had eaten, the pack horses were loaded and another day of riding began.

They were now getting into more mountainous terrain,

and at times the clouds obscured the sun. Thunder rumbled in the distance, sounding as if some angry giant were afoot.

"Your thunder god is waking up today," Robert said to his Indian guide.

And indeed the god semed angry, for at that moment, the clouds blossomed with rain and spilled over on the red-clay soil of the piedmont, drenching every crack and crevice of the land.

Day after day, they rode in the relentless rain. Swollen streams were a constant hazard, and the earth, softened by the torrents, became a red, sucking, living monster, terrifying the horses as they sank to their knees in the mud. At times, Robert wondered whether it would not have been wiser to sail to New Orleans as the trapper had done, instead of traveling by land. At the rate they were going, they would not be saving much time. And problems multiplied as the days went by.

Part of their supplies had been washed downstream when one of the pack horses, caught by a whirling eddy, lost its head and struggled in a frenzied attempt to be free of all encumbrances.

It was even difficult to find fresh game for their meals. For days they had almost tripped over animals darting before their path, but now the animals had disappeared into hidden recesses to wait out the storm, and it was only when an occasional rabbit became too hungry for caution that Running Wolf was able to provide meat for the roasting spit.

During that time, they came across a few scattered settlers, invariably bogged down in the mud, with a drenched family staring dejectedly from a wagon filled with their possessions. The three men did what they could to get a wheel out of the mud, but they never tarried long or stopped by day except to give the horses a rest.

A few Indian braves of the Chickasaw tribe eyed them as they crossed one of the streams, but after returning Running Wolf's silent greeting, the Indians moved on, seemingly not interested in them or their horses beyond a mild curiosity.

But one evening after the weather had cleared and it looked as if they might have a chance to stay dry, they saw two men coming through the shadowy half-light toward their campsite.

Hector's hand tightened on his gun while Robert watched the men's progress with an unobtrusive vigilance.

"Good evenin' to ya," said one of the rough-looking fellows with an unsuccessful attempt at an engaging smile. "Smelled your cookin' a ways back and we just sorta followed our noses."

For a moment, Robert stared at the strangers without speaking. Finally he said in a courteous voice, "Then, I gather you have not eaten?"

Both men shook their heads and with ravenously hungry glints in their eyes, they peered at the meat as it hissed over the hot coals.

The courtesy of the wilderness forced Robert to invite them to share the meal.

"Now, that's mighty nice of ya," one of the men said as he seated himself on a boulder near the fire. "Caleb Black is the name, and this here's my partner, Squint Hudson. We been out so long, we run low on supplies."

"Are you hunters?" Hector asked.

"Well, reckon ya could say that. But now we're on our way to the land office at Cahaba," Caleb volunteered while his partner's eyes roved over the campsite. "They're givin' away lots of land just for the askin,' and me and Squint here thought we might try our hand at agraculture."

No one voiced comment at his information. They watched his partner, who was now staring at the freshly built lean-to a short distance from the fire. "Looks like you'll be mighty comfortable tonight."

Robert nodded and his attention returned to the meat. It was done and conversation was forgotten in the more important business of filling their empty stomachs. Robert apportioned the two strangers their share of the meat and they tore it in strips and swallowed great hunks with a minimum of chewing.

When the meat was gone, Caleb and Squint wiped

greasy fingers on their tattered shirts and, at a signal from Caleb, they both stood up.

"Much obliged for the meal. Reckon we'll get on now to make our own camp. Maybe we'll meet up again sometime, seein' we're travelin' in the same direction," Caleb said.

Robert said nothing in answer to his remark, but bade them a good evening and stood with Hector, watching their departure.

As they disappeared, Hector turned to his cousin. "Robert, I don't tru—"

But Robert held his finger to his lips in a warning gesture and Hector froze.

In a few minutes, with silence still enveloping them, Robert and the Indian put out the fire and started to the lean-to. A puzzled Hector remained by the pile of smothered ashes while the two younger men stuffed pine boughs under the blankets in their temporary shelter. Robert removed his hat and placed it on the side of his saddle that lay on the ground.

In the increasing darkness, the still bulk, covered by the blanket, resembled a man stretched out for the night with his head resting on the saddle. Comprehension came to Hector, and he too removed his hat and placed it over his own saddle on the ground.

All three moved away from the lean-to, Running Wolf to tend to the horses and guard them, and Hector and Robert to hide behind the brush on the other side of the campsite and wait for what might come.

The moon climbed high and the night was quiet. Then the quietness was broken by a fleeing of small animals. A cracked twig, a soft oath, gave signal that someone was afoot in the woods, and coming closer.

Suddenly the dummy figures, stuffed with pine boughs, were attacked by Caleb and his rogue friend. As the two realized they had been duped, the air was filled with angry oaths.

Robert and Hector, framed by the moonlight, stood up with their weapons to face the two men and Caleb and Squint lunged at them.

Rifle fire reverberated through the woods and both

Caleb and Squint fell to the ground. Quickly, Robert walked to the still body of Caleb Black. He removed the knife from the man's hand and hurled it into the forest.

As Hector bent over Squint's body, he said, "Robert, I believe this one's still alive." With that pronouncement, the man, Squint, taking Hector by surprise, moved suddenly and with one final effort drove his knife into Hector's thigh, causing him to gasp in pain.

"Are you all right?" Robert called out anxiously. By the time Robert reached the older man's side, Squint Hudson was still.

"I'm afraid I've been wounded," answered Hector in a dazed voice as he attempted to staunch the flow of blood from his leg.

For the next several days they traveled slowly because of Hector's wound. The older man was stoical, and it was only in a fleeting grimace when his horse jarred him that he gave any indication that he was in pain. But the traveling did not help the wound. Hector had lost much blood and, off and on at intervals, he continued to bleed, the red fluid soaking through the strips of cloth tied around his thigh.

Robert was relieved when they finally reached the garrison at Arkansas Post. He had known he was getting close to civilization because of the increased traffic on the rutted cattle road, as well as the presence of a road at all. True, they had crossed a few traces running north and south, but they had been following a bridle path westward for so long that Robert was convinced he would never come across a civilized road until he was back home in Charleston.

"Now for a doctor to attend to your leg, Hector—and then, you can rest while I find news of Jacques Binet."

Within a few hours, they had been received cordially by the commander of the fort, Major Blount, who had also invited them to dinner; Hector had been examined by the fort's doctor, who was much concerned with the condition of the inflamed, swollen thigh; and Robert had found disturbing news of the trapper, who had already passed the fort on his way up the Mississippi.

He had driven them hard over the past weeks, and now Robert found it difficult to relax after the disappointing news that he had missed Eulalie. But a warm bath, a shave and clean clothes elevated his spirits and he felt closer to Eulalie than at any time in his journey. It would not take long to catch up with her, for he was determined to leave the fort as soon as possible to start upriver.

But would Hector be able to travel? His leg was alarmingly infected from the dirty knife wound, and if he were not careful, he could lose his leg.

And after he found Eulalie, what then? Would she ever forgive him?

Robert was aware of the punishment ahead of him— his atonement for selling Eulalie as a slave. He was destined to a lifetime of agony in seeing her and yet knowing that she could never be his wife again, because of what had happened.

But he pushed that thought from his mind as he and Hector walked to Major Blount's house for their dinner appointment. He was concerned only with the problem of finding Eulalie.

The major leaned back in his chair, after finally pushing himself away from the dinner table.

His massive front protruded from his tightly buttoned uniform, and his great bulbous nose resembled a treasure map sketched in red, broken lines.

"That was a delicious, well-cooked meal, Major Blount," said Robert as he rose from the table.

"Far better than what we've eaten for the past few weeks," Hector added.

"Rather enjoyed it myself," answered the major. "Most times it's a choice between roast beaver or boiled head of moose. Glad to get some bison steaks for a change."

Dr. Rolfe, the post doctor, who had joined them for dinner, found a place by the fire and proceeded to light his pipe.

"How long do you plan to stay at the post, gentlemen?" the major questioned.

Robert hesitated, looking at Hector.

"If my cousin does not mind waiting at the fort to

give his leg time to heal, my guide and I will leave tomorrow morning. I'm anxious to catch up with Jacques Binet as soon as possible, since he has . . . something of mine in his possession."

Dr. Rolfe agreed. "It would be much healthier for Mr. Tabor to remain here for a while, and there is plenty of room in my house. I would welcome him as a guest, as well as a patient."

"That's extremely kind of you, Dr. Rolfe," Hector answered. "Let me think it over and I'll let you know by tomorrow morning, if that's soon enough."

"Certainly."

"I'm not surprised that you're searching for Jacques Binet or that he has something of yours," Major Blount volunteered. "He would steal the rosary from his dying mother if he had half a chance. After his fight over the squaw, I gave him a choice of either leaving the post or being locked up in the stockade."

Robert stiffened but asked in a casual tone, "A squaw, did you say? Do you know which . . . tribe?"

"Oh, could have been a Quapaw or Osage—they all look alike to me with their black hair and dark eyes. But come to think of it . . ." His eyes narrowed in remembrance. "This one was particularly pretty, even in her dirty clothes."

Major Blount saw that both Robert and Hector were interested, and he began to elaborate.

"I have enough trouble keeping the peace between this conglomeration of humanity—Indians, runaway slaves, half-breeds and outlaws—without the added burden of someone like Jacques Binet. These squaw men are all savages, drinking and fighting. And since there are not enough women to go around, the men steal them from each other when they get drunk."

Hector watched Robert's reaction and hastily countered, "But I have heard that many of the traders have taken squaws as wives and have become good family men, living well-ordered lives with their half-breed children."

"I suppose there are a few," conceded Major Blount,

"but most of them are like this trapper scoundrel. When they get tired of one squaw, they swap her for another."

Robert scraped his chair as he suddenly stood up.

"Thank you, Major Blount, for your hospitality. It's getting late, so we'll say good night. Good night, Dr. Rolfe."

Dr. Rolfe stood up and shook hands with both men. Robert heard Hector's quiet conversation with the doctor. ". . . and since I would only slow him down, I have decided to take you up on your offer, Dr. Rolfe. I'll move in tomorrow, if that's convenient."

Robert became aware again of Major Blount's voice. ". . . and be sure to get a decent birchbark canoe. It's the best means of travel upriver," the man advised.

The major watched the two men disappear down the muddy walkway and then he closed the door against the cold night.

CHAPTER

8

THE horses were left with Hector at the fort and, on the next day, Robert and Running Wolf set out by boat for St. Louis.

Robert was disappointed that he had been unable to acquire a birchbark canoe. He had to be content with a dugout, but he had been assured that he would have better luck when he reached St. Louis.

The hollowed-out cottonwood hulk was heavy to handle and it sat low in the water. Still, the two men made good time against the current, and with each mile traveled, Robert's heart filled with hope.

He and Running Wolf drove themselves hard, staying on the river each day until sundown. Sleeping only a few hours each night, they got up early and were ready to cast off when the sun provided first light.

The river was now a strange sight, with the clear Mississippi water refusing to mix with the muddy red water emptying from the Missouri. Almost as if not on speaking terms, the two waters flowed separately, side by side, forced to share the same river bed.

Somehow it became a portent of his relationship with Eulalie—so near and yet so distant, their lives flowing in the same direction, but never together. He was determined to do everything possible to shorten the time when he would be able to rescue Eulalie from the man who had bought her as his slave.

At last, Robert and Running Wolf arrived in St. Louis, but again, Eulalie's rescue was denied him. Jacques Binet's party had already left St. Louis.

Still pushing themselves, they filled their newly acquired lightweight canoe with fresh supplies, and Robert and the Indian once more set out on their continuing quest. Aching muscles were a poor reason to slacken the pace, Robert thought.

The world was silent. No sound of bird or beast disturbed the air. Only the rhythmic pull of oars slicing through the water matched the movement of clouds gathering in the gray, muted sky above.

"There is a chill in the air, Running Wolf," Robert commented to the Indian. "I wouldn't be surprised if we had snow later in the day."

The Indian nodded, but Running Wolf's attention was more on the water than on the sky.

"What's wrong?" Robert asked, noticing the alert, listening expression on the Indian's face.

"Trouble ahead. Can you sense it?"

Robert stopped his paddling and listening. The exchange of rifle fire suddenly cut through the wilderness, echoing and re-echoing down the length of the river. Robert took up his oar again and together the two paddled more rapidly.

When they made the second horseshoe bend, Robert saw the long canoe. It was caught on a sandbar and Indians on the riverbank were shooting at its occupants.

"Your relatives?" Robert inquired cautiously, looking toward the redskins at the river's edge.

"No," the Indian replied. "Enemies."

The occupants of the long boat had no chance unless they could free themselves from the sandbar. Robert and Running Wolf placed their oars inside the canoe and took up their rifles to join in the fight. With each shot, their canoe dipped from side to side.

From the corner of his eye, Robert saw a savage's head appear in the water beside the long boat. And then a woman took an oar to drive off the menace in the water.

Robert's heart gave a leap. Could the woman be Eulalie? He was too far away to see her clearly, but she was small with dark hair.

When the second band of savages emerged from the woods, Robert became too busy to keep his eye on the woman. Having spotted the canoe downstream, the Indians now concentrated their fire toward Robert and Running Wolf.

At first, the bullets sang over Robert's head and dived harmlessly into the water behind the boat. Then the canoe was ripped in several places by bullets. Water crept into the canoe, but the fighting continued, with Robert and Running Wolf bringing down one savage after the other. And then, suddenly, the remaining Indians disappeared into the woods.

The canoe was sinking fast. Robert and Running Wolf jumped into the water to pull it toward the bank. Concerned with the sinking boat, Robert did not notice that the other boat was now free of the sandbar and moving away from them until he heard a voice shout over the water.

"Jacques Binet thanks you, *mes amis!*"

Jacques Binet—at last, he had found him.

"No, wait!" Robert shouted. "Wait! Eulalie—wait!"

But the boat moved out of sight and Robert was powerless to follow, either by boat or on foot.

So near—so near. Once more, a feeling of utter frustration swept over him and he banged his fist into his open palm. "Damn! Damn!" he muttered to himself in complete despair.

Cold and hungry, Robert kept watch while Running Wolf dozed for the first part of the night. Later it would be his turn to sleep.

He and the Indian had made as little noise as possible when repairing the canoe earlier in the evening. The frame of white cedarwood laths lashed together with rawhide thongs had not been damaged. And so the small holes in the birchbark had only to be caulked with spruce gum to make it float again. Robert's jaws ached from the chewing of the spruce gum to get it soft enough to smear over the holes. It would have been so easy to boil the gum, but they did not dare light a fire because of the Indians lurking in the forest nearby.

A soft wet layer of snow covered the blanket that was draped over his shoulders, and Robert shivered. He reached into his jacket for another piece of beef jerky to relieve his hunger—a far cry from the sumptuous dinner at Arkansas Post with Hector a few nights past.

The two men, anxious to catch up with Jacques Binet, continued traveling up the Mississippi, past the limestone bluffs, but the boat containing Jacques Binet and his friends had disappeared. Finally the heartrending truth dawned on Robert—the trapper must have left the Mississippi for the Missouri River soon after the Indian encounter.

Now Robert and Running Wolf were too far north to turn around and follow them. The river had frozen and they were stranded for the winter.

The meager warmth of the trapper's cabin seemed to enrage the howling blizzard outside. The wind, with its curving, icy fingers whipping through the chinks between the logs, struggled to choke the heat of the fire. Running Wolf picked up another log from the large supply stashed in a corner of the room. As he placed it upon the hearth, the embers took heart again with fresh vigor.

Robert lay on a pallet in another corner of the cabin. His eyes were glazed with fever and he tossed back and forth, until another burst of coughing left him gasping for breath. Still, he struggled with his nightmare.

"Lili . . . Lili," he called in his delirium. "Wait! Don't leave me!"

The howl of wolves outside disturbed him and, listening to them, Robert slowly pulled himself into an upright position.

"Running Wolf," he whispered, seeing his friend bending over the cooking pot at the fire, "how long . . . have I been . . . like this?"

"Six days, my friend."

He lay again full-length on the pallet, still listening to the wolves. Robert remembered then that he and Running Wolf, cut off from their search by the frozen river, had sought shelter for the winter in a deserted trapper's cabin not far from the banks of the river. In order to survive, they had become trappers themselves, subsisting on the meat and storing the furs on tall pole stands outside, stacking the furs together and waterproofing the bundles with large strips of bark.

The wolves were now gathered at the bases of these inaccessible stands and were howling their frustrations in an eerie wilderness symphony that penetrated the cold evening air.

Robert lifted his head as the sounds waxed and waned, feeling the same desolate anguish deep within his own throat—silent, hurting, vibrating the cords of his empty heart. Eulalie . . .

Slowly he mended, but it was many days before Robert was able to venture outside again. The rest of the winter was spent in trapping furs and in trying to stay alive.

At last the spring thaw came to the once frozen wilderness country, and the river lost its icy covering to become a busy, swollen torrent rushing toward the trading posts. The canoe, loaded with furs, was launched upon the water. The Indian and Robert, toughened and lean from the hard winter, began the trip south.

There was no food left, so each day Robert and Running Wolf fished in the river or trapped fresh game. Their ammunition supply had dwindled and they dared not waste their few remaining shots, since they were in dangerous territory. A panther, a group of marauding Indians or robbers were of much more danger than mere hunger.

Robert had heard tales of trappers, with their rich stores of furs, being preyed upon by those unwilling to spend a cold winter in the wilderness, but more than willing to relieve the trappers of their winter's work. A well-placed shot, a pushing of a body into the river or a deep ravine, and greedy men became owners of a fortune for which they had expended little energy.

And so, for these reasons, the two men made a habit of stopping in the early afternoon to cook their one meal of the day, so that their fire would not be so obvious as it would have been in the dusk. Then they would paddle downriver, away from the cooking site, to spend the night in relative obscurity and safety.

On the fourth day of their journey downriver, Robert and Running Wolf stopped as usual to build their fire and roast the two large fish that they had caught for their supper. After the bones had been picked clean of the white, flaky meat, the men sat in companionable silence. And Robert turned again to the problem facing him.

Six months or more—and still he had not found Eulalie. Back to Arkansas Post to get Hector and then to start over again, gathering any information he could. It was the only way to continue the search—until he could remove Eulalie from the hands of Jacques Binet.

Where could she be, this dark-eyed girl-wife, whose image refused to fade from his mind? It would seem, after so many months, that she would cease to haunt him, but for Robert, there was no respite.

Robert's brain, occupied by thoughts of his wife, barely registered the movement of the Indian as he leaned over to smother the cooking fire.

But a sudden roar brought his haunting reverie to a halt. Not more than ten yards from Robert stood a reddish-brown grizzly bear. For a split second, he and the bear eyed each other. And then the bear was on the move, coming toward him.

Robert had no time to take careful aim. He quickly grabbed his gun and fired. The bear did not stop. With an angry roar, the animal, merely wounded, swept his giant paw over the man's body, knocking him to the ground and leaving a tattered, bloody trail across his chest.

Stunned, Robert lay on the ground, his rifle out of reach.

Running Wolf, seeing what had happened, shouted at the bear and advanced toward him, attempting to distract him from the quiet, bleeding body stretched prone before him. At the same time, the Indian picked up his own rifle that lay beside the huge rock.

With another roar that filled the woods, the bear lumbered toward Running Wolf. The Indian held his rifle steady, aiming for the bear's throat. Running Wolf calmly pulled the trigger, but the rifle misfired.

The Indian stepped back, but it was too late. The bear lifted Running Wolf off the ground and flung him through the air, into a pile of rocks at the water's edge. The broken body of the Indian lay still.

Clawing at his wound and bellowing with mounting pain, the grizzly turned again toward Robert. Robert sat up, groping for his knife and shaking his head to clear his stunned vision. He was ready when the bear lunged. The knife struck flesh and the bear fell. But the weight of the bear crushed the breath from the wounded man. A fiery agony spread to every part of his body before total darkness brought release.

CHAPTER
9

THE burning pain was enough to keep Robert from opening his eyes. He didn't care where he was. His one wish was for death to come quickly. Better that than to breath in an agonized labor; for with each gasp, the pain radiated through his chest and down his spine, to linger in his left thigh.

He felt a stick prod him in the side and he winced and opened his eyes at the same time. It was dark, with a mere slit of light invading the enclosure where he lay. The sickening odor of stale bear grease mixed with herbs came from his chest and filled his nostrils. He turned his head and was sick.

An Indian with a grotesque headpiece and mask squatted on his heels in the corner of the tent and slowly withdrew the stick. The Indian stood up, rattled the gourd in his hand and walked out of the tent opening while muttering some incantation.

Within a few moments, the tent was filled with Indians, all gazing down at him and speaking in strange, guttural syllables to each other.

Why had they moved him to this place? Why had they not killed him where they had found him? Were they waiting to have some fun before putting an end to his life? He had heard how some Indians baited and tortured their prisoners before putting them to death. At that instant, Robert no longer cared what they did to him, if only they would get it over with quickly.

But nothing happened except that he was fed and cared for. Although the Indians appeared from time to time to stand and watch him, there was no expression in their eyes during the long days that Robert lay helpless in the tent.

Then, one morning, when his breathing was becoming less labored, a tall Indian brave, followed by four others, walked into the tent.

They murmured to him, but he did not understand. Suddenly, the four squatted down, each grabbing an arm or leg, as the tallest brave tightened a leather noose around Robert's neck.

He struggled and protested the choking sensation, but he was no match in his weakness for the five Indian braves. Then they released him and he was able to breathe again.

In relief, Robert realized they had not tried to kill him. But now, he knew they intended to keep him a prisoner.

The leather noose around his neck was looped by its own long leather rope plaited back to a tree outside the tent. It took some time for the plaiting, and finally Robert heard the metallic sound of a stake as it was driven into a tree, wedging the rawhide ends deep into the crevice. They were making sure that he would not escape.

They need not have bothered with securing him so soon. With the barest exertion of even sitting up, Robert felt a great weakness. It would be some time before he would be able to stand, much less walk a few steps.

As the days grew warmer, Robert sat outside the tent and drank in the sun. The wounds across his chest where the great bear had ripped him were now tender scars, but his ribs still pained him. He limped when he attempted to walk the short distance that his leather rope would take him, and it was not many paces before he felt the need to rest again.

The squaws and children were curious, and would come to the edge of the clearing to stand and watch. Some brought little gifts of food, a handful of berries or nuts. And one old squaw, with an uncertain, toothless smile, gave him a pair of moccasins. She touched his hairy beard, as if for luck, and quickly withdrew.

Ironic that they treated him almost as a talisman—as if by killing the grizzly, he had assumed an overwhelming importance in their lives. Yet he was their prisoner. Their awe did not extend to the act of freeing him.

Were they one of the tribes that worshipped the bear god? And by his own hands had he destroyed their deity? No wonder then that they thought he had a powerful magic in him that had to be contained with rope and wedge.

Robert had lost track of the days, but he knew he was getting stronger each day. He began to plot his escape, but he was smart enough to limp when he walked outside and to pretend he was far weaker than he actually was. He did not want the Indians to know how strong he was becoming, so he took most of his exercise inside his tent at night when no one could see.

From time to time, he looked at the iron stake in the tree to see how well the leather was embedded in the crevice. When no one was looking, he tried several times to dislodge it, but his strength had been insufficient.

The Indians had been careful to keep all sharp objects away from him, down to the small rock he had found in the clearing. Even then, it would have taken a long time to cut through the leather with a small, dull rock. And they examined the rope off and on—for teeth marks, he suspected, as if he could chew his way to freedom.

The summer storm came up suddenly. With a rattle of thunder, the clouds opened to breathe down cooling drops of rain. In the rapidly approaching darkness, the Indians scattered to their tents. Then the lightning began, noisy, deafening, and it was at that moment Robert realized the time for escape had come.

Silently, he crept out of his own tent and made his way to the tree that kept him a prisoner. He sat down on the wet ground and braced his feet against the tree. Wrapping several lengths of the leather thong in each hand, he began to pull against it.

The rain-swollen leather was too difficult to dislodge. Robert continued, stopping and starting, relaxing and straining. But the stake driven into the crevice would not budge. His hands and arms ached from the strain. Angry red patterns cut into his skin from the leather.

The peals of thunder were coming closer together and the sky turned yellow with light. Robert sat still and listened, afraid he had been seen, but no one came to check on him. Then methodically he began again.

His hands were now raw and bleeding, and the leather turned to red, but he persisted.

He was coming to the end of his strength and still he was a prisoner. Was there no way he could get loose?

The next flash of lightning revealed the heads of two Indian braves peering from their tent. Seeing them look in his direction, Robert crouched low against the tree until the light was extinguished in the ebony sky.

Robert waited, but the Indians did not come to stop him. Just as he was ready to give up, Robert felt the slight movement against the wood. Was it possible . . .

With fresh heart, he squeezed the remaining strength from his muscles and gave a powerful jerk to the leather. He suddenly shot backward to the ground. He was free!

Forgotten were the berries and nuts he had hoarded in his tent to take with him. Forgotten were his bleeding hands. He ran from the camp, with his leather rope still around his neck and the metal stake in his hand.

The momentary flashes of light from the storm showed him the way, and he hurried to get as far from the camp as possible before collapsing in a heap in the underbrush.

Robert slept by day and followed the path of the river by night, until he felt he was far enough away to be safe from his captors. Now it was time for him to find a boat to take him downriver.

He wondered if Hector were still at Arkansas Post waiting for him, or whether, when he and Running Wolf did not return, he had given up and gone back home.

A sadness filled his heart at the evident death of his friend Running Wolf. It was a twin sadness, to roost side by side with the sadness for Eulalie.

For three days, there was no traffic up or down the river. Robert considered himself fortunate when he finally found an old raft that had foundered on the bank. After making it riverworthy, lashing it anew with the same leather that had been his bonds, he cast himself upon the river, with a long pole to speed him on his way.

The iron stake proved useful also. He became adept at spearing fish with it, and it provided him supper several times when he would have gone hungry without it.

Robert knew he was an awesome sight, with his reddish-gold hair and beard grown so unruly, with his clothes in rags and the Indian moccasins the only whole item of clothing about him. He hoped that when he eventually met someone he would not be mistaken for a grizzly bear. At the thought, he laughed aloud, the first laugh in months.

The apparition coming toward him on the river was a strange sight. Robert saw that it was a flatboat, being poled by a black man. Sitting under a yellow canvas that had been used as a sunshade was a white man in an exotic sedan chair. And another figure he could not see clearly was sitting fishing from the side of the flat boat.

Robert watched while they drew nearer, and then he roared with laughter; for all at once he recognized his cousin, Hector, as the man in the chair.

He shouted his name and the man started from his seated position, putting his hand over his eyes to shade them from the sun. He peered at the man on the raft.

"Robert!" Hector shouted. "Robert, is that you?"

Within moments they were side by side, and Robert jumped from the raft onto the flatboat.

"Careful," Hector said as the boat gave a sudden pitch. "You'll drown us all. And we have gone to some trouble to find you."

Looking at the grinning black man clearly for the first time, Robert noticed it was Moses, his runaway slave. And the other smiling figure was his woman, Feena, who had disappeared the same time as Moses.

"Looks as if I have to do everything, while you go off into the wilds for the winter and decide to stay even longer," Hector gibed at him with a laugh. "And I have good news for you."

"Good news? You can't . . ."

"Eulalie is safe," Hector interrupted. "Seems she persuaded the trapper to leave her at the convent in New Orleans before he started upriver . . . told him she was a nun and that he would burn eternally in hell if he kept her, but if he let her go, she would pray for his soul every day. It was lucky for us that he is a superstitious Papist who can't get to heaven without someone's praying him in. And it seems I have to find your own people for you too. They were looking for Eulalie, also." His hand indicated the black man and woman.

Moses reversed the boat's direction and occasionally used the pole to keep them from getting too close to the banks.

For some time, the two men conversed. Hector related how he had found Moses and Feena, who had gotten to Arkansas Post too late to travel upriver to look for Eulalie; how they had traveled with him in the spring to St. Louis, where he had found Jacques Binet; and how they had decided to look for him when he did not appear.

In turn, Robert told Hector of the hard winter spent in trapping furs, the death of Running Wolf and his own capture by the Indians.

"Even the furs are gone," Robert commented ruefully, "so I have nothing at all to show for the winter."

Hector's eyes twinkled. "Well, my winter was vastly prosperous. Seems everybody was resolved to lose money to me at cards during the long, cold evenings at Arkansas Post. After selling the horses, too, we have more than enough to travel in style to New Orleans, pick up Eulalie at the convent and sail for home."

CHAPTER

10

I T was the last of July when they arrived in New Orleans. There had been much traffic up and down the Mississippi, with adventurers of every size and shape, appearing in outlandish costume and by outlandish means of travel— Germans, French, Italians, English. The summer madness, Hector called it; for once the government had purchased the land from the French, people were eager to explore it.

The weather was oven-hot and humid in the city. Fever was rampant and Robert was impatient to get Eulalie and return home. He prayed that she was well.

The carriage stopped at the convent gates and Robert, resplendent in a new linen coat and fawn-colored breeches, a snowy white cravat and shirt, and polished boots, stepped down to ring the bell hanging beside the gates.

"My name is Robert Tabor. I wish to see the abbess," Robert said to the black-clad figure before him.

"Mère Agnes is ill and can see no one."

"But it's urgent. It's my wife."

"Then perhaps Soeur Louise can help you." The nun unlocked the gates and Robert walked into the cloister, following the small, hooded figure.

"Will you please wait here in the garden?" the woman asked. "I will tell Soeur Louise you are here."

Robert sat down on a stone bench in the shade of the mimosa tree and waited. The coral vines climbed the walls and a peaceful calm seemed to wipe out all knowledge of the gay, wicked city outside the walls.

Robert was nervous. For so long he had lived for this day, thinking it would never come. At last, Eulalie was his again. But suppose she would not forgive him? Suppose she wished to remain at the convent and not return to Carolina with him? Of course she would return. He was her husband and she was obliged to do what he said. He would not allow her to stay another day within these walls.

As the figure approached him, Robert stood.

"I am sorry that Mère Agnes is ill and cannot see you, Monsieur Tabor," Soeur Louise explained. "But if your business is urgent, perhaps I can help you."

"Sister, I have come for my wife."

All the things that Robert had carefully rehearsed left him, and he had babbled the first words that had come into his head, like a nervous schoolboy who could not remember his day's lesson.

"Your wife, monsieur?" she questioned.

"Yes. Eulalie Boisfeulet Tabor. It has been some months now, but I have only recently found out that she is here. Will you please take me to her?"

Soeur Louise's lips tightened and her eyes were not kind. "It seems to be a little late for that, monsieur. But come, I will take you to her."

He followed her through another gate, into a much larger enclosure. Robert frowned as he saw the tombstones and mausoleums of a graveyard. Why was she stopping here?

"You could not have known, monsieur," she said uncertainly when she indicated the tomb before them.

The metal nameplate was shiny and new. Robert stepped closer and read the name—Eulalie Boisfeulet Tabor. He stared at it, unable to comprehend at first. And then the cold, sickening realization racked his body.

"No! It isn't true." Robert shook his head and in an

angry, intimidating manner he faced Soeur Louise and his voice demanded, "Tell me it isn't true! Eulalie is *not* dead."

The nun, cautious of the sudden violence of the tall man before her, took a step backward. "I am sorry, monsieur. It happened almost three weeks ago. There was nothing we could do to save her."

Robert turned back to the nameplate and his hand reached out toward the letters that spelled the name of his wife. The nun beside him was forgotten until she spoke again.

"You wish to be alone, monsieur? I will return in a short time."

Robert nodded. Alone, he went down on his knees and placed both hands on the cold slab that encased his lost love. The tears rolled unchecked down his bronze cheeks.

"Eulalie," he whispered. "Eulalie—"

For some time, he was still. Only the slight twitch of the muscle in his jaw and the wetness of his cheeks betrayed him.

Tormented for so many months by the image of soft brown eyes and an uncertain smile hovering about her sweet lips, Robert had lived on hope—hope that he would be able to find Eulalie and make it up to her for her ordeal. But now life offered an additional cruelty—to deny him atonement for his sin in selling her as a slave. Crushed was his hope, and Robert's heart was filled with despair.

In sorrowful silence he knelt until the soft rustling of the habit announced Soeur Louise's return.

"Are you . . . all right, monsieur?" she asked in a voice free of emotion.

Robert stood as if in a daze, aware of his grief, nothing else.

"Monsieur Tabor, what do you wish to do . . . about the child?"

He did not understand. "The child?" he repeated.

"Yes. Your son, monsieur. The convent cannot keep him forever. This is no place for a growing boy."

A child! Then Eulalie had died giving birth to a son. But was it his, or was it Jacques Binet's? He had no way of knowing.

"Bring him to me," Robert asked, his eyes suddenly grown hard.

The baby was brought into the garden and Robert gazed at him in the sister's arms. The fuzz upon the child's head was black, the color of Eulalie's hair. But Robert saw no other resemblance to anyone he knew in the tiny, helpless bundle of flesh that squirmed and whimpered in protest against the strong afternoon light.

So this was to be his atonement—to be responsible for Eulalie's child and never to know whether he or Jacques Binet was the father.

Abruptly he turned from the baby and said to Soeur Louise, "I will make arrangements and come for him tomorrow, sister."

"Do you wish to employ the same wet nurse that he has now, monsieur?"

Robert had not thought of that. He had no experience with this sort of thing.

"Who is his nurse now, sister?"

"An unfortunate young white woman who lost her baby the day before Jason was born," the nun replied.

"Jason." He said the name slowly.

"Your wife called him that when he was born. But to get back to the nurse . . . "

"Yes."

"Her husband, who was a visitor to the city, was killed in a duel, and she had nowhere to go, so she came to the convent. She has no money of her own, and for this reason, you would be doing a deed of charity to employ her."

"What is the woman's name?"

"Florilla. Florilla Hines."

"Would she be willing to travel to Carolina?"

"I am sure she would, monsieur, if it meant employment even for the next year. Would you care to see her?"

"No. Just tell her to be ready when I come for the child tomorrow afternoon."

He turned on his heel and, without looking back, he opened the gate, walked onto the banquette and climbed into the waiting carriage, while the clamor of the convent's bell lingered in his ears.

Feena did not like the woman, Florilla, and the way she looked at Robert Tabor. Her blue eyes were too bold, even if her corn-colored hair was bound in a style suitable for a widow.

Heartbroken that her *petite* Lili was dead, Feena protected and cared for Jason the same way she had cared for his mother, and she resentfully gave him up to Florilla only when he was crying with hunger.

On board the ship home, Robert Tabor paid no attention to either the baby or Florilla. He and Hector remained together, and at other times he paced restlessly up and down the deck.

The trip was uneventful, and within a week they had landed at Charleston.

With the malaria season in full force, Robert did not go immediately to the plantation house. Surrounded by the treacherous bog that bred this peril to life from May to the end of October, Midgard was too unhealthy for the baby and his wet nurse.

Robert installed Jason and Florilla in a rented townhouse in Charleston, where the cool breezes from the Atlantic could bring relief from the summer heat. And giving the new overseer, Gil Jordan, an ample supply of the medicinal bark of the cinchona tree to ward off the bouts of malaria, he left the man to run the plantation and see to the crops.

Robert propelled himself into a constant circle of activity, while he continued to ignore the child. He joined the Monday Night Club, the Friday Night Club, the Literary Society and the St. Cecilia Society and raced his horses against the young bloods with a reckless abandon.

When cold weather came, Robert shut up the townhouse and moved back to Midgard.

The haunted look on his face was still apparent, but Robert's initial frenzy was beginning to lessen. He became involved in politics, taking sides with the Jeffersonian

Republicans, much to the chagrin of some of his more staunch Federalist friends.

Arthur Metcalfe, who had greeted him when he first sailed home, was elected to the state legislature, and he and Robert spent hours arguing the issues of the day when the house was not in session.

Again hot weather enveloped Midgard and Robert moved into town until the danger of malaria subsided. And when the time came, he journeyed down Biffers Road to the plantation. Jason, Florilla and Feena traveled in the carriage, but Robert preferred riding alone on horseback.

The baby, Jason, was now two years old. His hair, black when he had been born, had lightened to a golden brown, and his eyes had gradually changed to that strange topaz of a jungle lion.

A strong and sturdy boy, he no longer needed Florilla as a wet nurse, but she remained in the house, acting as governess.

One afternoon in early November, after Jason had awakened from his nap and Feena had dressed him, the black woman led him down the stairs out to the piazza, to play in the yard.

Though it was unusual for him to be home at this time of the day, Robert sat on the piazza. Seeing them coming toward him, Robert called to Feena. "The boy—he is getting along well?"

Feena took the child and led him to Robert. The little boy stared solemnly at the big man before him.

"He is well, monsieur, and getting more like his father every day."

Robert frowned. "Do you believe *I* am his father, Feena?"

She looked him squarely in the eye. "If monsieur would only take time to look, he would not have to ask that question. The eyes would tell him."

The man scrutinized the boy's face, as if seeing him for the first time. The topaz eyes of the child stared into the topaz eyes of the man, who was now kneeling beside him.

The joyous smile spread across the man's face and he impulsively embraced the little boy.

"Careful, monsieur. Your arms are strong. You will crush your son if you do not watch out."

He released the boy and stood up.

"Is he talking yet?" Robert inquired.

"A few words, monsieur."

"Horsie—horsie," the child said, pointing to the animal being led to the front by a groom.

Robert picked Jason up in his arms. "Would you like to ride the horse, Jason?"

The little fellow gave a squeal of delight as he was lifted up to sit with Robert on the horse.

Feena watched while man and child rode slowly down the avenue of magnolias.

"At last," the woman said under her breath, "Jason has a father."

CHAPTER

11

THE young girl placed the flowers upon the tomb, near the plaque marked "Eulalie Boisfeulet Tabor."

Such a large tomb for such a little body, she thought.

She sat on the small stone seat supported by cherub's wings and sadly tried to remember the time over two years before when her baby had died. Because of the fever, she still could not recall everything that had happened.

She and Mère Agnes had become ill at the same time, and Soeur Louise had nursed them both back to health.

"It's the result of the fever, my child," Soeur Louise had reassured her troubled mind. "It does strange things to the brain."

"But I was so sure that I had a son," the girl protested. "I can still feel him in my arms."

"You had a daughter, Eulalie," the nun corrected her. "Her little soul is now in heaven with the angels."

Soeur Louise had been so kind to her when she first came back to the convent.

"He must not know that I am here. Promise me— promise me, if Robert Tabor ever comes to take me away, you will hide me from him." Her lips had quivered with fright.

"Hush, *ma petite*. Don't be so frightened. You are safe with us."

Eulalie remembered the shock when she first discovered that she was going to have a child—Robert's child. She had not been long at the convent. Everything had been too upsetting for her to notice the signs at first. She thought it was the aftermath of being so sick on the ship.

She had tried to wipe out the degrading memory of being sold to the trapper, and of that first night when Jacques Binet had drunk himself into a stupor. That was the only thing that had saved her—that and her *mal de mer* almost the moment they had boarded the *Jasmine Star* for New Orleans.

How disgusted the trapper had been with her inability to travel well on the water. Whenever he came near her, she had been forced to use the bucket by her pallet on the floor of the ship's cabin.

And when she had vowed to him that she was a nun, mistakenly sold as a slave, he was furious.

"Take me back to the convent, monsieur," she had begged over and over, when she was able to lift her head from the pallet. "The sisters will repay you."

"I do not want ze money," he protested. "Only you—as my woman. *Non,* I weel not geeve you back to zem."

"Do you wish . . . eternal damnation, monsieur?" Eulalie questioned.

The sudden fear was apparent in his eyes, and Eulalie took advantage. "For that is what you will receive, if you keep a bride of the church for your own . . . use."

He was defeated and she knew it. To soften the blow, Eulalie promised, "I will pray for you every day of my life, Monsieur Jacques."

The day that Jacques Binet had left her at the convent, he had said, "Do not forget your promise to me, leetle nun."

"I will . . . remember, monsieur," Eulalie replied.

He had gazed at her regretfully. "Such beauty, wasted here in a convent. Eet is sad, *non,* that you do not travel well on ze water. Otherwise, I would be tempted to risk even damnation."

He had shrugged and left.

"But father, I lied to him," Eulalie confessed to the priest. "I was not a nun, but a married woman."

The priest had heard her confession and had exacted a penance. She must pray for the man every day of her life, as she had promised him.

Eulalie should have felt better, but the malaise that had started on the ship persisted. Soon it was apparent to Mère Agnes and the others that there was a reason for it. Eulalie was with child.

Her time of delivery and the fever had come almost together. Soeur Louise, so patient and efficient, had nursed her back to health, but there was nothing she could do to save the tiny baby.

Later, Soeur Louise, seeing her interest in caring for the sick, had taken her under her wing, to teach her all she knew.

But still, she had not taken her vows. Eulalie did not know why she was holding back. Both Mère Agnes and Soeur Louise had hoped that by now, with nothing to stand in her way, she would relinquish all worldly ties and commit her life to God.

Was she bound forever to Robert Tabor, in spite of what he had done to her? And did she still nourish a small spark of hope that he would search for her and eventually find her here at the convent?

But it was now 1812. It had been three whole years since Jacques Binet had left her at the convent. No—Robert had not cared enough. He would have come if he had wanted her to return as his wife.

She must forget him. She must make a stronger effort to erase all thought of Robert Tabor from her mind.

Yet, had she not already tried that by working each day from first light to the evening bells? For theirs was no cloistered life of mere meditation and prayers. Rather, it was a working order of nuns, of teaching and healing, with the daily instruction of girls and young women, and the caring of the sick in the hospital attached to the convent.

But even with her hands constantly occupied, Eulalie's mind refused to forget Robert. It was as if his tawny eyes, that had once held her captive, were still sweeping over her, still capable of making her tremble with ecstasy, still making her afraid. . . .

The stone seat was hard, and the dampness in the air crept over the graveyard. Pushing her memories to the back of her mind, Eulalie arose to make her way into the chapel and there to kneel and pray for Jacques Binet. . . .

Early the next morning, Eulalie took her accustomed place at Soeur Louise's side, to work with her in the hospital. All day she performed her tasks with graciousness and a smile. Soeur Louise, trying not to show too much pride in Eulalie, said in a sober voice, "God has given you the gift of healing, my child. Do not abuse it, but always use it for His glory."

"I will . . . try to do that, Soeur Louise," Eulalie replied.

"Have you spoken to Mère Agnes . . . about your vows?" Soeur Louise continued.

"No . . . not in the past few weeks," Eulalie said. "I—I have been thinking—"

"There is nothing to keep you from them, child," Soeur Louise interrupted. "I have told Mère Agnes how well you are progressing. I know she will be pleased when you truly become one of us."

For the rest of the day, Eulalie thought of the words the sister had spoken to her. Now, down on her hands and knees, scrubbing the floor of the dispensary, Eulalie knew she could put off the decision no longer.

She owed the sisters so much; for had they not purchased her from the Frenchman? Eulalie shuddered to think what would have happened if they had refused. To be the trapper's mistress—or even to be buried in some remote wilderness beside her own dead child—

No, she had waited long enough. There was nothing to stand in her way. Eulalie would tell Mère Agnes that she was ready now to take her vows.

A sense of peace came over her at the decision. She would always be protected—never to know heartache again.

The door to the dispensary squeaked as it was opened, and Eulalie, glancing up, saw Soeur Thérèse, who was puffing from the exertion of walking to the dispensary. "Eulalie, Mère Agnes wishes to see you immediately."

Eulalie smiled and arose from the stone floor. How pleased Mère Agnes would be, Eulalie thought. She removed her long apron and followed the plump, elderly sister. They walked down the familiar corridor and Soeur Thérèse knocked at the door to Mère Agnes's quarters.

"Come in," the voice responded to the knock. The two quickly entered and Eulalie knelt before the woman enshrouded in black.

"You may sit here," Mère Agnes commanded Eulalie, indicating the chair beside her, while dismissing Soeur Thérèse.

The room was filled with shadows of the diminishing day, but Mère Agnes made no move to light the candle on the table. She seemed content to sit in the semidarkness.

Eulalie waited for the woman to speak. The authoritative voice began.

"Eulalie, you are to leave for the Carolinas with Père Ambrose tomorrow."

Seeing the stricken look on Eulalie's face, Mère Agnes explained in her authoritative manner. "We have received a request for help from our order's convent in Columbia. Half the city is ill, and the dispensary is inadequately staffed for an epidemic."

Eulalie tightened her fingers as they lay clapsed in her lap. She could not go. It was asking too much of her to return to Carolina.

"I . . . I cannot, Mère Agnes. Please—please do not ask it of me."

With a softened voice, Mère Agnes said, "If there were someone else to send, I would do it. But Soeur Louise is needed here." And then she added, "When the crisis is over, Eulalie, you will come back to us."

"But my vows, Mère Agnes. I wish to stay here and take my vows."

The smile was fleeting upon the abbess's face. "I am glad you have finally made up your mind, child, but there is no rush. You have waited over two years," the nun reminded her. "A few more months will not matter."

Eulalie, sitting in silence, rebelled at the thought of leaving the safety of the convent. Then a deep voice from the corner of the room shattered the silence.

"Our Lord went where He was called, my child. Would you deny His sick and helpless, when it is within your power to do His work?"

Eulalie turned with a start and saw the priest in the shadows. His eyes were compelling, and Eulalie, knowing that she was no match for either Mère Agnes or the priest, acquiesced in a small, barely audible voice, "N-non, mon père. I will go."

The abbess stood. "And now, Eulalie, you may leave me—to prepare for the journey."

The carriage swayed back and forth, and Eulalie, bruised from the harshness of the roads, attempted to find a more comfortable position. It was impossible.

She glanced at the priest seated opposite her. Father Ambrose remained impervious to his surroundings. It was as if he were in another world, with the discomfort of the present world unable to penetrate his saintly flesh.

Finally, Eulalie could no longer stand the isolation imposed upon her. "Père Ambrose," she ventured, and when he looked up, Eulalie continued, "This city that we are going to—what is it like?"

The priest closed the book he was reading. "It is a planned city, child," he explained, "built upon a large square, just like your Vieux Carré. But the streets that divide the square into sections are much wider than the cobblestone streets of New Orleans. In fact, they are so wide that there is little possibility of carriages colliding with each other."

"How far is it from Charleston?" Eulalie asked the question uppermost in her mind.

"About three days' journey. I do not know the actual number of miles," the priest answered before opening his book again.

For the rest of the day, Eulalie, peering from the small curtained window of the carriage, glimpsed bits and pieces of landscape as they passed by.

It was a dangerous time to travel. The British not only

had blockaded the harbors along the coast but had also stirred up the Indians. With each mile, Eulalie expected to be stopped by painted warriors and to be pulled from the carriage and massacred.

But the Indians did not bother them. After days of constant, uncomfortable travel along the coastal route, they turned inland, and finally one evening at dusk, they arrived in a city that smelled of death and disease. Bonfires were going and the fumes of sulfur caused Eulalie to gasp for breath. She held her handkerchief over her nose, but even then the stench of the streets filled the carriage.

They had reached their destination.

CHAPTER

12

*E*XHAUSTED from the trip, Eulalie had no trouble going to sleep that evening. When the new day began, she was put to work in the dispensary.

Faced with a steady stream of the sick and the dying, Eulalie had no time to think of anything but the ones who needed her care. Patiently, she administered to them and was rewarded when one took a turn for the better and cheated death of one more victim.

But the long, demanding hours took their toll. She grew thin and wan, and her brown eyes lost their luster.

"You cannot heal the world alone, Sister Anne," one of the other nursing nuns gently chided her. "You must take time to eat and get enough rest, or you will fall ill also."

Eulalie was touched at her concern. And inwardly she smiled at the name she was called—Sister Anne.

It had taken her a while to get used to the name that Mère Agnes had given her to avoid any possibility of being recognized. Yet Robert Tabor was miles away. There was little need to be afraid now; for she was far too busy to leave the confines of the convent.

The nun's words went unheeded as day after day Eulalie attended the sick. It was as if by denying the needs of her body, the restlessness of her soul could be quieted. Each day Eulalie grew thinner, her face more wan, until her unhealthy pallor came to the notice of the reverend mother.

"Sister Anne," the mother began, "you are to be commended for your dedication to the sick. But there is no need to neglect your own health. The fever is now abating and it is not necessary to work so hard."

The nun stopped speaking in order to look at the girl.

"I am told that you have not set foot outside the convent since you arrived here. Is that so?"

"Yes, reverend mother," Eulalie answered.

"Then you must take time each afternoon for a brisk walk and fresh air. We cannot have you getting any paler or thinner, or there will be nothing left of you."

And so it was that Eulalie, at the insistence of the reverend mother, found herself outside the convent. There was little space in the walled-in garden at the street side —little space to do anything but sit and meditate, and the reverend mother had insisted upon a long walk.

At first, Eulalie was uneasy. She kept looking over her shoulder for the familiar face, for a familiar footstep, but she saw no one whom she recognized. Because of this, she began to relax and to enjoy her afternoon walks, to notice her surroundings, the city built to bring together the dissenting factions of low-country slaveowning aristocrats and of upcountry farmers and merchants who had no slaves.

Eulalie passed by the empty plot of land where the new capitol building was to go, and she tried to imagine what the land had looked like while it was still the old plantation built along the banks of the Congaree.

"They took a damn fine plantation and made a damn poor town," one fierce dissenter commented loudly on the street corner, protesting the moving of the capital from Charleston to the middle of the state. Eulalie hurried from the group standing at the corner, so she would hear no more of the rough conversation.

It was now the third week of November. Soon the town would be bursting at the seams, for it was time for the legislative body to gather in the capital for its annual session. There had been talk of postponement because of the epidemic, but since it was on the wane, the governor had called it for the usual time.

Eulalie glanced toward the sun, already beginning its slow descent from the apex of the sky. She hurried down the street to the convent.

Fresh air and exercise, with additional sleep, had produced the desired effect. Although Eulalie was still far too thin, she looked much healthier, and as she walked into the dispensary to take up her afternoon duties, her eyes were alive with a sparkle that had been missing earlier.

Eulalie sat in the dispensary and waited for the last patient of the day to be seen before she locked the door. The conversation between the two women remaining in the outer room was loud and penetrating.

"This is goin' to be an excitin' time," one woman commented. "My husband said he wouldn't miss bein' in Columbia this session for anything. With that new Governor Alston takin' over—folks say he voted for himself in the legislature and that's how he got to be governor, by just one vote over his opponent. And those two enemies, Alistair Ashe and Robert Tabor, tearin' each other apart on the house floor about everything from public education to Mr. Madison's War. 'A mighty fine show, I can tell you,' he says to me just last night."

Eulalie's pulse began to beat rapidly as the name stabbed at her. *Robert Tabor,* her husband, in the legislature? And his overseer, Alistair Ashe, here too? How could that be? He was not eligible to serve in the legislature. He owned no property. And did the woman say that he and Robert were enemies?

Eulalie fled from the dispensary and took down her valise to pack her few belongings. It was a poor time to travel, with winter upon them. The sea would be rough, if they allowed her to sail back to New Orleans—that is, if there was even a ship willing to run the British blockade. Else, she would have to endure the torrential rains and muddy roads if she went by carriage. But whether by ship or carriage, it was imperative for her to leave Columbia. She could not risk being seen by either Robert Tabor or Alistair Ashe.

Tomorrow—I will get permission to leave tomorrow. Eulalie clutched the comforting thought to her breast, as she lay exhausted upon her narrow cot and drifted off to sleep.

"Sister Anne, Sister Anne, wake up." The hand shook her gently. "Reverend mother has need of you."

Eulalie was dreaming. Her body felt warm from the sunshine of the garden. Completely disoriented, she did not at first realize where she was, or why she was being waked in the middle of the night. As she sat up and slipped out of bed, her bare feet touched the cold floor. Then, she remembered. She was not safe in the cloister of New Orleans with Mère Agnes and Soeur Louise. She was in the same city as her husband, Robert Tabor. With a feeling of alarm, she put on the robe over her long white gown and hurried to answer the summons.

"You . . . you sent for me, reverend mother?" Eulalie asked sleepily.

"Yes, Sister Anne. You are needed at once. A little boy has become violently ill during the night and his father has asked for your help. The man has heard of your excellent ministrations during the epidemic, and if you will care for his child, he will reward the convent amply for our poor. While you remain in his house, I will release you from all duties here."

"But, mother . . ."

"Go with God, my child. The carriage is waiting. Pack your things and do not waste time."

Eulalie was dismissed and there was nothing to do but obey. And as for the valise, it was already packed.

The few remaining leaves of the yellow hickory in front of the convent were suddenly stripped from the limbs of the tree by a strong gust of wind. The dry, rustling leaves rolled in the wide street and, as if caught on an invisible string, were drawn together to the other side and then back again, before scattering in diverse directions.

Eulalie climbed into the waiting carriage. She removed the leaf still clinging to the hem of her dark cloak as the carriage, caught in the wind, started off. It lurched and then rumbled unsteadily down the wide avenue of the raw, provincial city.

The vehicle passed by the deserted rough wooden sidewalks where she had walked earlier, on past the flickering street lamps, until the darkness of the night prevented Eulalie from seeing any more.

Then the houses began to emerge, like gray and white images superimposed against the dark, rough embroidery of the troubled sky. The carriage slowed and stopped in front of a two-storied white clapboard house surrounded by a vertical iron fence.

"Here we are, ma'am," the driver said, placing the stool on the ground for her to alight.

Standing by the carriage, she looked up at the house, which was aglow amid its darkened neighbors. One light, with its reflection wavering, seemed magnified by the glass that framed the front door of the house. The wind whipped her nun's habit against her body, and Eulalie shuddered.

Hesitating at first, she stayed by the carriage while the driver set her valise on the porch. Then Eulalie walked slowly up the steps.

As if someone inside were waiting for the sound of footsteps, the door opened. A look of relief came across the black servant's face when she saw Eulalie. "They're waitin' for ya, miss," she said, opening the door wider. "Come on in and I'll git your valise."

Another light came toward her from the shadows of the long hall. With an air of impatience, the fair-haired woman holding the lamp beckoned to Eulalie and said, "Come with me, sister. He's in the nursery."

The woman led the way up the stairs. Eulalie followed her until they stopped in the narrow upstairs hallway.

With her eyes traveling over the girl in the nun's habit, the woman said, "I told him that it was not necessary to send for anyone, but the child's father insisted."

At the remark, Eulalie knew that the woman did not want her in the house. She said nothing in reply but waited for the woman to open the proper door.

The fire on the hearth was burning steadily in a soft, warm glow. With a sudden snap and wheeze, the resin ignited and sent sparks against the fire screen, to silhouette the small bed and the servant keeping vigil in the room.

"Stand up, Effie, when I come into the room," the fair-haired woman said in a harsh tone to the seated servant. "And move the other lamp so the sister can see the child."

A sullen look appeared on the servant's face, but she quickly obeyed and brought the lamp from the table to hold for Eulalie.

Eulalie stood, looking down into the face of the flushed, fevered child, his golden curls wet with perspiration and his little round cherub face marred by pink blotches from the fever.

As Eulalie knelt beside the bed, the child began to jerk convulsively. Quickly she thrust her fingers into the child's mouth to hold down his tongue and at the same time commanded, "Some cold water and towels—at once."

"Don't just stand there. Do as she says," the woman admonished the young black girl. "No, leave the lamp on the table, Effie," she continued in an exasperated voice.

"I declare, I don't know what I'm going to do. She doesn't have the sense she was born with . . . "

Eulalie shut out the droning, hard voice and watched the child as he grew quiet again.

"When did his fever begin?" Eulalie asked.

"About two days ago," the woman responded.

When the servant returned with the basin of water and towels, Eulalie removed the little boy's nightshirt.

"What are you doing?" the woman asked in a suspicious tone, while coming closer to the bed.

"I am attempting to bring the fever down, madame," Eulalie answered as she began bathing the child's feverish body in the cold water.

Seeing the child shiver, the blond-haired woman said, "You will only give him an inflammation of the lungs, bathing him in cold water. I think you had better stop before you kill him."

"You are his . . . mother, madame?" Eulalie questioned, puzzled at the woman's manner.

"I . . . I soon will be," the woman answered defensively. "And when his father gets back from the apothecary's house, I will see that he sends you on your way. Everyone knows that the cure for a fever is hickory ash mixed with brandy—*not* freezing a body to death."

Eulalie, already tired from the long day and having her sleep interrupted, had no wish to argue. Her thoughts were being taken off the child by the interference of the woman.

"Madame, you seem to forget that I did not come here by my own will. But there is no time to waste in arguing. If you wish to see the child well again, then you will please leave the room."

The woman's eyes glinted as she looked at Eulalie.

"It won't be for long, I assure you," she said in a threatening voice. "His father will have something to say about this."

Ignoring the woman's comment, Eulalie turned to the young black servant. In a firm voice, Eulalie said, "Effie, you will please sit outside the door and see to it that no one disturbs us for the rest of the night."

At the gentle command, Effie, with a broad smile, replied, "Yes ma'am. I sho' will."

The blond woman flounced from the room and, surprisingly, did not come back.

The storm that had threatened earlier came to fruition, loud and fierce. Rain beat against the windowpane and the wind howled down the chimney of the nursery.

The riderless hobby horse standing in the corner was caught in a sudden flash of lightning. It moved slightly and cast its shadow upon the wall, the toy a lonely sentinel for the child delirious with fever.

All through the night, Eulalie, keeping watch by the bed, repeated the bathing of the child's body. When the early-morning sounds drifted up the stairs, the child slept peacefully, his fever lowered for a short time.

In exhaustion, Eulalie leaned her head on the bed. The rain was steady and hypnotic. The fire had long since gone out and Eulalie wrapped her nun's habit closer to her body.

Her eyelids grew heavy. For just a few minutes, she thought. She would close them for a few minutes. She was so tired. . . .

The headpiece of her habit slipped and the pins, binding her luxuriant black hair into a tight bun at the neck, fell out, leaving the dark strands to fall in a curving caress across one cheek.

The door to the nursery opened and, as the footsteps came nearer the bed, Eulalie sat up, rubbing her eyes.

"Is my son better?" the man's deep voice inquired anxiously.

Eulalie's eyes, velvet-soft and wide, focused on the man standing before her. She suddenly gave a little cry of alarm, as recognition penetrated her brain. Standing before her was Robert Tabor—Robert Tabor, with his topaz eyes boring into her.

He stared at her incredulously, and then grasping both her hands, he brought her to her feet.

"No," she whispered, frantically looking for some means of escape.

"You! What are *you* doing here?" he asked in a hoarse voice.

"You . . . you sent for me—to take care of the boy."

He shook his head, dismissing her answer. "How can you come back from the dead?" he demanded.

"I . . . I do not understand what you are saying."

"You are supposed to be dead. They told me at the convent that you had died."

"You came . . . to the convent?"

"Yes."

There was a painful silence while the two stared at each other. Eulalie tried to remove her hands from Robert's grasp, but he refused to let her go.

She could not bear the searching, piercing eyes, stone-hard and pitiless, sweeping over her and her nun's habit, creased and wrinkled from the night's vigil. Searching for something to fill the awkward silence, she looked again at the sleeping child and said, "I . . . I did not know that you had a son."

"My son, Eulalie? He is *our* son," he corrected. *"Our* son—whom you did not love enough to keep."

His voice broke with bitterness.

"That is not true," Eulalie responded in a trembling voice. "I have no son—I have no daughter either; for her little body is buried in the cemetery of the convent."

"You mean . . . you did not know of Jason?"

"Jason?" she asked. The name had a familiar feel on her lips.

"Or was it convenient for you to forget that you had ever borne my son?" he taunted.

"I . . . I had the fever for many weeks, and I remember almost nothing of what happened. Soeur Louise told me my . . . daughter had died."

By this time, the tears were streaming down her cheeks. Her vision was blurred and she could not see the man clearly. "Is he truly . . . our son?"

"Do you not remember?" His voice had lost its former harshness.

Eulalie shook her head and her lips moved to form the word. But there was no sound, only tears continuing to flow from her sad brown eyes.

At her obvious distress, Robert realized she was telling the truth. She did not remember.

Roughly enfolding her in his arms, he leaned down to touch her hair with his lips. "Forgive me—forgive me," he murmured over and over.

The moment was filled with too much emotion for him to bear. He released her suddenly and the giant man fled from the room.

CHAPTER

13

I HAVE sent word to the convent that you will not return. They will understand that I wish you to take your rightful place here."

Robert's voice was distant and his manner formal.

Eulalie sat quietly by Jason's bed.

"What *is* my rightful place, Robert?"

At the question, Robert's eyes showed a controlled anger. When he finally spoke, Eulalie felt his anger meted out in every word.

"You are my wife, Eulalie—chosen for me by Uncle Ravenal. But do not worry. After what has happened, I would not ask you to perform any wifely duties. The only thing I require is that you remain in my house and give the *outward* appearance of domestic bliss."

His words lashed at her. He had not been so selective when he thought her a slave. But as a wife, she was found wanting. His message was clear—a wife in name only.

Feeling degraded, Eulalie replied, "And if I do not choose to remain—"

"Surely, you would not desert your own son, whatever you think of his father," he replied in an even icier tone.

"No, I cannot desert my own child, can I?" Eulalie said in a sad voice.

The sun had gone down and the flickering flame of the lamp made dancing patterns on the draperied window of the nursery. From a distance, the sound of a bell floated up the stairs and penetrated the quiet.

"It is time for dinner, Eulalie," Robert said, standing up. "Come."

"I . . . I would prefer a tray in the room, Robert. Jason might wake at any time. And he is still hot with fever."

"Mrs. Hines can sit with him while you come downstairs," he responded, brushing away her excuse.

"I am too tired for conversation."

The faint circles under her eyes became obvious to Robert for the first time. He stared at her tired face and in a more compassionate timbre, he said, "I will not force you then, Eulalie."

He started out the door but stopped. "Is there anything you need for the night?"

She hesitated. "If there is a cot somewhere in the house, I would like it moved in here."

"I will see to it."

He turned and closed the door behind him.

Eulalie had felt drained all day from the emotional encounter of that morning. And now, this. She could not go through another confrontation with the giant who was her husband. Better for her to stay in the nursery with Jason.

She had been afraid of ever seeing Robert again. And she was still afraid, now that they had met face to face. But there was nothing she could do about it. She was in his house, eating the food he provided and taking care of his child. Her child too, she thought. The baby was hers, too, taken from her arms to be given to Robert.

Eulalie did not blame Soeur Louise. Had she not begged to be protected from Robert? To be hidden away, if he should ever come to look for her? Yet, the payment for her request had been cruel. Two years lost. Two years without holding the baby in her arms, without nursing him with her own body.

Eulalie's eyes rested on the sleeping child. She marveled at his perfection and his angelic face. A fierce maternal instinct swept over her as she lovingly touched his dark-golden hair.

"Jason," she whispered softly, "Jason." Her lips curved in a smile as the name entwined around her heart.

If she could only leave and take Jason with her. But where? She could not go back to the convent in New Orleans. She would have to find another place to live— she and Jason—apart from Robert.

Eulalie's eyes showed their sadness. Robert would never allow his son to be taken from him now. And she could not leave without the child.

"You would not desert your own son." Robert's words flooded her thoughts. No, she was caught for the time being. She would be forced to stay because of Jason. But later?

On the fourth day, the child's fever broke and it was difficult to keep him in bed. By evening, he was tired and irritable, so Eulalie fed him some broth and rocked him to sleep, singing the words her *maman* had sung to her as a child. *"Au clair de la lune, mon ami, Pierrot . . . "*

Jason's eyes drooped, and flickered open off and on before remaining shut. Eulalie sat looking down at him, at the little face that was now covered in red spots. The worst was over.

Getting up carefully so as not to disturb him, Eulalie placed Jason in his bed and covered him with the soft quilt. He moved and whimpered but then relaxed.

Eulalie felt hungry. She knew it was almost time for Effie to bring her supper tray to her. Feeling tired, with her garments wrinkled from the long hours of sitting, Eulalie removed the habit and washed her face with water from the ewer. Then she put on a fresh habit that one of the girls had washed and ironed for her that morning.

At the small dressing table, she sat brushing her hair when the knock sounded.

"Come in," Eulalie called softly.

The door opened and, with her back to the door,

Eulalie said, "Just put the tray on the table, please." She continued brushing her lustrous black hair.

"There is no supper tray, Eulalie," the deep voice informed her.

Surprised, she turned and saw Robert towering in the doorway. "I am told that Jason's fever has now subsided, so there will be no more excuses for you to eat alone. You are to dine downstairs tonight."

"But he cannot be left alone," Eulalie protested, quickly binding the long strands of hair into a severe bun.

"One of the servants will sit with him," Robert argued, coming into the room.

Eulalie, nervous at Robert's staring, picked up the headpiece of her habit and, adjusting it on her head, hid the hair that she had just pinned.

Robert was now standing beside her. His eyes narrowed as he inspected her. "Do you not have anything else to wear, Eulalie?" he asked.

"Am I not suitably dressed for dinner, Robert?" Eulalie asked in return.

The deceptively demure answer caused him to smile.

"The only thing of importance is that you will dine downstairs tonight. But I see that I have been remiss in regard to your clothes. I will remedy that tomorrow."

Taking her by the arm, Robert guided her to the door. Eulalie sighed. She could no longer avoid him. He had seen to that.

The woman who had met her at the door that first night was already waiting at the table.

"You have met Mrs. Hines, I believe," Robert stated.

The woman stared at her coldly, but Eulalie inclined her head to acknowledge her presence, taking no note of her behavior. There was something faintly familiar about her. Had Eulalie seen her before coming to Columbia? She tugged at her memory, but nothing came of it.

"Mrs. Hines traveled from the convent with Jason. She has been much help with him these past two years," Robert explained.

"Then I am grateful to you, Mrs. Hines, for caring for my son," Eulalie said.

"*Our* son, Eulalie." Robert's voice corrected her.

Florilla, bringing the attention back to herself, broke in with an affected modesty. "I was happy to help with Jason." But the glance toward Eulalie was hostile and belied the soft answer.

Immediately after the meal, Eulalie left the dining room to return to the nursery. The look of disappointment on Robert's face was quickly disguised as he walked to the stairs with her.

Eulalie paused and turned to him. "Robert, is . . . Feena well?"

"Yes, she is fine," he answered.

"I . . . I thought she would be here with Jason."

"Florilla—that is, Mrs. Hines—felt that she was not good for Jason. 'Making a baby out of him,' she said, so we decided to leave her at Midgard."

"I would like Feena to be here with me," Eulalie added softly with an imploring look.

Robert frowned but answered, "I will send for her tomorrow, if that is what you wish."

"Thank you," she said with a hint of relief in her expression.

He took her hand and held it in his. Eulalie's pulse quickened and hastily she withdrew her hand. "Good night, Robert."

He stood and watched her walk up the stairs. Remaining in the hallway, he waited until he heard the nursery door open and close. Then Robert retraced his steps down the hall toward the library and came face to face with Florilla. Outside the dining room she had stood, silently taking in the exchange between Robert and his wife.

The next morning, the jingling of harness and the snorting of impatient horses at the front entrance heralded Robert's departure. He was leaving the house earlier than usual.

Within an hour, he was back. Voices downstairs broke into the steady hum of servants singing as they cleaned, and then the sound of the carriage departing once more told Eulalie that she was alone and safe for the day.

In a few moments, Effie came into the nursery, bringing with her several boxes wrapped with large pink ribbons.

"Miz Tabor, Mr. Robert lef' these clothes for ya. He said ya needed to put 'em on right away 'cause you're goin' to have comp'ny in a little while. And he says I'm to help ya."

So the nun's habit *did* bother Robert, Eulalie thought. And if she were to have visitors, it would be hard to explain why the wife of Robert Tabor was wearing the garb of a nun.

"And Mr. Robert said you was to move into the green bedroom, so I guess you'll want me to take these boxes there now."

Eulalie glanced at the sleeping boy and then meekly followed Effie down the hall to the designated bedroom.

Opening the largest box, Eulalie pulled out an ankle-length blue silk dress trimmed with ruffles at the hem. She felt the soft material, so different from the black, coarse weave of the garment she was wearing.

Eulalie had an urge to put the elegant dress back into its box, but she knew that Robert would be displeased if she disobeyed him and kept on the crow's dress that he so despised.

Without being told, Effie brought hot water into the room, and when Eulalie had bathed, she dressed and bound her hair in another style, softening the severity that was at variance with the dress Robert had chosen. Slipping her feet into the soft, heelless shoes, she was barely ready when the heavy knocker sounded at the door.

Who could it be, to be calling at such an early hour?

She did not have to wonder for long. And soon it became apparent that it was not a social call, as she had first imagined.

The woman introduced herself with a slight accent and a flurry of hands. Maggie—the buxom owner of the most exclusive dress shop in Columbia.

As an advertisement of her talents, she wore a dress, well designed and executed, although it was somewhat spoiled by the widening circle of perspiration under the arms, caused by her constant activity.

With the help of a small black boy, dressed in a red velvet suit, the woman brought the boxes from the carriage and up the stairs. Dresses were soon spread across the sofa in the adjoining sitting room of the green bedroom.

When his duty was completed, the boy sat unobtrusively on a cushion on the floor and watched the proceedings.

"Don't mind him," Maggie said to Eulalie when she glanced in the boy's direction. "He's used to this and thoroughly bored by it all."

But Eulalie was the one not used to dressing and undressing before an audience. Soon, though, her attention was diverted by Maggie and she forgot the boy while the woman discussed the clothes she had brought with her.

As she pulled the sparkling white ballgown over Eulalie's head, Maggie continued her chatter.

"You and Theodosia Alston will be the two most beautiful ladies at the ball this weekend."

"The ball? Is there to be a ball? This weekend?" Eulalie felt uneasy.

"Now, surely, Mrs. Tabor, you haven't forgotten the social event of the season—the ball in the senate chamber, with all the wives determined to outshine each other. Why, I've been busy for ages, making up gowns from the latest Paris fashion journals. And Mr. Tabor was explicit this morning about what he wanted you to wear."

"I . . . I have been away." Eulalie's voice trailed into a small wisp of sound.

Maggie pinned the waist of the gown and then began to measure the hem. "I understand that you've been visiting friends in New Orleans. Guess that's why you haven't heard all the gossip.

"And such a shame about your luggage, too. Your husband told me you would need everything from the skin on out."

Eulalie was embarrassed, and to pass the attention from herself and her lack of clothes, she quickly said, "The one you mentioned—Theodosia. May I inquire who she is?"

"That's Governor Alston's wife. She's had a hard time

lately, with the scandal and all. Theodosia Burr, she was
—Aaron Burr's daughter—but a finer, sweeter lady you
never saw.

"It hurts us all to see her looking so sad. She lost her
little boy this past summer—the only child she had. And
looks like there's no chance of her ever having another."

Maggie filled her mouth with pins, and for a while that
precluded any more information from her lips.

By the time Maggie left, with the small black boy trailing behind her, Eulalie had three day dresses finished, as
well as the lavender evening gown. Eulalie had promised
to come into her shop for the rest of the fittings that week.
Robert had left no doubt concerning her clothes, Maggie
revealed.

And, according to Maggie, Robert expected her to go
out to dinner that evening. Yet he had not mentioned it
the night before when she was downstairs. Had he made
up his mind during the night? Even so, he could have left
a note, instead of having her discover it from the dressmaker.

Although she would rather stay at home with Jason,
Eulalie knew that she would be ready at the proper time.
There was no need to make Robert angry over anything
so insignificant as dining out. What frightened her was
the formal ball, and the possibility of meeting Alistair
Ashe, the former overseer.

For the rest of the morning, Eulalie stayed with Jason.
He had talked very little while Eulalie had taken care of
him for the past week, but he clung to her each time the
servants or Florilla came to relieve her for an hour or so
at a time.

That afternoon, when Florilla appeared in the nursery,
Jason was unusually obstinate. He refused to be parted
from Eulalie.

"Come with me, Jason," Florilla commanded.

The child thrust out his lower lip in a pout. "No!" he
protested and held on to Eulalie.

"Mrs. Tabor, Robert asked me to take Jason for the
rest of the afternoon and evening, since you are to rest
before getting dressed for dinner. But you are making it

difficult for me. Naturally, he doesn't want to leave you since you have spoiled him so."

Had she spoiled him? She had only wanted to take care of him. But quickly, Eulalie leaned over and, kissing her son, she said, "Go with Mrs. Hines, Jason."

"No!" he bellowed. "Don't want Mama." The child stared at Florilla with a bellicose expression.

Eulalie blanched at her child's words. He had called Florilla "Mama." The fair-haired woman had the grace to be embarrassed, but she offered no explanation to Eulalie. Instead, she reached out for Jason to propel him along with her.

By this time, the child's face was red and he was sobbing. "Jason want to stay with Eu-lie."

His distress tugged at her heart. Eulalie could not abandon him.

"He is still ill, Florilla. And it's not good for him to get so upset. I'll give him supper in my room, and when he is asleep I'll bring him back to the nursery."

"Very well, Mrs. Tabor," Florilla said. Her words held disapproval, but already Jason was quiet, holding out his arms for Eulalie.

She carried him down the hall into the green bedroom, and after seeing to his early supper, Eulalie put on the pale-yellow fleece dressing gown and lay on her bed beside Jason.

"Oh, Jason," she said softly. "Am I really spoiling you?"

But he was already asleep, and soon Eulalie closed her eyes too.

At the faint knocking sound, Eulalie stirred. But she was not sufficiently awake to answer.

Looking down at mother and son together, Robert stood over the bed. The child had one hand across Eulalie's breast, and his little chest rose and fell in peaceful slumber. Eulalie stretched and opened her eyes, large and soft from sleep.

"You have only a short time to get dressed, Eulalie," Robert warned. "I will take our son back to the nursery."

She stared uncomprehendingly at Robert while he leaned over to pick up the sleeping child. Gently bending

Jason's arm away from Eulalie's body, he lifted him in his arms.

Eulalie was now awake. She sat up, pushing her long hair from her face. "I will be ready soon, Robert," she promised, yawning.

Carrying the little boy down the hall, Robert was thoughtful. I am jealous of my own child, he admitted to himself. Remembering the way Jason's hand had rested on the woman's soft body, Robert was plagued with all the old longing and desire. Then the specter of Jacques Binet loomed in his mind.

Would she tell him the truth? wondered Robert. Would Eulalie confess to being the trapper's mistress, if he required her to answer? Even longing for the truth, Robert knew he could not question her yet. It was too soon.

CHAPTER

14

*E*ULALIE stood before the cheval glass and critically viewed her appearance.

Her black hair, parted in the middle and brought back to a chignon at the neck, missed severity only by the exquisite oriental comb decorated with purple iris set in gold. But the style went well with the lavender velvet evening gown with its oval neckline, high waist and short puffed sleeves.

Self-consciously, Eulalie placed her hand across the low décolleté of the dress. Maggie should have made it more modest. Eulalie was not used to the fashionable, sophisticated dresses of a married woman, especially after having worn a nun's habit for so long.

Well, she would just have to keep the shawl around her for the evening.

Eulalie turned from the mirror and, walking to the bed, picked up the matching shawl and put it around her shoulders. It was a beautiful shawl, Eulalie confessed to herself, of lighter mauve than the dress, and lavishly embroidered at the edges with gold thread.

Hurrying from the room, Eulalie walked down the hallway and descended the stairs to the lower floor. At the base of the stairs, Robert stood and watched her descent.

"No one would mistake you for a nun tonight, Eulalie," he commented when she had reached his side.

At his words, she drew the shawl closer to her. And at her action, Robert laughed.

"Do not be so modest about your beauty, Eulalie. For you will have to get used to being stared at. We are already late and people will think that it is deliberate—that you are a vain minx, seeking admiration."

"That is not true, Robert," Eulalie answered. Her face was serious in its protestation. "And I have no wish to wear such an indecent dress. But it is all I have except the three day dresses."

"Eulalie, I was but teasing you. And as for the gown, it is exactly right for tonight. Do not be so embarrassed," he scolded.

She sat in silence while the carriage took them to their destination, to the large Greek Revival house that was lit with party lights.

Eulalie and Robert were late, and it was her fault for sleeping too long. As they arrived and were greeted by the host, dinner was announced and she and Robert were immediately separated.

So many people—and she knew no one except Robert. Seated far down the table from him, Eulalie could not see beyond the second candelabra. Robert would be no help to her tonight. She managed to smile at the older man at her side and to answer his attentive questions as best she could.

"I am pleased that Robert has decided to share you tonight. I was not aware that his . . . wife was in Columbia for the seating of the assembly."

"I have not been long in Columbia, monsieur," Eulalie answered with a slight accent.

"Charming," the man commented. "You sound charming, Mrs. Tabor. I take it you are French?"

Eulalie nodded. "I lived in New Orleans, monsieur, before coming to Carolina."

"Did you say New Orleans?" The man on her left

leaned over to join in the conversation, and at the soothing small talk, Eulalie began to relax.

She listened as the two men became embroiled in the issues before the legislature, and the news of the war with the British on the Canadian border.

"Our apologies, Mrs. Tabor, for speaking of forbidden subjects at the table," the elder man said, stopping the discussion.

"Oh, but I am so interested. Please continue," Eulalie urged.

"I am afraid our hostess will blackball us both from her sumptuous table, if we keep on."

The man on her left concurred. "When a man has the opportunity to enjoy beauty and fine wine at one sitting, he should not waste it in talking of politics."

On through the eight-course meal, the men paid cavalier tribute to Eulalie. And although he made no attempt to speak to her, the young sandy-haired man across the table also watched her every move. Making a half-hearted effort to be civil to the ladies on his left and his right, he incurred the disapproval of both. The two began to pout and glare at Eulalie.

"Mrs. Tabor, have you met Mr. Arthur Metcalfe?" The man on Eulalie's right added, "He and your husband are great friends."

"Then I am delighted to meet a friend of my . . . husband's," she answered, acknowledging the man across the table from her.

"We have been good friends ever since we were at Mr. Waddell's School for Boys," Arthur Metcalfe offered. "But I am disappointed that Robert chose to keep you a secret from me. May I be so bold as to ask how you met?"

Eulalie nervously fingered the ivory lace on the table-cloth. The conversation was becoming too personal. "My *maman* was married to Robert's uncle, monsieur. That is, after my own papa died."

"So you are the one who was at Midgard when Robert returned from Paris."

"Yes, monsieur," Eulalie answered, no louder than a whisper.

How much did the man know, if he was Robert's good friend? Had Robert confided in him? Frantically looking down the sea of faces toward Robert and hoping for rescue from the uncomfortable situation, Eulalie received another shock.

Familiar dark pinpoints from colorless gray eyes focused on her and would not cease.

Her face lost color and she gripped the arm of her chair. Alistair Ashe, the overseer. She was seated at the same table with Alistair Ashe, the man who had dragged her to the slave market, the man who had pushed her to the ground and treated her with such indignity.

"And what is your opinion. Mrs. Tabor?" the man beside her asked.

"I'm . . . I'm sorry. What—was your question?"

Seeing her pale countenance, Arthur Metcalfe bent toward her, his blue eyes and boyish face showing concern.

"Are you all right, Mrs. Tabor?"

She stifled her shivering and replied feebly, "The . . . the room is . . . suddenly cold."

The host and hostess stood up. Dinner was over. Eulalie in a daze heard Arthur's voice. "Go to the fire in the drawing room, Mrs. Tabor. It is a cold night for one used to the sultry weather of the Gulf."

The men remained at the table for brandy and cigars while the women excused themselves and followed the hostess into the elaborate drawing room. Eulalie forced herself to walk slowly, although she wanted to run and not stop until she had reached the safety of the white clapboard house with the iron fence.

Why had Robert brought her? Had he known that his former overseer was to be present also? And how much longer would she have to stay before she would be free to leave?

Eulalie, following the rest of the women, did not see Alistair Ashe and his quick conversation with his blond wife. Neither did she see the finger pointed in her direction.

"I believe everyone knows everyone else," Mrs. Kirkland, the hostess, commented, "except for Mrs. Tabor."

She took Eulalie's arm and guided her to the groups of women clustered around the drawing room.

"Mrs. Ashe, may I present Mrs. Robert Tabor? Mrs. Tabor, Mrs. Alistair Ashe—Polly."

Polly Ashe smiled at Eulalie in a cool, insulting manner, and when Eulalie walked on with her hostess, the blonde woman immediately began whispering to her companions.

Somehow, Eulalie got through the introductions, but the room echoed with whispers and titters.

"Mrs. Tabor," one woman asked, "why is it we have not seen you before? Has your husband been hiding you?"

The plump woman seated beside her muffled her laughter with her white lace handkerchief.

"I have been away," Eulalie replied. "And also, our son has been ill."

"New Orleans, was it not?" another guest questioned. "You're a native of New Orleans, I believe?"

"Yes."

"A Creole family?" the same woman continued.

"That is correct."

"Tell me, Mrs. Tabor—is it true that all Creole families have at least a drop or two of *Nigra* blood?"

Again the smothered laughter pervaded the room.

Before Eulalie could answer, her hostess interrupted. "Come, ladies. You know better than that. Most are fine old aristocratic French families or descendants of Spanish grandees."

Mrs. Kirkland turned to one of the younger women. "Anna, will you play and sing something for us, while we are waiting for the men to join us? The music is on the harpsichord."

"If Mrs. Tabor will turn the pages for me," she replied. Anna smiled in her direction, friendliness and kindness showing in her eyes.

Gratefully, Eulalie sat on the bench beside Anna and listened to her sweet, untrained voice, as she accompanied herself. For a while, at least, the open hostility was over.

Soon the men came into the drawing room, and many gathered close to the ornate harpsichord to listen to Anna, with their eyes wandering to Eulalie as well. Robert stood to the side of the hearth, conscious of the admiring glances in the direction of the two beautiful women—one dark, one fairhaired, suitable foils for each other.

"You . . . saw him?" Robert asked on the way home.

"Yes," Eulalie replied.

"And you met his wife, Polly?"

"Yes."

"It is not surprising that he quickly married her after his brother, Gregory, died. Now Alistair possesses not only his dead brother's wife, but also his plantation."

Eulalie did not respond to the information Robert supplied.

The look of reprieve on her face had not escaped Robert when he had said his goodbyes. And now as he gazed at the small, still figure beside him, he realized the emotional beating she had taken in seeing his former overseer.

Eulalie bit her lip to still the trembling and clutched tightly the reticule in her lap until her fingers ached. The silence between them was an awkward companion all the way to the white clapboard house.

When the carriage stopped before the iron fence, Eulalie was handed down from the carriage and, without waiting for Robert, she ran into the house, up the stairs and into the safety of the green bedroom.

Robert, walking slowly down the narrow hall, paused and listened at the closed door. Delicate sobs reached his ears. He frowned, taking a step nearer the door, and then stopped. Finally, he walked on to his own bedroom, where he tossed and turned restlessly before dropping off to sleep.

Robert was not the only one troubled by the episode of that evening. The next day, he was met by a concerned Arthur Metcalfe.

Sitting in the library with the glass of brandy in his hand, Arthur broached the subject immediately.

"Robert, there are some ugly rumors around town concerning your wife. If what I hear being planned is the truth, you must take care to protect her."

Surprised at the seriousness in Arthur's voice, Robert asked, "What have you heard, Arthur?"

"Alistair Ashe is telling everyone that the girl is your quadroon mistress—that you were never married to her. I know there is some mystery, that you have a son. Yet, you never mentioned a wife to me. If you do not choose to tell me the entire story, I understand. I just want to make certain. She *is* the former Eulalie Boisfeulet and she *is* your wife, isn't she?"

"Yes, Arthur. Eulalie was my uncle's stepdaughter and she is now legally my wife. But go on."

"Ashe has gotten the ladies incensed with his vicious lies. They feel insulted that you would bring your mistress to dine with them. I'd rather fall into a nest of water moccasins than be within a mile of those women when they think they've been insulted."

"And what has been planned?"

"The wives say she should be run out of town. If I were you, I would send the girl back to Midgard immediately."

"No, Arthur. She will remain here. But I will see that she comes to no harm."

"You weren't in the drawing room last night to protect her," Arthur argued. "Anna deLong said she had never heard the women so catty before. And with Ashe behind this, it will get even worse. You realize, of course, that he will do anything to see you discredited and shamed."

"His personal vendetta is with me, Arthur—not with Eulalie."

Abruptly setting his brandy down, the sandy-haired man, vexed with Robert's answer, replied, "Well, don't say I didn't warn you, Robert."

CHAPTER
15

*F*OR two days a subdued Eulalie remained in the house with Jason. It was raining anyway—a good excuse not to venture outside. And now that the child was almost well, he needed a different type of attention, a constant watching to make sure he did not get too tired. Eulalie had seen it happen—the complications that could strike later, more devastating than the initial disease.

Eulalie could tell that Florilla did not like this concern that she showed for her child. But she was not usurping Florilla's place. She had nothing to fear. Eulalie was merely taking her rightful place as Jason's mother. Her rightful place? As a mother, yes. But not as a wife.

Eulalie sighed. Robert did not want her as a wife; yet he was providing her with all the luxuries that a wife could expect.

She stood and gazed at the elaborate ballgown that Maggie had finished and delivered to her that very morning, now waiting to be put on. Of shimmering white, with silver leaves embroidered down the center for the skirt and silver lace tiers of ruching stiff at each side, the dress lay regally across the bed, barely touching the deep forest-green coverlet. And the silver slippers at the foot of the bed gleamed and waited for her feet.

Gazing down at her hands, Eulalie saw the result of Effie's labors to turn her work-worn hands into the hands of a lady. She reached up and felt the coiffure that she had been so proud of earlier. And then a sense of guilt overcame her. How easy it was to be seduced by material things, to forget that she had no right to them.

A need to atone grew larger as she counted her sins. She had succumbed to the sensual feel of silk undergarments against her skin, forgetting the coarse, scratchy material of the nun's habit; she had dismissed the lessons of service she had learned at the convent, taking too much pleasure in the improvement of her hands; and worst of all, she had forgotten to pray for Jacques Binet, as she had promised.

Eulalie made up her mind. She would not go to the ball. She would not masquerade as Robert's wife, in the finery he had provided for her. He could return the dress to Maggie and send back the jeweled chain of sapphires and diamonds that had arrived that morning.

And at home, she would be safe from the humiliation she had suffered two evenings previously.

Robert had not even been aware of her shame at the dinner, of how the women had treated her. Only Anna with her kindness had made the evening bearable, after those colorless gray eyes had found her and precipitated her humiliation. Anna was the only one who had shown her any sympathy at all.

Walking to the wardrobe, Eulalie took out one of the nun's habits, slipped it over her head, and then knelt upon the floor.

Robert did not knock. She heard his footsteps and sensed his presence even before she opened her brown eyes.

"I did not realize, Eulalie, that you took your devotions so seriously as to risk making us late again." His face was set and his eyes projected dangerous glints of anger.

Still on her knees, Eulalie looked up into his face. "I am not going, Robert." Her voice was soft but firm.

"Were you not taught at the convent, Eulalie, that a wife's first duty is to her husband?"

"I am not your wife, Robert. At least, not—"

His face, red with anger, stopped her words. In horror, she saw him as he leaned down, as his hand went out swiftly. In one crushing motion, he wrapped his arms about her, to lift her from the floor and to set her firmly on the bed. Her teeth chattered at the sudden jolt, at his rough handling.

"There is no need to remind me that you are not a wife to me. But I will not have anyone else knowing it, to pity me because my wife is *not* a wife. I will be back in five minutes, Eulalie. If you have not made a start toward removing that ugly crow's dress and putting on the gown I have chosen for you, I will dress you myself. Five minutes, Eulalie. That is all the time you have."

The door slammed and, hastily, Eulalie hopped off the bed. She dropped the nun's habit to the floor and, taking the ballgown from the bed, she struggled into it.

How could she get it on by herself in five minutes? The fastenings were too intricate for her to handle alone. But her pride stood in the way of calling for help from Effie.

The door opened again. Hands touched her from behind. The deep voice taunted, "The time is up, Eulalie. I see I shall have to help you."

Whirling around to face him, Eulalie spat out the words. "You didn't wait five minutes, Robert. You didn't give me even the small amount of time you promised."

"Did I not?" His voice, suddenly losing its anger, held an amused nuance, and the change maddened Eulalie even more.

"Kindly leave my bedroom, Robert. I do not need your help."

"No?" Robert's eyes held hers. "That may be so. I am not used to being a lady's maid. But since I do not wholly trust you, Eulalie, I will remain until you are ready." And his hands continued their action until the fastening was complete. Then he let her go.

Eulalie felt his all-seeing tawny eyes on her, and it

made her clumsy. She dropped the hairbrush, but before she could retrieve it, he picked it up and held it out to her. Her hand touched his and she quickly drew back from the contact. Smiling at her reaction, Robert laid the brush before her on the table.

It did not take her long to repair the several curls that had gotten out of place. When she had finished, she stood up, saying, "I am ready, Robert." The haughtiness was apparent in her voice.

"I think not."

Eulalie swiftly turned to the mirror. What had she forgotten? Frowning, she scrutinized her appearance in the cheval glass.

"The necklace, Eulalie. You have forgotten the necklace I had the boy deliver to you this morning. Where is it, Eulalie?"

"On the chair . . . next to the door."

In a swift movement, Robert crossed the distance, took the chain from the box and, before Eulalie could demur, fastened the jeweled necklace around her long white neck.

"Turn around, Eulalie," Robert ordered in a gruff voice. "So that I may see if you are presentable."

The imperious command to submit to his inspection angered Eulalie further. Dangerous sparks flashed from the dark-brown eyes, and Robert felt her smoldering resentment.

"Yes, master," she said, making a mock obeisance to him.

Two steps and she was caught, his hands gripping her arms in a painful grasp. "Don't ever do that again, Eulalie."

His reaction shocked her, even more than her own behavior. Too ashamed to meet his eyes, she cast her own eyes downward and waited for the giant hands to release her. His uneven breathing matched hers, as the seconds became an eternity.

Taking their time, the hands loosened and trailed sensuously down her arms. Eulalie shivered and stepped back.

"One day, Eulalie, you will learn not to be so impulsive. You can only get into trouble this way, as you should know by now."

The blush slowly blossomed over her face at his words. And subdued, Eulalie followed him out of the room—going where she had had no intention of going, following meekly her husband—in name only.

The capitol was brilliant with a thousand candles. Vast urns of red camellias filled the senate chamber, and garlanded festoons of holly and ivy hung on the walls. In jeweled splendor the women came, escorted by elegant, distinguished partners, and an air of gaiety pervaded the staid, formal senate chamber.

But Eulalie, hesitant to enter, hung back, her eyes searching the room for Alistair Ashe. Thankfully, she did not see him anywhere. In relief, she began to view the room with interest, getting her first glimpse of the governor and his wife, Theodosia Alston. Maggie had been right. She was the most beautiful lady in the room.

With amusement, Eulalie recalled Maggie's words— "You and Theodosia Alston will be the two prettiest ladies at the ball." How reckless of Maggie to include her in the same breath as the governor's lady.

Robert, standing at Eulalie's side, watched her, noticing the gradual change in expression from aversion to delight in the scene of pomp and glitter before her.

"Oh, look, Robert," she whispered, her eyes big with wonder. "Isn't he the most splendid fellow?"

Reluctantly Robert took his eyes from her to follow her discreet hand. And then he laughed. "That, Eulalie, is Mr. Crowley, from the upcountry. He's quite a dandy, all five feet of him. Peacock would have been a better name for him than Crowley."

But already, Eulalie's attention had been diverted, with Mr. Crowley completely forgotten.

Robert's topaz eyes narrowed as he studied his wife beside him. She looked so innocent, so virginal. No one would guess . . .

The three years in the convent must have done that to her, after Jacques Binet had left her there. If he had not known better, Robert would have sworn that she was untouched.

Robert knew if *he* had been Jacques Binet, he never would have released her to the sisters. He would have taken her with him, wherever he went, fighting to keep her constantly by his side.

But he was not Jacques Binet. He was Robert Tabor, her husband, whose pride would not let him forget that another man had known her charms, her soft body.

"Robert, is . . . is anything wrong?"

He quickly erased the bitter expression from his face.

"No, Eulalie. Nothing is wrong, except that we have not danced."

He smiled at her and, leading her to the edge of the dance floor, he joined the set for the next quadrille.

When the quadrille was over, Robert took Eulalie by the hand to lead her through the crowd of people to Joseph Alston, the governor, who stood on an elevated platform with his wife, receiving guests.

"Well, Robert, what have we here?"

The governor's eyes twinkled in his strong, dark face as he stared at the girl beside Robert.

"May I present my wife, Eulalie Boisfeulet Tabor."

Governor Alston held out his hand to take Eulalie's smaller one in his. He was not tall, but he was sturdily built, his neck well developed and his prominent brow half-hidden by dark curls that had refused to be brushed into submission. The man exuded power, and Eulalie was aware of it as his sharp eagle eyes swept over her and his hand tucked hers under his arm to move her along to his wife a few paces away.

"Theo," the man called gently, waiting for his wife to turn. "May I present Robert's wife, Eulalie. You must take this beautiful young thing under your wing. I can already see that she could encounter trouble with some of the less handsome ladies."

"Yes, Joseph," she answered, smiling at him. "She is far too pretty for her own good."

"Boisfeulet . . . Boisfeulet." The governor said the

name several times, searching for some answer that eluded him. "Are you from New Orleans, my dear?"

"Yes, Governor Alston. I grew up there but left the convent school to be with my *maman* when I was almost sixteen."

"Genevieve Boisfeulet. That's the name I was trying to recall," he said with a pleased expression. "Do you happen to be Genevieve Boisfeulet's daughter?"

"Yes, but—"

He laughed at the surprise written on her face. "How did I guess? Because you remind me very much of her. She was a beautiful woman."

In an atmosphere of conspiracy, he leaned over and said, "Would you like to meet one of your relatives, my dear?"

"A relative?" Robert questioned. "I was not aware that Eulalie had any relatives outside France."

"Then it will be my pleasure to introduce them. Go,. Robert, and fetch Arthur Metcalfe's cousin. You know the one—Desmond Caldwell, the representative from Chester County. No, leave your wife here, Robert. We will look after her while you are gone."

The evening was turning out vastly different from what she had expected. Eulalie waited while Robert went in search of Mr. Caldwell. And she waited for Joseph Alston to tell her how he knew her *maman.*

The man who returned with Robert was almost as tall as he. But he was thin and ascetic while Robert was muscular. The middle-aged man looked toward Joseph Alston with penetrating ice-blue eyes above the dark bushy sidewhiskers that hid a large part of his face.

"Mr. Caldwell," the governor began with obvious enjoyment, "is not your second wife a Frenchwoman from Santo Domingo?"

"That is correct, Governor Alston," the man replied with no trace of the accent that gave away the governor's low-country identity. "She fled that island during the last slave rebellion and came to Charleston with many other French refugees."

"And her surname was Longchamp?" the governor questioned further.

Desmond Caldwell nodded, the puzzled look matching the others surrounding Joseph Alston.

"Then, it is my pleasure to introduce you to a distant cousin of your wife's. Eulalie Boisfeulet Tabor, whose mother was also a Longchamp before her marriage."

"This comes as quite a surprise," Desmond Caldwell said. "I will be pleased to apprise Julie when I return home that she has a lovely young relative here in Columbia.

"My dear," he continued, turning to Eulalie, "it is a pleasure to meet you. And I hope that you will be able to visit us in the upcountry, after my wife recovers from her slight indisposition."

Everyone began to talk at once, but Joseph Alston, already tired of his role, stepped down from the platform and guided Theodosia through the roped-off area to lead her onto the dance floor. And Robert, bidding Desmond Caldwell good evening, claimed Eulalie for the next dance.

No matter in which direction Eulalie went, Robert was at her side, or watching her every move. Even when she danced with other partners, he stood protectively at the edge of the dance floor, observing her every turn.

But toward the end of the evening, Eulalie slipped away to the room reserved for the ladies, so that she might repair the silver lace that had come loose from her ballgown at the lower edge. And it was impossible for Robert to follow, with Eulalie already in the middle of a group of women walking in that direction.

She lingered in the cloakroom until the others had gone. And when her mission was completed and the lace pinned into place, Eulalie headed back to the senate chamber.

The hallway was dark, with only a few candles to give light along the way. Quickening her steps, she hastened toward the muffled sound of music coming from the senate chamber. So deserted—the long hallway.

"Mrs. Tabor," a voice called softly from the shadows.

Instantly recognizing the voice, Eulalie stopped, her eyes searching for the owner of the voice.

The woman stepped into sight.

"Florilla, what are you doing here?" Eulalie asked. And then panic seized her. "Is it Jason? Has something happened to him?"

Coming closer, with her hooded cape shielding her face, Florilla answered, "Yes. I'm afraid he's taken ill again. And he keeps crying for you."

So what she had feared had come true.

"I will get Robert at once," Eulalie said.

But Florilla shook her head and said, "No. You must hurry. There's a carriage already waiting for you. I'll find Robert to tell him you have gone. And I'll ride home with him."

Florilla took Eulalie's arm and guided her down the dark hall to the back entrance where the carriage was waiting . . .

CHAPTER

16

ROBERT watched the groups of women returning to the senate chamber, but Eulalie was not among them. She had been gone an unusually long time. What could be keeping her?

The ball was nearly over and he was anxious to leave. Already, Joseph Alston had left with Theodosia, his wife. It was common knowledge that she was departing the next day for Georgetown, where the *Patriot* lay anchored, despite the British blockade, for its trip to New York. Her father, Aaron Burr, had reentered the country under an assumed name and was awaiting his daughter's visit and the new portrait she was bringing him.

I must have Eulalie's portrait painted, Robert thought, in the same shimmering white ballgown she is wearing tonight. He would request her, though, to wear her hair long and unbound, as he first remembered seeing her. But the portrait would be for no one else. Only for himself. A pity that Jeremiah Theus was dead. He would have been able to capture the soft elusive look of those brown eyes and the pearl translucence of her skin.

Now visibly worried, Robert headed for the hallway. Perhaps Eulalie had become ill and even now needed help. She had watched over Jason so unceasingly. It would not do for her to become ill now that Jason was well.

Seeing Anna deLong, Robert reduced the space between them.

"Anna," Robert began, careful to mask his growing concern, "would you be so kind as to see if Eulalie is still in the ladies' room? I am ready to leave and she has not returned."

"Yes, Robert. I shall be happy to find her and give her your message."

Robert relaxed and waited for Eulalie to accompany Anna. But when Anna returned, she was alone.

"I have looked everywhere that I thought she might be," the woman apologized to Robert, "but I cannot find her."

At that moment, Arthur Metcalfe, on his way out, stopped. Seeing the dark frown on Robert's face, he asked, "Has something happened?"

Then, looking around at the dispersing crowd and not waiting for an answer to his first question, he said, "Where is Eulalie?"

"She seems to have disappeared," Robert answered in a flat voice.

"But her shawl is in the ladies' room," Anna added.

"Then she must still be in the building, unless she has been . . . abducted." Arthur looked troubled as he spoke.

At the last word, Robert turned pale. He remembered the warning that Arthur had voiced earlier. Moving quickly, they began to search the building, Anna and her husband, Richard, now at her side, and Arthur Metcalfe with Robert.

The porter with his lantern helped them in their search. But combing the entire building and all its rooms, they found no trace of Eulalie. So the careful search outside the building began.

It was at the back that Robert saw something silver gleaming in the mud. He reached down to pick it up and his stomach lurched. The silver slipper. Eulalie's silver slipper, crushed in the fresh tracks that had been made by a carriage.

So Arthur's warning was genuine. Despite his watchfulness, someone had taken Eulalie away.

Run out of town! Run out of town! Over and over the phrase rolled in his mind. And the memory of another night, a rowdy crowd and the same words spoken, pervaded his mind, and he saw the same nightmarish scene, but with Eulalie as the victim. But surely they would not do to a woman what had been done to the thief caught stealing—tarred and feathered and run out of town on a rail. No one could be that harsh to a mere girl who had done no wrong.

Without waiting for the others, Robert dashed to his carriage. He gave the horses their heads, and the vehicle hurtled toward the old abandoned blacksmith shop at the south edge of town.

With blood in his eye, Robert drove on, fearing, on the one hand, that he would find Eulalie at the suspected scene and yet hoping, on the other hand, that he would not have to continue his search throughout the night. Each minute lost put her in graver danger.

The drunken, milling crowd presaged his fears. Yelling obscenities, as at a bearbaiting or cockfight, the men spurred on the clandestine activity taking place.

Jumping from the carriage, Robert motioned for a young boy at the edge of the crowd to hold the reins. He shoved his way through the mob that had reached a feverish pitch in their shouts. "Tar her! Feather the loose woman," they jeered.

The stench of tar was upon his nostrils. And the sickening odor of unwashed bodies, seeking diversion in their humdrum lives, hung heavily on the cold blanket of air.

The crowd, seeing the angry giant pushing his way to the center of the blacksmith shop, parted and broke off their taunts.

Then Robert saw her. Her gown had been stripped to her waist, and already her breasts were covered with the mixture of tar and feathers. With a feral growl, Robert grabbed the two culprits holding her. Before they knew what had happened to them, they lay sprawled on the ground, stunned from the cracking of their heads together.

Tilting the cauldron of tar, Robert poured it over them

and then dumped the box of feathers on top, covering them from head to foot.

Now respectful, the crowd, cowed by Robert's actions, began to slip away, fearful of reprisal for their own behavior.

Robert and Eulalie were alone. Eulalie, with rescue an actuality, swayed and, except for Robert, would have fallen to the ground. The sticky mixture clung to his hands as he caught her and wrapped his own cloak about her body to hide her partial nakedness.

The carriage moved slowly through the muddy streets. Robert's eyes kept returning to the girl who lay slumped beside him, her head against his chest. A fierce, protective anger welled up in his spleen and overflowed.

Alistair Ashe—he was the instigator. And already, Robert was planning satisfaction.

Finally the journey was over. The carriage halted before the iron railing and Robert lifted the woman in his arms and stepped to the ground. Up the stairs into his own bedroom he carried her and he laid her on the bed, unmindful of the coverlet.

"Effie," Robert shouted. "Come here quickly."

The young black girl ran to the master's bedroom, and when she saw Eulalie with her eyes closed and the condition she was in, she began crying.

"Lawd a-mercy, Mr. Robert. Is she . . . dead? What did dem mean 'uns *do* to 'er?"

"Hush, Effie. She's not dead. But she needs attention. Go to the cellar and bring up the gallon jar of turpentine."

"But what'll I tell the folks waitin' in the parlor, Mr. Robert?"

"You'll tell them nothing, Effie, except that I will be down presently. Say nothing else. Do you understand, Effie?"

"Yes suh, Mr. Robert," she answered, "but they sho' is goin' to think it's mighty strange, seein' me with the jar of turpentine."

Exasperated, Robert was careful and gentle in his instructions. "Go into the parlor *first,* Effie. Give them my message and *then* go get the turpentine."

Her face brightened. "Yes suh," she said and left the room.

Robert used the turpentine to remove the tar from his hands, and quickly changing into fresh clothes, he started downstairs.

Effie sat with Eulalie and waited for Robert to return. "Stay with her until I get back. And say nothing to the other servants about this."

He assumed a calmness he did not feel and walked into the parlor. "Eulalie is safe. I have brought her home," Robert told them.

"Thank heavens," Anna deLong replied, still holding onto her husband's arm. "Is she . . . hurt at all, Robert?"

"Just badly shaken up. Thank you for helping tonight. I won't forget it."

"We . . . we brought her shawl with us. It's on the chair by the window, Robert," Arthur Metcalfe remarked.

The three stood up to take their leave. Too well-bred to ask Robert what had happened, they left the white clapboard house, still unsure what had actually occurred.

As soon as they were gone, Robert walked back upstairs. He did not look forward to the next hour.

"She's awake, Mr. Robert," Effie said. "You want me to stay and help?"

"No, Effie. Just bring me lots of towels and hot water. And then you can go to bed."

"Jason? Is Jason all right?" Eulalie's feeble voice shook as she tried to talk.

"He's fine, Eulalie. Don't talk. Save your strength."

His tawny eyes, smoky from emotion, looked down at her. "This is going to burn, Eulalie, but there's no other way. I will be as gentle as I can, but before I start, I want you to drink this."

"Yes, Robert."

He hoped the laudanum would help. But he was afraid to give her too much . . . so meek, her spirit crushed. If she could respond with anger or crying, it would help. But she lay there, silently submitting to the torture, with the vast anger belonging to Robert for the sacrilege that had been committed. But Eulalie was lucky that they had not gotten to her face, and for that, Robert was grateful.

Gently he worked, removing small dabs of tar at a time, methodically pulling the feathers from the loosened black mixture. But when he reached the last layer next to her skin, the pain grew worse. And by the time he dipped her into the soapy warm water in the old brass tub, Eulalie could keep quiet no longer. She screamed with pain, and the sound cut Robert to the heart.

Her translucent skin was red and raw, and small patches exuded moisture where the skin had once been and was no more.

Robert wrapped her in towels and, throwing the ruined coverlet to the floor, pulled back the sheets on the bed to receive Eulalie's aching, exhausted body.

All through the night, Robert sat by the hearth, keeping the fire going. The moans of a troubled Eulalie were answered by the whining of the wind in the trees. Back and forth, the sounds intermeshed until, toward morning, the wind rested.

A tearful Florilla was waiting when Robert went downstairs for breakfast.

"Robert, I have been incredibly stupid," she said, dabbing daintily at her tears with the lace handkerchief.

"You are not the only one, Florilla," he commented in a dry tone. "What is it that *you* have done?"

She looked at him in surprise, forgetting to shed more tears. "You . . . you mean, Eulalie—that is, Mrs. Tabor —hasn't told you?"

"Told me what, Florilla?" he asked with an air of impatience.

Relief showed in her cornflower-blue eyes, and she began her story.

"Mr. Ashe approached me yesterday and . . . and asked me if I would help him with a surprise party for Mrs. Tabor."

Robert's face showed his anger at the mention of the man's name.

She hastened on. "I thought he was a friend of yours.

I had no way of knowing . . . " She twisted her hand-kerchief in her hands.

"Go on with your story."

"Well, he said everyone in Columbia wanted to give your wife a fine welcome—and if I could get her away from the ball, they would all be waiting for her. And it would be such a nice surprise, he said.

"It was much later last night that I found out what happened, and that . . . that he was not your friend, but your worst enemy. Oh, Robert, if you only knew how I have berated myself!" She was again shedding tears. "And to think how I played into that evil man's hands!"

Her body was trembling and she turned her back to him, as if the confession were more than she could bear.

"Control yourself, Florilla. We are all at fault. But she is safe now."

"I . . . I know you will not want me to stay after this."

"Nonsense, Florilla. You have been with Jason for over two years. And very helpful with him. But we will both have to be a little less stupid and be more protective of both mother and son."

"Oh, thank you, Robert. You don't know how much this means to me, to know that you don't blame me entirely for what happened."

She smiled up at him through eyelashes glistening with tears, and with a slight sob, she walked tragically out of the dining room.

Florilla's confession confirmed Alistair Ashe's guilt. To think that he had deliberately done this, even after Robert had gone privately to him, entrusting him with the story of what had happened between him and Eulalie. And that he, Robert, was entirely to blame. Blast it! He never thought he would have asked a favor of anyone, much less an enemy, but his concern for Eulalie had made him swallow his pride. He had not wanted her to be hurt any more. And Ashe had not been gentleman enough to remain silent.

There was only one course to take. He would see him dead for what he had done to Eulalie, or die, himself, in the attempt.

Later that day, Feena arrived from the plantation. All the way, she had been wild with joy. Her *petite* Lili was alive!

When she walked to the strange white clapboard house, everything was remarkably quiet. Was Lili ill? Was that why the house seemed dead?

"Mamselle Lili has sent for me," she announced proudly to the young girl at the door. "Please take me to her."

"You mean Miz Tabor?" the girl asked.

"*Mais oui*—Mistress Tabor—Mamselle Lili. *Vite!* Don't just stand there looking at me. I am in a hurry."

Feena walked up the stairs, along the dim hallway, following the girl to the closed door of the bedroom.

"Mr. Robert said no one was to go in theah, 'cept Effie," the girl explained, doubtful that Feena would be allowed entry.

"Then she is ill. I will take care of her as I always have. *Ma petite* Lili, it is Feena," she called out, knocking at the door.

The heavy carved door opened a tiny bit, and when the other girl had left, Effie let Feena in.

"*Mon Dieu,* what have they done to you, mamselle?" an indignant Feena asked, shocked at the condition of Eulalie's skin.

"It was all a . . . mistake, Feena," Eulalie replied, wincing at the pain when she moved.

"Mistake is right. Whoever did this made the big mistake. Feena fix them, all right."

"No, Feena. Promise me you won't do anything. You would be sent away, and I need you."

"That mush-faced hussy, Madame Florilla—She had a hand in this. I feel it *here.*"

Feena banged her fist against her breast. And not waiting for Eulalie to confirm or deny it, she continued her tirade.

"She's a no-good woman. The minute I laid eyes on her, I knew. But now that you are back, things will be different. Madame will no longer rule this house. When will you get rid of her, *ma petite?*"

"It is . . . not my place, Feena. Robert was the one to hire her. He must be the one to let her go."

"Humph! Then you'd better put the idea in his head. Men cannot see through such a sly one. But a woman knows—and I know she will only cause trouble in this house between you and your husband. But now, you must rest. I will go downstairs to boil a poultice for you. Your skin will heal without a blemish, mamselle. Feena will vouch for it."

Eulalie lay quietly, waiting for Feena to return with the healing balm for her skin. But she did not go to sleep. Rather, the events of the previous night spun slowly through her mind. Nothing seemed real, except Robert . . . Robert, with the fierce look on his face. Even the dark scowl at Midgard when he had jumped the fence and almost run her down was nothing in comparison to the expression when he saw what the two men had done to her.

And he had been so gentle while removing the tar from her body. When she had cried out from the stinging of the turpentine, he had soothed her with loving words, as if he were calming a fretful Jason.

To think that his giant hands could be as dexterous as any nurse's. Eulalie remembered their insistence long ago, moving over her body, demanding her response to his lovemaking. Now she had seen another side of Robert Tabor.

She put her hand to her cheek, where she had felt his lips. Or had she only dreamed that he leaned over during the night to kiss her? She could not be sure.

CHAPTER

17

*F*LORILLA came to me this morning, Eulalie, to explain her part in what happened last night."

Robert stood before the window, looking down at the still-soggy ground, shadowed by the late-afternoon sun.

"Oh?"

Eulalie, dressed in a soft wisp of a gown, sat up in bed, her hair covering the pillows at her back. She waited for Robert to continue.

"I have no reason to believe that she knew what Ashe had arranged, so I have given her permission to remain as governess for Jason."

Stunned at his words, Eulalie was silent. Robert had not even bothered to get her version of what had happened, before absolving Florilla of any criminal intent. But whether she had known what was planned or not, Florilla had been cruel to tell her that Jason was ill. Now it was too late to mention that to Robert. He had already made up his mind to keep Florilla in the house.

"But there is no need for Jason to have a governess, Robert. I will take care of him from now on."

"You are in no condition to watch after anybody for a while. No, Florilla will earn her keep. Jason is already causing her some consternation, since he can't get in to see you. I'm afraid you have spoiled him, Eulalie, in the short time you have been in the house."

"But why is he being kept from me, Robert?"

"He would not understand your being hurt. It would only scare him and upset him. And I know it would be too painful for you even to hold him for a few minutes. No, it's best if he does not see you for the next few days."

The knock sounded at the door and Robert called out, "Yes? Who is it?"

"It is Feena, monsieur, to help Mamselle Lili back to her room."

Walking to the door, Robert opened it a few inches, not wide enough for Feena to enter.

"That will not be necessary, Feena, since *Mrs.* Tabor will be staying in here from now on. You can start bringing her clothes from the green room, instead."

"Oui, monsieur," Feena said, chuckling, as the door closed.

Furious at the servant's dismissal, Eulalie climbed out of bed. She held to the large mahogany post until her head could clear.

"Robert, you had no right," Eulalie choked, "to tell Feena that. There is no need for any of my clothes to be brought here. I . . . I do not plan to stay in this room."

"As you wish about the clothes, Eulalie," Robert retorted. "You will not be able to wear them for some days anyway. But you *will* remain in this bedroom, Eulalie, whether you like it or not."

Eulalie let go of the post and took three faltering steps before she stopped, her body swaying from dizziness. Quickly, Robert reached her side and took her arm to steady her. She cried out in pain at the touch.

"You are not able to manage alone. Stop torturing yourself and get back to bed." His voice was curiously gentle.

Defeated, she let Robert help her to bed, but not before the tears began.

Seemingly unmoved by her tears, the golden-haired man exploded. "You are acting as spoiled as Jason, Eulalie. However disagreeable it is for you to share this room with me, that is exactly what you will do. The servants have enough to gossip about as it is, without our having separate bedrooms."

Eulalie buried her face in the pillow and made no effort to check her angry sobs. Soon the door slammed and she was alone.

"It is natural, *ma petite,* for a husband to want his wife with him," Feena said, hanging up Eulalie's clothes beside those of Robert.

"He didn't even ask me about Florilla. He made up his mind without even talking with me. He . . . he thinks I'm spoiling Jason and . . . and he didn't consult me about this room, whether I wished to stay or not." Eulalie wiped her tears with the edge of the sheet.

"All men do that, mamselle. They do not think it necessary to *ask* their wives anything, before making up their minds."

"But I am *not* his wife, Feena."

"Ah, so *that* is the big problem, *n'est-ce-pas?* Well, do not worry. With my poultices taking effect, you will soon be well. And then, when your skin is healed, we shall see how strong Monsieur Robert is, in resisting you."

"But I do not want . . ." Eulalie stopped, her face turning red with embarrassment.

Feena laughed and helped Eulalie out of her gown.

"Already the skin is looking better," Feena remarked.

The door opened and Feena, turning to Robert, asked, "Do you not think so, monsieur?"

Robert stepped closer to the bed and gazed at Eulalie, who was reaching frantically for the fresh gown that Feena held.

"Much better, Feena," he said, smiling. "Your balm is working its magic, I see."

Eulalie glared at Feena and ignored Robert and his comment.

Preoccupied with his thoughts, Robert vaguely registered the movement in the large mahogany bed. Ready to blow out the candles, he glanced toward Eulalie to bid her goodnight before stretching out on the cot near the hearth.

"*Now,* what are you doing, Eulalie?" Robert asked, annoyed that she was again out of bed.

"I am praying, monsieur, for Jacques Binet, as I promised." She knelt by the side of the bed, with only a portion of her long, dark hair visible from across the room.

The candles went out and Robert's voice cut through the room. "Then you will do it in the dark. I will not be subjected to watching my wife praying for such a bastard."

In the darkness, an annoyed Robert listened to the whispered sounds of his wife. Then, the quiet, sweet voice spoke clearly. "Good night, Robert."

"Good night, Eulalie. Sleep well."

Before dawn, Robert, careful not to awaken Eulalie, tiptoed from the bedroom into the adjoining alcove, where he dressed.

He had not told her about the duel, knowing it would upset her. With luck, he would be back without Eulalie knowing he had gone—that is, if Ashe did not kill him, instead.

The sun rose on the east banks of the Congaree, its brilliance sifting through the heavy, gnarled oak trees. The cheerful chirping of birds was incongruous over the sinister strip of sandy earth where death was meted out according to the gentlemen's code.

And it was there at Dueling Oak near the riverbank that the small group gathered—Robert and Arthur, his second; Alistair Ashe and his second; and the surgeons, waiting in the background to pronounce the severity of the wounds that were sure to come.

The horses, tethered to the saplings not far off, nervously pawed the ground and snorted, anxious to be free of the carriages.

The odor of the river, the strength of the early-morning breeze against his face and the taste of vengeance bombarded Robert's senses while he waited for the signal to begin.

Narrowing his eyes, Robert peered toward Alistair Ashe, who stood arrogantly not twenty paces from him, slowly drawing up his flintlock dueling pistol to eye position and gazing down the barrel toward his adversary. Once a member of the infamous Charleston Dueling Society, Ashe had had much practice on similar well-worn stretches of ground, with his opponent quaking before him.

But Robert Tabor did not quake. With a coolness derived from total hate of the man who had so insulted his wife, Robert stood his ground and calmly waited, his tawny topaz eyes watching Alistair Ashe, like some jungle lion waiting certainly for his prey.

Nothing less than death would satisfy Robert, and Alistair Ashe, facing the giant golden-haired man, sensed this. For the first time, Ashe knew fear. His colorless gray eyes became wary, and to hide the sudden trembling that invaded his limbs, he quickly changed gun positions.

As the sun burst forth over the trees, Arthur's voice reviewed instructions. "Five paces, and then the signal to fire at will."

Each man nodded in affirmation to indicate he understood. Standing back to back, they began the walk down the sandy path that separated them momentarily from death.

Increasingly nervous, Ashe walked down the path, his grip on his pistol causing his knuckles to turn white. Small beads of perspiration popped out on his forehead, and he swallowed, trying to rid himself of the fear that clung to him, threatening to take over his once calm and sure pistol hand.

"One . . . two . . . three . . . four . . . " Before Arthur had finished counting, Ashe suddenly whirled around and aimed his pistol toward Robert.

And Arthur, seeing this breach of the code, yelled, "Foul!"

Hearing Arthur's warning, Robert turned to see what had gone wrong, and at that moment, heard the sound of the shot and, surprised, felt the piercing of fire in his arm.

The sudden spurt of blood invaded the sleeve of Robert's coat. With a steely look toward the white-faced Alistair Ashe, Robert held his arm again his body and, slowly taking aim at his enemy, released the shot that sent Alistair Ashe plummeting to the ground.

The surgeons rushed to the victims to attend to their wounds. But Alistair Ashe was beyond help.

In the carriage, Robert sat, with an anxious Arthur by his side, while the surgeon probed for the bullet. It was not deep, and with its removal, the doctor bandaged Robert's arm. He could do no more.

The sun was still barely above the east bank of the Congaree when the carriage slowly worked its way up the street and then crunched to a halt before the white clapboard house where Eulalie slept, undisturbed.

Arthur Metcalfe helped Robert out of the carriage and guided him up the steps to the heavy front door. "Robert, let me come in with you," Arthur urged.

"No, Arthur. I'll be all right. Eulalie might awake and I don't want her to know."

"Do you think you can keep it from her, with your arm in that condition?"

"I shall try, Arthur. The best thing you can do for me is to go to Joseph and file your affidavit, showing Ashe for the cowardly poltroon that he proved to be."

"You won't have anything to worry about on that score, Robert. Ashe's second intends to corroborate what happened." Arthur, unhappy at being dismissed, asked, "Can I send a physician to see you this afternoon?"

"No. All they know to do is to bleed and purge, and heaven knows I've lost enough blood already."

Slowly, Robert walked into the house and began the ascent of the stairs. Pale from loss of blood, he clasped his hand over his left arm where he had been wounded. The jolting of the carriage had started it bleeding again. Halfway up the steps, Robert had to stop and rest. He was breathing heavily and his legs were not responding as well as they should. But after a few minutes, he was at the top of the stairs, facing the closed door to the master bedroom.

A fresh shirt and linens to bind his wound were what he needed—and if Eulalie were still asleep, she need not know.

He twisted the knob. The door came open and he walked into the room. Eulalie was still asleep, one arm outflung and hanging over the edge of the bed. Restraining himself from touching her, Robert opened the drawer of the highboy and pulled out a clean shirt. Now for the linen press in the hallway.

He was almost to the door again when the room began to whirl about him. Trying to steady himself, he reached out toward the wall. But his fingers, unable to grasp hold, edged down the white wall, and with a loud thud, his body plunged to the floor. The sudden draft from the hall caused the partially opened door to slam shut.

At the noise, Eulalie sat up and rubbed her eyes. The room slowly came into focus. But the far wall was different. A large stain—it had not been there when she went to bed. It looked almost like . . . blood. With increasing horror, she gazed at the smeared handprint and, following its red-fingered trail, she saw Robert on the floor beneath it. Eulalie screamed in terror.

"What is the matter, *ma petite?*" The voice penetrated the closed door. Then, Feena, not getting an immediate answer, rattled the door open and with Effie and Florilla right behind her, gazed incredulously at the trail of blood leading to the unconscious man on the floor.

"*Mon Dieu,*" Feena exclaimed in horror. "Monsieur Robert has lost much blood."

Eulalie, bending over her husband, said in a distraught voice, "I will need help in lifting him to the bed. Effie, go and get Jimbo and Willie to help me. And Feena, my scissors and case—where did you put them last night?"

The two black women disappeared, leaving Florilla staring at the wounded man on the floor. Her eyes narrowed and with venom she turned to Eulalie and whispered, "How does it feel, Mrs. Tabor, to be responsible for your husband's death?"

"He is *not* dead, Florilla," Eulalie denied, with tears in her eyes. "And I did not know—he fought Alistair Ashe, didn't he?"

Florilla confirmed her suspicions and bitterly quizzed, "Why did you have to come to Columbia? Both Jason and Robert would have been much better off without you. You should have stayed in New Orleans."

It was hard enough to bear without Florilla's accusations. The tears escaped down her cheeks, as Eulalie said, "Go to Jason, Florilla. He is probably awake from all the noise. And there is nothing you can do here."

Willie and Jimbo came with a wide-eyed Effie, and after Robert had been lifted from the floor to the bed, Eulalie dismissed everyone but Feena, who stood at her side, tearing the strips of linen to bind the wounded man's bleeding arm.

By the time Robert opened his eyes, he was lying in bed with his arm rebandaged. He looked at Eulalie sitting beside the bed. "I had not intended for you to find out," he said apologetically.

"Robert, why? Why did you do it?" Eulalie asked, the agitation filling her voice.

"Ashe insulted my wife. I could not let him get by with it."

"And . . . and he is . . . dead?" she asked, shivering involuntarily.

"Yes."

"But you might have been killed, too."

"Would that have mattered to you, Eulalie?"

"Of course it would matter, Robert. I could not live, knowing that you had died because of me."

"Your little nun's conscience, Eulalie?"

His question went unanswered. Instead, Eulalie became lost in the past, with the words that Feena had spoken to her—how long ago?

"He will have to have a strong sword arm to win you, *ma petite*."

But the actuality was not so romantic as the dream. In the dream, there had been no blood—no Robert—merely a shadowy figure, a figment of a young girl's imagination.

During the days that followed, Robert watched Eulalie, while he rested and pretended to read. Aware of her every motion, he knew she was not comfortable being in the same room with him, or sleeping on the cot that had been moved from Jason's room.

Blast it! He wasn't comfortable either, watching her kneeling each day at the same hour, knowing that she was praying for the man who had purchased her. It went against the grain and he wasn't sure how much longer he could stand it. But he would not let her go back to the green bedroom.

Looking up, he caught Eulalie's eyes staring at him thoughtfully. She quickly averted them, but not in time.

"What are you thinking, Eulalie?" Robert questioned, propping himself up.

"I thought I might go to Jason's room and spend some time with him, if you do not object, Robert."

"So now that I am mending, you are anxious to neglect me for our son."

Eulalie saw the smile but could not be sure if Robert was serious or teasing.

"I do not wish to neglect you, Robert. I am truly thankful that there seems to be no infection. But I have missed seeing Jason, and now that I shall soon be able to wear street clothes again, I thought—"

Robert interrupted her. "I have missed seeing Jason also, Eulalie. Ring the bell, and get Florilla to bring him in to see us."

Walking to the bell pull, Eulalie gave it a tug and waited for a servant to answer. When the knock came, Eulalie was at the door to give instructions to the servant.

When Jason was brought into the room, Florilla stood passively beside the door, ignoring the affectionate exchange between Jason and the parents he had not seen for a while.

"Florilla, you may leave him with us," Robert ordered. "When we're ready for you to take him again, we will call you."

Jason ran back and forth, climbing on the bed beside Robert and then hopping down to run to Eulalie on the cot. He could not be still. When he was with one parent, his eyes traveled to the other, until finally he took Eulalie's hand, led her over to the master bed and announced, "Bed, Eu-lie."

Momentarily at a loss and a little embarrassed at his

obvious solution to his desire to be with both parents, Eulalie did not move.

"I believe our son has invited you to join us, Eulalie. And judging from his face, you will either have to obey or be witness to a temper tantrum."

Reluctantly, Eulalie sat on the edge of the bed. Jason chortled happily betwen them, but then, noticing that Eulalie was not lying down as he and his father were, he attempted to lift her feet onto the bed.

"Madam, you must play the game all the way, it seems," Robert said, laughing.

"Eu-lie," Jason said, happily snuggling next to her, his face buried in her lap. She leaned over and kissed the back of his head.

"We're going to have to do something about that, you know," Robert advised. "He must not get in the habit of calling his mother 'Eu-lie.' It smacks of disrespect, doesn't it?"

Eulalie laughed and hugged Jason even harder.

CHAPTER

18

*F*OUR days later, with the help of Jimbo, Robert dressed and came downstairs. Except for the sling around his arm and the slight pallor to his face, there was no evidence of the duel. It had been kept quiet, and according to Arthur Metcalfe, the bereaved Polly had returned to St. John's Parish, a widow for the second time.

Arthur, a frequent caller during those days, now sat in the parlor with Robert, filling him in on the happenings in the legislature and the latest news of the war.

When Eulalie walked in, with Effie carrying the tea tray behind her, she heard only a remnant of the conversation before the men ceased talking. Eulalie glanced from one to the other as she poured the tea, trying to discern from their faces the seriousness of the news.

"Robert, are we in danger from the British?" a troubled Eulalie asked.

An assuring look swept over his face. "Napoleon is keeping the British far too busy for a full-scale war. The blockade is just a blasted nuisance, nothing more."

Eulalie relaxed, hearing his answer. And Robert, watching her, breathed easier. He did not want to alarm her with news of the recent commando raids on the sea islands close to Charleston. Far better to keep that to himself, until he could report back to Governor Alston after the holidays.

"And Columbia is too far inland to be in danger," Arthur reaffirmed. "As for Charleston, the state militia is guarding its harbor. So Midgard is safe."

At his answer, the troubled look reappeared on Eulalie's face.

"It wasn't safe the last time," Eulalie responded. "I remember Papa Ravenal's talking of the family silver being carried away in rice barrels by the redcoats."

"That was different," Robert replied. "Charleston had no adequate defense system then. It will be much harder now for a vessel to slip through the harbor and up the river. But enough of the war," Robert said, putting a stop to that part of the conversation. "Arthur, I believe you have some papers for me to look over?"

Eulalie picked up the tea tray and left the parlor as the two men bent their heads over the papers Arthur had brought for Robert.

It was the next afternoon that Eulalie sat in Jason's room, watching him ride the hobby horse in the corner. The child had not been up long from his nap.

He was a miniature of Robert, with no physical resemblance to link her as his mother. But her love for him grew greater each day. His topaz eyes were now bright with joy, and Eulalie herself felt his excitement and happiness. Jason had been the necessary diversion to get her through those difficult days spent in the same room with Robert.

Eulalie had been so self-conscious with Robert's gaze always upon her. And Feena had been no help, making comments about her skin and asking Robert's opinion.

So close in proximity, yet miles apart from each other, like two adversaries—Robert, with his smoky, insolent gaze traveling down the length of her yellow fleece robe one moment, and then changing to unconcealed distaste when she prayed for the man he hated—and not knowing what measure of reprimand he would take. But she had promised. She could not back down on a promise.

Just as she was thinking of him, Robert appeared in the doorway of the nursery.

"Eulalie, since the weather is good, I have decided to take you to Maggie's for the final fitting of your clothes. Three day dresses and two—" He stopped to correct himself. "Or rather, *one* evening gown, are not enough clothes for you. How soon can you be ready?"

"Are you sure you are up to—"

"Of course I am. There is nothing wrong with me, except for my arm in the sling. Another day or so and I'll be able to discard the sling. How soon, Eulalie?" he asked again.

"About a quarter of an hour, Robert."

"Good. I'll order the carriage."

The same little black boy who had accompanied Maggie to the white clapboard house let Robert and Eulalie into the shop. This time, he was dressed in bright-blue velvet, with a silk turban wrapped around his head.

"Neijee *does* give the shop class, don't you think?" Maggie said. "But so vain. He wants a lavender velvet suit to wear and has already selected my choicest feathers for his new headpiece."

The child grinned at Maggie's halfhearted protests over his extravagance and then plopped himself down where he could watch the fittings. He pulled out a piece of the smooth lavender velvet from under his jacket and stroked it with his fingers.

"Bee-yoo-tiful lady," the black child voiced, clapping his hands at intervals, as Eulalie changed from one gown to another.

With each new gown, Maggie delighted in parading Eulalie before Robert for his approval. He sat in the front of the shop, looking out of place, but seeming oblivious to that fact, his interest in the gowns making Eulalie extremely uncomfortable and shy.

"Now, for the best of all," Maggie announced, leading Eulalie back into the dressing room.

She relaxed when she saw the plain midnight-blue dress with the high neckline—a modest dress, more suitable for her than the low-cut ones that had been forced upon her.

When he saw it, Robert frowned and voiced his displeasure. "Maggie, I do not want my wife to look like a nu— nuthatch."

Eulalie knew from the hesitation in his voice that Robert had meant to say "nun" and had thought better of it.

"Wait," Maggie scolded. "You have not seen what goes with it. Close your eyes until I finish."

The white, translucent silk robe, embroidered with jeweled hummingbirds and silk flowers with garnet-studded centers, fell in loose wide sleeves and long flowing hem, covering the dark dress like a shimmering veil. A delicate gold nest with two of the jeweled hummingbirds was pinned in Eulalie's hair.

In a pleased voice, Maggie called, "You may look now."

Robert stared at the goddess before him. Her lips were tremulous and her dark satin doe eyes seduced his heart with their unsuspecting allure. The night of the harvest moon and the season of desire—once again he was succumbing to its spell.

Robert merely grunted and said aloud, "If you have almost finished, I will see to the carriage." And with those words, he stamped out of the shop.

"He . . . he did not like it, Maggie," Eulalie said in a distressed tone.

"Don't you believe that, Mrs. Tabor. I saw the look he gave you." Maggie laughed. "He liked the dress, but he had other things on his mind, like making love to his wife. If I were you, I would not keep him waiting."

Maggie was wrong, of course. He had looked at her with distaste, as if she were suddenly someone to be avoided. But she would not correct Maggie. Better to ignore her comment.

"I'd close the shop and throw the key down the well if Harvey ever looked at me like that. But that's highly unlikely." The dressmaker shrugged her shoulders and sighed. "Well, that was the last dress, anyway. I'll send all of them to you on Wednesday."

"Thank you, Maggie. You've been most kind."

"Not at all. It's a pleasure to dress someone who is so loved and protected by her husband."

If Maggie only knew the truth, Eulalie thought. The woman had taken it for granted that she and Robert were lovers.

Neijee held the door open for Eulalie and escorted her to the carriage, where Robert was waiting.

She glanced back at the small black child standing in front of the shop, watching the carriage. How many years older than Jason? Three? Four? If she had remained a slave to Jacques Binet, would her own child have been sold as a pet for some rich woman? Or dressed in velvet suits and silk turbans to open doors for snobbish customers?

Thoughtfully silent, Eulalie sat beside Robert, who ignored her. With one hand he expertly tooled the horses home. He was in an evil temper, and Eulalie, feeling this, shrank against the seat, wondering what had happened to cause such an abrupt change.

Desmond Caldwell was waiting for them in the library when Robert and Eulalie drew up to the house.

"I have just heard from my wife, Julie. She is so delighted over her newfound cousin that she has asked me to extend an invitation to you both to spend Christmas with us at Cedar Hill."

Eulalie's face brightened and she turned expectantly to her husband.

"Robert?"

But Robert shook his head. "Give our regrets to your wife, Desmond. There are things I need to see to in Charleston. We will be returning to Midgard for Christmas."

"I am sorry to hear that. Julie will be quite disappointed." Desmond hesitated before speaking again. "Would you then consent to Cousin Eulalie going alone for part of the holiday season? Since Arthur will be coming also, he can see her safely home."

Robert's answer was not long in coming. "Impossible, Desmond. Jason has been ill, and a child needs his mother with him."

"Quite so," Desmond agreed. "I had forgotten about the child's illness. Well, another time."

Feeling thwarted, Eulalie said nothing until Desmond had gone. Jason was well and could have gone with her to Cedar Hill. But evidently Robert did not wish her to visit her cousin. And she, herself, was not anxious to go back to Midgard. The memories there were too painful.

"When will we be leaving for Midgard?" Eulalie asked, with a suppressed dread.

"On Thursday," Robert replied and left the library.

Wednesday morning, an excited Maggie personally delivered the finished dresses to Eulalie.

"You will not believe what has happened." Maggie's large eyes shone with happiness as she shook a dress free from its confining box. "Harvey has finally asked me to marry him and he wants me to set the date right away, so that we will have Christmas together."

"Oh, Maggie, I am so happy for you," Eulalie replied.

"There is only one fly in the ointment."

"And what is that?" Eulalie asked, seeing the frown on Maggie's face.

"Harvey refuses to have slaves. He's from the up-country, you know. So that means that I shall have to part with Neijee. Would you like to buy him, Mrs. Tabor? Somehow I can't bring myself to put him up for sale for just anybody to bid on him. And he already dotes on you."

"But I have no money of my own," Eulalie explained.

"Your husband—he would buy him for you, if you asked him."

"I don't know. Maggie. How long do you have before . . . " But then, Eulalie remembered. They themselves were leaving for Midgard on the next day.

"Five days. We're to be married on Monday and leave Columbia on Tuesday."

"You'd better find someone else, Maggie, to buy him. I doubt that Robert would agree to it."

"Try, Mrs. Tabor. I know he would buy him if *you* asked him."

Through dinner that evening, Eulalie was unusually quiet. Her mind was on Neijee and Maggie's dilemma. And all day, she had not found the proper words to approach Robert.

"I thought you would wear one of the new gowns this evening, Eulalie. Are you not pleased with them?"

Eulalie looked up from her sewing. She had retired early to the master bedroom, where Robert was now staring at her, a puzzled expression on his face.

"You know I am . . . grateful to you, Robert."

"That is not what I meant. I do not want your gratitude, Eulalie. I only want you to have the things you have done without these last three years." His voice grew fierce. "Are they not to your satisfaction, Eulalie? Was there something else in Maggie's shop you would have preferred? Some trinket, or another gown, even?"

Neijee. Now was the time to tell him about Neijee. Eulalie quickly admitted, "Maggie *does* have something that I would like to purchase."

Affronted by her admission, Robert advised her, "It is still not too late. You could send for it in the morning before we leave. You should have spoken up while we were in the shop the other day."

"But you bought so much for me."

"What good is that, if you are not happy with what I selected?" Then, in an effort at lightness, he said, "We will consider this purchase one of your Christmas presents —to make up for the disappointment of not spending Christmas with your cousin."

Her look was cautious. "The price would be . . . most dear."

Robert dismissed her protest. "I think I can stand the expense," he said, shifting his weight with an impatience to leave the room.

"Do you not want to know what it is?"

"It's not necessary. Go ahead and get it. And have Maggie send me the bill."

Just before he closed the door, she managed to say, "Yes, Robert. And—thank you."

So she had done it. But what would Robert say when he discovered what she had purchased?

They loaded the carriages with luggage, tying the extra trunk on top. Jimbo and Robert checked the ropes to make sure they were secure.

It was early morning and Eulalie, standing by the carriage, looked anxiously down the street. If Neijee did not come soon, it would be too late.

Already, Robert was telling Jimbo to drive on with Feena and Effie and the baggage. "You have a heavier load, Jimbo. Go on and we will catch up with you."

"Yes suh," Jimbo said and started the horses.

"I don't know why you insisted on coming out so early, Eulalie," Robert told her. "At least get into the carriage to stay warm, while I take one last look in the house. I'll send Florilla out with Jason the last thing."

Robert walked up the steps just as another carriage passed Jimbo, traveling in the opposite direction.

Maggie, dashing down the street in the small phaeton, stopped by the iron fence. Neijee hopped out, and Maggie, struggling with his trunk, apologized to Eulalie, who had stood outside the carriage in spite of Robert's orders.

"I'm sorry I'm late. Everything went wrong this morning. You know how it is."

"It's all right, Maggie. You're here in time." Eulalie helped Maggie lift the small trunk onto the back of the carriage and strap it on.

"Be a good boy for Mrs. Tabor, Neijee," Maggie said, patting the little boy on the head.

The boy grinned and followed Eulalie into the closed carriage.

Her heart was pounding when Robert reappeared. What would he say when he saw Neijee? But Robert was too busy to pay attention to the travelers in the carriage. Once he had handed up Florilla and Jason, he went to the driver's seat on the outside of the carriage and began the journey.

CHAPTER

19

W HO is that?" Florilla asked, pointing at the small black boy seated beside Eulalie.

"This is Neijee," Eulalie replied. "An early Christmas present from Robert."

Her casual answer stopped Florilla from commenting further. Little did Florilla know that under her assumed nonchalance, Eulalie's heart was still beating much too fast. She dreaded the confrontation with her husband at the first rest stop. But by then it would be too late to send the child back to Maggie.

It was past noon when they finally came to the travelers' rest. Robert had already passed Jimbo and the carriage containing Feena and Effie.

"Everyone out—time to stretch your legs." Robert sounded in a good mood.

"Take Jason on in, Florilla. I will be there in a few minutes." Eulalie reached down for the small valise at her feet.

Robert put the stool on the ground and waited for the passengers to alight. Florilla first, then Jason . . .

He stamped his feet on the ground and blew warm breath over his cold fingers while he waited for Eulalie.

"Don't dawdle, Eulalie," he said impatiently. "You need to get to the fire to warm yourself."

While he stood waiting for his wife, he saw the black child from Maggie's shop hop down and run past to catch up with Jason.

"Eulalie!" The voice was threatening, and so she climbed down, letting Robert help her from the carriage. He made no move to release her when she reached the ground. "What is *he* doing in the carriage, Eulalie?"

"He is my early Christmas present—from Maggie's shop."

Robert looked at his demure wife standing beside him, with the stubborn lift of her chin barely disguised under her bonnet. He made no attempt to hide his anger.

"And you made sure I did not discover him until it was too late to turn around and take him back."

"Maggie could not keep him," Eulalie explained, her trembling hands hidden under her cloak.

"And so you took him without my permission."

"Yes, Robert." Her eyes stared down at her slippers, while she waited for his anger to intensify.

"Neijee is no stray kitten, Eulalie, for you to tuck under your skirts to take home. He is a costly slave who cannot possibly earn his keep for many years. He is too young to be put to work. But come," Robert said, losing part of his anger. "We will discuss it later."

The weather suddenly changed for the worse soon after they left the travelers' rest. Snow, mixed with sleet, began to fall, and the roads became a hazard, with the heavy carriages loaded to the hilt sinking down into the soft, sandy mire.

Though wrapped in a soft blanket, Jason whimpered from the cold. Even Neijee, with his black eyes peering out from the folds of his blanket, shook from the intense cold. And Robert, outside, faced the buffeting wind and sleet that chilled him to the bone.

Because of the weather, they arrived much later at the inn where they were to spend the night—wet, cold and hungry.

Robert had been in a bad temper all afternoon, impatient with the horses, impatient with Eulalie and now impatient with the innkeeper, who had nothing ready for them when they arrived.

Crowded with other travelers caught in the bad weather, the inn offered few amenities except a blazing fire on the hearth in the public room.

Gratefully, they gathered around the fire, trying to get warm and dry. And when at last the innkeeper's wife brought them all mugs of hot cider, they drank it down quickly, cradling their mugs with their cold hands.

Robert was forced to share a room with two other gentlemen, while Eulalie and Florilla shared a bed in the same small room that housed Jason. Neijee slept on a pallet near Jason, and Feena, Effie and Jimbo were given space near the kitchen.

"Dammit!" Robert complained, his temper short. "No man should be forced to spend the night with strangers."

By the next morning, the sleet had stopped and each mile traveled in a southeasterly direction brought milder weather. But the improved weather did nothing to improve Robert's disposition.

They did not travel on Sunday, so it was not until Tuesday that they reached Emma's Bog and the approach to Midgard.

The familiar dark terrain of Biffers Road closed in on Eulalie. She clutched Jason close to her, intimidated by ghostly memories of her last trip down the road to Charleston and the slave market. Jason struggled against the constriction and Eulalie loosened her hold on the child.

The sun shone brightly as the increasing speed of the carriage wheels brought them out of Emma's Bog. Now the exhausting, hard trip was at an end. They were at Midgard.

Bradley, the old butler, was ecstatic when he saw them.

"Mr. Robert, it sho' is good to have ya home. And Miss Eulalie too," he added. "A reg'lar fam'ly by now," he said to himself as he shuffled away to supervise the luggage being brought into the house.

"Watch that box, boy! If ya cain't be careful, Ah'll send ya to Moses for a field hand!"

Threatened with outside work, the final insult for a house servant, the boy became more diligent.

Robert left the house to find his overseer and to look over the plantation, while Jason was put to bed for his afternoon nap.

Eulalie, grateful for the shelter of her own bedroom, unpacked and hung up her dresses before resting. Shortly before time for dinner, she emerged, freshly bathed and wearing one of the more modest dresses—a blue wool with its long sleeves buttoned to the wrists.

Wild duck, quail, rice, spoon bread and peach preserves filled the dinner table, and more delicacies were brought by Bradley as the long meal progressed.

Robert, scowling, sat at the head of the table, peering down to the opposite end where Eulalie was quietly eating her dinner.

She was where she belonged, thought Robert, remembering the vacant space and the frustration he had felt when he had found out she had hidden from him upon his return from Paris.

But now, at the same table, she was no closer than she had been that first night.

Completely unaware of her powers to stir him, she sat, daintily eating the quail on her plate, breaking the small wing and lifting it to her mouth with her slender white fingers.

Her very actions were provocative, and even now Robert desired her. Attending to Florilla's inconsequential chatter far more than was warranted, Robert ignored Eulalie. Under his exaggerated attention to her, Florilla bloomed.

And when he got up from the table after declining the brandy offered by Bradley and announcing his intention to go for a walk, an encouraged Florilla said, "Would you mind some company, Robert? I declare, my poor bones have been so jolted the past few days that I feel the need of a walk too."

"You're welcome to join me," Robert answered.

The two departed the dining room together and Eulalie was left alone.

Jason was crying, and Eulalie, hearing him, went upstairs where Feena was watching over him. Neijee, asleep on the little cot in the nursery, raised his head. "Go back to sleep, Neijee. It's all right," Eulalie told him, and the child lay down again.

"Jason is tired from the long trip, mamselle," Feena said. "And he has to get used to sleeping in his bed again."

"Eu-lie," Jason cried, holding out his arms to be taken up.

She sat for a long time, holding and rocking him with her body, until he became quiet, his head heavy against her breast.

Sounds of footsteps told her Robert and Florilla had come back into the house. She waited until the house grew quiet again and then she slipped to her room.

Ready for bed, Eulalie began to unbutton the blue wool dress by the light of the flickering candle she had brought from Jason's room. Her eyes searched for the yellow fleece robe and gown that had been draped over her bed earlier. They were both gone.

She stopped and looked for the trunk and for the dresses. Nothing remained. They had all been removed sometime after she had gone downstairs for dinner.

Surely Robert had not done it. He could not expect her to sleep elsewhere. This was *her* room, hers from the time she had first traveled up Biffers Road with Papa Ravenal.

Her anger made her forget her timidity in facing Robert. Taking the candle, Eulalie walked down the hall and knocked on the door of the room that her *maman* had shared with Papa Ravenal.

"What is it?" Robert's voice called out.

Eulalie pushed open the door and walked in.

He sat warily in the chair by the hearth, a book in his hands, as if he had been expecting her.

"Robert, my clothes have been removed from my bedroom."

"*Your* bedroom, Eulalie?" he asked in the same dangerous quiet tone he had used in the river house. "I was not aware that you had a separate bedroom from your husband."

She glanced at the two massive beds, seeing the yellow fleece robe and gown carefully spread over the chair next to one of them.

"Surely, you do not expect me to—"

"I thought I made it plain to you, Eulalie. I will not have the servants gossiping."

"But that was in Columbia," she protested. "Now that we are at Midgard—"

"The same arrangements will be observed."

Furiously she grabbed the robe and gown and took to the concealed corner of the room hidden by the tall screen. Muttering to herself, she pulled off the blue wool dress and slipped the gown over her head.

Her brush was laid out beside his on the dressing table. Ignoring Robert still sitting in the chair, she removed the pins from her hair, the strands tumbling down to cover her shoulders.

Cold and in an ill temper, she walked to the rug by the hearth, sat down and began the chore of brushing the tangles from her long black hair.

It was going to be harder than she thought, living with him in the same room, subject to Robert's disturbing gaze at her every movement. He was only doing it to torment her, while making it clear that he preferred Florilla's company to hers.

Silhouetted by the fire, Eulalie continued her brushing until her hair was smooth and shiny. Then she walked to the window seat and, trying to erase her petulant thoughts, knelt and began her evening prayers with her back to Robert. She was not successful. Her prayer for Jacques Binet was automatic, with her mind still on her husband.

"Which bed, Robert, have you decided I shall sleep in?" Eulalie faced a scowling, dark, disturbing Robert.

"If you had behaved as a proper wife three years ago,

179

there would be no need to ask that question." His voice was dangerously low.

The color drained from her face at his answer that was no answer at all.

"You have a choice," he said, indicating both beds with his arm, which had recently been taken out of the sling.

As if he could not help himself, could not contain his frustration, Robert kept on, uninterrupted. "I am curious to know what choice you made with Jacques Binet, Eulalie. Did he allow you to choose where you slept? Or did he have you warm his own bed, as you warmed mine in the river house?"

His eyes held hers and forced her to recall the memory of his hands and his lips upon her body. At war with herself and her own emotions, she lashed out, "Don't speak to me of choices, monsieur. I have had few choices since my marriage to you."

Her French accent was noticeable in her agitation.

Angered by her reply, he grabbed her wrists, drawing her roughly against him.

"You still have not answered my question."

"I . . . I will not answer you."

Like a man demented, he goaded, "If he could enjoy your charms, why should I deny myself the same comfort? Lord, you have tormented me from the moment I found you in Jason's room . . . in your little nun's dress . . . in your ballgowns cut to show the soft curves of your breasts . . . In your sensuous, deliberate seduction by the fire, brushing your witch's hair . . . "

In uncontrollable rage, he crushed her in his arms, wildly kissing her hair, her lips, and the tender lobes of her pink-shelled ears.

"Madame, you are no nun, despite your fine prayers," he whispered in her ear. "You are a whore at heart, and I intend to treat you as such."

She gave a cry as he lifted her and carried her to the bed. "Robert," she pleaded, but there was no stopping him.

He ripped the gown from her and she lay naked upon the bed. But her body was not cold. There was a stirring fire within her, fanned to a roaring flame by his caressing her in every private place, his fingers and his tongue moving over her body, unwillingly responding to every nuance of his lovemaking.

The pulsating fire built up and exploded. Gradually the consuming heat slowed and died, leaving Eulalie ashamed and heartbroken, a prisoner in Robert's arms, with no comfort offered her for her lost soul.

CHAPTER

20

HUMILIATED each night by Robert's lovemaking, Eulalie struggled against her own feelings of desire mixed with hate. Her prayers intensified. By day, she was the nun, but at night, inflamed by her silent piety, Robert turned her into a trembling, loose woman, responding to his every whim.

"Let me go, Robert," she begged. "You are only keeping me to . . . to punish me."

"Where would you go, Eulalie?" he asked. "Back to some nunnery?"

"Yes."

"When will you learn," he said triumphantly, "that you were never intended to be shut away in some convent? Your body was made for a man to love. The sooner you stop fighting it, the better off you will be."

"Does it not matter to you, Robert," she countered, "that I would rather be left alone?"

"No, Eulalie. Your unwillingness makes it even more challenging. Resist all you want. But I warn you—you cannot hope to win against me. One day I will make you forget Jacques Binet and this hold he has upon you."

Delighted at the silent enmity between Robert and

Eulalie at mealtimes, Florilla was more than willing to play the hostess at table.

The encounters with Robert left Eulalie devastated and withdrawn, and she readily let Florilla usurp her duties as hostess.

A few evenings after their return, Robert, stung by Eulalie's indifference to him, turned to Florilla.

"You were at the convent in New Orleans the same time Jason was born?"

"Yes, Robert," Florilla answered.

"Then tell me, since Eulalie does not appear to want to remember—tell me whose child is buried in the tomb marked 'Eulalie Boisfeulet Tabor.' "

"Why, did Eulalie—that is, Mrs. Tabor—not tell you that she had twins—a boy and a girl? The little girl lived only a few hours. Jason was born first and was the stronger of the two."

A malicious glint was partially masked by her smile. "But as to whose child she was, I'm sure *I* could not tell you, Robert. I only caught a glimpse of the man who left her at the convent—a most unsavory-looking character. It was lucky for her that the children were not born among the Africans. I am told that when twins are born in that dark continent, both the mother and babies are drowned. The natives believe the woman has been unusually wicked with two different men."

Eulalie stared unbelievingly at the venom-voiced Florilla. She overturned the wine glass at her place in her hasty escape from the table.

With satisfaction, Florilla gazed at Eulalie's empty place.

Eulalie fled from the house in the darkness of the night. Where could she go, away from the constant bombardment and erosion of her self-respect? What did Robert want from her? Tears filled her eyes and she stumbled over an upturned magnolia root and fell to the ground.

The dampness of the earth soaked through her dress and she shivered from the cold. Eulalie pushed herself up and forced her body to move in a slower tempo.

"Eulalie," the voice called. But she did not answer. She began running again, trying to find a hiding place from Robert and the tremendous hurt that swelled and threatened to destroy her.

"Eulalie, come back," the voice called again. But Eulalie kept on, to find a hiding place.

The slave nursery—it would be deserted now that the babies were with their mothers for the night.

Down the path toward the nursery she went, the drifting clouds hiding the moon from view. Even then, she did not need a light. The whiteness of the sand in the pathway was enough to guide her to the cabin and safety.

The rocking chair was still in its place where she had rocked Cassius to sleep. Was he well, or was he one of the unfortunate ones who had not survived the fever?

Even in the nursery cabin, Eulalie could not escape her memories. For was it not here that her troubles had first begun—when she had been discovered by Robert and mistaken for a quadroon?

The embers in the crude hearth were almost out. Eulalie watched their last feeble glow before the redness disappeared, like the eyes of wild animals fleetingly seen in the forest glow for a time and then disappear. But she dared not stir up the fire. The puff of smoke from the stone chimney would give her away. Besides, nothing would ever make her warm again.

Shivering, Eulalie curled up into a small ball. Her hair tumbled down to her waist, free of the pins that she had lost somewhere along the way.

Briefly the voices and the light of flares along the pathway disturbed her sleep. Soon they were gone, leaving her in silent shadows.

Much later, the door to the cabin creaked open. Caught in the light of the flare, she blinked and shielded her eyes with her hands.

"Eulalie—thank God I've found you!"

Robert's voice was vibrant with relief. He flung the flare onto the hearth and Eulalie cringed as Robert lifted her in his arms.

Her reaction wounded him, and with a strangely tender, hoarse voice, he said, "I will not hurt you, Eulalie. Never again will I hurt you as I did tonight. You are safe from me, little nun."

The morning sun caught the hidden silver glints of the limestone marker in the family cemetery. Ravenal Tabor —born June 12, 1745; died July 3, 1809. Rest in peace.

Robert stared at the marker and in bitterness he said aloud, "Are you having your laugh, Uncle Ravenal?"

Robert's mind was on the past, on the last conversation with his uncle before leaving Midgard when he was twenty-one—eight years ago.

"Besides you, Uncle Ravenal," he had said in his arrogant voice to the man who had reared him as a father, "there are only two things in my life worthy to be loved —horses and land."

His uncle had chuckled at the statement.

"What about a woman, Robert? Is there any room in your life for a wife?"

"No. Oh, I daresay I'll have to marry one of these days, but I'll put it off as long as I can. And she will not take up much room in my life. I will not allow a bit of fluff to change anything I have planned. Use them, bed them and then forget them."

What a fool he had been! Eulalie had changed his life completely. He had even killed a man because of her. Forget her? She had eased her way into his heart and he could no more forget her than his own name. She was a part of him—but a part he did not understand. Always, he had taken what he wanted, regardless of the consequences. But Eulalie had defeated him.

He had not wanted to hurt her. He had been driven mad by her indifference and had given sway to the devil within him demanding obeisance.

But no more. She was too fragile to be treated in such a manner. From now on, he would have to curb his jealousy of Jacques Binet, or at least not show it in Eulalie's presence.

She deserved a better life than that. But even with everything that had happened to her, she still showed spirit.

Robert smiled as he thought of Neijee and of how Eulalie had gotten her own way over him.

It might not turn out so badly after all. At least, Neijee

could act as companion and valet to Jason. They seemed to get along well enough together.

Robert left the family plot, untied his horse from the sapling and headed down the road toward Charleston and his mission for Joseph Alston.

Eulalie awoke that morning and the first thing she did was to look across at the other massive bed. Robert was up and gone.

She had thought she would never get warm again. But now under the soft covers, with the staccato crackling of the fire sounding like music on the hearth, she felt snug and secure.

Not so, during the first part of the night. Trembling with cold and her fear of Robert, she could not hide her feelings when he carried her into the house from the nursery cabin. Gradually the fear and cold had receded as Robert, remaining by her bed, briskly rubbed her numb hands and feet until the circulation brought warmth and color again. Only then did Robert leave her to climb into the other bed for the rest of the night.

"So, *ma petite* is awake." Feena brought the steaming chocolate and the brioche to her bed. "A scare you gave us all last night, mamselle. Monsieur Robert was beside himself, fearing that you had gotten lost in the bog."

"I . . . I am sorry, Feena. But I could not remain in the house with Robert listening to Florilla's vile words."

"I understand, mamselle. That one—she can only cause trouble. Have I not said so before? It made my blood curdle to hear her apologizing to Monsieur Robert so prettily, when she saw how upset he was."

"Robert was upset?"

"*Oui*. His temper was something to see."

Eulalie sipped her chocolate and broke off bits of brioche to put into her mouth.

Was Robert upset over Florilla's accusation? Or was it her knowledge that Jacques Binet had left Eulalie at the convent that had upset him? He had forbidden her to speak of it to anyone, her being sold as a slave and taken to New Orleans on the *Jasmine Star* by the trapper. The only other one who had known it was Alistair Ashe, and he was now dead.

How astute of Florilla to feed Robert's doubts about her relationship with the trapper. And it was too late for Eulalie to explain. It seemed a miracle, but nothing had happened between her and Jacques Binet. She had repulsed him that first night and he had been too drunk to do anything about it. And then she was so seasick all the way to New Orleans that he had left her alone.

Why had she not explained this to Robert? Pride had stood in her way—fierce, cold and uncomforting pride—and now it lay between them like a two-edged sword. But if she *had* explained, would he have believed her?

But he *had* accepted Jason as his own son. Looking at them together, no one could say that Robert had not fathered him. It was obvious from those tawny eyes and golden hair. That at least made it easier. But suppose Jason had had black hair and her own dark eyes, instead? Would Robert have denied him his rightful heritage then?

Eulalie dressed and went to look for Jason. He was quietly playing with his carved blocks in the middle of the nursery floor, with Neijee down on his hands and knees helping him.

By evening, Robert still had not come home. Florilla and Eulalie sat in the dining room alone and were served dinner by Bradley.

"Mr. Robert said he might be late gettin' back from Charleston," Bradley said. "But Ah've got his supper saved, in case he hasn't eaten."

Eulalie was thankful for Bradley's presence, for she and Florilla had little to talk about.

By the time Robert returned to Midgard, she was in bed. Eulalie heard him close the bedroom door softly. She kept her eyes closed while the sounds in the bedroom told her he was getting ready for bed.

She heard his boots drop and within a few minutes the candle went out. Eulalie listened in the dark as he climbed into the bed opposite hers, and at the sound, her tense body relaxed and she fell asleep.

The letter from Maggie arrived the next day, brought to Eulalie from Charleston by Gil Jordan, the overseer. And included in the letter was the bill for Neijee.

She stared incredulously at the amount—fifteen hundred dollars. She had no idea that one small black boy could cost so much.

And now she must go to Robert and give him the bill. No wonder he had been angry with her when he realized what she had done. An impulse to protect the black child from a harsh master had prompted her to do what she had.

Robert looked up from his desk when Eulalie entered.

"Robert, I have the . . . the bill for Neijee. Maggie sent it." Eulalie's face was pale as she stood hesitantly before him.

His hand reached for the slip of paper.

"It seems I have received my Christmas present for many years to come."

Her attempt at lightness was ignored, while Robert stared down at the paper.

Finally he said, "So Maggie is now Mrs. Harvey Crowley."

Eulalie walked closer to look at the paper. "Crowley? Do you mean the little man who . . . "

"The peacock whom you thought so splendid at the ball." Robert's eyes twinkled in amusement. "A bargain for him, wouldn't you say? Now he will not have to worry about his clothes and the lack of silks and satins from France. Maggie can even do wonders with homespun, if it comes to that."

Eulalie laughed and the tense moment over the bill subsided. Robert placed the bill on his desk with the heavy paperweight upon it.

So he was not refusing to pay it, as she had been afraid he might.

"Thank you, Robert," Eulalie said, backing away from the desk, where he was once again absorbed in the report he was writing.

Already, holly and mistletoe had been brought in, in great quantities, to decorate the hallway and dining room.

Giant red berries of the holly brightened the walls of the low-country brick mansion, while the white berries of the mistletoe hung suspended from the candled chandeliers and over each doorway.

Feena, Florilla and Eulalie were busy stringing popcorn, cotton bolls and dried crabapples together when Jimbo carried the mammoth Christmas tree into the house.

Eulalie laid down the chain she was working on, to direct Jimbo. And when the tree was in the right position before the window of the salon, Eulalie went back to her chair and took up the stringed decoration.

Puzzled, she saw that only part of it was intact. The popcorn was gone.

"Jason! Neijee!" she called to the two hiding behind the chair opposite hers. Sheepishly they came out of hiding, their cheeks resembling fat chipmunks' cheeks with their hidden goodies.

With a severe look on her face, Eulalie said, "If you don't stop eating the popcorn, there won't be enough to decorate the tree. What a terrible-looking string this is!"

She held up the scrawny string. The two little boys giggled and ran from the room.

"Florilla, you'd better follow them," Eulalie said. "Feena and I can finish."

Florilla pursed her lips but got up from her chair. "Neijee is not a good influence on Jason," she commented. "Already Jason has gotten into more mischief in the short time Neijee has been here than he did the entire two years I have been watching over him."

Florilla swept out of the room with a disagreeable expression on her face.

"Pay no attention to her, *ma petite,*" Feena said when Florilla was out of sight. "She would rather have Jason sit in a chair all day, instead of running and playing, so that she would not have to exert herself."

Feena and Eulalie carried the decorated strings to the tree and soon the bare tree took on a festive look.

But presents—what would they do for presents? Eulalie had had little time to make anything. Stuffed toys for Jason and Neijee, and a frilled shirt for Robert. That would have been nice. But it was much too late to begin. She could not possibly finish by Christmas Eve. She could start on the shirt for another time, though. Perhaps for Robert's birthday.

It was then Eulalie realized she did not know either his birthdate or his age.

Robert took her to the shops in Charleston the next day, giving her money with which to buy presents.

"I will not need all this, Robert," Eulalie protested. But Robert shook his head and closed his hand around hers, forcing her to keep all of it.

Although it was the custom for the slaves to be treated with presents on New Year's Day, Eulalie wrapped the gifts for Neijee, Feena and Bradley and put them under the family tree.

Jason was delighted with the hound puppy, with his long ears flopping to the floor, his fat little stomach swaying from side to side.

But when Eulalie saw the pony Robert had bought for Jason, she was alarmed.

"A pony, at his age?" Eulalie questioned. "Is he not too young to be riding?"

"I was riding when I was his age," Robert replied, and that seemed to end the discussion.

She gave Robert a gold filigreed pocket watch that she had found in the goldsmith's shop. Knowing that Neijee had been her Christmas present from Robert, Eulalie did not expect a present from him under the tree.

"Open it, Eulalie," he said, handing it to her that Christmas Eve.

He watched as she removed the ribbon and paper from the small box. When she lifted the lid, the large ruby ring, polished in a high cabochon, sparkled at her.

Robert gruffly explained, "It is a delicate, mysterious stone, and must be treated as such—treasured, not for its hardness or brilliance, as a diamond, but for its rich, red color. The ruby almost always has a flaw, but its beauty seems to make up for it."

Eulalie wondered if he were trying to tell her something—to let her know that he was willing to forgive any indiscretion with Jacques Binet, even though there was nothing to forgive.

While she stared at the beautiful ring, Robert took it and placed it upon her left hand that was bare of any wedding band. He frowned as he suddenly realized what was missing.

It had been a long evening, with the exchange of presents, the reading of the Christmas story to Jason, with Neijee looking on, and the festive dinner that Bradley had served so well.

Up the stairs Eulalie went, conscious of the ruby on her hand and conscious of Robert, slowing his stride to match her slower walk.

Into the bedroom they both went, where the fire blazed on the hearth and the candles on the bedsides glowed.

Robert, standing back, waited for Eulalie to discover her other gift.

In the corner, beyond her bed, stood a beautifully carved prie-dieu with its soft blue velvet kneeling cushion.

"Robert?"

"For my little nun," he said gently. "I cannot have you wearing out your knees on the floor."

Tears came to her eyes as she once again voiced her gratefulness to him. But already he had turned his back, his hand on the gold filigreed watch. He opened the case, still warm from his body heat. Caressing the silk lining inside, his fingers remembered the smooth silkiness of Eulalie's body. Once again, he was overwhelmed by his desire for her.

CHAPTER

21

ROBERT had other things on his mind, as well. As a member of the Charleston militia, concerned with the defense of that city from attack by sea, he went into Charleston to check on how well the militia was responding to its duty.

The people in Charleston and the surrounding countryside had not forgotten the city's capture by the British during the War for Independence and the widespread destruction that had come to them at that time.

But it was ironic that many were incensed not so much with the indigo and rice crops being destroyed or the buildings burned as they were with the appropriation of the bells of St. Michael's by a British officer. It had been some time before they had gotten the bells back and they were determined that it would not happen again.

A large breastwork of sod, with a wide ditch before it, had been built to protect the city. And it was not only the men who had helped. Women and children had labored in its construction also.

After a tour of the waterfront, Robert sat in the Exchange with Arthur and Hector. The Exchange was almost empty, for little business was going on because of the blockade.

"I would feel a lot better if so many of our militia units had not gone to fight with the army in the north. A ragtail group of civilians cannot guard the harbor nearly so well as trained troops," Arthur expounded.

"Then the civilians will have to be trained better," Robert said. "The Federal troops are much too busy to come to our aid if the city is attacked. They have made that plain."

"What I can't understand," Hector grumbled, "is why the militia is limited to men between eighteen and forty-five. I'm much healthier than many of them, but because of my white hair, they look on me as a Methuselah."

"Too bad they couldn't have seen you on the Mississippi, Hector. They would know you are a power to be reckoned with," Robert teased.

"When was this, Hector?" Arthur asked.

A startled glance was exchanged between Robert and his cousin.

"About three years ago. I had a sudden . . . hankering to see this new land we purchased. Beautiful river country," Hector said. "Very wild, but beautiful."

Robert relaxed at his answer.

"Just hope the British don't have a hankering to explore either of our rivers," Hector added, getting back to the subject under discussion. "Farther south, I understand, their cutters have slipped into the numerous waterways and have raided some of the nearby plantations. They would really get some prizes if they found their way up the Ashley or the Cooper."

"We will have to see that the harbor is guarded well. If it is, there will be little chance for the British to send their smaller boats upriver," Robert said.

There was a lull in the conversation, finally broken by Arthur.

"How is Eulalie, Robert?"

"She is fine, Arthur."

"Julie and Desmond were both disappointed that she could not come to Cedar Hill. We had a fine celebration, as usual, but it would have been even nicer if you two had joined us."

Robert did not respond and Arthur, peering thoughtfully toward Robert, asked, "Has she gotten over her ordeal?"

"I think it will take longer than these few weeks to erase it from her memory."

"What ordeal, Robert? Has something else happened to Eulalie that I do not know about?" Hector was puzzled at the turn of the conversation.

"I'm sorry, Robert," Arthur apologized, getting up from the table. "It seems I cannot learn to hold my tongue. Shall I see you tomorrow?"

"No, Arthur. I will be going to Taborville to check on the mill."

"Then I'll see you when you get back."

Arthur walked out of the Exchange, leaving the two cousins together at the table.

Hector waited while Robert debated how much he should tell him of what had happened in Columbia.

As he left the plantation on horseback the next day, Robert thought of the mill workers and the snug little village of Taborville.

He had not been popular two years before when he built the mill upriver in the pinelands and hired the white workers.

"You are bringing in riffraff, Robert," one of his older neighbors complained. "And paying them good wages will give our slaves ideas."

"Do you not hire out your own slaves, Reuben?" Robert inquired.

"Well, yes, but—"

"But you get most of the money for their work," Robert finished, with an amused laugh. "Is it that my mill workers are free and get to keep *all* the money they earn that disturbs you?"

The man looked at Robert with startled eyes. Then his nettled expression disappeared. With a short ghost of a laugh, he said, "Maybe so—maybe so."

Robert slapped him on the back and they parted as friends.

Owning another man did not appeal to Robert, even though he had inherited a number of slaves. Yet there was nothing he could do about it, since the economy of the times hinged on the workers in the cotton and rice fields. But now that the exporting of those goods made possible by slave labor had been sharply curtailed, the chore of making those raw materials into finished goods rested on the mill workers, poor whites who had previously been left to starve in an economy of rich planters and slave laborers.

Robert had been able to employ a number of them, and the mill was thriving under the foreman, Ebenezer Shaw.

With pride, Robert rode his horse into the clean little village, the tiny houses set in neat rows along the road leading to the mill.

A school—that's what the village needed, now that the law for free public education, that he had worked so hard for in the legislature, had been passed.

It was time to put it into action in his own village. The next time he came, he would bring Eulalie. With her convent education, she would be able to help him set it up and hire a teacher.

Eulalie, feeling the warm sun at her back, held the small hand of Jason in her left hand, and Neijee's plump little black hand in her right one. They walked down the path, past the cabins on their way to the rice fields.

Moses had told her of the beautiful wild mallards that had been there for several days, feeding on the rice. Eager to show them to the two little boys, Eulalie had bundled them into their coats and set out.

The rice fields were a strange sight, with the spikes swaying in the slight wind, causing ripples to form in widening circles in the water. A lonely place with the slave towers rising up out of the water like giant obelisks.

A hundred years from now, when the rice fields might be no more, would people wonder what those brick structures were doing in the middle of the watery fields? Would they recognize them as havens of safety against the sudden freshets pushed by the tides, that could inundate the fields in minutes? With sadness, Eulalie remembered the new young slave who had not made it to the tower in time, but, three years before, had drowned in the watery grave.

It was a treacherous field, with water moccasins and an occasional alligator hidden among the amber blades of rice—but so beautiful, when the rice birds or the mallards flew down to feed.

"Look, Jason—look, Neijee. Do you see the ducks? There they are," Eulalie said, pointing to the left of the waterway.

"Ducks," repeated Jason.

"Ducks with green heads," Neijee added.

The three sat on the old brick steps that led to the waterway and watched, contented, until the sun in their eyes made the little boys restless.

Suddenly, the ducks flapped their wings, and in protest at some hidden danger, they left the rice field and flew away toward the sun.

What had alarmed them? Eulalie felt the chill of the late afternoon, now that the sun had moved to the edge of the waterway. The wind rose and rippled the waters even wider, and Eulalie pulled her cloak closer.

It was time to go back to the house. The false warmth was gone, leaving winter to whine and rustle through the naked branches of the crepe myrtle nearby.

Eulalie stood, waiting for the two little boys to finish throwing their pebbles into the water. Just as Jason's plopped into the shallow water, the giant bell behind the big house clanged and sent its frightening message over the plantation fields.

Something was wrong—terribly wrong. No one was allowed to ring the bell, unless . . .

Taking the boys' hands, Eulalie swept them along as fast as their plump legs would take them. Back to the house. They must get back to the house.

Had something happened to Robert? Had he been thrown by his spirited stallion? Pray God it was not so.

Her mind was in a whirl and she paid little attention to the whimperings of the two children, who balked at the fast pace she was going.

Eulalie did not remember that it had taken so long to get to the rice fields from the house. But, of course, they had not been in a hurry, but had enjoyed a leisurely pace, pausing now and again to rest.

The time taken to get back to the big house seemed interminable and Eulalie became conscious of the change in the landscape, the desolate, quiet air that now reigned over the land. No workers were mending fences in the fields; no horses grazed in the acreage beyond the house.

Eulalie was breathless as she came within sight of the house. In the late-afternoon sun, it stood lonely and deserted. The bell that had clamored its frightening message was now silent, with no sign of the hand that had tugged at it so frantically.

Eulalie, Jason and Neijee were the only human beings in sight. Everyone else had disappeared.

Hesitant to investigate with the two tired children at her side, Eulalie took them to the back of the kitchen, separated from the main part of the house. There they sat on the stoop, glad to rest while Eulalie went into the kitchen itself. There was no sign of the cooks.

The odor of freshly baked bread hung over the warm room. But the rest of the dinner was still undone, as if it had been hastily snatched from the fire before the cooks vanished.

Perplexed, Eulalie broke off two pieces of the bread to take to Jason and Neijee. If Indians had come, they might still be in the house. No need to risk the children. Eulalie would hide them and go see for herself.

The stone steps led down to the underground spring behind the kitchen. Since the cover was firmly anchored, there would be no danger of the children falling into the spring.

Neijee and Jason willingly went with her down the steps, while eyeing the bread she had promised them.

"You must be very quiet," she explained, "until I get back. Neijee, make sure that Jason does not follow me."

"Yes, madame," Neijee said, his mouth already full of bread.

Eulalie climbed back up the stone steps and walked toward the back of the main house. She slipped into the hallway from the side piazza, as she had done many times in the past, and without making a sound she crept up the stairs.

A board creaked, and Eulalie stopped to listen. It was only her imagination, she decided, when the sound did not come again.

Where could everybody be? Feena, Florilla and even Bradley?

Eulalie walked down the hallway on the second floor and paused before the door to the master bedroom. Impatient with herself for being so nervous, she put her hand out to open the door. Slowly, the knob moved on its own and Eulalie withdrew her hand quickly and stepped back.

Unable to take another step, as in a nightmare, she stood and watched as the door opened. A strange man, his arms filled with Robert's clothes, faced her with a surprised look.

Trying to stifle her cry of alarm, she turned and fled down the stairs, while the man shouted. Almost to the bottom of the steps, she saw two more men appear from the front part of the house, one carrying the cushioned needlepoint footstool that she had given to Papa Ravenal.

"Stop her!" the man at the top of the stairs directed to the men below.

But Eulalie, fleet as a young deer, escaped down the hall in the opposite direction, retracing her steps to the piazza and out onto the lawn.

The British! They had slipped upriver, and were now methodically stripping Midgard of everything that could be carried away.

The rumbling sound of a wagon grew louder down the lane from the slave cabins. Eulalie watched it turn in the direction of the river landing. So there were even more of them, with their cutter more than likely tied up to the landing pier.

Eulalie heard Jason crying, and she rushed down the

stone steps to quiet him. The spring house was no place to hide the children with the British swarming over the plantation. They would easily be heard.

Everyone else would be hiding in the bog. But Eulalie could not get to Emma's Bog. Biffers Road would be overrun with the enemy, looking for the cows and pigs that the slaves would have driven into the bog with them.

Where could she go?

With the two frightened children lagging at her side, Eulalie fled. She finally picked up Jason and whispered to Neijee, "Hold onto my skirts, Neijee. We'll have to run."

"I'm still tired, madame," Neijee whimpered, but he held on while Eulalie, burdened with the heavy weight of Jason, urged them on.

Back in the direction from which she had come, Eulalie ran, not knowing where she could hide Jason and Neijee. If only Feena or Florilla had been with her to help. Her arms ached with their burden and Eulalie was forced to put her child down and rest for a moment.

"Ducks," Jason said, looking overhead at the birds flying in formation.

That was it—to the slave tower in the rice field where they had seen the ducks. She would take the children there. And she hoped no one would think to look for them there.

At the edge of the water, Eulalie gathered up her skirts and tucked the hem into her ribboned waistband.

With a child under each arm, she plunged into the water, her feet sinking into the soft mud. At the first step, her shoes remained suctioned in the mud, and Eulalie proceeded through the icy water, shoeless and afraid of what she might step on.

But water moccasins hibernated in the winter, didn't they? Her foot landed on something soft and she moaned as it moved away, almost causing her to lose her balance.

As if that were not enough, her foot suddenly plunged into a hole and the water reached up to her skirts, soaking the edges at her knees. It was so cold—and no chance of getting dry when she reached the tower.

It was at least an hour later that the bell sounded again, this time a soothing sound, signaling all to return. The danger was over. But it was now too dark to risk taking the children out of the tower, Eulalie decided. They would have to stay until morning, with nothing but her own body heat to protect them.

They huddled together and the children slept. There was no sleep for Eulalie. Reconciled to the darkness and the cold, she waited through the night, and wondered if Robert had gotten back from the mill village. Would he be alarmed that she had not returned with the children? It was too bad that there was no way to get word to him that his son was safe. The tower should have a bell, also. . . .

The sun shining through the slits of the slave tower told her that morning had come. Eulalie removed her cramped arms from around the sleeping children and stood up. She was stiff with cold. Eulalie sneezed and at the sound, Jason and Neijee both opened their eyes.

"It's time to go home," Eulalie said lightly.

"Cold," Jason said, frowning exactly like Robert.

"I know. But soon you'll be warm."

Again, Eulalie walked through the marshy field, with one little boy under each arm. She was careful to anticipate each step before putting her feet down. The water seemed even colder and Eulalie sneezed once more.

"*Mon Dieu*—where have you been, *ma petite?* Monsieur Robert has been out all night looking for you."

Feena rushed to Eulalie's aid, taking Jason from her.

"We were hiding in the tower in the rice field," Eulalie explained. "It was too dark to walk through the water last night, so we had to wait until morning. Where is Robert now?" Eulalie asked.

"Ready to leave for Charleston. He was convinced the British had taken you and Jason with them.

"Remus," Feena called to the small boy by the fence. "Go and tell your master that the mistress is safe. Quick, boy, before he leaves."

The boy ran toward the stables, while Feena and Eulalie walked on to the house.

"Did the British take very much?" Eulalie asked.

"*Oui*. But you will see for yourself later. I'll send the boys to Florilla, then come to help you. A nice hot bath is what you need—and dry clothes."

After cleaning her feet in the kitchen, where Jason's Christmas puppy now lay asleep in the box by the stove, Eulalie walked into the house. Up the steps she went, feeling somehow guilty that Robert had searched for them all night without success.

Pushing her bedraggled hair out of her face, Eulalie quietly walked past the room she shared with Robert and into her old bedroom, where the metal tub sat near the hearth.

Soon it was filled with hot water, and Eulalie sank into its warmth, while Feena, helping her, finished the task of washing her long black hair.

The door opened and Robert pushed into the room, not stopping until he stood intimidatingly over her.

"You may go, Feena," Robert ordered. "I want to speak with my wife."

"*Oui*, Monsieur Robert," Feena replied, her eyes interested in following the path of Robert's gaze to Eulalie, only partially covered by the water.

"I looked all night for you and Jason," he said, frowning, when Feena had left. "Where were you hiding, Eulalie?"

"In the slave tower in the rice field," she answered guiltily.

"You walked through the water," he asked incredulously, "with Jason?"

"And Neijee too," she added. "But I held them both under my arms. They did not get wet, Robert."

"But you, Eulalie. *You* got wet and had to stay that way for the entire night."

Eulalie sneezed. "I am sure the ones hiding in the bog got wet, too."

"But they did not stay out there all night. They came home when the all-clear bell sounded."

"Would you have preferred it if I had tried to bring your son home in the dark?" Eulalie's voice rose in indignation. "There was no possibility that I could have found my way out of the rice fields without a light."

"I know, Eulalie." His voice was instantly contrite. "It was safer for you to stay the night. But it did nothing for my peace of mind."

"I am sorry, Robert."

Ruefully, he looked at her. "I think you had better give me a list of your hiding places, Eulalie. That will save me many wasted hours and much agony if I know where to look for you the next time."

Eulalie's chin lifted and her eyes became darker. "You sound as if I make a habit . . . "

She stopped, embarrassed, remembering the times she had run away from him—first to the river house, then to the nursery cabin. But she had not been running from him this time.

Eulalie shivered and reached for the linen towel by the tub. Robert took it and held it for her. Self-consciously she stepped out of the tub and he wrapped her in the towel. He was slow to free her from his hold.

With a gentle voice, Robert said, "Were you frightened, little one?"

She nodded, her eyes suddenly filling with tears. "When I heard the bell, I thought : . . something had happened to you." Her voice was shaking. "That . . . that you had been thrown by your horse. But when I came into the house, I saw them."

"They are gone, Eulalie. I doubt they will come this way again. If they do, we will be ready for them."

He picked her up in his arms and started out the door.

"Where are you taking me?"

"Why, to your own room, madame," he answered, walking with her down the hallway.

She was impatient to be put down. When Robert obliged, Eulalie took the gown draped over her bed, walked behind the screen and put it on.

When she stepped out, Robert was undressing. "What are you doing?" Eulalie asked, alarmed at his actions.

"I am getting ready for bed. I don't know about you, but *I* have been up the entire night. And now I intend to catch up on my sleep."

Shamefaced, Eulalie climbed into the other bed. What could Robert be thinking? That she suspected he was planning to make love to her? But evidently, it was not so. It was only on her mind, with the feel of Robert's arms about her. She sighed, snuggling under the covers, and in a few minutes, Eulalie was sound asleep.

CHAPTER

22

"THEY took his blue velvet suit, Miz Tabor, and he won't stop cryin'."

"Neijee? They took Neijee's clothes too?" Eulalie asked, while Effie helped her into the yellow fleece robe.

"Yes'm. And it's broken his heart."

"I'll make another suit for him—even if it isn't just like the one Maggie made. I must go to him to tell him."

"And will you see that I am suitably clothed too, Eulalie?"

Startled at the sound of Robert's voice, Eulalie looked toward the chair near the hearth. Her husband sat in it, his tawny, teasing eyes watching her and waiting for her to reply.

"I am sure your tailor can see to your needs much better than I, Robert."

The teasing look was gone, changed to a darkened frown.

"There is no need to concern yourself over the child. His clothes were much too fine, anyway, for his role here at Midgard. Effie can make him something that will be more appropriate. Can't you, Effie?"

"Yes suh," the servant agreed, but her heart was not in her answer.

Eulalie glared at Robert. And as soon as Effie had left the room, Eulalie retorted, "But Robert, he *loved* his velvet suit. You don't know how disappointed a child can feel when he has lost his treasured possession."

"Do I not, Eulalie?" he questioned. "I imagine it is little different from the way a *man* feels when he has lost something he . . . values."

His significant glance left no doubt as to his meaning. Eulalie blushed as she hurried from the room to comfort Neijee.

It was odd that the British had taken only the men's clothes and Neijee's. Eulalie wished they had taken hers instead of Neijee's. It would not have mattered that much to her.

Pacified by the promise of a new suit, Neijee stopped his crying and Eulalie went back to the bedroom. She did not feel well. A general weakness descended upon her, turning her bones to jelly. Climbing again into the massive bed in the now-empty room, Eulalie welcomed the sleep that obliterated her promise to Neijee, with its accompanying disobedience to Robert.

She awoke to the odor of gumbo, hot and tantalizing.

Eulalie sat up in the dimly lit room and as she did so, her head pounded and her throat began to ache. The weakness that she had felt earlier was still with her, and she quickly lay down again to avoid the lightheadedness that plagued her.

"Oh no, my pretty. You have been lazy long enough. Time for you to get up—at least long enough to eat something."

Robert held out his hand, waiting to help her out of bed.

"I don't think I can, Robert," she said, feeling the dizziness come over her again.

He looked at her flushed face and his hand went to her brow, where it lingered, conscious of the heat that almost burned him.

"Are you ill, Eulalie?" he asked.

"I will be all right, once I have eaten something. I am just weak from hunger. That must be all it is."

She moved to escape the feel of his hands, and at her action, Robert dropped his arm to his side, and made no effort to help her to the sofa where the small table had been set for two. The soup tureen took up most of the space of the table, leaving just enough room for the soup plates and pieces of brown bread at each end.

Eulalie's body trembled at the exertion of moving the few steps between the bed and the sofa.

Robert watched her with narrowed eyes, then gathered the quilt from the end of the bed and brought it to the sofa where she sat.

Gruffly Robert said, "Let's hope you don't get a chill as a result of your impetuous behavior," and he wrapped the quilt around her.

"But I am already too hot," she complained. "You are smothering me, Robert. Take it away."

He shook his head and wrapped the quilt tighter around her.

Removing the lid of the tureen, Robert dipped the ladle into the thick, spicy gumbo and filled her bowl. He then proceeded to sit beside her to feed her.

"Open your mouth, Eulalie," he ordered, treating her as if she were some helpless baby bird.

"I can feed myself, Robert."

He ignored her protest, continuing to spoon it to her lips. She had no choice but to open her mouth to eat it.

At intervals, he broke the bread into small pieces to pop into her mouth.

"I can well understand why Jason protests when someone else feeds him," Eulalie mumbled.

"Do you feel better now?" he asked, laying the spoon down by the empty bowl.

"Yes," she admitted, "except for my head."

"I'd better get Feena to take a look at you."

"It isn't necessary, Robert. I'll be all right. And besides, you haven't eaten yet."

"I'll eat after I find Feena."

"Really, Robert, there is no need to treat me like an

invalid. I am not apt to die within the next fifteen minutes. Sit down and eat your soup before it gets cold."

"Your tongue, Eulalie, has become as sharp as the weather," Robert commented. "I can only hope it's temporary, and that it will subside with your headache."

He sat opposite her, filling his own bowl with the gumbo.

Eulalie sneezed and coughed, and at the worsening sound, Robert deliberately put down his spoon, stood up, and without saying a word to her, left the room.

A short time later, he returned with Feena in tow. The black woman looked solicitously at Eulalie and scolded, "No more than I expected, mamselle, with staying in wet clothes all night. If you will see to the fire, Monsieur Robert," Feena asked, "I will be back soon with my kettle and herbs."

Robert hoisted another log onto the hearth, and Eulalie, wrapped in the quilt on the sofa, suddenly giggled.

Puzzled at her display of mirth, Robert faced her and said, "What do you find so amusing, Eulalie?"

"I was just thinking that it's a good thing Florilla is not taking care of me. She would be forcing me to drink brandy mixed with hickory ash." Eulalie turned up her nose and Robert laughed.

"It might not be a bad idea to drink the brandy. But to spoil it with hickory ash is enough to turn a man's stomach."

"Or a woman's," Eulalie agreed.

Soon, Feena was back with her kettle. While she fussed over Eulalie, preparing the mixture of herbs, Robert disappeared. It did not take long for the water to steam, and when Robert returned with the two brandy snifters in his hands, the kettle was singing, sending out its herbed droplets of healing vapor to all corners of the room.

"Feena, close the door as you leave," Robert ordered.

"*Oui*, monsieur," the black woman said, grinning as she gathered up her bag of herbs and tucked it into her apron.

"This one is for you, Eulalie." Robert held out the snifter with less of the golden liquid in it, keeping the other for himself.

Dubiously, Eulalie took it, while clutching the quilt around her shoulders.

"What are you trying to do, Robert? Make me into an imbibing wife?"

He laughed. "It would take more than one glass to do that."

Seeing her reluctance to drink it, he asked, "Have you never tasted brandy before, Eulalie?"

She shook her head. "It is not something that the sisters approved of. A little wine with meals was their only indulgence."

At the mention of the sisters, Robert's face darkened, and Eulalie, seeing this, speedily added, "And Papa Ravenal did not encourage anyone to drink his brandy. In fact, he kept it locked in the cabinet."

"I well remember," Robert said, the crease in his brow disappearing. "I do the same, and that is why the British did not carry it off with them yesterday, with everything else they took." The crease reappeared in his brow.

"But drink up, Eulalie. What happened yesterday is over and done with."

She put the snifter to her lips, taking one small sip. The taste was fiery and it took her breath away.

"What's the matter? Don't you like it?"

"It . . . it burns my throat," she whispered, her dark-brown eyes widening as she swallowed again.

"Perhaps you would find it more palatable with hickory ash?"

Shaking her head, and not certain if he was teasing or not, Eulalie quickly took another sip. It went down better than the first.

A curiously floating quality accompanied the finishing of the brandy.

"Good," Robert said, taking the snifter from her. "Brandy is much better for sleep than laudanam—and much less dangerous."

"But I am not sleepy," Eulalie said, letting the quilt fall to the floor as she stood up.

Robert reached down to retrieve the covering by the sofa, and Eulalie swayed toward him.

"The room is moving, Robert," she said. "Isn't . . . isn't it?"

With a laugh he steadied her, and uninhibited, she reached out her arms and encircled his neck.

He held her tenderly, gazing down into her eyes, half hidden by drooping eyelids.

"I think the brandy has gone to your head, Eulalie. And such a little bit. Who would have thought it?"

"Why do you always call me Eulalie and never . . . Lili?" she asked suddenly.

Unconsciously he tightened his hold on her. "For me, Lili no longer exists. You are Eulalie, my wife."

She shook her head. "When I was a child, I was never called Eulalie except when my *maman* was reprimanding me. Are you punishing me, Robert, when you call me Eulalie?"

"I—punishing *you,* Eulalie? Have you not been punishing me, instead—by running away from me, by refusing to be my wife? No, Eulalie is an appropriate name for a cold wife. Lili is a passionate woman, capable of stirring the fires inside a man's loins."

"My name is Lili," she said, obstinately dismissing his argument.

At her stubborn insistence, he picked her up and carried her to the bed.

"If Lili you want to be, then Lili you shall be," he said softly in her ear, caressing the lobe with his tongue.

Languidly she lay on the coverlet, with no strength to protest what he was doing to her. His lips covered hers, seeking and asking, while his hands, slowly taking their time, unbuttoned the yellow fleece robe.

Eulalie was so hot and her brain refused to function properly. Of their own volition, her arms tightened around Robert's bare shoulders. She felt his flesh upon her flesh. The rocking motion soothed her at first, lulling her into a false peace. Then, the mood changed; the tempo increased, until the mounting passion reached its peak. Robert moaned in exquisite rapture and then was still, his head upon her breast.

209

The kettle whistled and Eulalie, breathing easier, slept in Robert's arms until the morning.

In the early light, she stared at the arm across her bare breast and felt the knee next to hers. She and Robert, sharing the same bed? How had that happened? The last thing she remember was drinking the brandy.

Robert had deliberately made her drink it, taking away all her inhibitions. Reaching up to her flaming cheeks with her hands, Eulalie pressed hard, trying to remember what had happened.

But it was no use. Her memory had deserted her. How had she acted? What had she said? Or done? Had she behaved as the wanton? Oh, dear God, she prayed, how could it have happened?

Distressed, she closed her eyes, fearing to meet Robert's glance when he awoke. Her mouth felt fuzzy and her head began to ache, the pain starting behind her eyes and progressing to the top of her head and then down her back. Heat slowly pervaded her body and the tiny beads of perspiration popped out upon her forehead.

Eulalie heard the door to the bedroom open. The kettle, silent for a time, soon began its whistling song. Feena—Feena had come into the room.

Robert stirred, moving his arm. But Eulalie did not respond. She lay quietly, with the pounding of her head echoing in her ears, like waves of the ocean crashing upon a distant shore.

Then she began to tremble as a vast coldness took over her body and her teeth chattered. "So cold," she mumbled, unable to stop her body from shaking.

The giant strong arms went about her, wrapping the covers tighter. The warmth of Robert's body, pressed close, fed hers until the chill, appeased by the added heat, gradually abated.

Comfortable in his embrace she lay, until his hands began to move, caressing her body. Shocked at her initial acceptance, she pushed away from him. Her eyes flew open and she sat up to meet Robert's amused, knowing look.

Mad with herself, she glared at Robert and croaked,

"You did it deliberately. Last night you forced me to drink the brandy so you could take advantage of me."

At her accusation, Robert laughed.

"Your reaction was not one of . . . indifference, Lili. So do not delude yourself. You enjoyed my lovemaking almost as much as I did. The brandy merely served to strip away your prudish modesty."

He had called her Lili. Why? Not since the river house had he addressed her as Lili—always Eulalie.

She frowned. "Why did you call me Lili, just now?" she asked.

It was Robert's turn to stare at Eulalie. "Because you wanted to be Lili, last night. It seemed to upset you for me to call you Eulalie."

A faint awareness of what had happened crept over her. "If I asked you to call me Lili, I truly must not have known what I was doing." Petutantly she added, "I do not *want* you to call me Lili."

"You have changed your mind so soon?"

Her reaction amused him, and seeing this made Eulalie more put out with Robert than ever.

"I would appreciate it if you would leave my bed, Robert."

"Oh no, my sweet. Never again will I be that stupid."

"I shall hate you, Robert."

"Only for a short time," he replied. "For I shall see to it that you become so used to my attentions that you will not be able to live without them."

Her raised hand was caught in his, stopped in midair from accomplishing its purpose.

"Are you ready for another lesson so soon, my pet?"

She shook her head, alarm showing in her flushed face.

Again he laughed and, getting out of bed, he said, "A pity that I cannot remain with you. But my tailor must attend to my other needs today."

Robert left for Charleston and Eulalie sank back on the pillows, relieved that he had gone.

Throughout the day, she remained in bed, tossing and turning and occasionally drifting off to sleep until the renewed whistling of the kettle would awake her.

Her cough loosened, but her eyes watered and her nose turned pink.

That night, despite her protests, Robert climbed into bed beside her.

"Aren't you afraid to sleep in the same bed with me?" Eulalie remarked after sneezing.

"I'll take my chances," Robert answered. "Besides, you may get another chill during the night. If so, my added warmth would be welcomed, would it not?"

"But I am getting better. There is little danger of a chill."

"Then I am glad to hear it." Thoughtfully he added, "So I am not taking such an awful chance after all of succumbing to the inflammation."

It seemed that she could not win against him. For better or for worse, he was in her bed to stay.

CHAPTER

23

As soon as Eulalie was well, she began to plan Neijee's new suit. But she had no blue velvet, and she knew better than to ask Robert for money to buy the material. Probably she could not purchase it in Charleston anyway because of the blockade.

She would have to use material already on hand. One of her old dresses, perhaps. But she had no light-blue ones.

Thinking back over her wardrobe, she remembered the old lavender velvet dress packed away in some deep trunk—the same shade as the evening gown Maggie had made her to wear that miserable evening to the Kirklands'. She could see Neijee stroking that small strip of lavender velvet left over from her own gown. Yes, he would be more than pleased with the lavender.

But she would have to make sure that Robert did not see her sewing on it, for then he might be reminded of their conversation concerning Neijee's clothes.

Never before had Eulalie been so disobedient. Impulsive and headstrong, yes. But there was something about Robert that made her defy him. She had learned that when she grew soft and acquiescent to him, she was always hurt. If she refused to succumb to his charm, then he would not have the ability to hurt her. Each time she let her defenses slip, she lost.

The news that sprinkled slowly through the south of the battles with the British kept Robert's mind occupied, together with the numerous details of running the plantation.

He had begun the gradual replacement of the pieces of furniture taken by the raiders, and the restocking of the larder and storehouse with the hams and other staples that were needed to feed the family and the slaves for the rest of the winter.

Lookouts had been stationed at the river landing and along the approach to Emma's Bog to give alarm in case the British tried to surprise them a second time.

When Robert's three-day duty with the Charleston militia came due, he left Midgard, with the lookouts doubled at both the river and on Biffers Road.

"You are to stay close to the house, Eulalie," he ordered, "especially with Jason. And if the alarm is given, Jimbo has orders to take you and Jason north to Taborville. You would be safe with Ebenezer Shaw, until I could come for you."

"Yes, Robert."

As soon as he was out of sight, Eulalie rummaged in the trunks in the attic until she found the lavender velvet. Now there would be no need to work surreptitiously on Neijee's suit. She could sew in comfort by the fire in the master bedroom with both Jason and Neijee in the room. And there would be no need to hide the evidence of her sewing each evening. She could leave it out until she had finished.

Her sewing progressed well and the lavender velvet began to take shape. Neijee watched with obvious enjoyment, but Jason was more interested in playing with his Christmas puppy, which Feena had brought to the bedroom in its box and set by the hearth.

"Hold still, Neijee. I need to measure you one last time."

By early morning of the third day, the suit was finished. "It is for special occasions, Neijee, not to be worn for every day. Do you understand?"

With his eyes shining, Neijee said, "Yes, madame."

"Take it off then, and we will put it up."

"May I show it to Effie first?"

"If you like," Eulalie said, smiling at the proud black child. He ran from the room, leaving Jason and the puppy behind.

Eulalie stooped down to pick up the small remnants of the material and thread scattered on the floor. The portion of the dress that had not been used still lay across the bed—a sad melange of sleeves and bodice, with the merest suggestion of what had once been the skirt.

"Puppy!" Jason said, pointing to the little dog.

"Oh no," Eulalie voiced in exasperation, seeing the widening circle of moisture on the floor.

Busy cleaning up after the puppy, she did not notice the heavy footsteps until Jason squealed and ran to the one coming into the room.

Robert was home, far earlier than Eulalie had expected.

"What is going on?" Robert asked.

"Jason's puppy has had an accident," Eulalie explained to him, hoping he would not notice the velvet material on the floor. "If you don't mind, perhaps you and Jason could take him back to the kitchen, while I finish cleaning up."

"Come, young man," Robert said to his son. "Your puppy will have to stay in the kitchen until he learns better manners."

Eulalie hastily rolled up the remaining evidence of her sewing, stuffing the velvet remnants in her sewing bag.

"You are back early," Eulalie said, when Robert came into the room.

"Yes. The drill did not last as long as usual."

Robert stood inside the door, watching Eulalie and

215

trying to decide why his early appearance home had disconcerted her.

"Madame," Neijee said, running through the open doorway, "Effie thinks my new suit is bee-yoo-ti-ful."

Too late, the little boy saw Robert standing and scowling at him. He backed out the threshold of the door and fled down the stairs. And Robert, spying the dress, walked to the bed and picked up the desecrated remains.

A flood of temper washed over his face, turning it into an angry red.

"Did you not care for the dress I bought for you any more than this, Eulalie? To cut it up and make a suit for a slave?"

"But, Robert—"

"Do not bother to give me your excuses, Eulalie. God! How could Uncle Ravenal saddle me with such a firebrand—to deliberately go against my wishes—to have no more regard for a husband's gift than this—"

He shook his head, refusing to listen to any apology.

Robert strode out of the room, slamming the door behind him and leaving a trembling Eulalie, devastated by his temper.

There was only one way to show him she had not cut up the dress he had purchased for her. Eulalie would wear it that night, even though it was far too grand for supper *en famille.*

The rest of the day Eulalie spent with Jason and Neijee. She did not see Robert again until evening when he came into the bedroom to change clothes.

Darkness had come early and Eulalie sat at the dressing table with the candle glow upon her hair as she brushed it into a sleek chignon at the nape of her neck. She was conscious of Robert's steps, even with her back to him. Laying her brush on the table, she drew the yellow fleece robe tighter around her, as if it could protect her from the anger that Robert still exuded.

"I hope you will not linger, Eulalie," Robert said, putting on his coat. "It has been a long day and I am ravenously hungry."

"I shan't be much longer, Robert," she promised him, again taking up the brush. "Only a few minutes more."

As soon as he left the room, Eulalie hastened to the wardrobe and took out the lavender velvet evening gown that she had not worn since that first night out with Robert in Columbia. For her it had sad memories, and when she had completed fastening it and had draped the shawl around her shoulders, it was as if the old hurts were embedded in the texture of her dress.

But she must forget all that. It was behind her now.

The tall mahogany clock, inlaid with cypress, struck seven, its chimes slightly out of tune with age. On the final note, Eulalie walked into the salon where Robert and Florilla were waiting.

The fair-haired woman, taking one envious glance at the elegant Eulalie, said, "I did not know this was such a special night." And then gazing down at her own gray dress, she continued, "But of course, I have nothing nearly so grand to wear anyway."

"You look fine, Florilla," Robert assured her, his good mood suddenly restored. "I think my wife wished to prove a point tonight."

Robert grinned and, looking at Eulalie, he said in a low, intimate voice, "Are you waiting for my apology, Eulalie?"

Her eyes were sad and no smile came in response to the question.

The odor of jasmine clung to the room where there was no bouquet. And the desk where she had reluctantly signed the marriage document making her the bride of Robert Tabor loomed before her.

Now she stood in the ghost-filled room, with her husband waiting for an answer.

"An apology? No, Robert. I do not wish an apology."

The spark had gone out of her, and Robert, puzzled at the rapid change in her manner, watched the silent Eulalie throughout the meal.

What had happened to cause such a change? Had he been too severe with her that morning in his anger? Or was it the dress that brought haunting memories to Eulalie? He could not wipe out the sounds of those delicate sobs that had come from behind the closed door that night she had seen Alistair Ashe.

What was she thinking as she sat at the table opposite him now? Was she reliving those moments at the Kirklands', or worse still, the night of the ball?

Damn it! Had he not suffered too? Yet here she was, sitting at the table, as if she were completely innocent of any guile. She had disobeyed him, regardless. And he was ready to apologize for his own behavior when she was the one who was guilty—a wayward minx with a penchant for getting into trouble when she was on her own. Eulalie needed to be taken in hand and kept so busy that she had no time to disobey him or get into mischief.

Tomorrow Robert would go to Taborville and take Eulalie with him. That should assure at least one day when she would be safe from her own impetuosity.

She was kneeling on the cushion of the prie-dieu when he walked into the bedroom. Her long wavy hair cascaded over her shoulders, and from the back, in her demure nightgown, Eulalie resembled a young schoolgirl intent on her prayers. But Robert, seeing her profile as he moved toward the bed, became aware of her woman's figure, her lips moving slightly in the forming of her words.

One day he would make sure that only *his* name was upon her lips. Jealousy reared its head and Robert waited for it to subside.

Eulalie stood up, blew out the one remaining candle, and with the faint light of the coals from the hearth, she found her way to the mahogany bed where Robert lay.

Three days he had been away from her, and his body, denied her comfort those three days, demanded expiation.

"Robert," she whispered, feeling his exploring hands. "This is not the time for making love. Give me another day," she requested.

"Then you are not with child?"

"No, Robert."

His hands stopped and he turned his back to Eulalie. Blast the time of women, he thought. Trying to think of other things besides his desire, he welcomed sleep, but it was elusive.

Almost three years now, since Eulalie had borne Jason.

But no sign of another child. If she had another babe to look forward to, to plan for, it would take her mind off Jacques Binet and her constant prayers. But for the time being, he would have to think of something else to keep her busy. With expanding thoughts of the school in Taborville developing in his mind, Robert went to sleep.

CHAPTER

24

EULALIE awoke to find Robert's tawny topaz eyes surveying her, and she felt uneasy at his scrutiny. It seemed impossible that he had been so mild-mannered the evening before. Something was bound to happen. It was in his look. Eulalie had seen it before and was wary of it.

She scrambled out of bed, not waiting to find out what he might have in store for her, but she did not get far.

Soon after breakfast, the sun streamed through the library windows and the fire upon the hearth crackled, giving warmth to the room. Almost as if he did not trust her out of his sight, Robert had insisted that Eulalie come down with him, and hastily she had grabbed her needlepoint to give her something to do. The lessons taught at the convent were hard to forget.

It was not the room itself she resented, but the manner in which she had been told that she would have to share the library while Robert worked on papers with his overseer, Gil Jordan. No fire had been built in the upstairs bedroom, even though she would have preferred to remain there.

At Robert's summons, Gil Jordan came into the library,

respectfully holding his hat in his hand. There was no resemblance to the arrogant Alistair Ashe. He would not expect an invitation to his employer's dinner table. It was enough for him to have a roof over his head, food to eat and a living wage for his hard, honest work.

Despite herself, Eulalie became interested in the discussion, and reluctantly she understood why Robert had forbidden Jason to come into the library with her. He would have been too much of a distraction.

But Jason's tantrum at being kept out was still fresh in Eulalie's ears. Luckily, Neijee had come to her aid and Jason's protest had dwindled away at the whisperings of Neijee, while Florilla took the two with her.

Plans for the new crops of sea-island cotton, the plowing of fresh land north of the bog and the repairs to some of the slave cabins kept Robert and his overseer for the first portion of the morning.

When the overseer had gone, Robert looked at Eulalie and said, "I want you to go with me to Taborville this morning. The carriage will be at the front in a half-hour. And you're to wear your cloak trimmed with ermine."

Not pausing for a reply or protest, he walked out the door, then suddenly stopped and added, "Get the girls in the kitchen to pack a lunch for us. I'm not sure what time we will get back."

"May we take Jason with us?" Eulalie asked, not wanting to be the subject of Robert's entire attention on the trip.

"No. He would only be in the way. And the trip is too long for him. Better for him to stay here with Florilla."

He strode out the hall and the noise of his boots disappeared.

Eulalie sighed and folded her needlepoint, putting it in its stand. There was no need to protest or refuse to go. With that look in his eye, Robert would have lifted her bodily into the carriage if she had demurred.

Immediately the girls in the kitchen went to work to fulfill Robert's request for food for the trip.

Eulalie went upstairs to the cold bedroom and opened the wardrobe where her two cloaks hung side by side.

"Wear your cloak trimmed with ermine." Could she not decide for herself what to wear?

Perversely, she pushed back the finer cloak that Robert had purchased and pulled out the serviceable black cloak she had worn from the convent. She changed into the midnight-blue velvet high-necked dress that he had also not cared for, and then she ran downstairs to the outside circular drive, where Robert waited impatiently beside the phaeton. Seconds later, Effie brought the basket filled with food and handed it up to Eulalie.

They had passed through the avenue of magnolias before Robert turned to Eulalie at his side.

"I see that you did not wear the cloak I requested."

"It is too fine, Robert, to wear on such a dusty trip. This one has always been . . . serviceable and warm enough."

Seeing the frown still on his face, Eulalie said, "Tell me about Taborville, Robert, and the mill."

At first, she thought he was not going to answer. Then he complied. "I have about thirty workers and a foreman whom you have already heard me mention—Ebenezer Shaw. He lives in the largest house, but the others in the village have good, sturdy little houses—finer than anything they've lived in, in the past."

"What do the people do in the mill, Robert?"

"Some work with the gin. Others spin the cotton into cloth . . ." He began explaining the operation of it to her, and she settled back and listened.

"I have also found something for you to do, Eulalie, that, I hope, will keep you busy, so that you will have no time to get into further trouble."

She looked at him with a frown on her face, not liking his words that sounded almost threatening, but she waited for him to explain.

When he did not, she finally asked, "What is it, Robert, that you want me to do?"

"You'll find out after we get to the mill," he countered.

So he was not going to tell her immediately, but make her wait. If that was the way he wanted it, then she would ask no more questions.

Silent and miffed at his secrecy, Eulalie sat in the

phaeton. But her mind puzzled over what he had said. Did he expect her to learn about the spinning looms and the separation of cotton fibers from seeds, or was there another purpose in bringing her with him?

She gathered her black cloak around her and rearranged the carriage blanket, but she was still cold. Robert took his eyes off the road to watch her activity, but said nothing.

It was mealtime when they arrived at Taborville, and all the men, with the exception of the foreman, had gone home to eat. Ebenezer Shaw sat in his office, eating his meal, when Robert walked in.

Eulalie, waiting just inside the main door with the lunch basket in her hands, saw Robert coming toward her. "We'll go to Shaw's to eat our lunch, and he'll join us there a little later. He thought you might be more comfortable there than here in the mill, since the men are due back at work in a few minutes."

"That is considerate of him, to offer his house," Eulalie said, getting back into the phaeton.

The carriage drew up to the house where the whitewashed well stood in the side yard. The dirt-swept front yard was lined with rocks, also whitewashed, and a bare young crabapple tree grew in lone isolation near the front door.

Inside, Eulalie was surprised not only by the cleanliness, but also by some of the really good pieces of furniture.

"One of the village girls comes over regularly to clean," Robert explained, "since his wife has been dead for several years now."

Eulalie took the basket from Robert and carried it to the kitchen table. But Robert, already at work with the fire in the parlor, had other plans.

"We'll eat in here by the fire," he suggested, so Eulalie, taking the basket from the table, walked into the parlor with it. There was no suitable table there and as Eulalie looked around, Robert moved the small, roughly woven cotton rug near the hearth and motioned for her to sit.

"Do you mind a picnic by the fire?" he asked, his eyes

amused at her frown. "Or are you too prim and proper for such rustic accommodation?"

She shook her head and knelt to spread out the tablecloth that Effie had enclosed. Robert added another log to the fire, and then, sitting crosslegged, he waited for Eulalie to fill the plates.

Robert was hungry and he enjoyed the food. Soon his plate was empty and then he sat watching the dark-haired woman.

Aware of this sudden intimacy, Eulalie was disconcerted at Robert's jungle eyes traveling over her dark-colored dress, now that she had removed her cloak.

He recognized the dress at once—without the magnificent, shimmering robe of silk. On purpose, she had worn it with her nun's cloak, and yet her severe grace stirred him, even in his amusement at her stubbornness in wearing it.

His hand reached out of its own accord and he sensually ran his finger along her neck, to end in a caress at her earlobe.

"Another piece of chicken, Robert?" she asked, inadvertently brushing his cheek when she turned her head.

"No, my love. My appetite for *food* has been satisfied. Have you finished?" he asked, looking down at her plate.

"Yes," she said, hurriedly getting to her knees. "I'd better clean up and put the remaining food back in the basket."

But she got no farther. Tense and apprehensive, Eulalie felt his arms draw her back down beside him.

"There's no hurry," he whispered, his hands moving to loosen the hooks of her dress.

"Robert," she said, her dark eyes widening, "the foreman will be here soon. Surely, you would not—"

"Wouldn't I? Did you not say one more day, Eulalie?"

"But not here, where anyone can walk in."

"Shaw will not walk in on us without knocking." He pushed her gently to the floor, his desire already impatient for fulfillment.

The glow from the logs diffused into warm rays over her body, while the cold floor beneath the thin rug rose up to give her a strange duality—hot and cold, wanting yet not wanting this powerful, arrogant man to make love to her.

"No, Robert," she protested for the second time. "I am not a kitchen wench to be thrown to the floor and . . . and pleasured."

"That you are not, Eulalie," Robert agreed. "A kitchen wench doesn't usually protest so much," he teased.

His answer only made her angrier, and Eulalie attempted to free herself from him. She was still miffed from his behavior of that morning, and Robert, sensing her stubbornness, abruptly removed his hand and sat up. With his back to her, he walked to the fire and, removing the firescreen, poked at the logs, sending fresh sparks up the chimney.

Relieved to be left alone, Eulalie sat up, brushing her hair with the back of her hand, and then fastening the hook of her dress that had come undone.

The foreman, with quite a lot of noise and stamping of feet, fumbled at the door after knocking, rattling the knob, and finally walking into the house.

"I trust you had an appetizing lunch, Mr. Tabor," he said with heartiness.

"Most enjoyable, Shaw," Robert replied. "Thank you for the use of your house."

"My pleasure, Mr. Tabor." The foreman stared at Eulalie, his frank eyes appraising her up and down with relish.

"I believe you have not met my wife. Eulalie, this is Mr. Ebenezer Shaw, my foreman."

"How do you do, Mr. Shaw," she said softly with as much dignity as she could manage from her sitting position on the rug.

At his continued interest in her, Eulalie lowered her eyes to the floor. "Bound for you, Mr. Tabor, to pick the prettiest filly in the corral, eh?"

"Quite so, Mr. Shaw," Robert agreed, holding out his hand to help Eulalie to her feet. "And she will be a great deal of help in starting the school for the mill children here in Taborville."

Clearly startled at his announcement, Ebenezer Shaw said, "But the older children already work in the mill."

"They will be taught with the younger ones, nevertheless," Robert replied, his voice firm. "Perhaps for only two hours a day—but we shall see."

"What do you want me to do, Mr. Tabor?" the foreman asked.

"Eulalie needs help with the school—a young woman who has *some* education, at least. Later on, she can be replaced by a better qualified teacher, but for now, the important part is to begin. Do you know someone already here in Taborville who would be suitable?"

The man's furrowed brow indicated he was deep in thought. It was not up to him to decide the merits of a school. Just so it did not interfere with the running of the mill.

"There is a young girl—Jessie Tilbaugh—whose father has recently started working here. A cut above the others, if you know what I mean. Only he has fallen on hard times."

"And the girl?" Robert asked, interrupting the family history.

"She would be suitable, I should think. Do you want me to send for her?"

"Yes," Robert replied. "Mrs. Tabor could interview her here, while I go back to the mill with you to discuss our business."

Turning to Eulalie, Robert instructed her. "If you think the girl is intelligent enough, then engage her and make a list of supplies for the school for Mr. Shaw to purchase."

So this was what Robert had in mind to keep her from getting into trouble again—to be sent to Taborville, to teach the mill children.

Stunned at his decision to be rid of her, she sat with her twisted handkerchief in her lap and waited for the rapid beating of her heart to slow to a normal rate.

But what about Jason? Would she be allowed to bring him with her? She could not bear it if she were separated from him again.

Fighting back the tears, Eulalie went to the door at the sound of knocking, to admit the girl, Jessie Tilbaugh.

"Come in, Jessie," Eulalie said, disguising her sadness

with a smile. "I am Mrs. Tabor. My husband thinks you might be able to help us."

The troubled look on Jessie's face vanished at Eulalie's words, and seated in the parlor, she listened carefully to what Eulalie had to say.

Satisfied that the girl would make a good helper, she asked, "Are you interested, Jessie?"

"Oh, yes, ma'am," the thin, red-haired girl answered, her eyes sparkling. "That's what I've always wanted to be—a teacher."

Eulalie spent the next hour with Jessie, and together they determined the number of children who would be involved and made lists of supplies adequate to last for several months. By the time Robert appeared with the phaeton, they had finished.

But when Eulalie began to relate the results of the interview, Robert cut her short, saying, "Tell me later. There is something far more important to attend to right now. One of the men has gotten his arm caught at the mill. I'd like you to take a look at it, to see what needs to be done."

Forgetting her own heartache, Eulalie quickly donned her black cloak and went with him.

The injured man rested on a crude bench, his arm hanging loosely by his side. Luckily, the bleeding had stopped, but the arm, misshapen, was now beginning to swell.

When Robert came into the room with Eulalie, the men who had stopped work to gather around the injured man moved back to allow her room to examine the man's arm.

"Do you have some brandy here?" Eulalie asked.

"I can get some for ye," one of the workers volunteered, moving rapidly out of the room.

"I will need two straight pieces of smooth wood, no longer than the lower part of his arm, and some cotton strips," Eulalie said, turning to Robert.

He glanced in the direction of the nearest man.

"We'll see to that," the white-haired, bent old fellow said, taking his friend with him.

When the first man came back with the brandy, Eulalie took it and held it to the injured man's lips. "To help with the pain," she said gently.

Eulalie straightened the rapidly swelling arm and placed the two wooden splints about it, and with the dexterity of the years spent at Soeur Louise's side in the convent dispensary, she wrapped it neatly and encased it in a sling tied about the man's neck.

"That is all I can do," she told him. "But make sure you keep the arm warm. And do not try to use the arm for several weeks."

"Thank you, Miss," the man said before being helped out of the room to be taken home.

It was later while waiting in the carriage that she overheard Mr. Shaw's remark to her husband. "A fine wife you have, Mr. Tabor—not only decorative, but useful too. I know a fellow who's still crippled from getting his arm broken in a fight last year. Lucky for my man that Mrs. Tabor was here."

Eulalie, cold and subdued from her trip to Taborville, wanted nothing more than to get warm again by the fire and to be left in peace when they reached Midgard. But Florilla, waiting for them when they returned, saw to it that her wish was delayed.

"I finally found them in the river house, Robert, dressed up in clothes from an old trunk. It was all Neijee's fault, I am sure, urging Jason to run away from me. He could have drowned in the river, if I had not located them. Robert, I think you should sell Neijee before it is too late."

The two children, knowing they were being reprimanded, hung their heads in shame, while Florilla held tightly to each child.

Jason, his lower lip in a pout, suddenly struggled against Florilla's grip and wailed, "Eu-lie."

Eulalie moved toward him, but Robert put out his hand to stop her.

"No, Eulalie. Stay where you are."

By this time, Neijee's dark eyes had filled with tears, and Eulalie, her heart going out to the two naughty little boys, looked up into Robert's stern stone face.

"Please, Robert. Do not be so hard on them," she begged, with an effort to keep her tremulous voice under control.

Striving not to be swayed by her imploring look, Robert spoke to her far more sharply than he had intended.

"Do not interfere, Eulalie," he said. "I will take care of this with Florilla. Go on up to the bedroom and I'll join you later."

She was dismissed with no one to remain as advocate for the two little boys. A hurt expression dulled her dark satin eyes as she slowly left the hallway and climbed the stairs.

Eulalie sat alone, picking at the food on the tray. Too tired to eat downstairs, she had asked for food to be sent up to the room.

No doubt Florilla and Robert were at the dining table, discussing what was to be done with Neijee. He had not allowed her to have a part in the discussion, just as she had had no say as to whether she wanted to be sent to Taborville to teach the children.

How would she be able to stand it? Apart from Jason and Neijee? She knew now that Robert would not allow her to take Jason with her. The mill children would be a reminder every day of her loss.

Wearily she put on her nightgown and climbed into bed. When Robert came in, she was asleep.

Walking to the bed, he held the candle high and peered into Eulalie's tear-stained face, her eyes shuttered by dark, long lashes, and her hand stretched out in silent supplication.

He drew in his breath at her beauty and her vulnerability. God—how she had turned him into jelly when she had looked into his eyes, begging him for compassion, not for herself, but for the two children whom she loved. It was all he could do not to give way to her and grant her anything she wished.

Not wanting to disturb her after her long, hard day, Robert blew out the candle and climbed into the other bed for the night.

CHAPTER

25

I S this yours?" Robert held out the small circlet of gold for Eulalie to see.

Recognizing it as her wedding ring that she had hidden over three years before in the portmanteau, she said, "Yes. Where did you find it?"

"Jason was playing with it. I presume he found it in the river house," Robert replied, "when he and Neijee ran away yesterday. I think you had better put it on, before it is lost again," he added.

She reached out her hand for it, but instead of giving it to her, he held onto her hand and, slipping the ruby from her finger on her left hand, he placed the band gold where it belonged. Then he put the ruby on her right hand.

Eulalie, held by his mesmerizing glance, saw the changing of his topaz eyes into a smoky, opalescent glow.

But still hurt at Robert's treatment and not wishing to remember the circumstances that had caused a stranger to put it upon her finger during the proxy ceremony, she hurriedly withdrew her hand from Robert's grasp and lowered her eyes.

She was not a wife, tenderly loved and cherished by

a husband. In the foreman's house in Taborville, it had been the same as in the river house—Robert had treated her as some slave to do his bidding, with no regard for her own feelings of embarrassment.

A loving husband would never say to his wife, "Madame, you are a whore at heart and I intend to treat you as such," as Robert had that first night they had returned to Midgard from Columbia.

Eulalie's eyes filled with tears, her heart sad that she was soon to be discarded like some excess piece of baggage that he did not want. But how soon, she had no way of knowing.

Robert, seeing the tears and misunderstanding their message, abruptly left the room.

Back and forth to Taborville Robert went, to check on the building of the school. The day it was due to be finished, with the desks in place, he took Eulalie with him.

The crabapple tree in the foreman's yard was now a mass of pink blossoms, blooming earlier than usual.

Would the school have trees around it also, Eulalie wondered? And where would she stay? In one of the small houses near the school?

The bell was being hoisted into its niche as Eulalie and Robert drove down the road.

"How do you like it?" he asked, turning to her.

"It is very nice, Robert," she admitted, trying to show some enthusiasm.

Inside, he walked along each row of new desks, the smaller ones set in the front, the larger ones toward the back.

"Would you like to see the living quarters?" Robert asked.

Numbly she nodded her head.

"I thought it would be better to have them in the school itself, rather than in a separate house. That way, the school can be taken care of, and the fire built before the pupils report each morning."

Robert opened a side door from the large schoolroom and waited for Eulalie to precede him into the next room.

It was furnished with a bed and dresser and a wash-basin with ewer. A small rocking chair stood near the window. And under the bed was a white porcelain chamber pot.

"Do you think it looks comfortable, Eulalie?" he asked, watching for her reaction to the room.

"Yes, Robert," she managed to say.

"You do not seem very enthusiastic. Have I forgotten something?"

"It would be nice to have a curtain at the window, for privacy," she said hesitantly.

"Of course. Bound for a woman to notice that. I will have Ebenezer Shaw see to it. And now, I'm sure you're anxious to check the supplies to see that everything is in order before school begins."

"When do you wish the school to open, Robert?" she asked, wondering how much longer she would have with Jason.

"In about a week. That will give them a good start before summer."

Eulalie unpacked the slates and chalk and the reading primers, setting them on the teacher's desk in the front of the school, while Robert removed the globe from a separate box and assembled it on its stand.

"Jessie will be here in a few minutes. I'll leave her to you, Eulalie, to give her any instructions. She already has the list of pupils, and you might want to put their names on the books and discuss the first few weeks' lessons with her."

Robert left the school, taking the phaeton with him, and Eulalie, walking back into the living quarters, gazed at the austere little room that reminded her of the room in the convent.

Jessie lovingly touched each new slate and primer when she came. "I don't know who's the most excited, Mrs. Tabor—the children or me—about school starting next week."

"We will go on Saturday before school starts on Monday, Eulalie. That way, we can make sure that nothing has gone wrong," Robert told her on the way home. "So do not plan anything else for that day."

On Friday, Eulalie packed her small trunk, leaving most of the beautiful clothes that Robert had ordered for her hanging in the wardrobe. With the black cloak from the convent, she chose four dresses that would be serviceable, putting in also her slippers and two white nightgowns.

With that task completed, she sought out Jason, to spend her last afternoon with him.

The week had gone slowly for Robert. He could not understand Eulalie's withdrawal, and it had worried him all week.

When had it started? After their first trip to Taborville? Perhaps it had been a mistake to try to interest her in the school.

She had certainly shown a lack of enthusiasm for it, which had surprised him. But despite that, she had done everything he had asked her to do—seeing that Jessie was well prepared, and that the supplies and books were adequate.

But there was something troubling her, and he could not put a finger to it. Neijee? Was she still worried about Neijee and the comment that Florilla had made?

But surely Eulalie did not think that he would sell the child just because of the episode in the river house, with Jason. No, there must be something else.

Finding the wedding ring? There was a hurt look in her eyes as he placed it on her finger. Perhaps it had stirred up all the haunting memories—of not wanting to become his wife, and of the three years after being taken to the slave market and sold. Or maybe it was a combination of the two.

His own leg served to remind him occasionally, especially when it rained, of the hazardous trip up the Mississippi and of his capture by the Indians. And when it did, he realized he was short-tempered. How much more would a young girl be affected by such memories—to be tied forever to the man who had sold her and left her to fend for herself. No, he supposed that with all she had been through, Eulalie had a right to be moody at times.

Robert ordered the phaeton to be brought to the circular drive, and then he sought out the overseer for a last word with him before leaving for the day.

When he came back, within sight of the house, Eulalie was already outside with Jimbo checking the straps that bound the small trunk to the rear of the vehicle.

Now what was she doing? Robert frowned but refrained from asking. Burned by the fiasco of Neijee's suit, and his assumption that Eulalie had cut up the dress that Maggie had made for her, Robert was in no hurry to repeat his mistake. She would tell him in time what she was taking to Taborville with her.

During the trip, Eulalie said few words, speaking only when he required an answer to a question. And the closer they got to the mill village, the more despondent she looked.

Beyond his feet, to the right of the box of books he was taking to add to the small library of the school, Robert had hidden the rifle from Eulalie's sight, covering it with the extra blanket.

Robert had kept from her the massacre at Raisin River of the wounded prisoners left behind by the British. And he hoped that Arthur would not mention it in front of her the next time he came to visit. But if Tecumseh, already a brigadier general in the British army, succeeded in persuading the Indian nations in the south to join them, no one would be safe from terror.

He kept his eyes mainly on the road, but occasionally flicked them toward the woods, alert for any sign of sudden activity.

As they approached the entrance of the village, Robert relaxed his grip on the reins. He must not stay too long, for with Eulalie at his side, it was important to get home before dark.

They were met at the mill by Ebenezer Shaw, who followed them to his house in his own vehicle. There the aroma of food greeted them as Jessie opened the door.

Despite the small breakfast Eulalie had eaten, she was

not hungry. But she smiled and allowed her plate to be filled by Jessie.

"Is everything in order at the schoolhouse, Jessie?" Robert asked the girl.

"Oh, yes sir," she replied. "And one of the older boys has already volunteered to come early every morning to build the fire and ring the bell."

"Good," Robert said. "I have brought some books that I had at Mr. Waddell's School when I was a student there. You might be able to use some of them later."

"Thank you, Mr. Tabor."

"I'll take them to the school after lunch and leave them on the teacher's desk. Eulalie," he said, turning to his quiet wife, "would you rather stay here and rest, or will you come with me?"

"I'll come with you, Robert."

"And Jessie and I will pick up the last box of supplies from the mill," Ebenezer Shaw said, "and meet you at the schoolhouse. We have the curtain to put up, as well," he added.

Eulalie's face, with her large sad doe eyes, upset Robert. She had almost dwindled to nothing from eating little all week, yet she had not complained. Robert had waited for her to tell him what was troubling her, but so far she had said nothing. If she had not confessed to him by the time they reached Midgard, he would let it go no longer. She would make herself ill if she continued this way.

"Is the trunk to go into the school, Eulalie?" Robert asked, stopping the phaeton by the front door.

"Yes, Robert. Will you please take it into the living quarters?"

So that was it. She had probably selected some of her old clothes for Jessie, knowing that the girl would need them when she started teaching.

Ebenezer Shaw arrived soon after Robert took in the trunk, and while the man, with Jessie's help, hung the curtain at the window, Robert carried the wooden box filled with books to unpack near the large desk.

"Well, there seems to be nothing more I can do until

Monday morning," Jessie said, and then waited for Ebenezer Shaw after bidding Eulalie goodbye.

"I'll see you at the mill in a few minutes, Shaw," Robert called from the schoolroom, waving his foreman on.

Eulalie, feeling desolate and alone, sat in the rocking chair in the little bedroom off the main part of the school. Her trunk had been placed at the end of the bed. She could hear Robert's footsteps, and suddenly she knew she could not face him.

She quickly rose from the chair and stared out the window, seeing nothing.

"Eulalie?" the voice sounded from the open door.

"Goodbye, Robert," she managed to say, unable to disguise her growing grief.

Hands touched her shoulders and drew her around to face him.

"What do you mean, goodbye?" he asked, seeing the large tear gather on her lashes and then spill down her cheek.

"Do not make it any harder for me, Robert. Just . . . go." And she turned her back to him again.

"Without you, Eulalie? Where would I go without you?"

"Back to Midgard."

Suddenly it hit him. Had she completely misunderstood him? Did she think he was leaving her to teach the mill children?

Robert racked his brain to remember what he had said to her to cause such a misunderstanding. And his words rose up to smite him. "I have found something for you to do—to keep you out of further trouble."

He groaned and drew her to him again. "Did you think I meant to leave you here, little one? That I would be so cruel as to take you away from Jason?"

Her sobbing against his chest answered him. And his heart was heavy, realizing how little she trusted him.

He stroked her hair and, speaking gently as he would to a child, he explained, "I merely wanted you to help Jessie. I never intended anything else." And in her ear he whispered, "Jason is not the only one who could not do without you. I could never send you away from me, Eulalie."

Slowly and certainly, he reassured her, until the sobs quieted. He found his handkerchief and gently wiped away her tears. "Shall I put the trunk back in the phaeton, or would you rather leave it here for Jessie?"

"For Jessie," she murmured, taking the handkerchief from him and blowing her nose.

The cover of the phaeton hid her from view when Robert stopped at the mill. "I will be only a few minutes," he said, climbing out to tie the reins to the hitching post.

True to his word, Robert reappeared after a short time, and getting into the vehicle, he left the mill road and headed south to Midgard and home.

The afternoon sun steadily sank into the pines by the edge of the road, until finally it plummeted beyond sight, leaving in its place the dark, stippled shadows of twilight.

The coldness of the air honed the fine sounds traveling from the inner regions of the woods, and Robert, with a feeling of being watched, edged his foot closer to the rifle hidden under the blanket in front of him.

Not wishing to wake up Eulalie, who had gone to sleep, he continued the steady pace set by the two matched bays, neither rushing them nor holding them back. Next time, if Eulalie traveled with him, he would make sure to have two post riders as well, to protect her.

The sudden hooting sound in the woods was answered by a similar call farther down on the other side of the narrow roadway.

Robert's progress was being dutifully noted; yet no one had made his appearance, or tried to impede him on his journey. But now he could no longer allow Eulalie to sleep. It was too dangerous, knowing for certain that something could happen at any moment.

"Eulalie," he called softly. She stirred but did not open her eyes. "Wake up, Eulalie," he said more urgently.

"What . . . what is it?" she asked, making an effort to keep her eyes open.

"We are being watched," he answered. "Nothing to get alarmed about, but I think you should be awake."

His words acted as a stimulant, and she sat up immediately.

"Who do you think it might be?"

"Probably just a few Indians on their way home from hunting."

"Do you think they intend to harm us?" she whispered.

He shook his head. "Not unless—" Robert bit off his words.

"Unless what, Robert?" Eulalie asked, suddenly afraid.

But he did not answer. Instead, he asked, "Can you handle the horses?"

"Yes."

With her affirmation, he turned the reins over to Eulalie, and then leaned down, picking up the rifle, still covered by the blanket. His eyes peered from one side of the road to the other, until the carriage passed out of the dense wooded area of pines, and into the bleaker stretches of hardwood trees, bereft of their leaves.

Another hooting sound greeted them, but this time it was behind them, and after a few minutes, when no answer was forthcoming farther down the sandy road, Robert took over the reins again.

Neither one talked for the rest of the trip, and when, with the last vestige of light, Eulalie saw the plantation house loom as some giant shadow on the land, she took a deep breath. When she had left the house that morning, she had been desolate over her separation from Jason. But now she would be with him again. Eulalie had won reprieve and her heart was thankful.

CHAPTER
26

THE school at Taborville was left in Jessie's hands, and Robert's attention now turned to the guarding of the Charleston harbor.

After the raids upriver by the British, the citizens had watched the harbor well, but now with the disappearance of the British fleet and news of its harassment to Chesapeake Bay farther north, they became lax, their attention shifting to other matters.

But Robert, Arthur and Hector were aware of the danger of becoming too used to the constant passing of the blockade ship off their coast. Fort Moultrie was little defense, and unless someone set up a communications system from the outer rim of sea islands, the British fleet could easily slip into the harbor again without a soul being aware of their coming. And Robert was in no hurry to be victim again to the stripping of his plantation.

Determined to do something about this lack of vigilance, Robert met with Arthur and Hector at the Exchange to explore possible solutions to the problem.

"What about the old lighthouse at the end of Tabor Island?" Hector asked as they sat at the table in the Exchange. "Is it in working condition, or do you think we could get it into shape to use, if it isn't?"

"It's in just as bad shape as Uncle Ravenal's summer house on the island," Robert replied. "Of little use in its present state. The last time I saw the lighthouse, its prisms were broken, and it would be impossible to get a replacement."

"But even without the prisms," Arthur countered, "couldn't it be used with lanterns to give a signal?"

"Do you think the lanterns could be seen as far as Fort Moultrie?" Robert asked.

Arthur, familiar with the fort, answered, "Yes, I'm sure of it, especially if someone were posted on the parapet."

Robert nodded and then raised another question. "The lanterns could only be seen at night. What about the daytime?"

"Mirrors," suggested Hector. "I'll bet my phaeton against yours that mirrors would work."

Arthur became enthusiastic at Hector's suggestion. "We could certainly try it," he said. "The fort itself isn't much defense, the way it's situated."

"No, it isn't," Robert agreed with a laugh. "I heard the other day that Mr. Langford's cow walked over the sand to the walls and fell into the fort. The poor boy on duty was scared to death—thought he was being attacked by the British."

Hector and Arthur joined in the laughter, and then in eagerness the men sat and planned how they would go about setting up their communications system from the island to the fort. By trial and error they would determine the best method, so that Charleston and its harbor would be protected from surprise attack. It was galling to all three that the British were using their own back door— Spanish Florida—to launch marauding attacks upon villages all along the coast.

When Robert visited Tabor Island three days later, it had an eerie air and the deserted house seemed to whisper loudly of earlier times, of secrets embedded in the three-foot-thick walls of tabby—oyster shell and lime.

Robert looked at the overgrown orange trees, cassina and sea myrtle, and he recalled the excitement he had felt as a boy when Uncle Ravenal had told him about the Franciscan friars who had come from Santo Domingo almost three centuries before to convert the coastal Indians to the cross, only to be massacred for their efforts.

And it was on the foundation of the old mission that Uncle Ravenal had built his summer house—out of the same materials the friars had used.

Back and forth to the island Robert went with a cargo of workers to repair the house and clean the area of rank undergrowth. A colony of wild pigs was rid of its fiercest members and the steps to the top of the lighthouse were strengthened with new wood.

In the middle of the renovation, Eulalie, who had remained at Midgard during that time, received a second invitation to visit Cedar Hill and her cousin, Julie. Robert did not have an excuse to refuse. For with the Catawbas and Waxhaws remaining friendly to the Americans, there was no danger in the upper regions of the Carolinas. The danger lay farther south, toward Georgia and Alabama.

Robert looked at the letter and then at Eulalie, who sat waiting to hear if Robert would allow her to accept the invitation.

He felt guilty that he had not let her spend Christmas with the only relative she had, and noting the sad eyes that had been that way ever since they had heard the tragic news that the *Patriot* had gone down in a storm off Cape Hatteras, with Theodosia Alston aboard, he said gently, "Would you like to go, Eulalie?"

"Oh, yes, Robert." And then her face lost its vivacity. "But you are busy with the island."

"That does not necessarily mean that you and Jason could not go. If I could arrange it, making sure that you would be safe on the journey, then I see no reason why you should refuse, this time."

"Thank you, Robert," she said, brightening. "How soon do you think it would be before you know?"

Her eagerness to leave him hurt him. "In a few days, and then you can send word to Cedar Hill."

He walked closer to her and stared into her eyes, aglow

with anticipation. "I would never let you go alone by water, Eulalie. It is a good thing the entire trip can be made on land."

And so it was that two weeks later, Eulalie and Jason, accompanied by Florilla, packed and left in the well-sprung carriage belonging to Arthur Metcalfe.

Robert tried to smother the jealous feeling that it was his best friend Arthur who would be a constant companion to Eulalie for the next month, while he, Robert, would be without his wife and child.

But what could he do after Arthur, intent on a visit with Desmond, had volunteered to accept the responsibility of seeing that Eulalie and Jason reached Cedar Hill safely?

Could he tell him that he did not trust him? That he would prefer strangers, rather than his best friend, to look after his wife? At least Florilla would be with them to serve as chaperone on the trip. And perhaps the visit would bring some color back into Eulalie's pale cheeks.

Eulalie, dressed in the cloak with ermine trim, sat in the carriage with Jason at her side. To think that she would finally get to meet her cousin! Her excitement over the trip transferred itself to Arthur, who sat opposite her, indulgently watching Eulalie as they left the circular drive of Midgard.

Robert, with a scowl on his face, remained standing in the drive until Arthur's carriage disappeared from sight.

Aware of Florilla's narrowed glare, Arthur suddenly straightened his cravat and, reluctantly taking his eyes from Eulalie, pretended to be interested in the view from the window.

It did not take long for the rhythmic swaying of the carriage to lull Jason to sleep. His head found a resting place on Eulalie's lap, while his plump little body curled up on the seat between Eulalie and Florilla. Eulalie covered the child with the carriage robe and then gently stroked his golden curls with her hand while he slept.

They were headed toward Columbia, a three-day trip,

and from there, northward across the fall line and into the piedmont section of the state. Five days in all, if the weather held good.

"When you become tired of riding, Eulalie," Arthur said, "let me know and I'll have Enoch stop the carriage for a while."

"Thank you, Arthur, but I am sure we can manage with the rest stops that you think necessary."

The journey was the same that Eulalie had taken in December; yet the land looked different when approached in the opposite direction, from Charleston to Columbia. With no freezing rain or snow to mar the sandy road, it was much more comfortable than the earlier trip, and the familiar inn where they were to stop for the night appeared almost deserted as the carriage drew into the yard.

It was already dusk when Arthur, carrying the sleeping Jason up the steps to the inn, was met by an effusive innkeeper.

"I have given you and your wife adjoining rooms, Mr. Metcalfe," he said in a voice anxious to please, "and the child and his governess the room across the hall."

Startled at the innkeeper's announcement, Arthur responded in a low voice, "I will take the room across the hall, sir. And the ladies may have the adjoining rooms."

"As you wish," the man said, resigned to the vagaries of the gentry when they traveled.

Each place they stopped on their way, the same mistake was made, the innkeeper believing Eulalie to be Arthur's wife. Embarrassed at first, the sandy-haired man attempted to correct the mistake, but by the third evening, he had grown accustomed to it and seemed to be enjoying it.

"I hope this does not disconcert you too much, to be thought my wife."

His blue eyes, alive with amusement, stared at Eulalie, seated across from him in the private parlor. Their dinner, brought to them by the innkeeper's daughter, was half finished, and Arthur reached over to pour more wine into Eulalie's goblet.

"I believe the only one who is embarrassed is Florilla,"

Eulalie acknowledged. "She does not approve of our traveling together or eating apart from the public dining room."

Arthur snorted. "I will not have you stared at by the other travelers. And as for Florilla, I don't care for her. It's a wonder you can stand to have the woman around. Why did you hire her in the first place, Eulalie?"

"Robert hired her," she explained without thinking, "when he discovered Jason at the convent."

Eulalie bit her lip, realizing she had said too much.

"Discovered Jason? What do you mean, Eulalie? What convent? Do you mean Jason is a foundling?"

"Oh no," Eulalie said, quick to protest his last question, without answering the first.

He stared at her thoughtfully and then repeated, "What convent, Eulalie?"

"Arthur . . ."

"Please do not try to hide anything from me, Eulalie." He looked into her troubled eyes and gently reminded her, "Are we not bound together as members of one family—you, Julie, Desmond and I? I will not take advantage of any confidence you impart tonight, I promise you."

"It was in New Orleans," Eulalie answered in a soft embarrassed voice. "When Jason was born, I was ill with fever."

"And you did not return with him when Robert brought Jason back to Carolina?"

"No."

"Why, Eulalie? Surely Robert would have waited until you were well."

"Soeur Louise told Robert I was dead."

Incredulously, Arthur looked at the girl across the table from him. Remembering Hector's words about his traveling up the Mississippi, Arthur said, "Eulalie, what was Hector doing on the Mississippi? Was he looking for you and Jason? Did you . . . run away from Robert?"

Confused by his questions, Eulalie nervously swallowed and pushed back the wine glass from its position beside her plate. And Arthur, so close to the truth, kept up the verbal assault, until Eulalie broke down, with almost the entire story forced from her lips.

"Please, you should never have forced me to tell you, Arthur," Eulalie said, seeing the dark anger spread across his gentle features. "Promise me you will forget it."

"To think that he sold his own wife . . . " Arthur was not listening to her.

"But he did not know I was his wife. It was my own fault, because I was so frightened after Hector's visit. I should never have hidden from him—and all this would not have happened."

"You do not have to stay with Robert, you know—against your will. Julie and Desmond would be happy to take you in, Eulalie. You and the boy, as well."

"But Arthur, you don't understand—"

The door opened and Florilla walked in from the adjoining room, cutting off Eulalie's reply.

"Jason is finally asleep," the governess announced, "so I have come to enjoy the glass of wine you offered me earlier."

On the fourth day, the sandy soil gave way to the red earth of the piedmont, and seeing this, Eulalie's excitement increased. The banks along the side of the road, studded with hidden bits of mica catching the attention of the afternoon sun, became a tomahawk red, as if painted by some giant brush dipped in blood.

The landscape was unprincipled, wild, and the carriage slowed in its progress, as the horses plodded up and down the terrain and struggled to keep their footing in the slippery red mud.

"I have never seen earth this color before," Eulalie commented.

"It is rich land, make no mistake, Eulalie. It is good not only for farming but for its valuable minerals. You know about Desmond's gold mine, do you not?"

Arthur's comment whetted Eulalie's imagination. And Florilla, at the mention of gold, suddenly looked up. "Did you say gold?"

Arthur nodded. "Desmond found the first nugget along

245

the creek bank near the falls. He has been looking for the main lode, but so far, he has not been able to find it. So he continues to dig along the eroded banks—with the Indians' help."

"He has Indians on his property?" Florilla's voice was fearful.

"Yes, Florilla, but you need not worry. They're friendly. And besides, you won't be seeing them anyway. The mine is some distance from the house."

By the fifth day, Arthur looked for the creek that heralded the beginning of Desmond Caldwell's land, and when he spied it, he said enthusiastically, "We're almost there, Eulalie."

At his words, Eulalie leaned forward, gazing from the window of the enclosed carriage to watch for the first sign of the house on Cedar Hill.

Up the hill the carriage went. And then, getting to the top of the ridge, the vehicle turned and ambled along a level road lined with giant cedars, the private drive belonging to Desmond Caldwell. The house, aptly named for its location, came into sight beyond the cedars. It was a large gray rambling plank house, with high steps and a covered porch surrounding the house on three sides. Ivy grew in an undisciplined expanse, fanning out from the base of a magnolia tree that shaded the porch on the front side.

The carriage did not stop until it reached the side yard and the second set of steps. The cellar door underneath the steps stood partly open. Someone must have gone into the cool place for a ham strung from the rafters, and had neglected to close it. Other buildings were apparent in the distance—a corn crib and a barn, as well as the paddock where the horses and mules lazily grazed.

The horses hitched to the carriage snorted and turned their heads toward the paddock and the grain that would be waiting for them.

Enoch, the driver, laughed at their impatience and restrained them until Arthur could climb out and help the women and Jason from the confines of the carriage.

"Leave Jason for me to carry in," Arthur commanded,

seeing Eulalie lean over to pick up the sleeping child from the carriage seat.

She obeyed him and with one swift glance to make sure he would not fall from the seat, Eulalie stepped to the ground, followed by Florilla.

Desmond, hearing the commotion in the sideyard, hurried onto the porch to greet them. But Julie, Eulalie's cousin, was nowhere in sight.

Far different from the planters' elegant houses in the low country, the wooden rambling house nevertheless had an elegant simplicity about it—a feeling of comfort and total relaxation that welcomed the tired travelers.

"I am happy that you have finally arrived. We have been looking for you all day," Desmond said to Arthur, who was watching Enoch remove the trunks from the top of the carriage, to be handed down to the waiting handyman.

"We would have been here sooner," Arthur teased, "but your red hills, Desmond, slowed the horses considerably."

"Ah yes—low-country horses," Desmond quipped, "not used to the challenge of our rugged terrain."

The two men looked at each other with affection in their eyes. Then Desmond, turning to Eulalie, said, "But come. Julie has been waiting impatiently for a sight of you for the past week. She's in the parlor."

"Florilla, will you come too?" Eulalie asked, but Florilla, shaking her head, began to act her role as governess. "I think I'd better take Jason on up to his room, if someone will show me the way."

The young white girl, hanging by the door, came forward at Desmond's request and led the way up the stairs to the second floor for Florilla and Arthur, who still held the sleeping child in his arms.

Down the wide hallway in the opposite direction of the stairs, Eulalie went with Desmond, at last to meet this lost cousin face to face.

The serene, dark-haired woman seated in the parlor by the fire held out her arms in a welcoming gesture when she saw Eulalie. And the girl, delighted to see her relative, went to the woman and embraced her affectionately.

In amusement, Desmond stood and listened as the two women lapsed into French. The sound of Arthur's footsteps made Eulalie and Julie aware of the two men and, in apology, the two broke off conversing in their native language.

"I can see they will have no time for us, Arthur," Desmond said. "These two will be quite occupied getting to know each other, so rather than being ignored, I have arranged a quail shoot tomorrow in your honor. At least the hunting dogs will heed our voices."

Julie, looking at her husband, smiled, and then in a serious tone she said, "I am afraid I have already forgotten my duties as hostess, keeping Eulalie here when she is so tired from her trip. Tanna, show Mrs. Tabor to her room," Julie said to the girl nearby, and turning back to Eulalie she said, "We will have plenty of time after dinner to become acquainted. But I know you will wish to freshen up now and rest after your trip." And looking in Arthur's direction, she said, "Arthur, you are in the same room as last time, so you can find your way, can you not?"

"Yes, Julie. Do not worry about me. I could find it with my eyes closed."

Satisfied that both Eulalie and Arthur were taken care of, Julie quietly spoke to her husband. "If you don't mind, Desmond, I think I should like to go up also."

Desmond leaned over and lifted his wife in his arms. It was only then that Eulalie realized that her cousin could not walk.

"What happened to Julie?" Eulalie whispered after Desmond disappeared with his wife up the stairs. "Arthur, why can she not walk?"

"It was a carriage accident," Arthur answered. "But they have not given up hope. One day, perhaps, she will walk again."

CHAPTER

27

IT was the next day, when Arthur and Desmond were on the quail shoot, that Julie confided in Eulalie, telling of her narrow escape from Santo Domingo during the slave uprising.

"I was lucky to reach the ship," Julie said, with pain still evident in her voice. "If it had not been for Maman Noire, I would have been killed with the rest of the family. But she hid me until the blacks finished ransacking the house and left, and then in the middle of the night, she smuggled me to the harbor."

"Was that when you had your accident?" Eulalie asked.

Julie shook her head. "No, it was several years later, after I had met Desmond and married him. It is ironic, *non,* that I survived the massacre, only to be thrown from a runaway carriage?"

Eulalie sat and listened while Julie related the events leading up to the accident.

"Desmond and I were on our way to Chester. He had business to attend to, and I wished to do some shopping. We started out late, but it did not matter, since we were to spend the night with friends. As we came closer to the town, we saw a gathering crowd, and they were laughing at this little man who was down on his hands and knees, begging for help from the crowd.

"Desmond stopped the carriage because he recognized the man. It was Aaron Burr, who was being taken to Baltimore to be tried for treason. He had escaped his captors, but when they apprehended him, he threw himself on the mercy of the crowd."

How strange, Eulalie thought, to be hearing of the proud and frail Theodosia's father like this. How sad his disgrace must have made her. And now he would never see her again. With a feeling of sadness, Eulalie waited for Julie to continue.

"Because of his respect for Joseph Alston, Desmond did not wish to see his father-in-law in total humiliation, jeered by the crowd, so he gave the reins to me and went to the man's aid, taking him inside the nearby building until the man could compose himself.

"In the excitement, the horses became frightened and I was unable to control them. Before Desmond could return to the carriage, the horses lost their heads and began racing down the road. I only remember a terrible whinnying and the sudden loss of balance before the carriage turned over."

Eulalie sat silently, aware of the swinging pendulum of the clock. But Jason's excited voice penetrated the room. Eulalie could hear his steps as he ran toward the parlor.

"Eu-lie," he called excitedly. "Eu-lie, look."

In his arms he held a small black kitten, its eyes still shut. Florilla, coming hurriedly behind him, was clearly not in a pleasant mood.

Eulalie took the kitten from Jason and held it gently, listening to its tiny mews.

"He's beautiful, *mon petit,*" Eulalie said. "Show him to Cousin Julie, and then you must carry him back to his *maman.* Already he is crying for his supper."

Jason solemnly took the small kitten for Julie to see, and then reluctantly walked to the waiting Florilla.

That evening, with the men home from the quail shoot, Julie, Eulalie and Florilla sat at the dinner table and listened to the enthusiastic recalling of the successful hunt.

"I hope you like quail, Eulalie," Arthur said, staring at the girl in the rose-pink silk dress. "For we bagged enough for a feast tomorrow."

"Just so I do not have to prepare them," she said, turning up her nose.

He laughed and leaning closer, he said, "I cannot imagine anyone so beautiful being *allowed* in the kitchen."

His low-voiced compliment made her blush, and Julie did not help when she acknowledged it to all at the table. "My cousin *is* beautiful, isn't she, Arthur?"

"Yes, Julie. It seems to run in the family—this dark hair and the alabaster complexion," he announced gallantly, looking at the pleased Julie.

"Oh, I am so sorry," Florilla apologized at the sudden clatter of her fork hitting the floor.

"Tanna will get you another one," Julie said, motioning for the young white servant.

"And what did you find to occupy your time today, Mrs. Hines?" a polite Desmond inquired.

"Oh, Jason and I explored the land. He found some kittens, and then he played on the lower limbs of an old gnarled apple tree." She smiled sweetly at the man seated at the head of the table.

"So he has found the tree," Desmond commented. "You remember it, Arthur, do you not? You used to play in it yourself when you were a boy, visiting us in the summer."

"I remember it well," Arthur replied. "It caused many a summer complaint—those green apples. What is it about an apple tree that draws a boy to it like a magnet, I wonder?"

"Not merely the fruit, I suspect," Desmond said. "It's the way that particular tree's limbs spread out in all directions, making it so easy to climb. I remember one summer you gave your mother quite a scare, Arthur, finding you at the very top of the tree. One slip, and you would not have gone back to Charleston with her."

Arthur laughed. "I remember the discipline more than

anything else. For the rest of the summer, I played only on the lower limbs."

The time passed much too quickly for Eulalie, with neighbors dropping by to call in the afternoons and occasionally staying for dinner. During the day, Desmond and Arthur were either at the mine or riding over the farmland that had been planted with fresh crops of corn and cotton. And one day, Arthur rode into Chester with Desmond, but by evening, they were both home again.

It was an enjoyable time for Eulalie, being with Julie, and the happiness showed in her face.

"I will be sorry to leave, Julie," Eulalie said. "I have so enjoyed being with you, and Jason has loved playing in his apple tree."

"And I don't want you to go, my dear," the dark-haired woman answered. "But I know your husband is impatient for you and Jason to return." Taking her hand, Julie continued, "But you will be welcome whenever you can come for a visit."

"I wish you could come back with us, to Midgard," Eulalie said wistfully.

"I am not a good traveler," the woman explained. "And Desmond wants me to begin a new treatment soon. That is why he makes me rest each afternoon." She looked up at her husband in the doorway. "You see, he has come for me already. And I cannot help but obey."

The loving look that passed between them caused a small ache in Eulalie's heart. Not that she was envious of her cousin—she was happy for her. It was only that all her life she had dreamed of exchanging the same loving glance with a husband who adored her. But Robert did not adore her.

Feeling suddenly lonely, Eulalie sought out Jason. It was not difficult to find him, for she knew that he would be at the apple tree with Florilla watching over him.

Down the side steps she went, passing by the clump of rocks at the edge of the yard. Crossing over the carriage drive, she walked past the paddock, down toward the meadow where the giant apple tree spread its gnarled branches.

Florilla sat on the log, with the sun at her back. The woman, unaware of Eulalie's silent tread, called out, "Very good, Jason. You're almost to the top."

Alarmed at the woman's words, Eulalie gazed at the apple tree and looked for some sign of Jason. And then she saw him, clinging to a branch far above the ground.

"One slip and then you would not have gone back to Charleston with your mother." The conversation at the dinner table mocked her, now that she was staring at her own child, precariously clinging to the high limb.

Without a word to Florilla, Eulalie hurried past her and called to Jason, "Be very still, *mon petit*. I am coming to help you."

Immodestly tucking her skirts up, Eulalie began to climb up the old tree to her child. It was slow, and once she missed her footing and hit her chin on an outstretched branch, but she dared not take her eyes from Jason. As if she could will him to remain safe until she could reach him, she watched him as she climbed.

"Eu-lie," he wailed, now frightened at the height.

"Hold on, Jason. I will be there soon."

She continued crooning to him as she climbed each succeeding limb, until she was at last within his reach.

Before she was ready for him, the frightened child let go of the limb and hurled himself at Eulalie. With chubby arms, he grabbed her around the neck and, burying his golden-crowned head into the hollow of her throat, he began soaking her with his tears.

His precipitate action stunned her, causing her to lose her balance. Even as the sagging limb creaked in protest at the weight of mother and child, Eulalie frantically reached for the next lower limb. Her arms, feeling jerked from their sockets, wrapped themselves around the smooth-barked wood that now stopped her unexpected plunge.

A small, dead twig, jutting out from the higher limb, grazed her cheek. And all the time, Jason clung to her with the instinct of the primitive young, intent on survival.

Breathing heavily, Eulalie rested until the trembling in her legs eased. Then, feeling with her foot, she took one limb at a time, laboriously making the descent, until she and Jason were on solid ground.

Untucking her skirts, now torn in places, with the scratch across her cheek an angry red, Eulalie smoothed her flyaway hair, and holding onto Jason's hand, she walked toward Florilla, who had stood by the log and silently watched the progress of mother and child.

She did not attempt to disguise her anger. "As soon as we return to Charleston, I will see that Robert dismisses you."

Florilla merely smiled at Eulalie's threat. "Robert will not dismiss the woman he was planning to marry," she retorted.

Noting the drain of color from the dark-haired girl's face, the woman pressed her sudden advantage over Eulalie. "He only took you back because of Jason. And if Jason were no longer . . . around, then he would have no reason to keep you. He would have no hesitation in sending you away the second time."

"That . . . that isn't true," Eulalie said, defensively fighting against the malignant words.

"In fact, he would probably be relieved if you did as Mr. Metcalfe suggested. I am sure your cousin would take you in. And it would be good riddance for Robert. You know, of course, that he never wanted to marry you."

She did not wait to hear any more. Unable to dispute the woman's words, Eulalie fled from the meadow, with Jason trying hard to keep up with her.

"Eulalie, what in the world has happened to you?" Arthur took one look at the disheveled girl and his face showed concern. "And where is Florilla?" he asked, looking toward Jason.

The lump in her throat kept her from answering, and seeing how upset she was, Arthur took Jason's hand and said, "I will take the boy to Tanna."

Eulalie ran into the house and up the stairs to her bedroom, where she tearfully flung herself across the bed. But she could not shut out Florilla's taunts. They reaffirmed what she had feared. Robert did not love her. But Florilla—had Robert actually planned to marry the woman? Was that why she had always addressed him as

Robert and never Mr. Tabor, as a governess should? Because they were intimately bound together? And too, Jason had called Florilla "Mama" when Eulalie had first come to the house to care for him when he was ill. Did that not prove that Florilla was already certain of becoming Jason's mother and Robert's wife?

Someone knocked at the door, and Eulalie raised her head from the pillow to listen. If she did not answer, then the person would soon go away.

But Arthur, standing outside the bedroom door, did not allow Eulalie to shut herself away. He called and knocked so persistently that she was forced to open the door to him.

"You will have to confide in me, Eulalie. I cannot bear to see you so unhappy." He stepped inside the room and closed the door.

"Arthur, it is not proper for you to be in my room," she protested.

"Where shall we go then, Eulalie, with your face stained with tears? Down into the parlor for Julie and Desmond to see, as well as the servants?"

"N-no," Eulalie admitted.

"It is far more important for you to tell me what has happened. Do not worry about the impropriety of my being in your room."

She walked away from him, toward the window. Never would she repeat to anyone what Florilla had said or done.

"I do not wish to go back to Midgard," she said, stifling a sob.

"If that is all that is troubling you, Eulalie, then do not cry." He sounded relieved. "I told you before that you would be welcome here at Cedar Hill. It is not necessary for you to return to Robert, if it causes you so much distress."

Arthur walked to the window and took Eulalie's hand. "Would you like me to talk with Desmond and Julie about it?"

"Yes."

"Then wash the tears from your face, Eulalie. And give

me a few minutes before you come downstairs. Everything should be settled by then."

He let go of her hands, and Eulalie, still standing by the window, heard the bedroom door close. Doing what Arthur suggested, she went to the basin and poured some water from the pitcher, to wash her tears away.

After she had changed her torn dress and recombed her hair, she went hesitantly downstairs to the parlor.

"My dear, we are so happy that you have decided to stay longer," Julie greeted her.

Three days later, Enoch readied the carriage, strapping the trunks on top, but Eulalie's was replaced by the solid black trunk belonging to an elderly widow, a neighbor of the Caldwells', who was delighted at the unexpected invitation to travel as far as Columbia where her sister lived.

Florilla and the widow sat in the carriage, while Arthur said his final goodbyes.

His kind blue eyes rested on Eulalie. "It seems strange that Florilla has chosen to go back to Midgard when Jason is remaining here. Will you be all right, caring for Jason by yourself?"

"Yes, Arthur. And I prefer it this way," Eulalie replied softly.

Still lingering at her side, Arthur appeared to be debating with himself. Suddenly he moved closer and whispered in a low voice, "If you ever wish to . . . to divorce Robert, I have friends in Augusta who will help you. There would be no chance at all that the South Carolina legislature would grant you a divorce, especially with Robert as a member."

Too shocked to reply, Eulalie stepped back, and Arthur, afraid that he had said too much, hurried to the carriage.

Two weeks slowly dragged by, each day weighted with uneasiness. Not sure that Robert would allow her to stay at Cedar Hill for an extended visit, especially since she had kept Jason with her, she watched and waited for a letter. But so far, none had come.

The words that Arthur had said at departure further

disturbed her. Divorce—why had Arthur mentioned such a thing? It was against the principles of her church. It was impossible for her to secure her freedom from Robert.

But what if Robert wished to free himself of *her* in order to marry Florilla?

Eulalie sat on the log in the meadow and pressed her hands over her forehead to shut out the frightening thought.

The voice sounded behind her. "Desmond told me you would probably be here, Eulalie. Your trunk is packed and we will be leaving within the hour."

She stood up quickly, and whirling around to face the unexpected intruder, she met Robert's tawny, stormy eyes gazing at her with a disturbing intensity.

"Robert . . . " The name trembled on her lips as she hastily moved back to avoid him.

"You do well to shrink from me, Eulalie. For at this moment, my one desire is to shake you until your teeth fall out."

He took a step toward her, and Eulalie, conscious of Jason's swinging on a lower limb of the apple tree, hurried to the child.

"Jason," she called, "it is time for us to go into the house. Come and we will find Tanna to give you some milk and cookies."

The child obediently climbed down, but seeing Robert, he bypassed Eulalie and ran to greet his father, wrapping his arms around one muscular, booted leg.

Robert swiftly lifted him into his arms, giving him a swing, and Jason laughed with pleasure.

"So, at least *you* are glad to see me," he said, ruffling the child's curls.

"Apple tree," Jason said in response, pointing to the tree. "Jason climb high."

Robert nodded and put the child down. "But the tree-climbing is over for the day, Jason. Run and find your milk and cookies while I speak with your mother." Robert gave the child a pat on the seat of his pants, and Jason, on chubby legs, ran from the meadow toward the house.

Eulalie started to follow, but Robert stood in her path.

"He can find his own way, Eulalie. Before we go back to the house, there is something I want to say to you—words not intended for other ears to hear."

"Did you . . . have a good trip, Robert?" Eulalie asked, hoping to postpone the confrontation.

"No, Eulalie. It was a damned inconvenience, as you well know. But if you hope to—"

"You came alone?"

In three strides, he had her in his grasp. Gone was the civilized veneer that had masked his face. Gone was any attempt to control his anger.

With a hoarse, strident voice, Robert lashed out at her. "Did you think I would be such a nincompoop—to free you so that you could marry Arthur? Or that I would allow you to hide here indefinitely with my son? No. Whether you wish it or not, your place is at Midgard. And I was a fool to allow you to make this trip in the first place. You will find, Eulalie, that your sad, dark, doe eyes will not have any effect on me from now on—"

"Robert, my arm . . . "

He looked down at the slowly spreading redness and he immediately released her.

While Eulalie stood rubbing her arm, he continued speaking, his hands now clasped together behind his back.

"Arthur understands that if he attempts to help you in any way to gain your release from me, I will personally see to it that he pays for it dearly."

Eulalie, with her small valise in her hands, solemnly walked to the parlor to bid Julie goodbye.

"I was afraid that Robert would not be pleased at your extended stay, Eulalie." Julie's troubled eyes looked at her cousin, while her hand reached out to take Eulalie's.

The small pouch was transferred to her hand, and Eulalie, surprised, looked down at the small leather bag.

"Desmond and I wish you to have this, my dear."

Realizing what it was—nuggets of gold from Desmond's mine—Eulalie shook her head and tried to return it. But Julie pressed it again into her hands.

"Take it, Eulalie, and keep it in a safe place. Desmond

and I will feel better, knowing that you will have some money of your own if you ever need it."

At the expression on Julie's face, Eulalie knew that Robert had come for her. She did as she was told and quickly bent down to stuff the pouch into her valise.

"Are you ready, Eulalie?"

"Yes, Robert. I am ready."

CHAPTER

28

$\mathcal{T}$ HERE was no attempt to make the return trip comfortable. Speed seemed to be the only consideration. Robert, in his unconcealed anger, drove the horses hard and made few stops along the way. And Jason, as if sensing the explosive situation between his parents, was fretful, adding to the bombardment of Eulalie's nerves.

Each time they rounded a curve at a fast pace, Eulalie's stomach protested, but she should not have been surprised at the queasy feeling. She had never been a good traveler, and it was especially true now, with the carriage hurtling over the roads, never slowing for any obstacle.

At the few stops, she made no effort to question Robert about Neijee, even though he was uppermost in her mind. She would just have to wait until she reached Midgard, to see if the black child were still there. If Florilla had had anything to say about it, Eulalie knew that Neijee would already be sold.

Florilla—Robert had not mentioned her either. Yet it was apparent that the woman had relayed the conversations between Eulalie and Arthur, for Robert seemed to know everything that Arthur had said to her—the conversation that night at the inn, over the glass of wine, and

Arthur's hurried whisperings on the day of his departure from Cedar Hill.

Eulalie sighed and curled up on the seat with Jason, and, thankful that the child had at last gone to sleep, she too closed her eyes and slept.

Abruptly she awoke. The carriage was no longer in motion. Eulalie sat up, reaching out for Jason, but she was alone.

Alarmed, she gathered her cloak about her, ready to leave the carriage when the door opened and Robert appeared.

"So you are awake."

"Jason—"

"He's already being taken care of by the innkeeper's daughter. You have no need to worry about him."

Her relief was obvious, and Robert, showing a sudden gentleness, said, "You were so soundly asleep that I took him in without waking you. I am sorry if you were alarmed, Eulalie."

"Just so he is all right," she managed to say, her senses now quickened by the contact with Robert's arms as he slowly lifted her from the carriage to the ground.

Robert stood with his arms still about her, until Eulalie freed herself from his embrace and hurried up the steps to the inn.

She sat warily across the table from him, watching his movements as he helped her plate from the platters piled high with enough food to feed ten people.

"Were you going to say something, Eulalie?" Robert asked, holding the ladle in midair.

She pulled her robe closer to her body. She did not like this intimacy of eating with Robert, when she was wearing so little. But it had been so late when they arrived at the inn that it was ridiculous to dress for dinner again after the bath that had removed the grime of the dusty road from her aching body.

"I do not . . . you are giving me too much, Robert," she responded hesitantly.

With his topaz eyes boring into her, he retorted, "You are easily satisfied, Eulalie, if this is all you require. A result of too many years at the convent, no doubt. As for myself, I intend to make the most of the meal. It's the first decent food I've had in several days."

He placed her plate before her and filled his own with a hearty helping of each dish.

Eulalie sat toying with her food while Robert demolished his dinner, helping himself to a second serving from the bounty spread before them on the oak table in the privacy of their room.

"Some wine, Eulalie?" Robert asked.

She quickly shook her head, remembering the last time that she had shared an evening drink with Robert and what trouble it had made for her.

Almost as if reading her mind, Robert laughed. "I forgot. It has an unusual effect on you, doesn't it, my dear?"

"I don't know what you mean."

His smile disappeared. "Come now. You must not pretend with me, Eulalie. We both know how it affects you. Are you afraid that the spirits will betray you into becoming a loving wife again, anxious to share my bed?"

"That is not fair, Robert, for you to remind me of my . . . weakness."

"Your weakness? Do you consider making love a weakness?" He leaned toward her and she immediately drew back. "Is that why you refuse to partake of even a single glass of wine with me, when you had no such hesitation with Arthur?"

His face lost its earlier pleasantness. "You had no compunction in pretending to be Arthur's wife and in drinking a glass of wine with *him*. Yet you refuse to engage in so much as a toast with your own husband."

Eulalie lifted her chin and the dark eyes glinted dangerously. "Perhaps it was more pleasant with Arthur. At least he was not the unfeeling oaf that *you* have been this entire trip."

Angered at her barb, Robert stood. "Eulalie, I am warning you . . . "

She pushed away from the table and standing on unsteady legs, she gazed defiantly at him. "I am not afraid of you, Robert. Even though you beat me, I will not partake of anything else at this table with you. I am tired of being told what I should eat, and what I should drink. I am tired from the bumpy roads and the lurching carriage, and the lack of consideration as to my comfort. So if you will excuse me, sir," she said, "I will go to bed, to find what comfort I can in sleep, since I am sure that tomorrow will be no more pleasant than today has been."

He caught her before she had taken many steps. "What devil's spur is in your side, Eulalie? Are you hoping that I *will* beat you, so that you can use it against me in your bid for freedom? I am afraid you will be disappointed, my dear," Robert added, with sarcasm enveloping his words. "The law does not frown on a husband's beating his wife when she deserves it. But there are other ways to subdue a shrewish woman—much more pleasant to a man."

Her feet no longer touched the floor. And Eulalie, with her face far too close to his, struggled against him. "You would not—"

"But I *would*, Eulalie," Robert interrupted. "You are my wife, however much you want to deny it. And I have been celibate much too long for comfort."

"But I am tired, Robert. Can you not have pity, tonight?"

He looked down into her dark, murky eyes, and there was no trace of pity offered her.

"No, Eulalie. Since you already think of me as an unfeeling oaf, I shall not disappoint you."

"But Jason—"

"Is being watched over, as I mentioned earlier."

The alien bed, with its feathered mattress, creaked with the weight suddenly cast upon it.

Robert's lips were demanding, and Eulalie, remembering what Florilla had said, was determined not to give in. Robert did not love her. He was merely showing her that he was master.

Eulalie moved her head to the side, but she was no match for Robert. He deliberately enticed her with his teasing lips and her body shivered under his expert hands.

I will think of something else, Eulalie said to herself, trying to shut out the sensations Robert evoked. Neijee—Soeur Louise—Feena and Jason—she pulled each one from her brain, to keep her mind from Robert and her own body.

His fingers caressed her breasts and then moved to her back, making a slow, sensuous descent along her spine, until she could no longer remain unmoved.

Her brain now refused to think of anything but Robert and what he was doing to her. Eulalie moaned, and at his mercy, she raised her limp arms from her side and they became alive, tightening around his neck, holding his body closer to hers.

It had been so long, and her body ached—not from the day's arduous travel, but from the unrequited pain that yearned for the release that only Robert could give her.

Just when she thought she could stand it no longer, the slow, throbbing sensation began. Robert's words, whispered in her ear, were unintelligible. But his actions required no words. He had done what he had set out to do—to subdue her completely, and this time she had no excuse at all for her behavior.

The storm outside began, slowly at first, with a whisper of wind among the trees. Rain delicately pelted the roof and windows of the inn, and Eulalie, drowsy with sleep, listened to the musical sound that lulled and soothed her toward deep sleep again.

Her feeling of safety was rudely shattered by the flash of lightning that penetrated the room. And when the thunder that accompanied the flash of light moments later crashed upon her ears, she jumped in fright.

Beside her, Robert stirred, and Eulalie was again in his arms. But this time, his arms brought comfort to her.

"The storm will pass, Eulalie. Don't be frightened," he murmured in his sleepy, husky voice.

Eulalie relaxed against him and closed her eyes again, to drift slowly into a dream state. Far off, thunder resounded and the noise of doors opening and closing vaguely registered in the back of her brain.

Robert, now awake, lay in bed with his strong, muscular arms around his petite, dark-haired wife. Such an enigma—she had fought him tooth and nail the evening before; yet here she was, hours later, curled into the curve

264

of his body, like some small kitten, completely trusting. It was enough to drive a man mad, never knowing how she was going to react to him.

He was not happy, behaving as he had. But her clear preference for Arthur's company had made him furious with her.

Nevertheless, he had no intention of imitating Arthur. Eulalie would just have to get used to him and his ways. An unfeeling oaf, was he?

Did she have no idea how he felt when Arthur returned to Midgard with the carriage empty, except for Florilla? The disappointment and then the fury at Florilla's insinuations about Arthur and Eulalie?

But Robert had made it clear to Arthur. Regardless of how Eulalie felt, he would never release her. She was his wife and would remain so—the mother of his son, Jason. And if he were smart, he would make doubly sure that she would never leave him.

He had missed being at the birth of his first son, but this next time . . .

Robert became aware of Eulalie's soft sweetness, and his desire grew as his hands began their knowing path along her body.

His heart quickened; his breathing became more rapid. And Eulalie, safe from the raging storm of the early morning, murmured sleepily, responding to his demands . . .

The kiss awakened her. Eulalie, expecting to see Robert's face, opened her eyes and looked into the childish round topaz eyes of her son.

"Jason," she said in a surprised voice. "How did *you* get into this bed?"

Chuckling happily, the child lay back on the pillow between his parents.

"He slipped away from his nursemaid when she was busy cleaning up after his breakfast," Robert explained.

"Does she know he is in here with us?" Eulalie asked her husband.

"Yes—and greatly relieved that I did not complain

to her father about it. But if he had come in any earlier, I might have complained."

Vaguely remembering his lovemaking, Eulalie felt her cheeks flush, and she was silent. In the silence, she became aware of the dull gray morning, punctuated by the steady drops of rain. Even with the curtains drawn back from the windows, the room was dim.

She could not look forward to the hours of travel ahead. It had been uncomfortable enough when the weather was nice, but with the storm's appearance, the roads would be difficult and rough.

"How long before we leave?" Eulalie asked, brushing her tousled hair with her fingers.

"Are you that impatient to get soaking wet?" Robert's raised eyebrow mocked her.

"No. I would much prefer . . ." Eulalie stopped. It would not matter to Robert *what* she preferred. But remembering what had happened because of her outburst the evening before, she took care to guard her tongue. "I only wanted to know how much time I have to get dressed."

Robert leaned back on the pillow, with his arms over his head. He stared at the ceiling, and in a peculiar far-away voice, he said, "There is no hurry for you to get dressed. I thought we might rest here today. With the roads in such a muddy condition, we would make little time anyway."

He glanced sideways at Eulalie and watched for her reaction. When none was forthcoming, he added, "Or should I act the *unfeeling oaf* again and drag you and Jason out of this warm bed, to brave the driving rain?"

Eulalie winced at the repetition of the words she had flung at Robert. But she did not acknowledge his use of them. Instead, she said, "I thought you were in a hurry to get home."

"It is not good for the horses," he replied matter-of-factly, "to drive them too hard. I think I'll let them rest today."

Her softening toward him ceased. It was his concern for his matched chestnuts that had prompted him to delay the trip—not any feeling for her. But at least it would

266

be good to remain at the inn for the extra day. She would not complain.

The knock sounded at the door and as Robert's voice answered, Eulalie quickly pulled up the covers.

It was the food being brought upstairs—the hot, steaming breakfast, whose aroma instantly filled the room and made Eulalie conscious of her extreme hunger.

The table had been pulled to the side of the bed, and Robert handed Eulalie a plate on which he had placed a portion of the buttered loaf.

"Would you care for some—" Robert stopped abruptly. "I forgot. You do not like to have food urged on you."

He turned his back to Eulalie and began heaping his own plate with eggs and sausages, slabs of bacon and steaming apples.

Staring unbelievingly at the ill-mannered Robert, Eulalie did not see the small plump hand that swiftly confiscated the slab of bread on her own plate.

When her eyes returned to her meager offering, she found the plate empty. "Jason," she scolded, "I thought you had already eaten breakfast."

He clutched the bread hard in his hands and crumbs fell upon the covers.

At the sound of her voice, Robert looked in Eulalie's direction. Seeing what had happened, the golden-haired giant laughed. "It looks as if you intend to fast this morning, madame."

Eulalie gave him a severe look and climbed out of bed, and walking around to the other side where the table stood, she filled her plate high. And Robert, seeming to ignore her action, leaned toward Jason, to spread scuppernong jam on the bread he had claimed from Eulalie's plate.

"Bacon," the child demanded, pointing to the meat in Robert's plate.

"Not so fast, my little glutton," Robert answered. "Finish the bread in your mouth first." He took the napkin and, wiping Jason's face, Robert removed the purple stain of the scuppernongs from the child's cheeks and chin.

Eulalie, seeing Jason with his cheeks stuffed with bread,

remembered Neijee and Jason together in the spring house the day of the British raid on the plantation. She could no longer keep silent about the black child. She had to know.

"Robert, is Neijee still at Midgard?"

"Where else would he be, Eulalie?"

At his answer, she was suddenly happy. "I just wondered," she said in a little girl's voice.

Robert grunted and handed a piece of bacon to Jason.

Smiling to herself, Eulalie began to eat, making up for the lack of food from the previous evening.

CHAPTER

29

IT was barely light when the carriage finally arrived at Midgard. At the sound of the horses in the driveway, the front door of the plantation burst open, and Feena and Bradley walked down the steps to assist Eulalie and Robert. This time, Jason was wide-awake and he hopped from the carriage to run into the house.

Eulalie caught a glimpse of Neijee, peeking from the open door, but instead of coming to greet her, he disappeared. He was probably glad to have Jason home again, Eulalie thought, trying not to feel hurt that he had ignored her.

Her attention returned to Feena, and she listened to the woman's words. "It is good to have you home, *ma petite*. I was worried when you did not come with Monsieur Arthur."

Glancing over her shoulder toward Robert, who stood with Eulalie's valise in his hands, Feena added in a lower voice, "But now that you *are* home, maybe Monsieur Robert's temper will improve and the plantation will be happy again."

The two walked side by side into the house.

"Did Florilla say anything to you, Feena, when she got back from Cedar Hill?"

"Not to me, mamselle. Only to Monsieur Robert. She had much to say to him—far too much."

"She must not be left alone with Jason," Eulalie confided suddenly to her old nursemaid.

Feena stopped in her climb up the stairs. She looked strangely at Eulalie, and at last she nodded as if she understood. "We will make sure that she does no harm to him."

With the sound of the men carrying her trunk into the house, Eulalie hurried on to her bedroom.

Dressed in the rose-colored silk, with her black hair pulled back in a smooth chignon, Eulalie sat in the dining room, opposite Robert.

The candles on the table flickered as the door from the butler's pantry opened.

Eulalie, expecting to see Bradley, gazed instead at the small black boy who struggled under the large silver tray. She watched his progress toward her. His silk turban, in palest ivory, set off the black satin of his skin, and his eyes shone brightly from his round face. He was wearing the lavender velvet suit she had made for him.

"Neijee," she said in surprise. "Your suit. You are wearing your new velvet suit."

"Yes, madame. You said I could wear it on special occasions."

"But today is not a special day, Neijee."

"I think to *him*, it is," Robert interrupted. "Have you not come home, Eulalie? Yes, I think it is a special day. Is it not?" Robert asked, addressing himself to the child.

"Yes, Mr. Tabor," the boy acknowledged.

Tears came to Eulalie's eyes as she helped herself from the tray that Neijee held before her.

"Welcome home, madame," the child's voice uttered.

"Thank you, Neijee."

Back and forth the child went, helping Bradley with the serving of the meal. And Eulalie, at the end of the table, sat quietly, eating her meal.

She should have been happy. She was at home with

Robert, Jason, Feena and Neijee. But her mind was uneasy, thinking of Florilla and wondering what the days ahead would bring.

Eulalie left the table and immediately went upstairs. It had been a long, soul-wearying day and she longed for the peace and quiet of the massive bed in the room that she had grown to think of as her own, even though she shared it with Robert.

Removing the silk dress, she hung it in the wardrobe and then sat down at the dressing table to remove the pins binding her long hair.

Automatically she reached for the boar's-bristle brush that she used every night, but it was not on the dressing table—only the silver-tipped one that she had used earlier before dinner.

It was in her valise, of course, still by the bed. With an exploring hand she reached inside, but the brush eluded her. In a hurry, she dumped the articles upon the bed and in relief she saw it. She had not left it at the last inn after all.

Staring down at the contents now lying helter-skelter over the coverlet, Eulalie looked for the pouch of gold nuggets that Julie had given her. It was not among the other things.

Frantically, she grabbed up the valise, turned it upside down, and shook it, but it was empty. There was no sign of the leather pouch.

"Are you looking for something in particular, Eulalie?"

"Yes, Robert. I had a . . . a gift from Julie. It was in my valise, but now it is gone." He walked toward the bed.

"Do you mean the leather pouch of gold nuggets, Eulalie?"

"How did you know?" Eulalie asked with a guilty expression replacing the anxiety.

"You forget. I was outside the door at Cedar Hill when Julie gave it to you."

Her mouth fell open at his confirmation. So he *had* seen the exchange.

"But do not worry, Eulalie. I took the liberty of placing it in the safe in the library as soon as we came home. That much gold should not be left lying around. It is too much of a temptation for someone to steal it."

"You put it in your safe?"

"Yes, Eulalie."

She did not thank him for his actions. Angry at his behavior, she said, "Robert, you had no right to take it from me."

It was his turn to display anger. "I have merely put it in a safe place. I have not taken it away from you, Eulalie. You have only to ask for it, when you think you need it."

His words did not reassure her. If she ever decided to leave, Robert would have to be the first to know. For she could not leave without the gold.

Feeling frustrated, she went behind the screen and removed her chemise. And as she struggled into her gown, she muttered under her breath.

"Did you say something, Eulalie?"

"No, Robert."

Robert had defeated her again. And not only by removing the gold from her valise.

She had not told him what she had suspected even before leaving for Cedar Hill—that she was *enceinte*. The same early-morning queasiness, the same wave of nausea at the sudden rounding of a curve when she was riding in the carriage had left no doubt. She was to bear Robert another child.

She was now bound to him more than ever, faced with having to stay on at Midgard, in the same house with Florilla, the woman Robert preferred.

But she could not stay, knowing that Jason was in danger. She would have to find some way of getting the gold nuggets out of the safe.

In the meantime, while she decided what to do, she and Feena would need to watch Jason carefully to make certain that Florilla did him no harm. It was a pity that the woman had not known that it was useless to hurt Jason. If she had been aware of the new babe, then Jason would not have been placed in such peril at Cedar Hill.

Of course! Why had she not thought of it? If Florilla

was told, then the danger would be transferred to Eulalie. And Jason would be safe.

But would Florilla inform Robert? Eulalie was not anxious for Robert to know. But would it not be to the woman's advantage to keep it a secret? Making up her mind, Eulalie walked from behind the screen and climbed into bed for the night.

Early on the following morning, Eulalie sought out Florilla. For Jason's sake she would have to remain outwardly calm in the woman's presence and not reveal the devastating mark that the taunting words, spoken at Cedar Hill, had left on her heart.

Walking down the hallway, Eulalie saw the fair-haired woman coming from her own bedroom adjacent to the nursery.

When Florilla saw Eulalie, she stopped short and stood fixed, while Eulalie approached her.

"Florilla, I need your help," Eulalie said, ignoring the surprised expression on the woman's face.

Florilla's eyes darted toward the closed door of the nursery and back again to Eulalie. "I was not aware that you were here," she said, continuing to scrutinize Eulalie. "And Jason?"

Eulalie frowned. Had Florilla not known that Robert was going to Cedar Hill to bring them back? But surely he had told the woman before leaving. What game was Florilla playing—to pretend that she did not know Robert's plans?

Dismissing the frown, Eulalie nodded. "Yes, Jason is here also. Feena took charge of him last night when we came home. He is probably being a sleepyhead this morning, after the long trip."

Casually, the girl came back to her primary purpose in seeking out the child's governess.

"Jason's baby clothes," she said. "The ones that came with him from the convent. Where are they stored, Florilla?"

"Why, in the attic, I believe, in one of the trunks. It was Marcey who laundered them and put them away when Jason outgrew them. Do you wish to see them?"

"I have need of them again," Eulalie replied. "Will you please see that they are brought down from the attic?"

Florilla, speechless for a moment, faltered, "There are . . . many other trunks in the attic. And since Marcey is no longer here, I might not be able to find the right one immediately. Do you wish to go with me to the attic?"

Remembering the narrow, dangerous stairs to the top floor, Eulalie shook her head. "Take one of the servants, Florilla. I dare not climb the steep stairs in my condition."

"Does Robert know yet?" Florilla asked.

Eulalie forced a smile to her lips. "Not yet. It is a little too early to inform him."

Eulalie turned from the woman and started walking to the master bedroom. "Oh, yes," she said, pausing to speak again. "When you find the trunk, just have someone bring it down to my old bedroom in the other wing."

She trembled as she closed the door to the room she shared with Robert, and catching sight of the comforting prie-dieu in the corner, she went to kneel on the soft blue cushion.

So she had done it. Now, perhaps, Jason would be safe for a while, and the danger transferred to her.

Her lips began to move in prayer. Eulalie's hands slowly relaxed their tense position against her breast and the trembling of her body gradually ceased.

Robert watched Eulalie carefully, hoping for some sign of her being with child again. But so far, there had been no indication—merely a shortness of temper, especially when Florilla's name was mentioned.

It was noticeable, even to him, that Eulalie avoided Florilla as much as possible. She was probably still miffed that the woman had come to him about Arthur. But he was grateful to Florilla. If it had not been for her, he might never have suspected what was blossoming between Eulalie and Arthur. And by the time he had caught wind of it, it might have been too late. Except for the mistake she had made about Alistair Ashe, Florilla had been quite reliable.

Eulalie would just have to become reconciled to having the woman around. For Robert intended for Florilla to be kept busy, helping to care for other children. And it would be good for Eulalie not to think that she could have her way with *him* all the time—that with just a look from her, he could be forced into satisfying her every whim, even to getting rid of Jason's governess, because of her tattling to him about Eulalie's behavior with Arthur.

No, Florilla would do very well. And Eulalie, with less responsibility, would be able to spend more time with her own husband.

In the midst of packing supplies for his trip to Tabor Island, Robert paused. There was nothing to prevent Eulalie from accompanying him this time. With each trip he had become increasingly charmed with the wild, untamed beauty of the island. And he knew Eulalie would enjoy seeing it too—the beach, the old lighthouse, the improvements he had made on the tabby house. And there was little danger that the blockade ship would weigh anchor near the island.

Abruptly Robert ceased his packing and went in search of his wife. "Eulalie," he called, walking up the stairs toward the west wing of the house.

Working in the privacy of the bedroom that had been hers before Robert married her, Eulalie had begun the repairing of the baby clothes that Jason had worn. Handling the tiny garments that the sisters had lovingly made at the convent brought back all the pain of the months before Jason's birth.

Robert's voice penetrated the closed door of the bedroom. Quickly, Eulalie put down the soft material on which she was sewing and opened the door to the hallway.

He frowned when he saw her. What was Eulalie doing in her old room? The guilty look on her face told him that she was keeping something from him. Because of it, he was more determined than ever for her to go with him to the island.

"What is it, Robert?" Eulalie asked, closing the door and standing in the open hallway.

"I am leaving for Tabor Island tomorrow. And I want you to accompany me."

"For how long?" she asked. "I have been busier than usual."

She was not anxious to be with him again, away from Feena and Jason. Besides still being miffed at him for taking the gold nuggets, she was afraid that the trip by boat might give her secret away, and she hoped to keep it from him as long as possible.

"For a few days. The weather appears to be nice. It should be a smooth, pleasant trip on the water," Robert responded. "You are not afraid, are you, because of Joseph's wife and the storm?"

"Of course not, Robert. I am not afraid of the water. When do you plan to leave?"

"Tomorrow morning."

"I'll be ready."

"Good."

"But I am not a good traveler," she warned.

The sparkling blue water, edged with a garland of white foam, made small slaps against the boat.

Blowing the hood of Eulalie's cap from her head, a gust of wind with its airy fingers tore her carefully demure chignon to shreds, so that her long, black wavy hair lifted above her like wings of a bird spread for flight.

"You resemble the figurehead on some proud Viking ship," Robert shouted above the sound of the sea.

Just then a large wave spewed over them, and Eulalie felt the salt spray on her face. She shrank from the wetness and quickly dabbed her face with her handkerchief. Disgruntled, Eulalie replied, "And I *feel* like some poor maiden lashed to the prow, soaked with every wave."

"Today it's quite calm in comparison to many trips I've made." His tone was reassuring.

"If this is calm, then I have no desire to be on the water when you consider it rough."

The motion was disturbing, and Eulalie felt the old familiar queasiness.

"Robert," she said. "I . . . I warned you yesterday. I am not a good sea traveler. I think I am going to—"

She barely made it to the side of the boat. And as she leaned over, she heard Robert's laugh.

Then he was beside her, holding her head. A few minutes later, feeling disgraced and wan, Eulalie tried to free herself from Robert's embrace, but he continued supporting her with his strong arms. Unable to move away from him, she buried her face against his chest and determined not to look at him.

"Do you always react this way, Eulalie?" he asked gently.

"Only when I'm—" She stopped and sighed. She had almost given herself away.

"It won't be much longer. Matthew will have us on the island soon."

Remaining in his arms, she listened to the strong pulse of his heart. And then she was being lifted from the boat and set onto the pier.

"Do you think you can make it, now that you're on land?"

"Yes, certainly. There is nothing wrong with me," she replied haughtily, glancing at Robert for the first time.

"Then why are you still green, my pet?" he asked with an amused twinkle in his tawny eyes.

His teasing infuriated her. "If I am green, it is all your fault. If you remember, you're the one who insisted I come."

"So I did," Robert admitted. "Once you have gotten your land legs, I think you will enjoy being on the island."

"I doubt it, monsieur," she said, walking unsteadily away from him.

Despite herself, she was drawn by the beauty of the island. Eulalie followed the path carefully laid out from the pier, and as she walked, she noted the unfamiliar green shrubbery and vegetation that had been pruned on either side.

Then the path divided, and Eulalie, uncertain in which direction to go, looked over her shoulder. But there was no sign of Robert.

Hesitating but a moment, she turned left. Suddenly, the old tabby house rose before her in lonely splendor.

Seeing it, Eulalie threw off her cloak and ran toward the house. Up the steps she went, onto the open tabby porch. She reached for the doorknob and it twisted noisily in her hands. She was so intent upon getting inside that she was barely aware that the house was not locked.

Slowly and almost reverently, she pushed open the door and walked into the deserted entrance. And once inside, she paused—as the strange feeling swept over her. She had been here before.

But that was impossible. Papa Ravenal had never brought her to the island—merely talked about it. Yes, that must be it. She had recognized the house from his description.

Eulalie hurried from room to room, seeing the evidence of the recent care the tabby structure had received from Robert's hands. And then she was up the steps, into a large open room. Looking out the window, she could see the pale-blue water that now looked placid and smooth from a distance.

"I see you had no trouble finding it."

Robert's voice behind her caused her to jump in fright. She had been so absorbed in her own thoughts she had not heard his footsteps.

"Robert," she said, turning to him, "is . . . is anyone else in the house?"

"Not for the moment. Hector is still at the lighthouse, but he will return in time for dinner."

"Am I expected to cook?" she asked, uncertain of Robert's reason for bringing her with him.

In amusement he replied, "No, Eulalie. I brought you here to enjoy the island—not to work. And I don't think the cook would appreciate your taking his job away from him."

Relieved at his reply, Eulalie said, "How long will Hector be here?"

"For three more days, until Arthur comes to replace him. But of course, we will have left by then."

"You are only staying three days?"

"Two days," he corrected. "You don't think I would

be fool enough to throw you and Arthur together again, do you?"

"*Throw* us together?" Eulalie repeated, feeling her anger against Robert growing.

"Yes. There will be no more secluded dinners with just the two of you, while I am on duty at the lighthouse. . . . Where are you going, Eulalie?"

"To the beach," she replied, "unless I have been forbidden *that*, too."

He did not respond to her gibe. Instead, he questioned, "You are feeling better?"

But Eulalie, peeved with Robert, hastened out the door without replying. Down the steps she went, retracing her course, until she had reached the divided path. She did not want to go back to the pier. So she took the opposite way—anywhere that she could escape. Florilla had sown the seeds well.

CHAPTER

30

HE found her on the beach. In utter relaxation, Eulalie stood, shoeless, her skirts tucked up and slightly damp.

She had evidently been wading along the edge of the water, and now she held a conch shell to her ear, listening.

The sun shone down on her tousled hair, capturing the sheen of the blue-black strands. Again Robert was reminded of the grace of the beautiful doe poised in a silent stillness, unaware of being watched.

Reluctant to disturb the picture before him, Robert stopped and gazed at the girl. Oblivious to everything else, Eulalie pirouetted, still holding the conch shell to her ear.

Her slight intake of breath and the fleeting frown indicated that she had seen him. And Robert was sorry at her reaction to him.

Speaking more severely than her offense warranted, he said, "It is not yet summer, Eulalie. Put your shoes on before you catch cold."

As if embarrassed to be caught without warning and reprimanded, she cast her eyes to the shoes waiting on the large gray rock, and hurriedly let down her skirts, while clinging to the shell with one hand.

He was at the rock before she reached it. And Eulalie found herself aided by strong arms and set upon the boulder where her shoes rested.

She stared at him strangely while he brushed the sand from the soles of her feet and then fastened the buttons of her slippers to encase her feet in the soft kid.

The wind began to blow from the sea—a sudden change from the pastoral quietness that Eulalie had enjoyed before Robert's appearance. Jumping from her perch on the rock, she felt the sharp buffeting of the sea breeze against her body. Her skirts rippled and billowed in the wind. Robert, already on his way ahead, paid no attention to her difficulty with her skirts.

She was far behind when he looked back. The sudden gust of wind made a sail of her skirts, and as she struggled to grab the flyaway material, Eulalie lost hold on the delicately fluted conch shell. It fell onto the hard-packed sand and, landing on its thin, translucent edge, broke into pieces.

Rapidly, Robert walked back to the girl.

"My shell—my beautiful shell," she lamented, her dark-brown eyes showing her distress. "I had wanted to take it to Jason, but now it's broken." She stared ruefully at the pieces at her feet.

Gentleness swept Robert's face. "I will help you find another one tomorrow, Eulalie."

"You will?" she questioned eagerly, looking up. "Do you think we will find one just as beautiful?"

"Even more so," Robert promised. "I'll take you to the lighthouse tomorrow and you'll be able to gather shells all along the way."

He drew her close to protect her from the wind, and unprotesting, Eulalie walked with him back to the tabby house.

That evening, Eulalie dressed for dinner in the yellow moiré high-waisted gown that Maggie had made for her. It concealed the slight thickening of her figure. But to make certain there were no telltale signs, she draped the matching yellow fringed shawl over her shoulders and tied the ends loosely in front. She gave one last glance in the half-length mirror before walking down the steps.

She followed the sound of men's voices coming from the front part of the house.

In the doorway she stood framed by the last light of the dwindling day, and Robert, seeing her, could find no evidence of the disheveled child from the beach. Before him was an elegantly clad woman, her hair in classical restraint, with no hint of its earlier unruliness.

When Hector saw Eulalie, he stepped forward to greet her. "My dear, what a pleasant surprise."

The other member of the militia also stood and waited to be introduced to Robert's wife. And soon the four of them were seated at the dining table together.

"Did Robert recruit you to take your turn at the lighthouse?" Hector asked Eulalie while helping himself to the meat before him.

Eulalie wrinkled her nose and laughed at his question. But Robert answered for her.

"No, Hector. Eulalie would be a detriment to the entire militia."

She glanced quickly at Robert with a displeased look. "Although I have no wish to be on watch, Robert, I cannot believe that the island or harbor would be any less safe if *I* were on duty to watch for the British ships."

"Perhaps *some* women would be effective," Robert admitted in his teasing manner. "But what would *you* do, Eulalie, if a British ship anchored here? Could you take up arms and defeat the enemy?"

The younger militiaman gallantly interceded in Eulalie's behalf. "If the British were met by someone as beautiful as Mrs. Tabor, I believe they would lay down their arms and surrender willingly."

Hector's laugh filled the dining room. "Then we had best let her take *your* turn tonight, Robert, since there are so few of us."

"You are on duty tonight at the lighthouse?" Eulalie bent toward Robert with the question on her lips.

"Just for a few hours. Long enough for Tom to come back for dinner and the others to get some rest."

It was nearly eleven o'clock by the time Robert returned from the lighthouse. Eulalie was still awake, listening to the sounds in the house. She was uneasy with Robert gone, even though she knew that Hector and the other two were both nearby.

As the door to the bedroom quietly opened, the candle by the bedside table flickered and Eulalie sat up.

"I had thought you would be asleep by this time," Robert said in surprise.

"I could not sleep," Eulalie admitted. "There are too many noises in the house."

Suddenly Robert grinned. "Then you can get up and help me find something to eat. I am ravenously hungry."

"I thought you said I didn't have to cook," she reminded him with a feigned pout.

"Woman, I have changed my mind. If the cupboard is bare, then you will have to come up with something."

"Mayhaps I can find some old bone to assuage your hunger." Eulalie giggled as she climbed out of bed.

He held the robe for her to put on and, catching its ribbons, he drew her close to him.

"It will take more than a bone to assuage my hunger tonight," he replied.

She looked up at him, but his teasing eyes told her nothing. Walking ahead of him with the bedside candle in her hand, Eulalie hesitated when she reached the downstairs hall. Which way was the kitchen? She had not ventured that far earlier.

"To the right, Eulalie," Robert advised her, seeing her pause.

She found the meat left over from dinner and cut a large chunk of it. With bread and honey and a glass of wine, Robert settled down to eat.

Eulalie sat at the old refectory table with Robert, watching him. The candle at her elbow made a sputtering sound and Eulalie put her hand up to shield the flame from the draft that passed through the room.

Eulalie shivered, and as she did so, she drew her robe closer to her body.

"Do you have a feeling that someone else is in this house?"

"You mean other than Hector and Tom?"

"Yes."

Robert laughed. "It could be the ghost of one of the friars from the old mission. Uncle Ravenal claims to have heard him several times. Perhaps the friar is hungry tonight, too."

"Now you are making fun of me," Eulalie complained.

"Would it be so surprising," he continued, ignoring her comment, "since we're in the only original part of the mission? Perhaps he was not hungry, only thirsty, and has merely gone into the spring room for water." He indicated the closed door, sealed by a long bar of wood across it, at the opposite end of the kitchen.

She did not like his teasing, and Eulalie stood, ready to depart with the candle. But he reached out and brought her to his lap instead. She pushed against him, but Robert would not let her go. Instead he kept her close to him while finishing the second glass of wine. And when the liquid was gone, he set the goblet down and gave her his total attention. Robert began to stroke the long dark hair, while his eyes traveled up to her face and then started their slow, wicked trail down the length of her body.

Caught like a hare in a trap, she could do nothing while his left hand moved intimately across her body.

"You are getting plumper, Eulalie," he stated. "Is there . . . a particular reason for it?"

Quickly she shook her head. "No reason, except that I have been eating more than usual."

At her answer, she veiled her eyes from him and, worrying the ribbons of her robe, hoped that he would not pursue the subject further.

Robert's hand stopped its caressing as he set her from him. His tawny eyes were unfathomable. What was he thinking? Did he suspect?

While they walked together up the stairs, Robert was silent, intent on guarding the meager light of the candle.

"You had enough to eat, Robert?" Eulalie asked, somehow anxious to break the silence between them.

"Yes, at least for the time being," he replied. Then, staring down at her from his great height, he added, "But I have another hunger that needs to be appeased."

There was no doubt what he meant when he looked at her in that way. She knew she would have to submit to his intense lovemaking, but this time in the strange tabby house that echoed the memories of earlier times. . . .

Robert kept his promise the next day and took her along the beach toward the old lighthouse. Before they reached the end of the island where the lighthouse jutted against the viridian sky, he pointed out the cache of seashells that had been washed ashore by the strong waves and left to air in the sun.

She was delighted at the vast number from which to choose. Eulalie picked up each one, turning it over in her hands, and when she found an imperfection, she discarded the shell for another one. Soon she had a collection of perfect specimens to take back to Midgard with her—large fluted ones, with their pink linings hidden under the slight coating of sand. Eulalie took her fingers and rubbed away the sand, revealing the smooth, convoluted texture of sea pearl.

The cries of the sea gulls overhead signaling others to join them in formation cut through the quiet air. Eulalie watched in fascination as they joined forces and flew toward the sea, only to divide again and go their separate ways back to land.

And although the blockade ship came into view on the far line of the horizon, Eulalie felt at peace on the island—and safe. It was too bad that Jason and Neijee were not with her to enjoy the beach. But they would be happy to get the shells that she carefully placed in the crate Robert had provided for her.

When it was time to leave, Eulalie did not want to go. But she obediently packed her valise and saw to the crate of carefully wrapped shells.

Matthew waited for them at the pier, and Eulalie, after saying goodbye to Hector, climbed into the boat, with Robert's help, and the watery journey began.

Robert stood in the prow of the boat, looking out over the water. Then he turned to Eulalie. "Before going back to Midgard, Eulalie, I plan to stop in Charleston for a day or so. Would you like to go to the theater while we are there?"

Eulalie's eyes lit up at his suggestion. She remembered the few times she had gone to the theater while living in New Orleans, but she had never seen a play in Charleston.

"Oh yes, Robert. I would enjoy it very much." Then her eyes clouded. "But I did not bring anything suitable to wear to the theater. I would have to send to Midgard for something, if there is enough time."

"That will not be necessary," Robert replied. "There are any number of shops in Charleston from which to choose."

"But that would be expensive, getting a gown just to wear one time. And I do not actually need another gown."

"No woman has too many beautiful gowns, Eulalie. And I have not taken you shopping for clothes since we left Columbia."

"Where will we stay?" Eulalie asked, now curious of their immediate destination.

"At the townhouse," Robert answered.

"You have a townhouse?"

"*We* have a townhouse. On Tradd Street. I purchased it several years ago after I brought Jason home from New Orleans."

She did not ask any more questions, and Robert watched her carefully and indulgently, wondering if her quietness was a prelude to her becoming seasick again. But this time, Eulalie managed well.

The water was placid, almost like spun glass, with streaks of white interspersed in the blue, and although the wind tugged at the dark-eyed girl, ruffling her hair and skirts, for Eulalie the trip was uneventful.

Soon they were tied up at the wharf near the warehouses that held the cotton and rice waiting to be slipped through the blockade.

While Robert went to the carriage stand to hire a vehicle to take them to the townhouse, Eulalie stood alone on the wharf.

"Eulalie—Eulalie."

She recognized Arthur's voice at once. With a smile she turned to face the man and watched while his quick strides voided the distance between them.

"Arthur, how good to see you." In delight she gazed at the sandy-haired man, but he did not return her smile. With a seriousness he reached out, took her hand and held it to his lips before Eulalie, with Robert's threat ringing in her ears, suddenly felt guilty at the encounter. She pulled back, letting her hand drop to her side.

"Robert and I have just come from the island. It's beautiful—but you know that already, don't you, since you saw it before I did."

"He came for you at Cedar Hill, didn't he?" Arthur accused, ignoring her comments about the island.

Eulalie's face showed a sadness. "Arthur," she cautioned, but she got no further, for the clatter of wheels on the dockside told her that Robert had arrived to collect her.

Arthur stood his ground when he saw Robert coming toward them. But Eulalie, noting the stormy look on Robert's face, took a step backward, away from him.

She felt uncomfortable to be the cause of this enmity between friends. But there was nothing she could do to counteract the feeling. Had Robert not left her alone on the wharf, with only Matthew to keep an eye out for her? Did he think she was responsible for Arthur's coming along at that particular time? No. If Robert wanted to make something of it, then let him. Her chin lifted, but she held her breath, waiting for Robert to speak.

"You are on your way to the island, Arthur?"

Robert's voice sounded normal and pleasant, and Eulalie, relieved, breathed easier.

"Yes, Robert. I understand from Eulalie that you both have just come from there. Anything you need to tell me before I shove off?"

"No. Hector will fill you in on the happenings. Sir George is still busy, harassing the poor townspeople around Hampton Roads with his rocket ships, so he should not come back this way anytime soon. You should have an easy watch."

Robert hurriedly put his hand under Eulalie's elbow and directed her to the carriage. Waving to Arthur in a final goodbye, he lifted Eulalie into the carriage and gave the driver a signal to depart.

CHAPTER

31

"WHO is Sir George?" Eulalie asked before the carriage had gone far.

"Sir George Cockburn, the plague of the coast," Robert explained. "He is in charge of the British ships of the line. He has a habit of scaring off untrained state militia with his Congreve rockets, and then sending marauding parties inland to plunder and burn the farmhouses and make off with the livestock."

His voice had gotten progressively harsher, and Eulalie watched the change on Robert's face.

"But if I can help it, he will do no such thing from the Charleston harbor."

"Was it *his* men who raided Midgard?"

"In all likelihood."

Robert silently fumed, remembering the capture of his ship—by Sir George's hands. That was degrading enough, without the stripping of his plantation as well. Had the man known whose land it was? Or was it coincidence that the one responsible for putting him in irons in the *Carolana* was also answerable for the plundering of Midgard?

"The man was also responsible for our marriage, Eulalie."

In surprise she looked up at him, waiting for him to clarify the words he had spoken.

"How . . . how was that?" she asked, unable to disguise the quiver in her voice.

"He confiscated my ship, the *Carolana*."

"Then you must dislike him intensely."

"I do," he confirmed.

The beauty of the day no longer mattered to Eulalie. And the time spent with Robert on the island became a shattered dream at her feet—like the broken pieces of the beautiful conch shell.

No wonder Robert had shown such determination in his repair of the lighthouse and setting up a watch for the British ships. He had a personal vendetta against the man who had cost him so much—his ship and his freedom.

And Eulalie, hurt by Robert's words, huddled in the corner of the carriage and closed her eyes, so that her husband could not see the tears threatening to spill. "He never wanted to marry you, you know." She could not get Florilla's words out of her mind. For had not Robert confirmed it himself?

And yet she was to bear him another child—in a loveless marriage. A marriage he had been forced into. And she was helpless to do anything about it, except to remain silent about her own love for him. She had tried not to love him, not to spend her days thinking of him. Yet everywhere she turned, she was reminded of him. When she looked at Jason, he was there. And when she tried to pray for Jacques Binet, she saw only Robert's face. Even kneeling on the cushioned prie-dieu, she remembered that Robert was the one who had given it to her.

When she encountered Florilla, she saw before her the woman who would have been Robert's wife if she had not been summoned from the convent to care for Jason. And worst of all, she could not forget the time spent in the river house with Robert's making love to her, and all the time, planning to sell her. . . .

The carriage stopped and Robert touched Eulalie on the shoulder. "Are you asleep?" he asked.

Averting her face, she sat up quickly, brushing her hand across her eyes.

"No, Robert," she answered in a soft whisper, "only tired."

Robert looked at the small figure beside him. In the short time since they had arrived by boat from the island, the spark had gone out of Eulalie. Was she thinking of Arthur, whom she had met on the wharf?

His face was set as he paid the driver and then walked with Eulalie to the door.

The two servants, alerted that he was coming, had hurriedly removed the white dust covers from the furniture and were now taking fresh linen to the master bedroom.

"After you have rested, I will take you into town."

"Would you mind if I did not go to the theater with you tonight, Robert?"

"Of course I mind, Eulalie." He gazed at her, but her face was a mask, revealing nothing to him. "Why this sudden change? You were eager enough when I first mentioned it." Robert loomed over her, and in an intimidating voice, he questioned, "Did seeing Arthur make you change your mind? Tell me, Eulalie. Are you pining so for his company that you have no wish to share an evening with your husband?"

The shake of her head gave quick denial to his accusation.

"Then let's say no more about it. I will come back for you in an hour."

Abruptly he spun around and made for the door, leaving her to find her own way in the townhouse.

She took an instant dislike to the townhouse. Set in the narrow street between two similar houses, it gave her a feeling of being closed in, especially after the stately wide expanse of the island with its beautiful view of the sea and sky.

Looking out the window, Eulalie could see no farther than the house directly across the street. There was little lawn, little greenery—nothing to interest her in the view.

And as she climbed the stairs to look for the bedroom, she hesitated at the first door that was open—the salon

291

on the second floor, with its rigid, delicate-looking furniture. How different from the comfortable old blue velvet chairs in the drawing room at Midgard. Not a single seat looked as if it would hold Robert's massive frame. Had he bought the furniture with the house?

Eulalie walked on, stopping at the bedroom beyond, but her valise was nowhere in sight. Just then the black servant appeared, and seeing Eulalie's hesitation, she said, "That's Miss Florilla's room, ma'am. Mr. Robert's is on down the hall. I'll take you there now, ma'am, if you'd like."

"Yes, please," Eulalie answered, feeling a stranger in Robert's townhouse.

Within the hour, Eulalie had changed clothes and was ready when she heard the front door open.

The horses waited impatiently on the street side, and Robert wasted no time in collecting Eulalie and seeing her into the carriage. It evidently had not entered his mind that she might not be ready when he had specified.

Did no one dare to balk at his commands? One day—just one day—he would not have his own way. But Eulalie, sighing, knew she had no strength left to defy him, for the present.

It was late afternoon and the streets were quiet; the calls of the Gullahs selling their wares of shrimp and fish and early spring vegetables had ceased. Instead their empty carts rolled along the cobblestones as they headed silently for home and rest. All too soon, their street cries would be repeated at the rising of the sun, to announce fresh wares for another new day.

The carriage drew up to a dress shop on a side street, and Robert delivered Eulalie into the hands of a Mrs. Windom.

"She knows what you need, Eulalie. And has promised to have the gown ready in time to wear tonight."

Robert took out the pocket watch she had given him at Christmas, looked at it and then snapped it shut. "I will be at the Exchange until five o'clock. If you finish earlier than expected, send a boy for me."

"You're not staying?" she asked.

"No, Eulalie. Mrs. Windom does not encourage husbands to remain in the shop while their wives are being fitted."

She gazed at the back of his golden head and watched him walk into the street.

"My dear, come with me. I have a lovely gown that should be just the thing you need."

Eulalie swung around to meet the interested eyes of the gray-haired woman, and she followed her to the back dressing room, where the pale gown of shimmering green was hanging.

"With your coloring, this gown should be quite effective. And it has a matching turban, as well." Peering into her face, the woman said, "Have you been in the sun, my dear?"

"Yes," Eulalie admitted. "Robert and I spent the past several days on Tabor Island."

The woman clucked her tongue in dismay. "That is asking for trouble. You must always shield your face. It wouldn't do *at all* to lose your complexion to the sun. Luckily, you have done little damage so far. But remind me to give you my cucumber-and-cream recipe for your face before you leave. Now, let's see to the dress."

The bell attached to the door gave a jingling sound, indicating another customer had come into the shop.

Mrs. Windom finished helping Eulalie place the dress over her head, and then she said, "I'll only be a moment. Let me see who has come in and I'll be back to fit you."

The woman left the small dressing room and Eulalie stood looking in the mirror at the pale-green gown. The ruch-trimmed back was cut in a V shape just below her shoulders. But Eulalie, holding the dress together, could not tell how it looked, until the woman returned to fasten it.

"Oh, Mrs. Ashe, how good to see you. I had not expected you until tomorrow."

"I could not resist coming in earlier, Mrs. Windom, to see if my new gown is ready."

Eulalie's face turned pale when she heard the name. There was no mistake. And the voice—Polly Ashe. It was Alistair Ashe's wife, here in the same shop.

"If you will have a seat, I'll be with you soon. I'm

the only one in the shop this afternoon, and I have promised Mr. Tabor to have his wife's gown fitted in time to wear to the theater. But it shouldn't take long."

"Robert Tabor? His wife?" Polly Ashe gave a harsh laugh. "You mean his slave, don't you, Mrs. Windom?"

"I don't understand, Mrs. Ashe. What is it you're saying?" the puzzled voice of Mrs. Windom responded.

"Does she have dark hair and brown satin eyes?"

"Yes—and very petite."

"Then that is the one. Surely you know the story, Mrs. Windom—of the slavegirl, Lili, that Robert Tabor lives with."

"There must be some mistake, Mrs. Ashe. He introduced the girl as his wife."

"Heaven help me, I should know what I'm talking about. Robert Tabor killed my husband because of her."

Eulalie, heartsick, did not wait to hear more. She dropped the pale-green gown to the floor and hastily put on her own dress. And as the sound of voices grew dimmer, she slipped from the dressing room and hurried to the street, the little bell giving a jingle as the door closed.

The Exchange—Robert said he would be at the Exchange. Eulalie looked up and down the street. She had no idea where the Exchange was located. And she could not stand in front of the shop, waiting for Robert, with Polly Ashe inside.

She started down the street, trying to remember the route the horses had taken. Three blocks and then a turn to the right—no, to the left. She hurried on, walking several more blocks, but the surroundings became increasingly unfamiliar. Confused, she stopped, turned around and retraced her steps, heading in the direction from which she had just come.

Again she found herself at the intersection of streets. This time Eulalie turned right, and two blocks farther down, she finally spied the sign that read "Tradd Street." A vast relief swept over her. Now she could get back to the townhouse and safety.

Her breath came in gasps, but still she hurried on, ignoring the sounds of a carriage behind her, until the high stone steps and wrought-iron railing of Robert's house suddenly appeared in front.

She reached out to grasp the railing, to walk up the steps that seemed to be moving in ripples before her. The house, at a strange angle, gave no welcome, but receded from her view, lost in the grayness that gradually spread over her like a mantle.

"Eulalie!"

"It is not surprising for a woman in her condition to have a fainting spell. There is no cause for alarm, Mr. Tabor."

The man's voice startled her, for Eulalie did not know where she was. She only remembered running from something. Then Robert's familiar gruff voice projected across the distance. And with it, an awareness of where she was—in the townhouse, with the soft bed cradling her tired body.

"I suspected as much," Robert said. "But she said nothing about it to me."

"A wife usually likes to keep it to herself for a while. Nine months is a long time to be fussed over. . . . You have other children, Mr. Tabor?"

"A son, Jason."

"And she had no trouble at that birth?"

Robert hesitated. "She became ill with fever almost immediately afterward."

"But survived. A strong constitution, no doubt. No—I think you are worrying unnecessarily, but if you would like me to see her at any time during the next months, I shall be happy to do so. Ah, I see she's coming around."

Eulalie opened her eyes and two men were gazing down at her. One was Robert, his tawny eyes showing concern.

"Well, my dear, you gave your husband a giant scare, fainting away as you did," the stranger confided. "But I have assured him it's quite normal, when one is expecting a child. Just rest for the next several days. Don't exert yourself. Do only what you feel like doing—and no more."

The man started toward the door, and Robert, walking partway with him, assured him, "I'll see to it that she gets enough rest."

Eulalie, lying very still, was the subject of Robert's quiet scrutiny. Tenderness welled up in him—and a feeling of triumph. She was bound to him more closely now, and at least for the next year, it would be almost impossible for her to leave him. This was what he had hoped for—to give her something more than Arthur to think about and plan for.

But he would have to be more tolerant of her sudden whims and desires, he decided.

Smiling at her, Robert said, "You seem to have gotten your way, Eulalie. The theater will have to do without us tonight."

"But Robert, if you wish to go . . ."

"Not without my wife, Eulalie. No, we will both stay in tonight. I, if for no other reason than to see that you get the proper rest."

And so they stayed in that night, with Robert seeing to Eulalie's comfort. He did not question her about her running away from the dress shop. He could see that she was upset, and he knew it would not be good for the child to upset her further. No, he would have to find out later what had happened, when she had had more time to calm herself.

"I suppose you will be seeing to the baby clothes, and anything else you need?"

"Yes. I have already started repairing Jason's clothes that the sisters made for him." She looked up, tugging at her lip and watching for his reaction to her confession.

"In your old bedroom? Is that what you were doing in the west wing?" He grinned at her, waiting for her answer.

"Yes."

"You do not have to use Jason's hand-me-downs, Eulalie," he said in a more serious voice. "If you wish, while we are still here in town, you can shop for the new babe—that is, when you feel better."

The shake of her head was vigorous. "I have no wish

to do any shopping. Jason's clothes will be more than adequate."

Puzzled at her reaction, Robert did not press the matter. Eventually, he would find out what had caused her to shun the shops in Charleston.

CHAPTER

32

T WO days later, Robert took Eulalie back to Midgard. And Eulalie, happy to be with Jason and Neijee again, unpacked the crate of shells to give to the two little boys.

With their happy warblings still sounding in his ears, Robert left the plantation almost immediately to see to the cotton mill at Taborville. He did not ask Eulalie to go with him this time. It would not be good for her to travel the rough road or to visit the school because of the misunderstanding that had taken place on the previous visit.

Jessie could manage until summer, and by fall, Robert would have hired a trained teacher. Now there was no need for Eulalie to be concerned with the school, for she had the new child to think about.

He felt smug at his success in getting her with child. Traveling along the road to the mill, Robert began to think about other arrangements for his family for the summer. He had planned to take them to Flat Rock before the malaria season started, but that would have to be changed, since Eulalie could not travel the distance in her delicate condition.

They would stay in the townhouse in Charleston,

Robert decided. It would be better that way, with Eulalie close to the doctor if she needed to be seen.

All afternoon Robert's mind was only partially on the mill and Ebenezer Shaw's report. Strange, that having been with his wife constantly for the past week he should be so impatient to finish his inspection and get back to Midgard and Eulalie.

It had been a long day, and traveling down Biffers Road on the last lap of his journey, Robert felt tired. It would be good to sleep in his bed that night. He was looking forward to a good dinner, some brandy to remove the dust from his throat and a decent night's sleep.

The movement in the bog caught his eye as his horse passed by. He stopped, trying to detect what it was. An alligator, foraging for food after its winter's hibernation? Or was it a slave, surreptitiously treading through the swamp?

Robert listened, and dimly across the bog came the sound of drums—voodoo drums. So that was it. In his absence, it had started up again. Was Feena responsible? He would have to put a stop to it before it got out of hand.

He galloped the rest of the way to the stables, handed his horse over to the waiting groom and hurried on into the house.

Florilla, lingering at the entrance to the side piazza, confirmed his suspicions. The slaves, called by Feena, had slipped from their cabins and were now gathering in the bog, under the cold moon.

A deep scowl marred his face as Robert went down the hall to the alcove next to the library, where the hip boots, designed to protect him from the snake-infested waters, were stored.

At the noise downstairs, Eulalie left the nursery, where Jason had fallen asleep. The front door closed with a slam, and Eulalie, expecting to meet her husband coming home, bumped into Florilla instead.

"I thought I heard Robert," Eulalie said. "Has he not come home?"

"Yes, and gone out again," the fair-haired woman responded. "He heard the voodoo drums and has gone to the bog to put a stop to it. Feena is *really* in trouble this time," she gloated.

"He went on foot?"

"Yes."

Eulalie was suddenly afraid for Feena. Why couldn't the black woman leave well enough alone, knowing that Robert would have no hesitation in selling her if she disobeyed him for the second time?

If that happened, Eulalie would have no one left at Midgard to protect her—or to love her, except for Jason and Neijee. And a child's love, sweet as it was, was not sufficient protection against a sly, determined woman.

Up the stairs Eulalie flew, leaving Florilla standing in the hall. And riffling through the wardrobe, she pulled out the black serviceable cloak she had worn from the convent. If she could get to Feena in time to warn her before Robert found her . . .

There was no way she could reach the black woman on foot before Robert. Her only chance of success lay in getting a horse from the stables and riding through the bog.

With the black cloak flapping against her legs, she ran to the stables. Thunderbolt, whom Robert had ridden to Taborville, was still tied to the post, waiting for his rubdown by the groom. Grabbing the lantern hanging on the rough wall nearby, she mounted the horse and left the enclosure.

Along the northern edge of the bog Eulalie rode, the lantern swinging dangerously close to her cloak. Then she plunged into the water, and the vegetation overhead closed in, obliterating the cold white moon.

The voodoo drums, their sound magnified over the water, acted as a guide. Following the hypnotic beat of the drums, Eulalie rode deeper and deeper into the bog, the horse sinking to his knees in the black mire.

Wisps of Spanish moss, hanging from the grotesque cypress trees, brushed across Eulalie's face, but intent on getting to Feena, she paid little heed except to brush them impatiently aside, urging the horse onward. And the cypress knees, jutting from the bases of the trees, stood guard over the watery domain—gruesome, frightening.

With the steady dropping of temperature, the mist of the bog thickened, until it began to rise in layers—floating banshees lured by unseen forces. The layers floated together and then separated, and when they came apart, Eulalie saw the glow of fire in the distance.

The horse waded onto higher ground, but still with the mist completely surrounding her, Eulalie knew her only protection from being hopelessly lost in the bog was in keeping sight of the light and in following the sound of drums—to Feena.

Suddenly the mist cleared, and there before Eulalie, silhouetted by the fire, was the circle of slaves.

The horse whinnied. At the noise, the slaves looked up, their eyes wide with fright at the unexpected intrusion. They dispersed, running in all directions, until only Eulalie remained, staring at the fire.

"Feena," Eulalie croaked in a low voice. "Robert is coming. Hurry back to the house before he catches you."

Her voice was met by silence, and there was no movement in the darkness beyond the fire.

Again she called, louder. "Feena, hurry! Robert will be here soon."

Eulalie frowned at the continuing silence. Surely if Feena were anywhere near, she would have answered. Could it be that the woman had not come to the bog after all?

Eulalie, with the awareness of what she had done beginning to seep into her mind, felt an urgency to flee as the slaves had—from Robert.

But she could not leave the bonfire unattended. She would have to put it out so that it would not spread. There had been little rain, and a spark could easily set off an inferno, wiping out the entire plantation.

Eulalie dismounted, still holding onto the lantern. Setting it upon the ground, she led Thunderbolt to the nearest sapling and tied the reins around the tree. The horse snorted and nervously pawed the ground.

A stained bowl lay deserted near the fire. With a shudder, Eulalie picked it up, realizing she would have to use it to carry water to quench the fire.

She walked to the edge where the swampy land sank

lower, and there she dipped up the fetid, stagnant water and took it back to the bonfire site. Five trips she made, back and forth, throwing the bowls of water upon the wood that hissed at each sprinkling.

The fire was almost out. One more bowlful and then she could start home. Eulalie gathered her dark cloak closer to her in the dim light of the dying embers and shuddered at the stillness deep within the bog.

She would not think about going home alone—with the black waters surrounding her. Did she not have the lantern and Thunderbolt? She should be safe enough.

But if her husband should find out what she had done, how angry he would be. Thinking about it, she hurried to finish with the fire and leave.

Eulalie stood facing the embers, with the bowl of water in her hand. Strong arms came from nowhere, suddenly enveloping her in an iron-tight grip. Eulalie screamed in fright and dropped the bowl at her feet.

"I have caught you red-handed. This time, you will not get off so easily!"

His angry voice echoed through the bog, yet holding her as some felon, Robert still exuded strength and comfort to Eulalie.

"Robert," she managed to whisper.

In surprise, Robert loosened his grip and turned her around to face him. He picked up the lantern at his feet and held it toward her face.

"Eulalie!" he exclaimed, recognizing his wife. "In God's name, how did *you* get here?"

"On . . . on Thunderbolt."

The horse whinnied in impatience, and Robert glanced in the direction of the animal emerging from the darkness.

"Who told you I was coming after your woman, Feena? Or have you suddenly decided to take up voodoo as one of your less worthy accomplishments?"

He did not expect her to answer. And no explanation came from her lips.

Grim-faced, Robert set the lantern down and walked toward the horse. "Well, at least I will not have to traipse through the bog on foot."

He untied the horse and swung his leg across the stallion's flank, and Thunderbolt moved away from her.

Eulalie, picking up the lantern, called out, "Robert you are not leaving me alone in the bog?" Her voice shook and her dark eyes gazed imploringly after him.

Silently, he headed in her direction, and leaning over, Robert scooped her up in his powerful arms and set her in front of him on the horse.

"Make sure you hold onto the lantern, Eulalie. We will need its light to help us out of Emma's Bog."

A silent Robert made his way out of the bog, guiding Thunderbolt through the thick mist. And all around him, minute sounds of the living swamp called out, reminding him of its deathly beauty.

Eulalie sat within the curve of Robert's arm, her body leaning against his, while he held the reins with his other hand. The lantern bobbed easily up and down with each cautious step of the horse.

At the sudden appearance of an owl flying from his hollowed-out tree, Thunderbolt, with his ears already pricked at the unearthly sounds emanating around him, snorted in fright and abruptly edged sideways. The lantern swung out from Eulalie's hand, but she clutched it hard and steadied it.

"Easy, easy," Robert called to the horse, keeping a tight grip.

The owl, swooping past them, lowered itself into another tree, and when it had reached its destination, it hooted and ruffled its feathers, while its large yellow eyes followed the progress of the horse—the Hiddle-diddle-dee, a bad omen for the night, according to the slaves.

Thunderbolt quieted and the lantern once again assumed its slow, rhythmic swing in Eulalie's hands.

The night was one of frustration for Robert. He was hungry and tired, and he resented being in the middle of the swamp instead of sitting down to a good dinner. And then finding his own wife when he had expected Feena was a further frustration. It was providence that he had come along when he had, finding Eulalie at the voodoo site before she had started out of the swamp. It would have been almost impossible for her, with no fire to guide her. And Thunderbolt could easily have thrown her. Yet, he realized if he had not been in search of the black woman, Eulalie would have been safe at home. She would not have come except to save Feena from his wrath. Who had told her where he had gone?

Robert did not look forward to the confrontation with Eulalie when they reached Midgard. But he would have to make it clear to her, without upsetting her unduly, that she could not continue to shield everyone on the plantation from him.

With the black waters and weird sounds surrounding her, Eulalie felt suspended in time. The hours in the bog had no relevance for her. Only Robert's arms, holding her safe against the dangers that threatened her, were real. That and his anger, which, however well concealed in his voice, vibrated against her with each step of the horse.

Would he send them both away? Eulalie *and* Feena?

Thunderbolt, with the double weight on his back, finally climbed the small embankment of dirt onto the narrow road that led to Midgard. Robert loosened the reins, for the surefooted animal was anxious to return to the stables and needed no guidance.

Up the circular drive Robert rode, and at the steps of the low-country brick mansion, he deposited Eulalie and took the lantern from her.

For a moment she stood watching, while Robert veered out of sight. Now that it was over, Eulalie was reluctant to go inside, to await the cold, hard eyes of her husband.

The front door opened and Florilla looked disappointed, seeing the girl in her black cloak walking across the piazza.

"He caught her, did he not?" Florilla asked.

"You are speaking of Feena?"

"Of course. Who else?"

"No, Florilla. Robert did not find Feena."

"So you were able to warn her."

"Feena was not in the bog, Florilla," Eulalie countered.

Eulalie walked past the woman, but Florilla's words reached out to disturb her.

"Feena will not always be as lucky as she was tonight,

Mrs. Tabor. Robert will eventually catch her and give her the punishment she deserves."

Eulalie, with a dejection that enveloped her, went on to the master bedroom, where she rid herself of the stained black cloak.

The water in the ewer was cold, but Eulalie used it anyway, washing her face and hands and sponging the rest of her body quickly before putting on her gown.

Then she climbed into bed, and by the lamp glow she brushed her hair and waited. But Robert did not come.

Voices downstairs indicated that he was in the house. Perhaps he was just now sitting down to supper.

Eulalie's nerves were finely tuned with the waiting. Thinking of the scolding that was in store for her, she continued brushing her hair, on and on until her arms finally protested. The brush slipped from her fingers and, sighing, she lay back on the propped-up pillows and closed her eyes.

"Eulalie—" The voice was soft in her ear, unlike the harsh voice and terrible visage of her dreams.

The man touched her arm. "I am sorry to wake you, but we will have to talk before this night is over."

Drowsily, Eulalie struggled to open her eyes. The giant was bending over her, helping her to sit up.

"Are you awake?"

She nodded, but slumped against him, murmuring, "Feena wasn't there, Robert. She wasn't in the bog."

"You know it was wrong of you to try to get to her, to warn her. I want you to promise me, Eulalie, never to go into Emma's Bog again."

"That won't be hard to promise. I was so . . . frightened."

She shuddered and Robert quickly drew her in his arms to keep her warm. Her head drooped against his chest, with her long, dark hair spreading over his arms. And her eyes closed again.

"How can I stay angry with you when you will not even stay awake, Eulalie?"

Exasperated at his mildness, he released her, lowering her to the pillows, and then tucked the quilt around her.

Eulalie's breathing became even as she drifted deeper in sleep, and for a long time, Robert sat by the bed and stared at his wayward wife whom he could not even reprimand properly, as an irate husband should.

CHAPTER

33

"BUT Mamselle Lili, I was not in the bog last night," Feena protested when confronted by Eulalie the next day.

"Then where *were* you?" Eulalie questioned.

A bland expression glided across the black woman's features. "With Moses, mam'selle."

At her confession, Eulalie hurried on with her next question. "How did Florilla get the idea that you had gone to Emma's Bog?"

Feena's black eyes closed in a suspicious slit. "Miss Florilla knows that while I'm around, *ma petite,* it would be hard for her to do you harm. Maybe she is trying to cause trouble and get rid of me."

Eulalie nodded. She had not thought of that. But it was possible.

"Then you must be extremely careful, Feena, not to give Robert cause for . . . dismissing you."

"*Selling* me, you mean," Feena said with a snort. "But do not worry. I have no intention of being separated from you. Just make sure that you do not go off looking for me again because of something that hussy has said."

A subdued Eulalie kept close to the house. The experience in the bog had left its mark on her, and somehow she felt drained.

And ashamed too. Eulalie realized she must have gone to sleep while Robert was scolding her the evening before. All she could remember was being in his arms. And then the sun had come up, waking her.

What had Robert thought of her, behaving as she had? Would he find some way today to reprimand her for her lack of tears and contrition?

It was past lunchtime. Eulalie sat in the drawing room and waited for Robert to finish his work in the library. She was getting hungry and she hoped he would finish soon.

A pity that it was not already evening, when Florilla would be with them at the table. Then Robert would have to be polite. But the governess had eaten early with Jason and was now putting him to bed for his afternoon nap. And so Eulalie would have Robert's entire attention. That was something she could well do without, especially after such an evening as the one before.

The steps sounded from down the hall and Eulalie looked toward the door. Robert, appearing before her, inspected her up and down before speaking, and she became self-conscious at his attention. She straightened the écru lace on her sleeve and began to pluck at a loose thread.

"You slept well, Eulalie?"

At the sound of his voice, she looked up and met his slightly mocking glance. Her face colored, remembering.

"Yes, Robert. And you?"

He nodded while taking a step nearer her. "We'll go into the dining room, if you're ready."

In the presence of the food, her appetite diminished. Eulalie sat opposite Robert and played with her food, while her husband ate in thoughtful silence.

"I have decided to take you and Jason and move to the townhouse by the first of May."

Robert's deep voice filled the room, and Eulalie, startled at his pronouncement, let her fork drop onto her plate. The words slowly sank in. He was planning to spend the summer in Charleston.

"I had hoped to go to the mountains," Robert continued, "but I dare not take you on such a long trip in your condition. Charleston will not be as cool as the mountains, but the house will be relatively comfortable with the sea breeze blowing in by late afternoon to cool things off."

"Do we *have* to go to Charleston, Robert?"

He was displeased at her question. "Well, you cannot stay here at Midgard. It's much too unhealthy for you."

"I stayed at Midgard the summer after Papa Ravenal died, and I was not ill."

"You would not have been allowed to do that if someone had been here to watch after you properly, Eulalie. I cannot let you run the risk of fever, especially now that you are expecting our child. No, I have decided. And we'll say no more about it."

Eulalie, seeing the thunderous look on his face, did not dare protest. She looked down again at her plate and absentmindedly rearranged the food with her fork, while thinking of the summer in Charleston.

It would be the same as in Columbia, with the same women in attendance. She had almost forgotten that painful episode in the state capital, but Polly Ashe had refreshed her memory. And now Polly had more reason than ever to spread the ugly rumors about her. No, she could not look forward to spending the summer in that city.

Eulalie thought of Tabor Island, the beautiful old tabby house and the white sand of the beach. What fun Jason and Neijee would have, gathering shells and playing all day. They could even take the pony and a cart, and the Christmas puppy, Rags, with them.

If only Robert would change his mind and let them spend the time of the malaria season on the island, instead.

Robert looked indulgently at Eulalie. For the past two weeks, she had been unusually submissive, and had begun acting as a wife should. But he was not certain that was a good sign.

Eulalie sat in the light by the window and bit off the knotted thread with her even white teeth.

Robert enjoyed watching her hands making their deft, graceful movements with the needle. And now, in the library, he laid down the accounts that Gil Jordan had brought to him to go over, to sit and stare at his wife.

Eulalie sighed, and Robert, seeing the disturbed expression on her face, asked, "What are you thinking, Eulalie, to cause you to sigh so noticeably?"

"I was thinking of the island," she confessed, "and wishing we could spend the summer there."

"We have been over this before, Eulalie. You must be near a doctor when the time comes for the baby."

"But that is not until the end of October, Robert. We will be home again by then."

"What if the baby should decide to come early?"

"Then Feena could be the midwife. She has delivered many babies, and I would have no trouble with her to take care of me."

"That may be so, but you forget, the British fleet could come back at any time."

With a puckish look, she gazed at him sideways. "Didn't you say we would have ample warning from the lookout in the lighthouse?"

Robert laughed at her argument and then presented another objection, while still indulging her.

"What about Jason? We would even have to take a cow along to provide milk for him."

Eulalie smiled and in an excited voice answered, "And we could also take the pony and a little cart for him to ride in. And Rags could go too, of course. Jason would love it so, playing with Neijee on the beach."

"Hold on, Eulalie. Don't get too carried away by your plans," Robert warned.

She left her place by the window seat and walked toward Robert, her eyes holding an unconcealed anticipation.

Taking her hand in his, Robert looked at her and in a more serious tone he asked, "You are not anxious to be in Charleston, are you?"

"No, Robert," she readily admitted.

He stared into the dark imploring eyes looking up trustfully at him. She knew how to use them, he thought in amusement, to get her own way. With his arms now wrapped around her, Robert spoke softly. "You argue well, Eulalie. And heaven knows, the tabby house would be a lot cooler than the townhouse."

"Does that mean we can go? Oh, thank you, Robert." Eulalie stood on tiptoe and impulsively kissed him on the cheek.

"I have not given my assent yet, Eulalie."

Uncertainty flickered in her brown doe eyes, but she did not take them from Robert's face. She was quiescent while his hand trailed along her arm, and drew her hand to his lips. She watched him and felt the tightening of his hand on hers.

"I might be more kindly disposed to your suggestion if you showed a little more ardor. What kind of gratefulness was that, Eulalie—a sisterly peck on the cheek? Can you not show more enthusiasm than that at the possibility of getting your wish granted?"

"Oh, Robert," she shrieked in happiness and threw her arms around him.

He lifted her from the floor and his lips sought hers in long, exploring fulfillment.

The only person unenthusiastic about the change of plans was Florilla. She much preferred being in Charleston for the summer. She did not relish watching after Jason on the beach or having her complexion ruined by the sun.

Neither did she relish this improved relationship between Eulalie and Robert. She had been so very close to getting Robert to marry her. But having Eulalie suddenly appear in Columbia had put an end to her plans for a while.

. . . And after she had been so careful not to let it slip that Eulalie was still alive and at the convent. It had been a stroke of luck for her that Eulalie had given her own name to the child that had died, and that the old nun, Soeur Louise, had protected her so fiercely from Robert.

Poor old nun—thinking that Florilla had been grieving for her own child. She had never wanted the baby in the first place. And she had hated all those months that her figure had been so misshapen. But the convent had served its purpose after Clem had gotten her pregnant and then run out on her.

Florilla looked into the mirror and adjusted the neckline of her dress, to make it lower. "Robert would have married me," she said to her reflection in the mirror, "if Eulalie had not come back."

She frowned and then immediately smoothed the lines with the stroke of her fingers. But Eulalie *was* back and Florilla would have to decide what to do next. It was too bad that her bargain with Alistair Ashe had not worked out the way she had intended, or that Eulalie had not met with a mishap in Emma's Bog.

But there was still time. And it might be even easier on the island than in the city. . . .

The first of May came to the plantation, and with it, the beginning hints of the malaria season.

Some said it was caused from the unhealthy miasma that rose from the swamps. Others blamed the mosquitoes. But whether carried by the air or the pesky, biting insects that swarmed as soon as the sun went down, it made no difference to Robert. He was still driven from his home. And that was what he resented.

Somehow, Robert had never gotten used to it—to be forced to live almost six months of the year away from the beautiful land that looked so peaceful and mild. But the land of white gold was treacherous and demanded a penance for the richness of the living.

It was almost as if the gods had planned it that way, saying, "We will give you a beautiful land, a fertile earth between two rivers, as an inheritance, to yield bountiful crops and make you prosperous. But we will also send a seasonal plague, so that you will not become too comfortable or possessive of the land."

Robert, looking over the beautiful plantation that was his inheritance, saw that all was in order. The milk cow, the pony and cart, as well as the bedding supplies and staples and luggage had all been sent ahead to the wharf to be loaded on the large boat for Tabor Island.

Now all Robert need do was give last-minute instructions to his overseer, before going on his way with his wife and child and their retinue.

"It looks as if we are emigrating to another country," Robert complained to Eulalie when he came for her on the wharf.

Eulalie lowered her parasol and smiled. "But it's a beautiful day, isn't it, Robert—to emigrate?"

He returned her smile and led her onto the plank, then lifted her into the boat. She watched while the others were helped on board—Jason, Florilla, Neijee and Feena. And soon the wharf became a small speck in the distance, and the busy sounds of the wharf were replaced by the sounds of the sea.

Eulalie gazed out at the calm, sleeping sea, with the sun dipping to the white-tipped edges of the softly lapping waves. It was peaceful, beautiful. Yet underneath was the dormant raw force that could be awakened by the wind to become a devastating power.

Robert is like that, she thought, seeing the calmness of his features and yet knowing that the surface was misleading. For the calm visage overlay the same hidden strength as the sea.

Looking out over the water, Eulalie, with her thoughts on Robert, was oblivious to the upheaval at the other end of the boat.

Rags, the young hound, began to yap at the heels of the Guernsey milk cow, and the black servant was hard pressed to hold onto the cow's rope. With a mournful sound, the cow lumbered away from the dog.

Robert moved quickly, removing the troublesome dog to the opposite end of the boat.

"Jason! Neijee!" he called, his temper rising. "Stop your running and go back to your seats."

With Robert standing over her, Eulalie suddenly looked up. "I think you'd better keep your mind on Jason, Eulalie," he said. "There'll be ample time later for daydreaming."

She started at Robert's admonishing tone and then reached out for Jason to sit beside her. Florilla hurriedly got up and said, "I'll get a piece of rope, Robert, and tie Rags to the railing."

"That would be helpful, Florilla," he acknowledged, using a much milder tone with her.

The difference in his voice was obvious to Eulalie, and it did not make her happy to be reprimanded in front of Florilla. Was Florilla not the governess, charged with looking after Jason? Why then did Robert not scold her too, at the lack of supervision? But then, Eulalie already knew the answer to that.

Jason squirmed in his seat, but with Neijee to distract him, he did not present a problem for the rest of the trip. And Rags, secured by the piece of rope, pulled at it for a while and then settled down at Eulalie's feet with a yawn before going to sleep.

It was a tiring afternoon, unloading the boat of all its stores. Back and forth the servants and Robert went, along the divided path from the pier to the tabby house, to carry the bedding, dishes, clothes and food.

Eulalie stood in the entrance of the tabby house and directed the servants as to where to put each load. She was tired from the long day's activities, but she could not complain. She had gotten her wish—to spend the summer on Tabor Island.

Effie stumbled under the large armload of linen. And Eulalie, going to her aid, took half the linen herself to carry up the stairs. Robert, at her side almost at once, stopped her and removed the burden from her arms.

In an exasperating tone, he said, "You are not to do the work, Eulalie. Leave that to the servants."

"But Robert, I was merely—"

"Merely being foolish," he finished for her, with the scowl spoiling his handsome features.

He dropped the load of linen onto a chair and, taking a companion chair, he placed it in the middle of the downstairs hall. Pointing to it, he ordered, "I expect you to remain in this chair, Eulalie, until everything has been unloaded from the boat. You can easily direct the servants from here. But you are not to carry anything yourself."

"Yes, Robert."

Turning his back on Eulalie, he called, "Florilla, get Jason and Neijee out from underfoot. Take them for a walk. And get that blasted dog out of everyone's way before he trips us all."

Despite the short, curt tone, Florilla smiled sweetly at Robert, but when he was out of sight, she grasped Jason's hand with a jerk, startling the child by her force.

Eulalie did not see Florilla's action. But Neijee, walking beside Jason, was aware of it—another offense by the fair-haired woman to be filed away in his child's mind.

Eulalie, sitting sedately in the chair that Robert had designated for her, smiled. She smoothed the wrinkles of her blue muslin dress while she recalled Robert's tongue-lashing of Florilla. And Florilla, charged with taking care of Jason, would not dare harm the child with Robert around.

When the kitchen supplies were all delivered, Eulalie sent Feena downstairs to put them away. Only a few more items, she thought, and then she would be free of the restriction Robert had placed on her.

She watched with interest when the prie-dieu was brought into the hallway. Robert had said nothing when she had placed it with the trunks in the bedroom at Midgard to be brought down, and she had watched as it had been loaded on the wagon to be taken to the wharf.

Now it only needed to be carried upstairs and placed in the bedroom of the tabby house.

"That's all, Miz Tabor," Effie informed her. "Everything's off the boat."

"Good," Eulalie responded, standing up.

"What ya want me to do now?"

The black girl waited for Eulalie's instructions.

"Why don't you rest awhile, Effie, and then you can help make the beds."

"Yes'm."

The girl disappeared and Eulalie was alone in the hall. She started toward the stairs and then turned around, remembering the prie-dieu. It was not heavy and Eulalie decided to take it with her.

Halfway up the stairs, the blue velvet cushion came loose and bounced down the treads to the base of the stairs, but Eulalie did not stop. She would have to retrieve it later, after she got the prie-dieu to the bedroom.

A white-faced Robert bounded up the stairs and snatched the prayer bench from her hands. His voice shook with anger, and Eulalie, surprised at his violent reaction, shrank against the banister railing.

"You deliberately disobeyed me, Eulalie."

"But I stayed in the chair, Robert, until everything had been brought in. Effie told me nothing was left on the boat."

"That is not what I'm talking about. You had orders not to carry anything yourself."

"It's a small thing, Robert."

At the head of the stairs he set the prie-dieu down. His arms reached for Eulalie and he held her fiercely. "A small thing," he repeated. "God! I thought you had fallen down the stairs when I saw the blue cushion. Don't ever scare me like that again," he said, his lips touching her dark, wavy hair.

It was several days later after they had gotten settled that Eulalie took Jason for a walk along the beach. And it was on that afternoon, with Florilla and Neijee accompanying them, that Eulalie saw the ghost.

He appeared from nowhere and stood in the late twilight, dressed in a flowing robe that seemed to be made from the shimmering essence of the thickening gray mist.

"Look, Florilla. Do you see the man?"

Florilla turned in the direction that Eulalie pointed, but he had vanished as quickly as he had appeared, leaving Eulalie with uncertainty—not sure that she had actually seen him, yet not sure that he was an apparition that had disappeared in the last sudden glitter of the dying sun.

"What man? I do not see anyone."

"He . . . he's gone," Eulalie replied, still staring toward the rock.

Florilla laughed. "You're going to have us all quaking

in our shoes if you see someone who isn't there. But they say the mind does strange things when one is pregnant."

By evening, Eulalie was sorry that she had mentioned the figure to Florilla.

They sat in the dining hall, and in a lull of the dinner conversation, Florilla turned to Robert.

"Are you aware, Robert, that your wife saw a ghost this afternoon?"

"A ghost?" he repeated with a raised eyebrow.

Eulalie spoke before Florilla could answer. "It was a trick of the light on the beach today, Robert. The gray mist gathered in such a strange way, like a robe. And it did resemble a man, for an instant, standing and looking out over the water."

"Did you see him too, Florilla?" Robert asked.

"See what wasn't there?" Florilla answered with a laugh. "I'm afraid your wife has much more imagination than I."

"Perhaps it was one of the gray friars from the mission," Robert teased Eulalie. "You remember you felt a presence here in the house not long ago."

"She's going to have us all frightened to death. I just hope the servants don't get scared and run off," Florilla said. "They're more afraid of ghosts than the British soldiers."

"Then perhaps," cautioned Eulalie, "it would be best to say nothing further about it."

Florilla said no more but sat silently, daintily spooning small bits of bombé into her mouth, thinking of the ghost and how she could turn the apparition to her own advantage.

Robert, looking at Eulalie, hesitated as if debating whether to speak. And then his voice penetrated the silence in the dining room.

"I do not wish to encourage your imagination, Eulalie, about the ghost, but if you are interested in the story of the friars who lived here, then you might enjoy seeing the contents of a strongbox that Uncle Ravenal dug up when he was building this house years ago. The box contained an old leather book, and listed in it are the names of some of the Indians who were baptized by the friars."

Eulalie immediately showed her interest. Her eyes sparkled as she said, "Oh, yes, Robert. I would enjoy seeing it. Is the book here in the house?"

"Yes. I'll get it for you after supper."

"But how did it survive all these years in such a damp place?" Eulalie asked.

"You forget. It was in the heavy metal box. Even then, the ink is faded and the pages are brittle."

Later that evening when Eulalie was ready for bed, Robert came into the room, carrying the metal box. It was of an unusual design with intricate metalwork, studded with iron tacks. Eulalie stopped brushing her hair and watched while Robert set the box on the table by the window. He lifted the lid and took out the book.

By this time Eulalie was at his side and she reached out to touch the old leather cover, tracing with her fingers the triangular metal pieces decorating each corner of the book.

Musty and fragile and its ink barely visible, the book almost came apart in Eulalie's hands.

"It is so old," Eulalie said in awe.

He smiled at her. "Yes, and I'm afraid you will not be able to make anything of it until daylight. And even then, you may not be able to read it, since it is not in English. But I forgot—that does not limit you, does it, Eulalie?"

"Languages change. I may not be able to, unless it is written in the classical Latin of the church." She stared at the faded pages and shook her head. "It is too dim to see by candlelight. I will have to wait. But thank you, Robert, for showing it to me."

CHAPTER

34

IT was the last of May, and Florilla, with her small valise clutched in her hands, waited for Robert at the pier. Discovering that he was going into Charleston, she had asked if she might go along also to do some shopping. And while she waited at the pier, Robert was busy seeking out Eulalie.

He found her sitting on the rock and gazing toward the sea. Jason and Neijee played on the beach nearby, with Feena keeping her eye on the two little boys.

"Are you sure, Eulalie, that you do not wish to go too?" Robert asked, standing beside the rock and looking at his wife.

She turned and shielded her eyes from the sun. "I am sure, Robert," she answered. "I have everything I need."

"I will be gone for several days. And I don't like leaving you here on the island."

"But I don't mind, Robert. Truly I don't—with Feena to help with Jason."

"It isn't that. It's the British," he informed her.

"But Tom and Rufus will warn me, if it comes to that. And we can easily leave in the other boat."

Robert shook his head. "So stubborn. Does it not matter to you, my fat little pigeon, that I will miss you?" He gently placed his hand on her rounded stomach.

Scandalized at his action, she jumped from the rock. Looking in Jason's and Neijee's direction, she protested, "Robert, the children . . . "

His arms went around her and he held her close. "Does it matter to you, Eulalie, that the children can see me making love to you?"

"Yes," she whispered loudly. "Let me go, Robert."

Robert glanced toward the two little boys, who were now standing and watching the proceedings with interested eyes. Reluctantly he obeyed her. "If I had more time, then I would remove you from their little prying eyes and take you where I could love you properly."

"But you do not have the time," she reminded him. "Is Matthew not waiting for you already?"

He nodded. "Matthew and Florilla both."

At the mention of the woman's name, Eulalie walked back toward the rock. "Goodbye, Robert, and . . . have a pleasant trip."

His hand reached for her. "What sort of goodbye is that, Eulalie? Come, you must be more concerned, even tearful, or I shall think you are trying to get rid of me."

Eulalie laughed, and lifting her face toward his, she waited for his kiss.

He walked slowly down the path to the pier. The time spent on the island had been good for Eulalie, he thought. She was healthy and seemed to be happy. And Robert was glad. But still, she was so unsophisticated, caring not one whit that her skin was now a golden tan. She had sat in the sun without benefit of bonnet or parasol—a far cry from the blond Florilla, who had wrapped herself in layers of clothes sufficient for an Egyptian mummy, and hidden her fair skin under a floppy bonnet as well as a parasol.

Seeing Robert coming toward her, Florilla smiled, and when he had helped her into the boat, Matthew cast off and headed for the Charleston harbor.

Robert was quiet, thinking of Governor Alston's order for the militia to guard the powder magazines near the harbor. Major-General Thomas Pinckney, in command in the southeast, must be uneasy at the movements of the

British fleet, especially with the Federal government announcing again that the state would have to defend itself in the event of an attack. State militia, Robert had observed, were notoriously unreliable, scattering for cover at the first round of shots or rockets. He hoped that they would never be put to the test.

Robert's attention turned to Florilla. It was awkward for him to have her staying in the townhouse at the same time he was in Charleston—especially without Jason, or Eulalie, his wife. But the woman deserved some time off from her duties as governess, besides one afternoon a week, he conceded. And he would be at the townhouse very little, with his duty at the powder magazines taking up most of his time.

The days that Robert spent in Charleston were busy ones on the island for Eulalie. She tried not to think of Robert and Florilla together, but to keep her mind on Jason and Neijee and see to the running of the tabby house.

The children had a large cache of shells and spent much of their time loading them into the cart to be pulled by the pony back to the tabby house and unloading them by the cassina bushes next to the porch. They stacked them carefully and jabbered happily in the time-consuming chore.

As long as they were busy with the pony and cart, they were good, but when they grew tired of working with the shells, Jason and Neijee reverted to their mischievous ways and led Eulalie and Feena into a steady, energy-draining chase.

Robert had been away for two nights when Eulalie awoke from a nap in the late afternoon. She had not meant to drop off to sleep, but the day had been long and she was tired. The house was quiet—too quiet—and when Eulalie searched for Jason, he was not to be found.

Both she and Feena started for the beach, sure that he had slipped out to gather more shells. But when they reached the beach, neither Jason nor Neijee was there.

"Feena, where could they have gone?" Eulalie asked,

now worried over their disappearance. "Do you suppose they slipped off to the creek?"

Eulalie shuddered even to think about it. She had heard the bull alligator only a few evenings before, bellowing his anger at some disturbance by the creek bank.

"That Jason is becoming a bad little boy," Feena said. "But so fearless. Last night he asked if he might bring Monsieur Alligator home with him in the pony cart."

At the alarm on Eulalie's face, Feena hastened on. "But more than likely, he has gone to the lighthouse to visit his friends."

Gazing toward the sun, Eulalie realized they did not have long to look for him. "Quick, Feena. Go to thé lighthouse while I search the creek bank."

"Mamselle Lili," Feena protested, "let me go to the creek instead."

"No, Feena." Eulalie hurried from the black woman and headed toward the creek, leaving Feena with no choice except to do as she was told.

The going was rough, with no carefully laid path to walk along. Eulalie picked her way through the scrubby brush, avoiding the prickly bushes that jutted out every so often.

If Neijee and Jason were at the creek, they would have to be reprimanded soundly before Robert came home. She could not have them doing such a thing again. It was too dangerous, for that end of the island was rampant with matted growth. She had seen several marsh tackeys at dusk one evening, and she remembered Robert's talking of the colony of pigs that had covered the island when he had first visited it.

The barking of Rags, the dog, first alerted Eulalie. The sound came from beyond the reeds adjacent to the creek.

"Jason! Neijee!" Eulalie called. "Where are you?" She pressed through the barrier of growth, dividing the reeds with her hands, and edged nearer the sound.

And then she saw the two little boys. Eulalie started to speak, but seeing the spellbound expression on their faces, she looked in the same direction as their fixed stare, at the large ugly animal that was walking toward them.

Its tusks were shaped in a dangerous curve. The brown

short-haired creature continued walking slowly from the watering hole. A wild boar—one of the most dangerous animals of the low country. And it was on the creek bank, much too near the children.

Eulalie stopped, hesitant to make another sound. If they remained where they were, silent and still, perhaps the animal would go away and they could get back to the tabby house without mishap.

But Jason, seeing Eulalie, moved, and the animal lumbered from the bank in a slow canter toward the boy.

"Jason! Neijee! Run! Run back to the house!" Eulalie stepped forward as if to protect the children, and the animal, sensing another presence, shifted directions and then hesitated, now that he had a choice. Which to attack? The woman before him or the fleeing, noisy children?

Eulalie stood, and for a moment she too came under the spell of the belligerent animal. But as the boar turned to pursue Jason, Eulalie came alive, picking up several pebbles at her feet to hurl at the animal. One hit him on the snout, and the bombardment diverted the animal's attention from the boy. The boar started toward her, and at his action, Eulalie also turned to flee.

The vegetation along the creek bank was lush and green, with tips of decaying logs jutting from the jungle floor of vines. She stepped on a log and immediately lost her balance, landing on the earth with a soft thud. Her foot twisted under her.

Neijee looked back and seeing Eulalie on the ground, he paused. "Go on," she ordered. "Take Jason back to the house. Hurry!"

His black eyes were uncertain until she said, "Find Feena for me." He then took Jason's hand, and together they vanished from Eulalie's sight.

She knew she could not remain where she was, a target for the wild boar. One attack by its dangerous tusks and she could be torn to shreds.

Eulalie attempted to get up, but her foot, wedged between the logs and matted vines, refused to come free. And as she tugged, a shooting pain told her that she had injured her ankle.

The boar was now almost upon her. Rags, the hound,

dashed back toward Eulalie, as if waiting for her to get up. And when she did not, he began barking and running up and down in the space between the wild beast and Eulalie. At the dog's actions, the boar stopped to reconnoiter. In a display of rising anger, the animal grunted and tore great clumps of matted greenery with his tusks.

The movement on the bank behind the boar was swift and noiseless. It was the bull alligator. Eulalie watched in increasing horror as the six-foot-long reptile, resembling another log on the creek bank, began its rapid, sliding descent. And the boar, intent on Eulalie, did not know that he too was being stalked by an enemy. A shrill shriek filled the air as the alligator opened his powerful jaws and dragged the wild boar into the water. At the thrashing of the animals in the creek, Eulalie frantically tugged at her foot, while Rags, frightened at the sounds and activity, ran to and from the creek bank.

The water, now discolored, rippled out in great concentric circles, until finally all was quiet. No sign of the boar—no sign of the alligator. The water returned to its smoothness, undisturbed.

She shivered at witnessing the primitive scene that had suddenly made the island an alien and sinister place. And Eulalie, still entrapped, prayed that the alligator had had enough to eat and would not venture out onto the banks again.

How long would it take Feena to start looking for her? When she did not find Jason and Neijee at the lighthouse, would Feena go back to the tabby house? And would Jason and Neijee be waiting there for her, to tell the woman about the wild boar?

Eulalie's ankle began to throb, and she felt dizzy. Even if she could get free, she was in no condition to walk back to the house. She would have to wait until Feena came to the rescue.

The cry of the gulls in the distance told her that the day was old. Cradled with threads of purple and deep mauve, the sun began its slow journey behind her, sinking lower into the sky with each passing moment.

The water in the creek slowly cleared from the sand and mud stirred from the bottom, and Eulalie, afraid to look back toward the water, nevertheless watched, and what she feared began to happen.

The waters rippled and the slit-eyed monster, with its great jaws and thrashing tail, slithered out of the water onto the bank.

At the reptile's appearance, Eulalie held her breath. Could alligators see well? Or did they follow their prey by sound and odor?

"Eulalie!" The frantic male voice cut through the quietness of the late afternoon. "Eulalie, where are you?"

She recognized the voice. It was Arthur and he was looking for her. Hope of being rescued now rushed over her; yet she was afraid to answer. If the alligator had forgotten about her, her voice might lead him to her. And which one would reach her first?

The alligator moved and Eulalie made her decision. "Arthur, I'm here," she shouted. "Near the creek bank. Oh Arthur, do hurry!"

"Keep calling, Eulalie. I'm coming."

"Arthur, the alligator." Her voice rose in terror. "He's coming toward me."

"Then run, Eulalie. Get away as fast as you can."

"I can't. My foot's caught."

Rags' excited bark drowned out other sounds. Eulalie listened, but Arthur's voice did not continue. Was he headed in the wrong direction, away from her?

At the activity of the dog, the alligator doubled the speed of his slithery walk. And Eulalie, seeing his slit-shaped eyes and his giant snapping jaws at closer view, sensed she was his next victim.

"Arthur!" she screamed. Then she closed her eyes, not wanting to see.

The shot rang out. And then another. Startled at the deafening sound so close to her, Eulalie jerked her eyelids open. Within a few feet of her, the bull alligator thrashed his powerful tail and then was still.

Hands reached down and lifted the log that trapped her foot.

"It's all right, Eulalie. You're safe. Nothing can harm you now." His voice was gentle, but Eulalie was too numb to respond. She sat where she was, with Arthur bent beside her, patting her hand in a sympathetic gesture.

"Mamselle, where are you?" Feena's voice came from the distance. Eulalie lifted her head but her voice would not come.

Arthur replied for her. "Here, Feena. Near the creek bank."

By the time Feena found her, Arthur had helped Eulalie to her feet. But Eulalie protested when the man made ready to carry her.

"I am all right now, Arthur. I can walk," Eulalie assured him. With Arthur supporting her, she tried to use her bruised foot. The ankle was too painful for her to put her weight on, and at the sight of the girl trying to hobble a few steps, Feena said, "You are hurt, *ma petite*." And then the black woman spied the bull alligator lying only a few feet away, with Rags cautiously sniffing about the animal.

"*Mon Dieu*," she said, her black face showing the horror she felt. "It is a good thing Monsieur Arthur came along when he did."

"Are the children at the house, Feena?"

"*Oui*, mamselle. Effie is with them. But they are very frightened."

Supported by Arthur, Eulalie took a few more limping steps before stopping to rest. When she stopped, Feena leaned down and examined her foot. "You plan to walk all the way back, *ma petite?*" she said in a censuring tone.

Eulalie nodded, but Arthur took issue with her. "She insists she can, Feena. But we shall see just how many steps before she gives up that idea."

Eulalie managed for a short distance, but it was slow and tiring.

"Are you ready to give up now, Eulalie, and let me carry you the rest of the way?" Arthur asked, seeing the pain in Eulalie's face.

"Yes, Arthur." Her voice sounded small and defeated. With her avowal, Arthur shifted his rifle over his arm and lifted her in his arms.

What a difference between Arthur and Robert, Eulalie thought as she was being carried. Arthur had been kind and gentle, respecting her wishes, until the walking became too painful. Robert would not have waited. He would have snatched her up like a child who didn't know her own mind, regardless of her protest.

Down the path, Rufus, the militiaman, ran with the gun in his hands. He stopped when he saw Arthur. "I heard shots. What happened? Has Mrs. Tabor been hurt?"

"She has had a slight accident to her foot," Arthur explained.

"And the shots?"

"There is now one less alligator at the creek."

"You mean—"

Arthur cut him off. "Rufus, I will tell you all about it later. Would you take my rifle to the lighthouse with you? I'll join you there, as soon as I see Mrs. Tabor safely to the house."

"Certainly, Arthur, if that is what you want me to do."

"It is," Arthur assured him.

Feena went ahead to boil her herbs for Eulalie's foot, and in the fast-falling shadows, Arthur followed the path toward the house with Eulalie in his arms. Exhausted by the terrifying experience, she rested her head against his shoulder and closed her eyes.

Robert and Florilla walked from the pier on their way to the tabby house. It had been a boring three days for Robert, and he was glad to be back on the island.

It was late when he had finished his duty at the harbor, but he had not wanted to spend another night apart from Eulalie.

Already the stars glittered in the heavens and the moon projected its distorted image upon the waters, while the sun still colored the western horizon.

Robert and Florilla came to the division of the path, and Florilla, seeing the man with Eulalie in his arms, turned to Robert and said, "I wonder who the two lovebirds are."

At her words, he looked up, and peering into the near darkness, Robert watched the approaching figures. As they came closer, he recognized them—his friend, Arthur, and in his arms was Eulalie, his wife, her long black hair cascading against the sandy-haired man's throat.

Robert's lips tightened, and in a stern voice he greeted them. "A very pretty sight, indeed. I suggest that you put my wife down at once."

CHAPTER

35

A HUMILIATED Eulalie lay across the bed, her throbbing ankle serving to intensify the pain and anger in her heart.

"I should have taken you into Charleston with me, Eulalie," Robert said. "It seems I cannot leave you for any length of time without your getting into trouble."

She ignored his comment, and in a soft voice quivering with emotion, she said, "You did not have to be so curt with Arthur, Robert."

"What was I to believe, Eulalie—seeing the two of you together, and remembering how anxious you were for me to leave the island? Did you think I would welcome the sight of you in another man's arms?"

"But I explained, Robert. I could not walk, and if Arthur had not rescued me, I would have been another meal for the alligator."

At the mention of Arthur's name again, Robert stiffened. "What were you doing at the creek? Had you gone there to meet Arthur?"

"To meet Arthur? Is that what you think, Robert?" Eulalie's voice ended in a harsh laugh.

"Your son slipped away from the house, and Feena and

I started out to look for him. It was getting late, so we went our separate ways—Feena to the lighthouse and I to the creek. Jason and Neijee were at the creek, with a wild boar bearing down upon them. It was to look for Jason, Robert—not to meet some . . . some lover."

With a bitter voice she continued. "Look at me, Robert. Did you think I was eloping with Arthur when it is already obvious that I am carrying your child? I am about as desirable to a man as a pregnant sow."

Robert laughed, and Eulalie, shocked at her own temerity, blushed.

"I agree that you would not make the most *virtuous*-looking bride, Eulalie, but do not underestimate your desirability, my pet. You will always be able to stir that flame of passion in a man's heart, regardless of your . . . fruitfulness."

His eyes traveled insolently over her and came to rest on the swollen ankle, now bound with compresses. "At least having to stay off your foot for a while will assure me that you are safe. And I will make certain that someone reliable is here to watch over you, if I have to leave again."

Her eyes darkened at his announcement. "Is that a threat?"

"I would regard it as more of a promise."

Petulantly, Eulalie said, "You make it sound as if I need a keeper."

"Well, don't you?" His voice was mildly teasing, and it irritated her even more.

"No."

Her voice was now devoid of challenge. She did not want to spar with Robert any further. Her hand crept up to her mouth, and she shivered, although it was hot in the room. The feeling of fright from the dangerous interlude had been pushed aside for a while, but now it was coming back, rushing to overwhelm her.

Robert looked at her critically for a moment, then turned heel and left the room.

She had been so close to death, but Robert acted as if

he did not care. He had expressed no sympathy or pity for her—only anger at Arthur, who had saved her.

It was then that the small needling thought pierced her heart. If something had happened to her, Robert would have been free to marry Florilla.

By the time Robert came back into the room, Eulalie was sitting in a tight ball, her hands clasped around her knees and her head leaning against them, with the wavy hair spreading in all directions over the demure white gown. And an involuntary shiver racked her body.

Hands brushed her hair from her face and lifted her chin from its resting place. Eulalie stared into the tawny eyes of her husband.

"Here, Eulalie. Drink this," he ordered.

"What is it?"

"It's brandy, but do not protest. You need it."

Without waiting for her to respond, Robert held the glass to Eulalie's lips, and meekly she drank the liquid.

When she had finished, Robert remained beside her, taking her in his arms when she shuddered again, and gently he stroked her hair.

"I had not realized how the experience must have frightened you." His voice was faintly apologetic.

The hint of sympathy in his voice did to her what his anger could never have done. It released the tears, the pent-up emotions of the day, and she was powerless to stop them.

For a long time, Robert held her close, soothing her and rocking her, until the tears were spent. Exhausted by the emotional outburst, Eulalie lay quietly, still protected by her husband's strong, comforting arms.

Why did she have to love Robert so much, to be tortured each day, knowing that he had not married her willingly?

Why could she not hate him instead, this powerful golden man who took away every ounce of pride she had ever possessed, who forced her into responding to him against her will and took great delight in her capitulation?

Eulalie, with no suitable answer to her question, sighed and finally drifted to sleep.

Robert spent the day on duty at the lighthouse. Visibility was poor because of the slanting rain. As he looked out toward the seaward horizon, he sensed the loneliness and isolation of the nearly deserted island. It seemed to be suspended in time, past and present undivided.

Robert could almost feel the presence of the Indians paddling in and out of the sea isles, as they had done years before the first white man had set foot on the land to claim it for a foreign power.

No wonder Eulalie had imagined the ghost—the gray friar of long ago. The island could do that with a person sensitive to the aura of yesterday. He had seen it in her face when he had brought the friar's book to her. And now, recalling Uncle Ravenal, Robert wondered if the old man too had felt it—this presence of an earlier unresolved time.

Uncle Ravenal had never explained why he had abruptly stopped going to the island. Or why he had left the friar's book in the house undisturbed. He had seemed to regard himself as an intruder on his own property, as if the island had belonged to someone else.

The crashing of waves upon the shore matched the restlessness of Robert's spirit and the storm going on inside him.

Seeing Eulalie in Arthur's arms had caused the old fear to reemerge—that uneasiness that she would leave him at the first opportunity. He had dealt with it quickly upon their return from Cedar Hill, making sure that she would not have the gold in her possession, but hidden in the safe. And when he learned of the impending birth of the child, he had relaxed, certain that she would be forced to stay at Midgard.

But jealousy made a man react with his heart and not his head. And each jealous action of his drove Eulalie further from him. When would he ever learn to keep his temper in check?

It had not been good to jump to conclusions because of the words Florilla had spoken. And he knew he deserved the scolding Eulalie had flung in his face for his treatment of Arthur. Deep down, could he not swear that

Arthur was too honorable to try to lure Eulalie from him, especially with another child on the way?

Robert would have to come to terms with his friend. He had no wish to alienate him further. He needed Arthur on the island to take his turn at the lighthouse. And where else could the man stay except the tabby house after his hours on duty?

No, he must show his gratitude to Arthur and attempt to heal the enmity between them, caused by his own jealousy. Let Arthur look at Eulalie as much as he wanted. Robert could stand it, remembering that *he* was her husband, the one who had the right to share her bed and get her with child. And lucky for him that Arthur had come earlier than expected and had been able to save Eulalie. God! What a close call she had had.

The ennui of the day enclosed Eulalie amid the steady downpour of rain. She was unable to walk downstairs, to do anything except sit in the upstairs bedroom and wait for her meals, embroider the shirt for Robert, and sleep. By afternoon she was tired of all three activities.

Eulalie hopped on one foot to look out the window toward the sea. She rubbed the vapor from the glass to get a clearer view, and her dark eyes scanned the water. There was no division between sky and sea, but one large gray expanse. Could Robert, on duty at the lighthouse, see any better? Were ships waiting, even now, for the storm to subside, so they could begin their plundering?

With the window closed against the rain, it was airless and humid in the room. The lit tapers of the candelabra on the small table, positioned to shed light on the delicate stitches of her sewing, now chased the shadows into the corners of the room. But the added heat from the tapers made Eulalie uncomfortable. She lifted her long, wavy hair from the nape of her neck. Maybe she would feel better if she sponged her face with water.

Still hopping on one foot, Eulalie reached the basin and ewer. Bracing herself against the marble washstand, she poured water into the basin, and, taking a cloth, dipped it into the tepid water and patted her neck and face with it.

The friar's book lay on the table where she had left it the day before. It was difficult to decipher, and Eulalie had made little headway in translating it. But one name had caught her interest. It had appeared more than once in the pages she had browsed over. Morning Tears. What a sad name for an Indian girl. What had happened to her, Eulalie wondered, after the friars disappeared? Had she gone back to her native ways, forgetting everything she had been taught?

Eulalie looked at the prie-dieu in the corner and, shamefaced, she realized she had spent little time in praying. Her thoughts had been taken up too much with Robert and Jason and the tabby house. Yes, it was much too easy to forget.

She closed the book and hobbled to the prayer bench, and that was where Robert found her when he came off duty.

He was wet from walking in the rain. He said nothing but stripped off his clothes and dried himself before putting on a clean white shirt and fawn breeches. Every few minutes, he glanced toward Eulalie, but she seemed oblivious to his presence.

So he waited for her to finish, trying not to show his irritation at being ignored. Was she still praying for Jacques Binet after all these months?

That was another thing he would have to put to rest, regardless of how hard it would be. Never would he taunt her again with the name of Jacques Binet.

Eulalie glanced up, and seeing Robert, she smiled. The gesture was worth waiting for, he decided.

"I see you have been reading the friar's book," Robert said, with his hand indicating the open pages. "Have you deciphered any more of it?"

"A little. The ink is better toward the last. The friar is telling the story of the mission, but there is such a sadness about it, Robert—as though a great tragedy is going to occur."

"You remember, Eulalie, most of the friars were massacred by the Indians," he reminded her. "I think *that* qualifies it as a tragedy, does it not?"

His words caused her to wince, and in a sad voice she said, "That could also account for the ghost on the beach."

"You have seen him again?"

"Yes. And I think I know which one he was."

"Which one, Eulalie?"

"Fray Roberto de Ore," she replied. "Strange, is it not, that he has *your* name?"

He looked at her cautiously and then broke into a laugh. "And is there a Eulalie in the friar's memoirs too?"

"Her name was Morning Tears," she replied. "I think she was in love with one of the friars."

"You must not become too wrapped up in the book, Eulalie. I thought it might be a diversion, but if it is going to upset you, then I will return it to its place downstairs."

"Oh, no, please don't do that, Robert. I have to find out what happened at the last."

He was relieved at her answer. Womanly curiosity, after all. Nothing more than that.

"Well, just remember, Eulalie. Whatever happened was a long time ago, far removed from our own lives here on the island. And don't take the ghost too seriously," he warned. "Every old house up and down the coast has its own resident ghost. But for the sake of the servants, I hope ours is a benevolent one."

"He would have to be, would he not?" Eulalie said, matching Robert's light tone. "And poor, too—to honor his vows of poverty, chastity and obedience."

Robert regarded her tenderly and helped her back to her place on the bed. With his arms still enfolding her, he whispered, "And what vows did *you* take, little nun?"

"I . . . I had not yet taken my vows," she replied seriously.

"It is just as well. For your rounded stomach denies your chastity. And you have never been one to obey willingly."

He caressed her throat and bent over to kiss her ear.

"But you have seen to it that I have kept my poverty," Eulalie responded.

He lifted his head and stared into her eyes, now twinkling with merriment. Robert laughed, remembering the pouch of gold, and he crushed her to him, demanding obeisance with his lips.

CHAPTER

36

EULALIE'S ankle began to heal, but she was still limited in her movements. Unable to leave the bedroom except when Robert carried her downstairs for dinner, she felt frustrated. She thought of Julie, her cousin, at Cedar Hill, unable to walk, and a new sympathy arose. Each day she prayed that the new treatment Julie was undergoing would be successful.

The friar's book fascinated Eulalie. She was certain now that Morning Tears was in love with the friar, Roberto. But the book told of the animosity of some of the Indians, and Eulalie, with her fingers touching the brittle yellow pages, could feel the pathos of those early days. And her mind remained on Fray Roberto de Ore.

She was coming to the end of the manuscript, and an inexpressible sadness took hold of her. The mood continued while she pored over the page. And then she reached the tragedy—Roberto was massacred and his body thrown into the sea by the Indians. And Morning Tears, seeing it happen, powerless to do anything about it, had calmly walked into the sea, following the young friar even in death.

The old man had recorded it hurriedly, judging by the look of the ink and the lettering. Eulalie closed the book.

That evening as she went to bed, tears filled Eulalie's eyes. The place beside her was empty. Robert was on duty at the lighthouse.

For a long time she lay in the darkness, unable to sleep. The story that she had read haunted her. Eulalie knew how Morning Tears must have felt, with her love for a man who had always been out of reach. For was that not how she felt about Robert, bound to him by strong ties, but unable to bridge the schism that divided them?

With a sigh, Eulalie closed her eyes. She felt the movement of the child, strong now, and in a protective attitude, she placed her hand upon her rounded stomach.

The stirring ceased and Eulalie dropped off to sleep. She was restless, and her sleep disturbed by jumbled dreams. On the beach she stood barefooted, looking out over the waves as the gray mist gathered and slowly took shape into a hooded shroud. It walked toward her, becoming more alive with each step. Unable to move, Eulalie waited, until the shroud stood before her, with the tawny topaz eyes of her husband, Robert, staring into hers.

All at once, Eulalie was enveloped in the gray shroud, her breathing cut off. She was being smothered.

She struggled, pushing against the material. With a sudden burst of strength, she managed to push it from her and, catching her breath, Eulalie screamed.

The room in the tabby house, half-lit by the brilliant moon, was witness to the sudden movement of the apparition as it escaped and slipped out the doorway.

Unable to distinguish between dream and reality, Eulalie sat up, terrified. She screamed again, and at the sound of her desperate voice, the house came alive.

"Mamselle Lili, what is the matter?"

Feena came running into the room, hastily donning her cotton robe.

"Someone was in the room," Eulalie cried, recognizing her old nursemaid's voice. "And they tried to smother me."

The candelabra was lit and brought to the bedside, and

the concerned, dark eyes of Feena stared into Eulalie's, unusually soft and vulnerable with fright.

Feena looked thoughtful while she sat by the bed, but she said nothing. The door, already open, was filled with another presence—Robert, who had just come from his lighthouse duty.

Seeing Feena so late at night, he said, "What is the matter?"

He looked from Feena to Eulalie, whose face still showed the effects of her frightening experience.

"I thought I heard someone scream," he said.

"It was the . . . the ghost," Eulalie whispered. "It tried to smother me."

"You have evidently had a nightmare," Robert said, his voice now grave. "I knew it would not be good in your condition to continue reading the friar's book."

"That was not the cause," Eulalie objected. "Someone tried to smother me."

But Robert, sending Feena back to bed, merely shook his head and tried to calm the hysterical Eulalie as best he could.

"You do not believe me, do you, Robert?"

The next morning, Eulalie sat at the table in the bedroom and sipped her cassina tea, made from the leaves of the bushes that grew near the tabby house.

"No, Eulalie. I think you have an overactive imagination. And that is why I have removed the friar's book. It would not be good for you to read any more from it."

"There is no more to read, Robert. I finished it last night," she admitted.

"Just as I suspected," Robert replied.

The incident with the ghost was soon forgotten by Robert, as his mind turned toward the war. Now at peace with Arthur, he welcomed his help at the lighthouse.

Hector, Rufus, Tom and Arthur all took turns on watch, coming back and forth to the island, and Eulalie, seeing that Robert and Arthur were friends again, relaxed and enjoyed the brief evenings they were together.

News had not been good. The British cutters were continually in and out of the waterways north and south of them, and the men, however much they tried to disguise it, were uneasy, realizing that Charleston's turn would eventually come.

And state politics were becoming increasingly muddled. Letters were exchanged between Robert and John Calhoun, a state representative in Washington. One of the original War Hawks, he had introduced Madison's declaration of war into Congress. John Calhoun was as adamant against the British as Robert was. Earlier in the year he had almost lost his seat in the Congress, along with Cheves and Langdon, because of Joseph Alston. Increasingly unpopular, the governor had now begun his feud with the state militia, to the detriment of the state.

Each time a letter arrived from Calhoun, Robert and Arthur would closet themselves, discussing the letter's contents in private, and Eulalie would feel left out. But now that her ankle had nearly healed, she was able to return to her enjoyment of the beach with Jason and Neijee. The wild-boar episode had made the children much less venturesome and they seemed to be content playing nearer the house.

The peace Eulalie experienced was soon disrupted by the constant bickering between Florilla and Feena, as their enmity grew ever greater.

They had never gotten along well together, but Florilla, after her visit to Charleston with Robert and Eulalie's encounter with the ghost, began to show her active dislike of Feena more and more.

One afternoon, Florilla, in a state of agitation, approached Robert.

"Robert, I would speak with you if you have a moment."

He had not slept well the night before, because of his duty at the lighthouse, and his weariness showed in his voice. "What is it, Florilla?"

She gave an embarrassed laugh and answered, "Really, I know it is nonsense but, nevertheless, it disturbs me."

"Yes?"

"This morning, I found a gris-gris under my pillow. Oh, I know voodoo doesn't mean a thing. It's only that I am alarmed that someone in this house would wish me ill."

Robert frowned, thinking of Feena. He knew there was no love lost between the two and he was aware of the increased animosity.

"Are you sure it isn't a love potion, Florilla?" teased Robert. "Put there by someone who wants you to fall in love?"

"No, it is black magic," Florilla affirmed. "Nothing to do with love."

Looking at her with penetrating eyes, he asked, "And do you suspect someone in particular?"

"Well, of course, we are all aware of Feena's interests. I overheard Effie the other day asking her for an amulet to keep the ghost away."

"I will speak with her, Florilla," Robert promised.

"Thank you, Robert. I knew I could call on you for help."

She retraced her steps and walked down the hall, smiling as she walked. The ribbons of her hat entwined her arm, and before she opened the door to the outside, she stopped to put on the oversized hat, even though the sun was hidden behind the clouds.

When Feena was later confronted by Robert, she denied all knowledge of the gris-gris.

"This is a warning, Feena. You have gotten into trouble previously with your voodoo. I thought you had learned your lesson. But if it continues—this pagan practice of yours—then something will have to be done."

Feena's eyes narrowed and her lips pursed together, but she said nothing. She did not put it past Florilla to have done it herself in an effort to place blame on Feena.

Two days later, Florilla kept to her room, complaining of a constriction in her throat. Food was taken to her at mealtime, and no one saw her except Effie, who carried the trays. Eulalie, busy with caring for Jason, finally went to see her at the end of the day and found the woman limp, wilted and very pale. In a hoarse voice, Florilla answered Eulalie's questions, and at the raspiness in the voice, Eulalie assumed the woman had come down with a summer cold.

"Would you like a poultice for your throat?" Eulalie suggested.

"No, Mrs. Tabor," the woman answered quickly. "I am afraid of Feena and her poultices."

"Effie can make it for you just as well," Eulalie reassured her, and soon the odors of the poultice crept from the kitchen situated beneath the first floor of the tabby house.

Bad weather set in, with rain and wind rattling against the window panes. Jason and Neijee played noisily up and down the stairs until Feena took them to the kitchen to help her cut out gingerbread men and bake them in the old wall oven.

In the parlor, Robert took out the chess pieces from the cabinet and set them on the game table.

Eulalie, sewing on a garment for her child, watched as Robert fingered the old pieces of carved ivory and black onyx. Leaving her sewing on the chair next to the window, Eulalie arose and walked to the table, where she picked up one of the pawns in her hand.

At her obvious interest, Robert said, "I don't suppose you know how to play the game?"

His face had a boyish, wistful expression, and in response to his question, Eulalie smiled and said, "It has been some time, but I think I remember."

"Then, madame, will you join me in a game?"

He stood and held a chair for her, and when she was seated, he asked, "Black or white?"

"Black," she replied, stating her preference of the pieces, and he immediately turned the chessboard until the black pieces faced her.

"You play very well, Eulalie," a surprised Robert complimented her after some time had elapsed. "Who taught you?"

"My *grand'pere*, the Comte de Boisfeulet," she replied. "But that was long ago, when I was a child. More recently, it was with Papa Ravenal that I played."

"I thought I recognized some of my uncle's tactics," Robert said with a laugh.

There was an intimate feeling between the two as the game continued into the afternoon. But Eulalie's mind, filled with other things, could not concentrate as well as it should, and with a mounting sense of disaster, seeing her queen vulnerable, she watched Robert sitting and pondering his next move. Suddenly, his giant hand reached out and closed around her queen. His laugh was one of triumph when he removed the piece from the board.

"You would do well to practice your—"

His sentence was left hanging with the sudden interruption of Florilla bursting into the room.

In her blue negligee, she stood inside the doorway, with an object grasped in her hand.

"I . . . I have found it," Florilla whispered dramatically.

"What have you found, Florilla?" Robert asked, frowning.

"The wax doll," she replied, holding out the image dressed in a wispy strip to match the color of her negligee, and a strand of long blond hair hanging from its head. "I took the pin out of its throat."

At the sight of the voodoo doll, Robert's face darkened, and he stood. A chess piece fell to the floor with his abrupt movement.

"Who do you think did this?" Robert questioned the fair-haired woman, yet knowing what her answer would be.

"It was Feena, of course. It has her mark upon it."

Eulalie, hearing Florilla's accusation, put her hand to her breast to still the erratic beating of her heart.

CHAPTER

37

N O, Eulalie. Do not leave the room."

Eulalie, already halfway out, stopped when Robert's words reached her.

"I want you to remain here while I send for Feena." He tugged at the bell pull, and Eulalie slowly passed the gloating Florilla on her way back to her seat near the window.

Robert took the wax doll from Florilla and said, "Since you have not been well, I will not expect you to stay."

At her dismissal, Florilla looked disappointed. But she managed to conceal it after the first faint flicker of annoyance, and with a delicate cough, she trailed from sight, her wispy blue negligee flowing behind.

There was a strained silence between Robert and Eulalie while they waited for Effie to give the message to Feena. Gone was the intimacy of the shared game. The game table now held the ugly wax figure that had intruded to ruin the afternoon.

Feena's steps were light, barely audible to Eulalie, who sat tensely waiting for the woman to appear.

"You sent for me, Monsieur Robert?" Feena asked in a wary voice at the threshold.

"Yes, Feena." Robert picked up the wax doll from the table and motioned to Feena. "Mrs. Hines said this is yours. Do you recognize it?"

She stepped closer, looking at the image.

"Where did she find it?" Feena asked.

"She did not say. Is it yours, Feena?" he asked again.

The black woman was hesitant. "The *doll* is mine, yes, but I do not know how Madame Florilla got it."

Eulalie, at the window, closed her eyes and held onto the chair at Feena's admission. She waited for her husband's voice.

"Pack your things, Feena. I am sending you back to Midgard."

"But Monsieur Robert—"

He held up his hand to silence her. "Nothing you can say will make me change my mind, Feena."

The woman, now frightened, walked toward Eulalie. "I did not dress the doll in that material, or put the hair on it. You believe me, Mamselle Lili?"

Before she could answer, Robert said, "That is another thing that I will not tolerate. You will not address my wife either as 'Lili' or as 'mamselle' any more. Eulalie is a married woman. No longer is she the young girl you have cared for all these years. And I expect you to remember that."

"Yes, Monsieur Robert."

A sad Eulalie stood up and walked toward Feena. "I will come with you, Feena, while you pack."

"Thank you, mam—" She stopped. "Thank you, *ma petite*."

Robert did not forbid Eulalie to leave with the woman. He stayed by the table after the two had departed, and in a sudden action, he picked up the sinister voodoo doll and crushed it in his hands.

Eulalie did not come down to supper. She stayed in her room, eating nothing and mourning the separation that had been caused by Florilla. Later, when Robert's steps announced his return to the bedroom, Eulalie turned her back and stared unseeing out the window into the blackness of the night.

345

"There is no need to show your displeasure, Eulalie. I know you are furious with me, but understand there was nothing else I could do in the circumstances."

"But I *need* Feena," Eulalie lamented.

"I have sent for Tassy to come from the plantation. And Effie can help you with Jason."

"But Tassy is not Feena."

Exasperated by her stubbornness, he said, "Just be happy that I sent her to Midgard in place of the auction block."

"It must be nice to be so powerful that anyone displeasing you can be removed from your presence and sold." Her eyes looked at him accusingly.

His hands reached toward her and then stopped short when she shrank from him.

"Will you never let me forget what I did to you, Eulalie?" he asked, clenching his hands at his side. "With your dark doe eyes staring at me that way? The past is past. And it would behoove you to turn your energies to making the present more amiable, instead of dwelling on the past."

"Is that an order, Robert? And what if *I* displease you? Will you send me away again as you did Feena?"

His scowl suddenly cleared and his smoky eyes were amused. "Are you baiting me deliberately, hoping I *will* send you away? No, Eulalie. No matter how shrewishly you behave, you cannot hope to win. You will stay here with me."

The nights that Robert stood watch, Eulalie locked the door to their bedroom. She had had two other encounters with the ghost in her bedroom, but because of Robert, she had not mentioned it. It was strange that it was only when he was standing watch at the lighthouse that the ghost appeared. But now that Jimbo had fixed the lock, Eulalie was not bothered.

She missed Feena, and so did Jason. But Effie was kind to the child, taking him for rides in the pony cart and helping with his shells when Florilla was free from her chore as governess.

Later, Eulalie sat with Jason on the beach, giving him

346

encouragement with his castle in the sand. Neijee, farther down from them, was digging his own castle and watching the water fill the moat he had designed.

"Feena was a bad girl," Jason offered. "So she sent away." Jason looked up at Eulalie with his big troubled topaz eyes. He continued digging in the sand. "Eu-lie, if Jason bad, will Papa send him away too?"

"No, my pet. You'll always be with us, whether you're bad or good," Eulalie reassured him.

"Flo'illa say Jason be sent away," he replied.

"Then she is wrong, Jason. Your papa and I love you very much. You'll never be sent away."

Relieved, the child began digging again. Eulalie, sitting beside him, was thoughtful. She must speak with Florilla. It was wrong of the governess to scare the child into being good.

"Jason," Eulalie said, "can you start calling me 'Maman'?"

He shook his head and answered at once. "No. You Eu-lie."

The child continued digging with his shell, scooping out the sand around him, and Eulalie, watching him, sighed and made no further comment.

"Madame," Neijee's voice called out. "Come and see my castle. I have finished it."

She arose and brushed the sand from her hands. "It's beautiful, Neijee, and I love the moat," she said, standing beside him and admiring his handiwork.

He smiled at her in delight and she returned his smile.

Robert, walking toward the beach, had much on his mind. It was now the last of July, two weeks since the feud between Joseph Alston and the state militia had reached its apex, resulting in the governor's abolishment of the militia.

Tired of their duties, two of the units had refused to guard the harbor. And when Alston had ordered the court-martial of those forty citizens, Judge Bay interrupted the proceedings. Nowhere did the law state any penalty for disobeying orders to defend the city, even though there were penalties for lesser offenses. Furious at the action, the governor had simply abolished the militia.

Robert was at a loss to understand the man's maneuver, leaving the harbor undefended. Perhaps losing his wife and son the same year had embittered him and done something to his reason. But now, Joseph had been forced into rectifying his actions.

Robert looked up and saw Eulalie standing beside Neijee. And then he saw Jason, happily playing in the sand.

Yes, losing one's wife and child could cause a man to lose his sanity. How clearly Robert remembered when he had believed Eulalie to be dead—and the hell he had lived in for those two years.

"So this is where you have spent the afternoon," Robert said, approaching the three figures on the beach.

"Papa, come and see," Jason squealed, running to him and tugging at his breeches leg.

The man took the child's hand and walked with him to his castle in the white sand. And although he commented to Jason's satisfaction, Robert was troubled.

He looked back where Eulalie was standing with Neijee, her gaze toward the sea. Even in peaceful moments such as this one, their eyes automatically turned to the far horizon, where British ships had been spotted several times, with the alarm flashed from the lighthouse to land. But each time the ships had sailed on, leaving them alone.

"Eulalie, come and walk with me for a while," Robert requested. "And Jason, you and Neijee go back to the house."

When the children had gotten beyond hearing, Eulalie's attention reverted to Robert. Seeing the grave expression on his handsome face, she asked, "Is there bad news?"

"I'm afraid so, Eulalie. The British have landed at St. Helena. This means that Joseph will have to do something about the militia."

Eulalie, making an effort to keep up with Robert's long strides, was not successful. She lagged behind, and seeing this, Robert slowed his gait.

"He has revoked his order to abolish the militia, but

he needs more power, to place them under the same regulations as Federal troops in time of war. Eulalie, Joseph has called the legislature into emergency session, to give him that power, and I will have to leave for Columbia tomorrow."

His words were alarming. Would they be allowed to stay on the island, or would Robert force them to leave with him?

"I debated about what to do with you and Jason— whether to take you into Charleston to the townhouse. But you would be in just as much danger there. And even more so, if the town is shelled. As an alternative, I have decided to let you stay here, and I have sent for Hector to be with you while I am away."

"So Hector is to be my keeper this time." Eulalie said softly, remembering their earlier conversation.

Robert stopped and took Eulalie's hand. "Do not be resentful. I am doing it for your own good."

"Just as you sent Feena away—for her own good?"

Robert stiffened at her remark. "God! Why can't you be more like Florilla? At least she knows how to please a man. She doesn't continually harp on a subject when it's already dead."

He glanced at Eulalie, with her dress wet around the hem. "Florilla would never let her dress get into such a condition, either."

His words hurt Eulalie, who quickly looked down and shook the sand from her skirt.

"And I suppose you admire her fair complexion, too?"

"Yes, I do. And she never forgets she's a woman. She's dignified and demure at the same time. You don't hear her raising *her* voice like some shrewish hoyden."

"And she also has kept her figure, not having it spoiled," Eulalie agreed sweetly, "by a demanding husband."

He looked at her ripening figure, with its obvious protrusion, and Robert's guffaw reached out over the water. A gull sitting quietly on a piece of driftwood took flight at its sound.

"You are a little minx," Robert accused in a softened

tone, "handed to me by Uncle Ravenal to drive me out of my mind."

Unsure of his meaning, Eulalie started walking to the tabby house. Robert stood on the beach, watching the indignant swing of her skirts as she moved. And he was reminded of the time she had hidden from him in the river house, driving him mad with desire.

CHAPTER
38

THE first day that Robert was away was unbearably long, and Eulalie, in that quiet dusky period when the sun had set, found herself alone on the beach. Eulalie did not know why she was drawn to that particular spot where Robert had found her the first time she visited the island with him.

She sat on the rock and watched the waves dissipate from roaring breakers into softly lapping blankets of foam that crept over the white sand of the beach.

And then with her eyes shut, she closed out everything but the memory of that day with Robert—the betrayal of her senses to his touch when he fastened her slippers and held her in his arms to lift her to the ground.

The cry of the gulls suddenly broke into her reverie. Eulalie opened her eyes. No longer was she the slim girl who had pirouetted with the conch shell to her ear, listening for the sounds of the sea. She was now large with child, awkward and slow in her movements.

Eulalie stared at her bare arms, browned by the sun. And her muslin dress, let out as much as the seams would allow, was wrinkled, with the hem still wet from the water at the edge of the shore.

No wonder Robert had given her such a disapproving look. His castigating words had made it plain. He preferred the simpering Florilla, who was incessantly concerned with the state of her complexion or dress.

"Well, if that's the way you want it, Robert Tabor," Eulalie said aloud, "more than one can act the part." She would show him.

Eulalie made up her mind. She would stay out of the sun. But that would not be hard to do, since it had started giving her a headache anyway.

And Florilla did not have exclusive use of concoctions to make her skin soft and white, she thought. Effie would be glad to make some more of the buttermilk-and-cucumber mixture she had used in Columbia to soften Eulalie's workworn hands.

"If that's what you admire, Robert," she continued talking to herself, imagining him in front of her, "then I will be the picture of elegance, with not a hair out of place, not a spot or wrinkle on my dress."

Eulalie twisted a strand of hair around and around her finger. There was only one thing wrong. No matter what she did, the truth remained. She was heavy with child and there was no way to disguise it. How could a body be elegant when it looked like a ripe melon ready to be plucked?

Sighing, Eulalie left her perch on the rock and walked toward the tabby house.

She met Hector on the path. "I was just coming to look for you, my dear. Robert would never forgive me if I didn't watch over you properly."

Eulalie felt remorseful at his words. "I am sorry if I gave you cause for concern, Hector. I was on the beach, and didn't realize how dark it was becoming."

"No need to apologize, Eulalie. I thought that's where you might be. And I would have joined you there except for Mrs. Hines."

Eulalie smiled at his polite words. It was obvious that Florilla was intent on enchanting Hector. Poor Hector, Eulalie thought. From the moment he had reached the island, he had been subject to Florilla's simperings.

And to think that Robert had held the woman up as a model for Eulalie to emulate.

Ten days—that's all the time she had before Robert returned. . . .

"Yes'm, I'll be happy to mix a batch for ya," Effie said when Eulalie approached her about the buttermilk-and-cucumber recipe. "But it won't do much good for ya if ya keep on sittin' in the sun."

"I have already decided. It's much too hot for me now to be on the beach in the heat of the day."

Effie agreed. "Don't take long to get a heatstroke in this kind o' weather. Best for *you* in yore condition to find a nice, cool place in the shade."

"That's what I intend to do from now on, Effie."

Eulalie looked at Effie and asked, "How long will it take to make the recipe?"

"I'll churn some milk jus' as soon as Jimbo brings it in tomorrow mornin'. Then I'll mince the cucumbers while I set the milk out to clabber. Should be ready in another day."

Jason and Neijee could not understand why Eulalie had suddenly stopped playing with them on the beach. But Hector took charge of them, and their protests soon dwindled. Jason, always pleased to see the white-haired man, began to follow him everywhere, and Hector seemed to enjoy the company of the little boy and his black companion, Neijee.

With Robert and Arthur in Columbia, other volunteers took their turn at the lighthouse. It was imperative that they keep a sharp lookout for the ships immediately south of them.

Eulalie did not see the men. The ones on duty now spent the nights at the lighthouse and had their meals taken to them there. So in the evenings, the dining table encompassed Hector, Eulalie and Florilla—no one else.

Effie, true to her word, brought Eulalie the mixture for her skin as soon as it was ready. On the next afternoon, Eulalie sat at the dressing table in her bedroom and watched while Effie slathered the thick cream on her face, neck and arms.

Sitting in her chemise, Eulalie complained, "But it smells so terrible, Effie." She stared at herself in the mirror—at the two brown eyes peering from the layers of white cream.

"You'll soon get used to the odor," Effie answered her. "And won't Mr. Robert be pleased when he sees the difference it makes."

"I doubt that he will even notice."

"Mr. Robert notices 'bout everything, when it concerns *you*," Effie commented.

The servant's remark made Eulalie feel even worse. Her dresses, with their unmistakable need for attention, had not escaped his eyes. But Robert had not offered to buy her any more clothes since that day she had run away from Mrs. Windom's shop.

She would have to see about letting her dresses out some more, or even sewing an extra panel in the front.

The afternoon ritual continued each day that Robert was away. Still Eulalie got no more used to the odor of clabbered milk and cucumbers as the days went by. She continued to wrinkle her nose in disgust, much to Effie's amusement.

"Won't be long now," Effie said. "Already feels like satin. Soon that skin'll be jus' as nice and white as a petal on a magnolia blossom."

Tassy was in the kitchen helping Effie to fix breakfast when Eulalie went downstairs early the next morning.

"I cannot wait any longer," Eulalie confessed. "I am absolutely starved."

Tassy and Effie both laughed. "You're eatin' for two," Effie assured her. "No wonder you're hungry."

Eulalie picked up a piece of fresh bread and poured a glass of milk from the pitcher on the table.

"Looks like she might even be eatin' for three," Tassy said, her eyes on Eulalie's shape. "Herself and two little 'uns."

"But that's impossible," Eulalie said, taking a sip of milk. "It's true that Jason was a twin, but do you think I might be having twins again?"

"Wouldn't be a bit surprised—the way you've mush-roomed out in the past few months. Jus' like that Miz Weekes over at Midland Hall. Pore Miz Weekes." Tassy shook her head in sympathy. "Never a one stays alive. They always comes too early."

Eulalie set the glass on the table. She had suddenly lost her appetite.

"Tassy, how many babies have you delivered?"

"By myself, ma'am—or helpin' Feena?"

"By yourself."

Tassy stopped what she was doing to count silently on her fingers. Her eyes rolled upward in concentration. "Must be 'leven or twelve," she answered Eulalie, "since this time last year."

No, it was impossible, Eulalie thought to herself as she walked upstairs to the dining room on the main floor. She wished she could talk with Feena about it.

Nine days elapsed, and on the tenth, Eulalie awoke with a feeling of excitement. Robert was coming home.

She listened for his footsteps throughout the day. But there was no sound except the children noisily tramping into the house. The afternoon passed and the sun went down. Still Robert had not come.

Delaying dinner for over an hour, Eulalie watched at the window until the sky grew dark. Finally, a disappointed Eulalie gave orders for Tassy to serve the dinner. Robert had evidently been delayed.

She went through the motions of eating, checking on Jason and then retired to her own bedroom for the night. Before she climbed into bed, Eulalie made sure that the door was locked.

Her muslin dresses, ready for her to wear at any time, were all hanging neatly in the wardrobe. And already her skin was less tan than it had been when Robert left. But it was too soon for Robert to notice any difference—except for her voice. When he came back, she was determined to keep her tone of voice demure and low, to be the picture of sweetness and shyness that he admired. That is, if she could stand it.

The banging on her door awoke her.

"Eulalie, for God's sake, open the door."

It was Robert, calling from the hallway. What was he doing home in the middle of the night?

Eulalie hastily scrambled out of bed. How long had Robert been standing outside, knocking to get in?

She reached the door and felt for the lock. Twisting it in her hands, she heard the click, and Robert on the other side, hearing it also, pushed open the door. With the candle held high, Robert stood glowering over her. He was in an evil temper.

"I am not used to having my bedroom door locked against me."

"It was not to keep *you* out, Robert," she said, still drugged with sleep. "It was to keep someone else ou—" Eulalie stopped abruptly.

"To keep *who* out?"

"No one, Robert," she answered. "I am surprised to see you this late," she added in a sleepy voice and stumbled back to bed while he set the candle on the table.

"You forget, Eulalie. I was a sailor, used to traveling by the stars. But finish what you were going to say," he ordered, coming to sit on the bed beside her.

She was sleepy and irritated at his manner of greeting her after being away for ten days. "But it's the middle of the night," she protested.

"It is *not* the middle of the night, Eulalie," he contradicted. "It only seems so to you."

"Can't it wait until tomorrow? I am so sleepy." Her voice was plaintive, but it did not deter Robert.

"No. By tomorrow, you will have thought up some ridiculous tale, bearing no resemblance to what you were ready to confess tonight. And I have learned to my detriment that what is left unsaid in the evening never gets resolved the next day."

His accusation served to wake her. She sat up facing him, her wide eyes flashing with annoyance. "All right, Robert. I was going to say I had locked the door to keep the *ghost* out."

For an instant he gazed at her without speaking. "I

was not aware that the door could even be locked," he stated, still watching her.

"It couldn't, until Jimbo fixed it."

"When was this?"

"After . . . after the ghost had bothered me several times, when you were on duty at the lighthouse."

"And you didn't deem it necessary to tell me about it?"

"You had said it was my imagination the first time it happened. If you didn't believe me the first time, how could I expect you to believe me when it happened again?"

Seeing her quivering lip, Robert stood up. "I think we will wait until tomorrow to discuss this, after all, for I am tired too."

She lay back against the pillows and closed her eyes. But she was now wide awake. Disappointment enveloped her. She was going to be *so* demure when he returned, never raising her voice. But the moment he had entered the bedroom, she had begun to behave like a shrew again. Would it ever be any different between them?

The next morning, Eulalie slipped downstairs before Robert was awake. She did not relish continuing the conversation that he had started earlier.

She was surprised to see Hector up so early. "Good morning, Eulalie," he greeted her. "How are you feeling this morning?"

"Just fine," she answered, her mind still on Robert and the previous evening. "And you?"

"All packed and ready to leave."

"You're going so soon?" Eulalie's voice sounded disappointed.

"There's no need for me to stay longer now that Robert is back—although I have enjoyed being here," he added.

"You were kind to come, Hector."

The dishes were laid out on the server, and Eulalie and Hector helped themselves to the fresh fruit, milk, bread and jam and slabs of bacon. For a while they ate in companionable silence. Then Hector spoke.

"Any time you want to get rid of Jason, you can send him to me, Eulalie. He's a fine little boy."

Robert, entering the dining room, spoke up. "Now why

should we do that when you're quite capable of marrying again, Hector, and raising a family of your own?"

The older man grinned at Robert. "It's too late for that, as you well know, Robert. But thank you for the compliment. Besides," he continued roguishly, "the only one I would have been interested in was already married into the family."

His exaggerated glance toward Eulalie caused Robert to laugh. "Take your covetous eyes off my wife, Hector. I thought I could trust you."

"Only up to a certain point," Hector teased.

After breakfast, Robert and Eulalie walked with Hector to the pier. Matthew was waiting to take the man back to Charleston. Settling himself in the boat with his baggage surrounding him, Hector waved at the figures on the wooden structure that jutted into the water. At last the boat disappeared from sight, and Eulalie and Robert turned and started down the path toward the tabby house.

Robert's glance took in Eulalie's neat appearance. And at the touch of his hand on her arm, he was surprised at the softness and smoothness.

"You got along well while I was away?" he questioned.

"Yes, Robert. Jason immediately attached himself to Hector. It was a blessing, since I can no longer keep up with our son. And you," she hurriedly said, "was your trip to Columbia successful?"

"Yes. The matter is now settled. The legislature gave Joseph the power he wanted. It is not likely that the militia will balk again at being on duty."

"I had thought you would be home earlier," Eulalie stated.

"So did I. But then I stopped to pick up my order from Mrs. Windom's shop. She had not finished one of the items, so it was necessary for me to wait."

They were in sight of the tabby house when Robert stopped. "Come now, are you not curious? Don't you want to know what I brought home?" Robert asked.

"Not the green dress?"

"No—although I would have purchased it too, if the woman had not already sold it."

"But I wouldn't have been able to wear it."

"Not now," he admitted, "but you could have saved it for later. Well, no matter—it was gone. But I hope you will be pleased with what I brought to you. Mrs. Windom will remove the extra material after the baby comes, unless you want to pack the dresses away for the next time."

Her words of gratitude froze on her lips. *"Next* time?" she croaked, staring at Robert with a disbelieving air.

His hand reached for her and drew her close to him. "I plan to have a large family, Eulalie—to start a dynasty of Tabors in Carolina." His eyes were teasing, and Eulalie glared at him and pushed herself from him.

"And I have nothing to say about it?"

"Of course you will have something to say about it. I'll leave the choice of names up to you, although I would like to have *one* son named Ravenal for my uncle."

"Perhaps you had better plan for another wife, Robert, while you're doing all your other planning—one who would be eager to bear your children."

"The wife I have suits me well enough," he said, the teasing now absent from his voice.

CHAPTER

39

So now she knew the role that Robert had assigned her—someone to bear his children, her position little better than the brood mare Papa Ravenal had purchased shortly before he died.

And with this knowledge came added despair. It did not require love. Robert could find love elsewhere while she, Eulalie Boisfeulet Tabor, could be left at home, conveniently *enceinte,* and hidden from view year after year. And Florilla, whom Robert admired, could keep her trim figure and his love.

"Don't you want to see your new dresses?" Robert's voice asked when she hesitated at the bedroom door.

A hot tear fell down her cheek and landed on her breast. "If it's all right with you, Robert, I will see them later," Eulalie managed to say before running down the hallway to avoid Robert's all-seeing tawny eyes.

A puzzled Robert stared at the nursery door that swung shut behind Eulalie. Now what had he done to cause her to go off in such a manner?

Was bearing his children so repugnant to her? Was that what had caused her to run from him, to shed her quiet tears elsewhere? The realization that he was not ever going to let her go, that she would always be trapped with no way of escape from him?

Robert thought of the young fawn he had tamed when he was a boy—how desperate the wild creature was to escape his hands at first. Yet his gentleness and patience had eventually won, and the fawn began to come willingly to him to nuzzle him and show her affection.

Eulalie was like the fawn, easily startled and ready to escape at the least untoward sound or awkward movement. How much longer before she would learn to trust him and come willingly, seeking affection?

Sighing, Robert realized he would have to leave his offering of the dresses to Eulalie, just as he had left the food in the clearing for the fawn at the edge of the forest. She was still shy of him. He spread the six beautiful dresses across the bed and walked out of the room to disappear down the path toward the lighthouse.

Eulalie, hearing Robert leave the house, brushed away her tears and walked slowly back from the empty nursery to the bedroom. She was ashamed of her behavior and her inability to hide her feelings. But was that not what Papa Ravenal had always teased her about? She could hear his voice now—"Lili, my dear, your eyes will always give you away." And she had not wanted Robert to see what she had been unable to hide.

The dresses lay on the bed where Robert had left them—thin, delicate Indian calicoes and muslins, suitable for a hot climate. And a large white sun hat decorated with flowers and colored ribbons rested upon the pillow.

Interested in spite of herself, Eulalie felt the gossamer material of the dresses with her fingers, and unable to resist trying one on, she removed her own mended dress and stepped into the white Indian calico.

It was soft and luxurious to the feel, and Eulalie's steps were lighter as she hurried to the mirror. She smiled when she saw her reflection. The pleated folds in front disguised her figure as her other dresses had been unable to do. She felt elegant and pleased—grateful that, even if he did not love her, Robert had noticed her need and provided for her. She would never have had the courage to enter Mrs. Windom's shop again, after hearing the conversation between Polly Ashe and the shop owner.

Eulalie removed the dress. She would wear it at dinner and hope that Robert would notice.

He had spent most of the day at the lighthouse, even eating his midday meal with the militia volunteers. But now, Robert, seeing the man off at the pier, began his trudge back to the house. On the pathway he met Jason and Neijee, accompanied by Florilla.

The woman seemed unusually glad to see him. Such a pity, Robert thought, that Eulalie could not show the same pleasure when he returned. Holding Jason's hand, Robert slowed his walk to accommodate the child's shorter steps, and Florilla, on his other side, chattered as they walked.

The sound of laughing voices announced Robert's arrival. Eulalie sat by the open window in the parlor. Her fingers, deftly stitching the soft white material, faltered at the sound.

"Eu-lie," the child's voice called out. "Where are you?"

"In here, Jason—in the parlor," Eulalie answered.

Jason and Neijee rushed into the room, their faces slightly dirty from their play.

"Madame, hold out your hands," Neijee instructed her.

"And close your eyes, Eu-lie," Jason ordered.

Eulalie obeyed them both, smiling at the same time. She felt something being pressed into each hand.

"Now may I open my eyes?" she asked.

"Yes," the two excited little boys chorused together.

Eulalie slowly opened them and stared at the offerings —a starfish and a small, exquisite pink shell.

"They're beautiful," Eulalie said, beaming. "Thank you very much for my lovely presents."

"We found them on the beach," Neijee confided.

There was a sound from the open doorway, and Eulalie looked up to see Robert standing there, observing the proceedings.

"I think Effie is looking for both of you, Jason," Robert said. "Time to get cleaned up, so run along."

Unprotesting, the boys ran from the room in search of Effie. Eulalie moved to put the starfish and shell on the window sill.

"Love offerings, Eulalie?" Robert asked, walking closer.

She nodded. "They always bring something to me when they go out on the beach. I never know what it will be, but the ritual is always the same. I have to close my eyes and hold out my hands." She smiled as she said it. "And I'm always afraid they will bring back something . . . alive."

Robert laughed. "Being on the island for the summer has been good for Jason. And it seems to have agreed with you, too."

Their eyes met, and Eulalie, suddenly nervous, was aware of Robert's scrutiny.

"The dresses are beautiful, Robert. Thank you." Eulalie's voice was now serious.

"Turn around and let me look at you, Eulalie."

Self-consciously she turned, aware of his continued concentration. She had used the cream mixture that afternoon and brushed her hair until every strand was lustrous. And now in the beautiful white calico . . .

"There is something different about you, Eulalie—something I can't seem to put my finger on. What is it?" he asked.

"I don't know," she said, "unless it is the new dress."

"No, it isn't that, although it has made a vast improvement in your appearance. You have a different look about you."

She certainly was not going to tell him how hard she worked while he was away to become more the type of woman he admired. It would be a blow to her pride if he ever found out about the buttermilk-and-cucumber mixture. For then it would seem that she was trying to compete with Florilla in making herself desirable—just for him.

"After the baby comes, I want to have your portrait painted, with the new baby in your arms and Jason at your side."

Surprised at his wish, she said nothing. And almost as

if she were not in the room, Robert, thinking aloud, walked back and forth from the fireplace to the oversized leather chair.

"I can see it now, with the garden at Midgard in the background, when the yellow jasmine is in bloom. With your dark eyes, you will resemble a picture of a madonna I saw in Paris, brought back by Napoleon from the war in Spain."

"Tassy thinks I may be having twins again, Robert, so you might have to pay for a larger canvas to get all of us in."

He stopped his pacing. With deliberate steps Robert was immediately at her side, frowning at her.

"And you, Eulalie? What do *you* think?"

"I don't know," she replied. "I feel the same as last time."

"If there is such a possibility," Robert said with a hesitant voice, "then I think it would be better if we all went to Charleston to stay at the townhouse, so that you can be nearer to a physician."

A haunted look appeared in Eulalie's dark eyes. "Robert, there is too much danger of childbed fever. I do not wish to have a physician in a crowded city attending me for the birth. It is much safer for me here."

"And who will attend you if something goes wrong, and the baby or babies decide to come before their time?"

"Tassy has helped Feena many times, and delivered some babies by herself. So if the baby comes early, we can rely on Tassy and pray that nothing goes wrong."

Robert was silent, lost in his thoughts, and Eulalie had no way of knowing what he was thinking. She went back to her window seat and took up her sewing. Concentrating on each stitch, Eulalie did not look up again until the room was empty.

Robert was unusually brooding at dinner. Eulalie felt his eyes on her throughout the meal, and it made her uncomfortable. She was glad when it was over and they had gone once again into the parlor.

With not enough light to sew, Eulalie became restless. She sat in a chair for a few minutes, but she was uncomfortable. And so she stood up, peering out the window at the shadows cast by the cassina bushes on the open porch.

Robert took the chess pieces from their hiding place and became absorbed in setting them up. Eulalie, glancing quickly at his action, diverted her eyes to the landscape outside the window. A revulsion came over Eulalie at the sight of the chessboard.

She had not touched the pieces since that day that Feena had been sent back to Midgard. The memory of the voodoo doll dressed in a strip of Florilla's gown, with the blond strand of hair, was still fresh in Eulalie's mind. She could still see the doll resting on the table beside her queen that Robert had removed from the board.

"Would you care to play a game, Eulalie?" Robert asked, forcing Eulalie to turn from the window.

"No, thank you, Robert. I cannot sit for long periods of time. It is too uncomfortable."

Florilla, as if sympathizing with Eulalie, remarked, "It is too bad that having a child makes a woman so restless, besides spoiling her looks. And sometimes, she never gets them back. But such is the lot of women," Florilla finished with a half-concealed gloating expression.

"My wife is even more beautiful *now* than she was the first time I saw her," Robert said quietly.

The compliment was overshadowed by his next words. "Florilla, since Eulalie does not seem to be interested, would you like to join me?"

"I have never learned to play, Robert," she replied. "No one ever took the time to teach me." She quickly pushed out of her mind the games of blackjack she had played in the saloon with Clem.

"I have lots of time tonight, if you would care to learn."

Florilla left her seat and went to the game table. With Robert's voice patiently explaining the positions of the pieces to Florilla, Eulalie slipped from the room. She would not stay and watch the two together for the rest of the evening, their heads bent intimately over the chess pieces.

Eulalie began to climb the steps to the bedroom. The movement on the landing caught her attention.

Amid the gray shadows projected on the walls, Eulalie

saw a fleeting movement of a gray shroud and a stark white face staring down at her. The ghost. It was the island ghost, but far different from the figure of her dreams, far different from the shimmering essence on the beach near the rock.

She did not wait to see more. With a cry, Eulalie turned and fled back down the stairs.

At the sound of Eulalie's frightened voice, Robert pushed his chair from the game table and headed for the hallway. He saw Eulalie's hasty flight and he held out his arm to steady her.

"Eulalie, what is it? Why are you so frightened?"

Shaking with fear, she managed to gasp, "The g-ghost. It was the ghost, Robert. And it's up on the stair landing."

Robert, with Eulalie clinging to him, took a step nearer the stairs. His deep voice rang out, echoing over the deserted hallway.

"Come down," Robert called. "Whoever you are, come down at once."

Florilla, standing farther back, joined Robert and Eulalie in watching and waiting.

Slowly the gray shroud appeared and floated down the stairs, with the coarse material dragging on the steps behind.

Eulalie, her eyes fixed on the moving apparition, shrank against Robert. The old steps creaked under the weight of the ghost as it stumbled and then righted itself. But ghosts were supposed to float, Eulalie thought. Unreal, gossamer things like the mist on the beach.

Now out of the shadows, the gray shroud descended and stopped. Two small faces, plastered with a mixture of buttermilk and cucumbers, were visible under the shroud. And Eulalie, recognizing the two children, called out in disbelief. "Jason! Neijee!"

Robert's hearty laugh rang out. "So that is your ghost, Eulalie—two small harmless boys, intent on some fun."

Jason's round topaz eyes and Neijee's, black as two bits of coal, stared at the three grown-ups.

"Neijee, where did you and Jason find the robe?" Robert asked.

"In the attic, Mr. Robert," the subdued little boy answered.

"And what is that mess on your faces?"

Neijee looked at Jason and the golden-haired child stared back.

"It is Effie's mixture of buttermilk and cucumbers," Eulalie admitted.

"Buttermilk and cucumbers?" Robert repeated.

Florilla, behind Robert, explained, "It is a beauty preparation, Robert—designed to make a woman's skin soft and—desirable."

"Does it belong to you, Florilla?" Robert asked, his eyes still amused.

While Florilla was shaking her head, Eulalie answered, "It belongs to me, Robert." Embarrassed that she had been forced to tell him, Eulalie spoke in a soft voice.

"To *you*, Eulalie?" Robert asked incredulously.

Eulalie blushed at his inquiry, while his eyes carefully took in her complexion. His hand went to her cheek and she closed her eyes as his fingers moved to the back of her neck, caressing where the wisps of curls were tied together with the ribbons.

Conscious of eyes directed at them, Robert stopped the movement of his hands and in a gruff voice ordered, "Florilla, see to the boys. And after their faces are clean, make sure they stay in bed."

The rustle of material swept past her as Florilla hurried to obey Robert. Eulalie, attempting to move from Robert's embrace, was restrained by his strong arms.

She stood in the hallway, abruptly silent, and stared at the buttons on Robert's white shirt. His familiar hand lifted her chin, forcing her to look into his inquisitive eyes —the same gesture he had used in the nursery cabin the day the fever had begun.

Finally, Robert's voice whispered, "Have you suddenly become conscious of being a woman, Eulalie? Dare I hope you were using the cream to make yourself more desirable—for me?"

Stung at his amusement over the ghost, Eulalie shook her head. "Effie insisted that I use it."

He did not force her to remain in his arms. At her resistance, he dropped his arms, releasing her.

While Eulalie, in a dignified walk, went up the stairs, Robert, with a disappointment scarcely concealed, stood where he was for a while and then slowly walked back and seated himself at the game table.

There was little light left to shine through the bedroom window of the old tabby house. Eulalie did not seem to notice, so intent was she on reaching the prie-dieu in the corner. She sank to her knees and bowed her head to ask for forgiveness.

She had used the mixture to try to make herself more desirable in Robert's eyes, as he had suspected. But her pride had forced her to deny the truth.

CHAPTER

40

SEPTEMBER had come—the month of hurricanes for the Carolina coast. It was hot, with the days passing in alternate fits of blazing sun and storm-soaked humidity.

In the parlor of the tabby house, Robert, Arthur, Florilla and Eulalie sat in silence. They were subdued because of the news of the massacre at Fort Mims. But no one mentioned the thoughts uppermost in all their minds. A pall had descended upon the room, its somber threat broken only by the creaking of the small rocking chair in which Eulalie sat.

It was early evening, and Eulalie, wearing the pale-blue muslin with white rosettes, had protested her presence. She was self-conscious about her size. But Robert had refused to let her hide in the bedroom when Arthur came. Robert's manner was a proud one, as if by flagrantly showing Eulalie off, he was not only announcing his claim to her but also proof of his virility.

"Why do hurricanes appear only during the month of September?" Eulalie asked, fanning herself with the ivory fan that had belonged to her *maman*.

"It has to do with the Bermuda High," Robert explained. "Charleston is on the fringe and has borne the brunt of the wayward winds many a time."

"Do you remember, Arthur," Robert said to his friend, "the time we were children and the streets of Charleston were covered with the remains of ships swept in by the high tides and winds?"

"I only remember hearing about it," Arthur responded. "I had spent the summer at Cedar Hill and had not returned to Charleston. But when I came home, I saw the devastation to the plantation. The rice fields were ruined that year."

Robert nodded. "We lost many trees around Midgard as well. Also much of the livestock." Turning to Florilla, he said, "Have you ever been in a hurricane, Florilla?"

"No, Robert, and I hope I never will. I am terrified of storms, especially on the water," Florilla confessed.

Eulalie sat quietly, thinking of Florilla. She had been such a puzzle ever since they had come to the island. At the appearance of the ghost in her room, Eulalie had suspected Florilla, but she had no evidence against the woman. After Neijee and Jason had masqueraded in the gray shroud, there was no further appearance of the ghost, for Robert had taken the shroud from the children.

Was it true, as Robert had accused, that she had let her imagination run rampant after reading the friar's book? And that the children, finding the gray cloak in the attic, had added to her fantasy? But she *knew* that someone had tried to smother her. She could not forget the feeling. And the two little boys would never hurt her.

Cedar Hill seemed such a long time ago, with Florilla's taunting words and the danger to Jason. At least she had not imagined *that*. Eulalie knew that the scene at the apple tree was real. Yet here Florilla sat opposite her, the picture of sweetness and femininity. And there had been no further attempt to harm Jason. Jason . . . Eulalie thought of the golden-haired child so dear to her, and her heart was heavy as her mind dwelt on the innocent children who were dead at the hands of the Indians.

"Is there something wrong with my appearance, Mrs. Tabor?" Florilla asked, seeing Eulalie's eye still on her.

Eulalie gave a start and straightened in her chair. "No,

Florilla. I did not mean to be staring. I was thinking of the massacre at Fort Mims."

So Eulalie put into words what they had all been aware of, what they had not talked about once during the evening. The silence and the mundane discussion of the weather had served as a mask to hide their real thoughts.

The land war in Canada and the north, so far away, had suddenly moved southward with the Indian, Tecumseh, accounting for the tragedy at the junction of the Alabama and the Tombigbee.

Eulalie's words stopped the reluctance to speak about the massacre in the women's presence. Robert looked at Eulalie, sitting calmly in her rocking chair. She had shown a sympathy for the coastal people when she learned of Sir George Cockburn's destruction of the ironworks and cannon foundry, and the plundering of St. Helena. But she had not been paralyzed with fear, as so many women would have been. And had she not decided on her own to take the risk of spending the hot summer on Tabor Island? Robert was proud of her for that. It demanded courage.

"It was Tecumseh's fault. If it had not been for him, Red Stick would never have massacred those helpless people." Arthur spoke aloud with anger, bringing Robert's attention back to the subject of the massacre.

"True, Red Stick was used by Tecumseh, but the blame does not stop with him," Robert argued. "The scalps of those five hundred men, women and children at Fort Mims were but the dowry price for the union between the British and Tecumseh. I have a feeling, though, that the marriage bed will not be comfortable for the British. They cannot help but wonder when Tecumseh and the Indian nations might turn on them and murder them in their sleep. But regardless of whose fault it actually was," Robert continued, "something will have to be done. We cannot allow another Creek uprising here in the south. People are more afraid of the Indians than of the British."

"I heard in Charleston today that Andy Jackson of the Tennessee militia has been appointed to march against Red Stick," Arthur informed Robert.

Surprised, Robert said, "Is he well enough, after his duel?"

"It was a flesh wound in the arm, as yours was, Robert. I think it will heal in time. But I understand the other man did not fare so well."

Eulalie, with a sudden movement, rose from her chair. "If you will excuse me . . ." Eulalie put her hand to her head to fight the dizziness.

Robert was out of his chair in an instant and by her side. Arthur stood, looking decidedly upset, as Robert helped Eulalie from the room and up the stairs.

"You do not have to stay with me, Robert," Eulalie said, while he laid the cool, wet cloth across her forehead. "You have Arthur to—"

"Arthur is not a guest, but a friend. He will understand when I do not return. Besides, Florilla is still downstairs to entertain him."

"But he doesn't care much for . . . " Eulalie did not continue, but Robert had an idea what she was going to say.

"I know that Florilla could not hope to replace you in Arthur's affections, but I expect when he realizes that you have retired for the evening, he will find some excuse to retire to the lighthouse."

Robert's voice was harsher than usual. Then it grew softer and contrite with his next words. "I will have to remember, Eulalie, not to discuss such unpleasant matters in front of you. Arthur and I were rather carried away, but I promise you that it won't happen again."

Robert looked down at her pale face, at the long, curved, dark lashes across the high cheekbones. She had completely lost the tan she had acquired earlier in the summer, and her delicate, wan features disturbed him. She was not so strong as he had thought. He would have to remember that.

Eulalie kept her eyes closed and let Robert go on thinking it was the talk of the war that had caused her sudden indisposition. She would not let him know that it was the mention of the duel, with the scene flashing through her mind, of finding Robert on the floor of their bedroom, the trail of blood down the side of the wall . . .

"Are you feeling better?"

Robert's words greeted Eulalie's awakening the next morning. She smiled at her giant of a husband holding the fragile porcelain cup of hot cassina tea under her nose.

"Yes, Robert," she said, sitting up. "But hungry, as usual."

Gratefully, she took the cup from him and began to sip. Eulalie missed the hot chocolate she was accustomed to, but there was little she could do about it. One day, when the war was over, she would be able to have as much chocolate as she wanted, or could afford.

"Tassy said it would be good for you to remain in bed for the day."

Eulalie lowered the cup from her lips. "But I feel fine. Just because I was dizzy last night is no excuse for me to be lazy today."

"Eulalie," Robert's voice spoke patiently, "there is some trouble at the mill. It seems that I will have to be away from the island overnight. And I would feel better about you if you rested for the day. I do not want to leave you, but it looks as if I have no choice."

"When will you be leaving?"

"In a few minutes. Matthew is getting the boat ready."

"Has Jessie started the new school year yet, at the school?" Eulalie asked, thinking of Taborville, with its neat houses and little white school at the end of the village.

"I hired another teacher—a trained one this time, as I had planned," Robert replied. "So Jessie is no longer responsible for the school."

Eulalie's eyes clouded at his admission. "You mean you let Jessie go, after all her work? Robert, you can't do that. She was so proud and anxious to teach. How could you be so cruel?" Eulalie asked, with a break in her voice indicating her distress.

"For your information, Eulalie, it was Ebenezer Shaw who did not want Jessie to teach any more." His voice was cold at her accusation.

"Ebenezer Shaw? What does he have against Jessie, when he was the one who recommended her?"

"He decided he did not want his wife to teach."

"What does that have to do with Jessie?" Eulalie asked, and then stopped. Her face lost its frown and she immediately brightened. "Do you mean Jessie is Ebenezer Shaw's wife?"

"Not yet. That event is to take place in about two weeks."

Eulalie laughed and pushed her hair back from her face. "I cannot believe that Jessie and the mill foreman . . . " She looked up at Robert with an embarrassed air. "Oh, Robert, I *am* sorry for misjudging you. Do forgive me."

"If you promise to spend the day in bed," he answered, his attempt at lightness only partially succeeding.

"I promise," Eulalie replied reluctantly.

Robert leaned over and kissed her on the forehead. He set the empty tea cup on the bedside table and walked out of the room.

The mill needed his attention, it was true. But one of the main reasons for leaving the island was to bring Feena back with him. The woman might not be the most obedient servant, but she was the one who could care for Eulalie best. And Robert wanted to take no chances with Eulalie's welfare.

The water was unusually calm beyond the sea isle, and though the clouds had begun gathering far off, there was little wind. Robert missed the sounds of the gulls flying back and forth in search of food, and their absence troubled him. If a storm was brewing somewhere out in the Atlantic, he would need to hurry back to the island and not linger during his visit to Taborville. Stop at Midgard on the way to tell Feena to pack, ride on to the mill, spend the night, and come back for Feena before the mosquitoes swarmed in the late afternoon. Yes, he would be gone only as long as absolutely necessary—and hope in the meantime that the British fleet stayed at Pamlico Sound.

She had given Robert her promise, but it was hard for Eulalie to remain in bed for the day.

There was nothing for her to do. Eulalie had finished making additional clothes for the new baby. They were now folded and hidden away in the small trunk near the window of the bedroom, along with the tiny garments that had belonged to Jason. And she had finished the shirt for Robert, as well.

Eulalie propped herself up in bed and reread the letter from Julie that had come the previous week. It had been handled so much that the edge of the paper was tattered and a small stain from spilled tea obliterated a word.

Eulalie did not know why she bothered to hold the letter in her hands, for she knew every word that her cousin had written . . . the treatments she was undergoing and her hopes that they would be successful. And the astounding news that she and Desmond were adopting an orphan child, already eight years of age.

No mention had been made of the gold that Julie had given Eulalie. Evidently, Julie believed that everything was right again between Robert and Eulalie, with the coming of the baby. What would Julie say if she knew that Robert had taken the pouch from her as soon as they reached Midgard, and had placed it out of her reach?

The barking of the dog outside told Eulalie that the boys were playing near the cassina bushes at the porch. And then she heard their high-pitched voices. Eulalie smiled to herself. The stack of shells had provided untold hours of pleasure for Jason and Neijee during the summer.

Soon it would be time for all of them to leave the island and return to Midgard. They had been lucky to spend as much time as they had on Tabor Island without being forced to leave because of the British.

With the children's voices quieter in the background, Eulalie closed her eyes. Julie's letter fluttered to the floor as Eulalie relaxed. . . .

"Madame, hold out your hand." The child's voice awoke her and Eulalie opened her eyes.

"Jason! Neijee!" Effie called in a loud whisper. "Come out of that room. Don't wake Miz Tabor."

But it was too late. "It's all right, Effie," Eulalie said, yawning. "I am already awake."

"Close your eyes, Eu-lie," Jason's voice commanded, ignoring Effie's admonishment.

She did as she was told, used to the game that had taken place all summer.

The small marguerite plant pulled up by its roots was pushed into her hands. At its feel, Eulalie opened her eyes, seeing the rapidly wilting leaves and drooping blossoms.

"We'd better get it in some water right away," Eulalie recommended to the boys.

Ready to climb out of bed, she was stopped by Effie. "No need to get out of bed, Miz Tabor. I'll take that and put it in a pot of dirt for ya. . . . You boys want to help me?" the servant asked.

"Yes," Jason answered, hopping happily on one foot to Effie, with Neijee directly behind him. They disappeared with Effie, and Eulalie lay back against the pillows and smiled. Nothing on the island was safe or secure with Jason and Neijee searching each day for some new treasure to bring to her.

Much later that evening, Eulalie closed the book she had been reading. Her eyes were tired, so she blew out the candle on the bedside table and settled down for the night.

The dappled light of the moon, shining into the room, rested upon the plant in the window. Its leaves were more vital, now that the roots had been buried in the soft damp earth by Effie. Eulalie hoped that it would live for the boys' sakes.

It was the wind in the night that woke her. The banging of the shutters against the window told Eulalie that the breeze coming in from the sea was strong. Another rainstorm on the way, she thought, getting up to move the earthen pot that held the marguerite plant. One strong gust of wind coming through the window could easily sweep the container from its resting place and break it into pieces.

Eulalie was restless; the baby stirred, and she lay for a

long time, listening to the wind and unable to go back to sleep.

A sudden loneliness, magnified by a longing for her husband at her side, seized Eulalie. Her hand reached out to the unused pillow where Robert's golden head had rested the night before. And a numbing fear slowly washed over her, inundating her with its ebb and flow, much like the delicate waves on the sandy beach that had destroyed Jason's sand castle.

But it did no good to feel this way—to be so afraid. Robert would be back. It was not as if he had gone forever. And did she not have Effie and Tassy and the children to console her until he returned?

It was merely the weather that caused her to feel this way—the sudden change in the atmosphere that made her skin prickle and troubled her mind.

She would count slowly, and if that did not put her to sleep, then she would pull out all the pleasant memories that were stored in the back of her mind. And soon it would be morning and she would be safe.

The doorknob moved slightly and Eulalie lifted her head from the pillow to listen. Was someone outside her door, attempting to get in? Just then, the sound of the chairs blown against the outside wall of the open porch reached her, and Eulalie relaxed. It was the wind—nothing more—traveling through the house, making its presence known.

She consoled herself with that knowledge and, finding a comfortable position on her side, Eulalie went back to sleep.

CHAPTER
41

IT was dismal and still—no sound of wind, no cry of birds—and the world was gray, the sky and sea newly wrapped in a colorless, dangerous gray, like the eyes of Alistair Ashe.

It was morning and Eulalie felt a heaviness in the air and a heaviness of body. She listened for sounds within the house, but no one seemed to be stirring.

She could not stay in bed a moment longer. One whole day and night had been enough. And she had promised Robert that one day only. Surely he could not object to her activity on the day he was to return.

Eulalie slipped on her white cotton lawn robe and walked to the window to stare out onto the sea. The wind, almost without warning, swept in from the water to land, softly at first, fluttering the palmetto fronds in a swaying movement, and then gradually it built up until Eulalie could hear the sound of Jason's shells clicking against each other.

The draperies blew out from the window and flapped against the wall, and Eulalie hurriedly lowered the window and lifted the earthen pot of flowers from the floor to the window sill, now protected against the wind.

The sound of the wind was far more soothing than the deathly stillness. A rain squall was building up. Would Robert have trouble getting back to the island in the rain? That was her only concern—not the storm itself. ,

Eulalie's dark eyes watched the sea responding to the wind. But it was nothing to get alarmed about. The waves were little higher than usual. She had seen it many times during the summer, when the smooth waters were disturbed for a time by the wind, and then quieted again when the sun broke from the fast-moving clouds overhead.

The plant on the window sill was still drooping, suffering from the shock of being transplanted. It needed more water to sustain it, and so Eulalie went to the basin stand for additional water. There was none left. She had used all of it the evening before.

Glad to have something to do, she took the water container in her hand, unlocked the bedroom door and started downstairs to the kitchen and the protected spring room.

The kitchen was deserted, and no coals glowed in the open hearth. It was even too early for the servants to be up and about. Walking to the door that gave access to the spring, Eulalie lifted the wooden crosspiece and set it aside, and leaving the door open, she walked into the dark room with its damp earthen floor.

How convenient it was, Eulalie thought, for the spring, visible at the other end of the island, to disappear under the subterreanean layers of shale and rock and to re-emerge in bubbling force underneath the house. Probably that was one of the reasons the mission had been built on that site.

With the gourd dipper, Eulalie filled the ewer with fresh water. To think that people had drunk from that spring for hundreds of years, maybe even thousands—the Indians first, and then the Spaniards. How many more before she, herself, had tasted it?

It was a wonder that the British, with their constant need for fresh water, had not taken advantage of the spring at the far end of the island to replenish their own brackish supply in the wooden barrels on the ships.

Suddenly the door slammed shut and Eulalie was caught in the darkness. She jumped at the unexpected closing and scraping of wood. Why did all old houses have to be so drafty anyway?

In the darkness Eulalie groped for the door. She pushed hard against it, but it would not open. The door was stuck.

Eulalie, still for a moment, thought she heard a rustling sound beside the door. Had someone put the crosspiece in its place, not knowing that she was inside?

"Tassy," Eulalie called, certain that someone was in the kitchen, "is that you? Unbolt the door. I'm locked in the spring room."

She heard the footsteps falter. And she relaxed and waited for the wooden bar to be removed to set her free. But the footsteps, when they resumed, grew fainter. The person was walking away from her, instead of coming to rescue her. Had they not heard her call for help?

"Tassy! Effie!" Eulalie called in a louder voice, this time using the names of both the servants. "Please come and unlock the door."

No one came to her aid. The footsteps disappeared and she was left alone and imprisoned.

How ironic that the same bolt she had insisted on keeping across the door to protect Jason and Neijee from falling in the spring was the instrument that now imprisoned her in the darkness.

She was impatient to be set free. How much longer before Jimbo would come into the kitchen with the load of wood for the hearth? And Tassy and Effie to follow, to get the coals ready to cook the breakfast?

Eulalie leaned her head against the rough, weathered planks of the wall and shivered from the coolness of the air. Except for the small sliver of light that crept underneath the door, she was in almost total darkness, and she did not like it—a dark, dank prison.

With no place to sit, Eulalie was uncomfortable. Shifting her weight from one foot to the other, she knocked over the ewer, the water spilling and soaking her slippers. Quickly she stooped and felt for the container. When her hands found it, she set it upright.

Why had she not stayed in her room until everyone was up? Then she would not have had to suffer this long wait for help to come.

The sounds above her indicated that someone was stirring. Good—it would not be much longer.

From the outside of the tabby house a sudden shout came—Jimbo's voice. His words were unintelligible to Eulalie, but the pitch of his voice indicated something was wrong. What had happened to cause Jimbo to become so excited?

Putting her ear against the door, Eulalie strained to listen. With a slam of another door, the voice grew louder and clearer. The black man's words traveled the length of the long hallway and down the old brick steps to the lower level.

"They's comin'!" he shouted. "They's landed on the island."

Who? Who had landed on Tabor Island? Robert? No, Jimbo would not sound so upset with the coming of the familiar boat steered by Matthew. Could it be—the British?

With the approaching storm the British would be too busy getting their ships to the open sea to ride out the storm far from land, Eulalie argued with herself. Too easily the vessels could be caught in the strong winds and sent crashing upon the shore. And besides, there had been no warning from the lookout in the lighthouse.

But regardless of who had come, the words uttered by Jimbo marked the beginning of frantic activity in the house. Eulalie listened to the rushing of feet hither and yon, and then the scream pierced the air, frightening Eulalie with its intensity. There was no doubt left in her mind. It had to be the British, who had surprised them after all, despite the careful watch.

At the noise, Eulalie called out, fearful for Jason's safety. But her voice did not penetrate beyond the lower level. There was too much activity above for it to be heard.

Weeping now, frustrated with her inability to free herself, Eulalie rattled the door again, and when it did not budge, she sank to the floor, crying out, "Jason—Jason."

The running continued up and down the stairs. Eulalie thought she heard Effie's voice. Then the house was silent. There was no sound except the wind outside, rising in pitch to drown out the soft, gurgling sounds of the spring. There was no one left but Eulalie, trapped in the deserted tabby house.

She tried to put out of her mind the things that had happened on the other islands—the stripping and plundering, and even taking the black servants to be resold in the West Indies. Poor Tassy and Effie and Jimbo and the others. Would they suffer the same fate? And what about Jason—and Neijee? The tears came anew when she thought of the two little boys, who would be so frightened. And she was not with them to comfort them.

The odor of burning wood was strong. And it grew stronger, permeating to the lower depths and into the kitchen. A new terror gripped Eulalie. The British must have set fire to the tabby house before leaving. And Eulalie, locked in the ancient room, was powerless to save herself and her unborn child.

Outside, the rain began—vying with the wind for pre-eminence over the island. The roar from the sea grew progressively louder as it sent its angry waters gushing over the flat land of sand and palmettos.

There was now no need to call for human help. She knelt and prayed on the earthen floor and waited to see which would destroy the house first—the fire or the sea. While she knelt, the water began seeping underneath the door from the kitchen. So now she knew. The sea had asserted its dominance.

"Robert," she whispered, "I am . . . sorry that I could not save your children." Eulalie stood, but there was no place to go, with the waters rapidly swirling around her ankles.

The low nagging pain in the small of her back mattered little. It was the pain in her heart that was all-encompassing. Never to see Jason again—never to be in Robert's arms again. The salty tears fell and mingled with the brine of the sea, already dragging her robe down with its weight.

"Madame! Madame!" the small, high-pitched voice called.

The sound barely registered with Eulalie. Her head drooped in tired defeat, as she wiped her tears with her sleeve.

"Madame! Where are you?"

Eulalie lifted her head and listened. Neijee? Could it be Neijee, still in the house?

"Neijee," Eulalie called, unsure that her mind was not playing tricks on her. And then louder, her voice growing stronger with a sudden burgeoning hope. "Neijee, I'm here—in the kitchen. I'm locked in the spring room."

"Madame, I am coming."

"Be careful, Neijee—the water—"

He was so small. Would he be able to get through the water in time and remove the wooden bar?

There was a splashing sound on the other side of the door. Eulalie waited.

"I cannot reach it, madame," the child cried, his voice revealing his fright.

"Get a chair, Neijee. Hurry, before the water gets any higher. You can reach it in a chair."

The roar of a fresh deluge of water blurred her words and enveloped her body to the waist. And outside the door there was a splash, a cry, and then the small voice was silent.

"Neijee, are you all right?" Eulalie called. But there was no reply.

The calmness that Eulalie had maintained left her. "Neijee," she screamed, certain now that the water had pulled Neijee underneath.

It was too much to bear. Eulalie, caught in an uncontrollable hysteria, screamed again and again, and she fought against the wooden door. Her efforts, ineffectual before the water surrounded her, were even more impotent, serving only to unbalance her, her feet moving out from under her, and the awkwardness of her body throwing her into the submerging waters.

Instinctively she fought against the swirling water, regaining her footing. But the effort was exhausting. Her breath came in short gasps, and the salt stung her eyes.

Blackness greeted her in all directions, and when her hands reached out for the weathered planks of the door, they felt nothing. She had lost her position, and now, disoriented, she was afraid to move, for fear that she would fall into the spring.

"Eulalie," another voice shouted, this time in the deep low-throated pitch of a man. The girl, caught in her nightmare, did not respond. Lethargy overwhelmed her. Soon now it would be all over.

"Eulalie, answer me," the voice demanded. "Where are you?"

"In . . . in the spring room, Robert." Her voice was soft, devoid of hope, for she did not actually believe that her husband was in the house, calling to her. Besides, she had no strength left. With her hand reaching into the air, she slowly sank into the waters.

The scrape of wood was a new sound, and the door, pulled open against the pressure of water, let in the small amount of light from the kitchen. A strong hand touched hers, pulling her fiercely from her watery grave.

"No, I am too tired," she whimpered. "Let me rest."

The hand was strong and would not let her go. "Robert?" she whispered, certain that the man was a figment of her imagination, like the ghost she had seen on the beach. But the grip of his hands hurt her. Did ghosts have the same feel of a man—flesh and body and heart rapidly beating?

"Neijee is gone. He tried to save me," she murmured over and over.

"Where is he, Eulalie?" the deep voice demanded of her. "Where did he go?"

"He is . . . drowned . . . only a minute ago, here in the kitchen."

It was not *her* voice telling him this. It was another voice outside herself, using her own lips to form the words.

"Matthew," the man said to the dark shadow beside him. "Find him. He must still be in the water."

The shadow moved and plunged underneath the water, while Robert waded against the current, fighting the flow that spewed from all directions, filling the kitchen.

Eulalie, looking back toward the area where the black man dived, saw him come up empty-handed. Again, he dived into the water, and the second time, he emerged, holding the limp, small body in his arms. Eulalie cried out and hid her face in Robert's wet shirt. . . .

She was lying on the bed upstairs, with Feena leaning over her, blocking the view of the drooping marguerite plant.

The pains were more rapid now, moving from her back to the pit of her stomach. Eulalie gripped Feena's hands and gasped until the pain subsided.

"Try to sleep, *ma petite,* between the pains," Feena urged her.

"The baby—" Eulalie whispered.

"Oui, the baby is coming—much too early, but Monsieur Robert has saved you. That is all that matters."

"Jason," Eulalie whispered.

"Shh. Jason is safe, mamselle. You need not worry about him."

At Feena's soothing words, Eulalie relaxed and slept, until another pain tightened into a constricting band, cutting off her breath with its intensity. She opened her eyes and reached for Feena's hand. But Robert was beside her instead, and she held onto him, while he stared down at her, anguish etched in his tawny eyes.

With each spasm, her pain became his pain. Why had he been so selfish, determined to bind her to him by any means? He wished that he could go back in time, to erase what he had done, so that her life would not be in danger now. Far better for her to be happy with someone else than to die, bearing his child.

Robert used the wet cloth to wipe the perspiration from her face. There was little water in the house—only the amount gleaned from each upstairs bedroom. And no food at all. If they were lucky and the wind did not turn inland again, they would be able to leave the island soon after the child was born.

A fierce anger grew in Robert's breast. Eulalie had been locked in the spring room by someone. Who had done such a dastardly thing, assuring her death with the water overrunning the island? Robert made his vow. He would not rest until he had found the culprit and punished him.

"I will sit with her now, Monsieur Robert," Feena said. "Try to get some rest, for it looks as if this will be a long day. I will call you when I need you."

His haunted face turned to the black woman. "Do you think everything will be . . . all right?"

"She is very weak," Feena replied, "and I am not sure about the baby, coming this early."

"Forget the child, Feena. It's my wife I care about. She must not die." His voice broke, and with a movement to conceal the anguish he felt, Robert turned his back to the woman and walked from the room.

Robert did not go far—only next door to the nursery, within calling distance if Feena should need him.

He watched from the nursery window while the wind gradually began its bombardment of the island. The house creaked and groaned; the palmettos bent toward the ground under the gathering force. The storm was merely beginning, turning its full wrath upon the island, instead of going out to sea, as Robert had hoped it would. And now the rains descended, spattering the window, so that Robert's view was blocked.

The old tabby house gave another groan, and Robert was uneasy. Would the house, on its three-foot-thick foundation walls, be able to withstand the assault of wind and rain? And the boat that he and Feena had come in— would it be dashed to pieces as well, leaving them stranded on the island?

Robert moved from the window and sat on the cot with his head in his hands. There was no telling how much stronger the winds would get during the night. And with the house already protesting, there was a possibility that it would not last through the storm.

They would all be safer at the lighthouse for the night. But dare he risk it—to take Eulalie from her bed in her condition? If they were only on his ship instead of land, he would feel better. Robert had ridden out many a storm in the *Carolana,* but he was uneasy on the land, knowing he had no control over the old tabby house. It was an inanimate thing that did not respond to his hands as a ship did.

The cough at the door interrupted his thoughts. Robert raised his head and stared at the small black boy. He was seemingly none the worse for his experience in the water.

"Pardon, Mr. Robert. I did not know you were in here."

"Come in, Neijee. It's all right," Robert assured him.

At the boy's hesitation, Robert stood. "I am just leaving." Peering at the child, Robert asked, "Have you gotten over drinking half the Atlantic Ocean?"

The small boy frowned. "That Matthew—he rolled me over the barrel so many times, I think my ribs must be broken."

Robert smiled a bitter smile. "I wouldn't complain, Neijee. Because of it, you're still alive. Be thankful that Matthew was able to save you."

"I *am* thankful, Mr. Robert—but I'm still sore."

"You'll feel better when you've had some rest," the man answered him. In the doorway of the nursery, Robert paused. "Where is Matthew now?" he inquired.

"In the kitchen, trying to rescue some food," Neijee said.

Still debating about the move from the tabby house, Robert went downstairs and called to Matthew. If the pony cart was anywhere near, he and Matthew could pull it to the lighthouse, with Eulalie inside. Robert had no hopes of finding the pony. But if the cart had lodged against something, it would not have been swept out to sea by the first flooding.

"Matthew," Robert called again, walking nearer to the kitchen entrance.

At the same time that a wet Matthew emerged from the kitchen in response to Robert's call, the house groaned and shifted. That was enough to make up Robert's mind.

"The storm is getting worse, Matthew. And from the sound of it, the house is not going to last."

"Aye. 'E be gone 'fore day-clean," Matthew agreed.

"We'll have to take refuge in the lighthouse, Matthew. And the sooner we start, the better our chances of getting there. See if you can find the pony cart, while I see to my wife and Feena."

The black man obeyed, while Robert went upstairs to inform Feena that they would have to move.

"But Monsieur Robert, it is not wise to move mamselle in her condition."

"The house is going to fall apart, Feena. I have no choice. Get everything together that you need. If Matthew finds the pony cart, we will take Eulalie in that, with the small trunk. Otherwise, we will have to carry everything in our hands."

Robert lifted the small trunk from the floor near the window and carried it down the stairs, setting it on the heavy mahogany table in the hallway where the waters could not reach it. And then he retraced his steps, going to all the bedrooms to gather as many quilts as he could find.

Matthew was lucky. The pony cart, still intact, was lodged between two fallen trees not far from the house. And at the news, Robert went inside while Matthew brought the cart to the sheltered side of the porch.

"Eulalie, we will have to move to the lighthouse," Robert whispered gently, wrapping her in a quilt. "You and Neijee will ride in the pony cart. I am sorry it will be so rough for you."

"Neijee?" Eulalie questioned in a weak voice. "But Neijee's dead—"

"No, my darling. He's very much alive. Matthew found him in time."

The smile lit up her face, only to disappear into another mask of pain. And Robert's heart was grim as he carried her down the stairs.

Matthew carried Neijee and, bracing the wind, he placed him in the cart near Eulalie, each covered with a quilt taken from the bedrooms.

Still, the driving rain came down, soaking them all. As Matthew and Robert began their slow journey across the island, Feena held onto the side of the cart, her dress caught in the gale that whipped her skirts around her legs.

Water swirled around their ankles. The wind howled

and the rains descended. The sky and sea poured out their wrath upon the island, but Matthew and Robert kept on, using their brute strength to force the cart toward its destination.

Feena stumbled over a log, but quickly righted herself, clutching to the side of the cart. Down the path the wheels of the cart rolled, stopped occasionally by the debris that littered the path.

The lighthouse was within sight when Robert sensed it —the giant intimidating wave, as tall as a ship. The roar was deafening, drowning out Robert's warning. Matthew saw it too and looked to Robert for guidance.

The golden-haired man, his wet clothes plastered to his body, dropped the yoke of the pony cart and leaned over to snatch Eulalie from the cart. Matthew grabbed the small black child, and with a command for Feena to run, Robert set out for the lighthouse—racing the giant wave that was eager to claim the lives of his wife and unborn child.

CHAPTER

42

*F*EENA looked back and her eyes grew wide with terror at the approaching wave. *"Mon Dieu,* save us all," she prayed, running faster than she had ever run in her life.

The door to the lighthouse swung open and she squeezed inside moments before the wave crashed against the door. Up the steps she climbed, directly behind Robert, who carried Eulalie in his arms. The lower portion of the winding stairway disappeared in the angry waters.

Robert did not stop until he had reached the top. And there in the room sparsely fitted with the two cots that the militiamen had used, Robert lowered Eulalie onto the bed and knelt beside her. His massive chest heaved in and out as he drew great gulps of air into his lungs. He had won the race, and now it was up to the lighthouse to shelter them from the storm. He could do no more.

"Robert," Eulalie whispered, her hand reaching out to touch him. "Robert."

He took her hand and held it to his cheek, his own giant hand trembling. Her hand tightened on his, with the pain.

"Feena, where are you?" Eulalie called.

"I am here, *ma petite*—beside you."

"I am frightened, Feena."

"*Le bon Dieu* will not let anything hurt you, *ma petite*. Has he not sent Monsieur Robert to save you—for the second time? There is nothing to fear now. So we will get on with having the baby, *n'est-ce pas?*"

"Yes, Feena."

Neijee and Matthew remained in the room next to the top while the birth of the baby was in progress.

Robert stayed by Eulalie's side, and Feena did not protest his presence. He took his wife's small hands in his, and immediately they tightened in pain.

Robert stared down in pity and in anger. She was so helpless. And it was *his* fault for deliberately getting her with child, *his* fault that she was stranded on the island without a doctor to care for her. He never should have listened to her pleadings to stay on the island. Robert should have taken her into Charleston long ago.

The dark doe eyes opened and looked up at Robert, but she did not seem to recognize him.

"But you don't understand," Eulalie said in a weak voice. "Arthur—Arthur, I . . . I love him."

Robert blanched at her words. Was this not recompense for his sins? To hear another man's name on her lips while she was bearing *his* child?

Sadness added to the pity and anger in Robert's breast. What could he do but sit and wait—to see if the gods would be kind to him—to wait to see if they would allow the only woman he had ever loved to live? That was all he asked for—for Eulalie to live, even though she loved another man.

Eulalie's deep moan echoed through the lighthouse, and Robert's face was moist with sweat. He closed his eyes and the tight grip relaxed. Eulalie's hands no longer held to his.

A small cry in the room aroused Robert from his listlessness. Surprised at the sound, Robert looked up. Feena held the squirming flesh upside down. Another spank and the baby's cry grew louder. His child had been born.

Feena carefully wrapped the baby in a strip of the

linen sheet that had covered the cot adjacent to the one in which Eulalie lay.

"It is a girl, monsieur—very tiny but alive. That is good."

Robert held out his arms for the small bundle, his heart turning over when he saw the golden hair, the pink rosebud mouth turned up in a display of temper at having been so rudely brought into the world.

"She is . . . beautiful, Feena. And I am thankful that it is over." He handed the child back to Feena and hastened to Eulalie's side.

"Eulalie," he whispered to the ashen-faced woman, "we have a daughter, my darling. I will love her and cherish her because you have given her to me." He leaned over to kiss Eulalie on the forehead, but another cry from his wife caused him to stop in midair.

Feena put the baby on the other cot and rushed back to Eulalie's side.

"Mon Dieu," Feena said. "Can there be another one on the way?"

The squirming infant on the cot was forgotten by both Feena and Robert. Doubly alarming for Robert, additional waves of pain passed over Eulalie's face. He grasped Eulalie's hands in his, and as in a nightmare, Robert relived the agony over again, with Tassy's prediction echoing in his ears, until, at last, the agony was over.

But this time, there was no sound as Feena held the newborn twin by its heels and spanked it. Time and again Feena tried, but to no avail.

Her voice was sad. "I am afraid, monsieur, that it is no use."

And as she had done before, Feena took a small strip of linen and wrapped the waxen-faced baby in it. "A girl-child too, but not destined to live. See how perfectly the little one is formed."

Hair black as coal—magnolia-petaled skin—the image of Eulalie. Robert gazed at the still small form and then took the baby from Feena. He placed it upon the cot where the other infant lay, and breathed into the baby's mouth, covering mouth and nose with his own mouth. With each breath of his, the baby's chest expanded only slightly. He stopped after a while to see if the child was breathing on her own. Her tiny chest was still.

With a last desperate attempt at bringing life to the child, Robert took his fingers and thrust into its mouth, as he had done once on his ship to a sailor who had fallen overboard. Robert cleared the mucus from the child's mouth and again placed his mouth over the infant's, breathing steadily in and out, taking another breath and exhaling, forcing the small lungs to expand.

The baby moved; a weak cry came from her throat, answering the stronger cry of the other child upon the cot.

The lighthouse was filled with the sound, and Robert and Feena looked at each other in triumph. On unsteady legs, Robert went to Eulalie. He knelt by her side, and while she slept, Robert caressed the long strands of black hair that were still damp from the rain. And finally, he too slept.

During the night, the wind subsided and the waters began to recede. The only disturbance that cut through the silence of the night was the cry of the hungry babies. Eulalie, despite her weakness, took them to her breast, and soon all was quiet again.

For the others, there was no relief from hunger and thirst, for the small amount of food and water brought with them in the pony cart had been lost, along with the baby clothes. There had been no time to retrieve anything before the wave struck the island.

Robert awoke at the first light of day and, careful not to disturb anyone, climbed to the top of the lighthouse and gazed across the expanse of sea and land. The tide was still running high, but minute patches of blue appeared scattered among the clouds. The beach was littered with debris from the storm—fallen palmetto trees and bits of lumber, no doubt from the servants' quarters that had washed away. The lifeless body of a marsh pony, sprawled in the sand, was the only sign of its former inhabitants.

Then Robert heard the gulls and he was glad.

When Robert climbed down the ladder to the room where he had spent the night, he saw that Eulalie was awake and already nursing the babies. She turned her head to watch Robert walking toward her. Her eyes were fathomless pools of black, magnified in size by the small wan face. But as Feena took the babies from her arms, Robert saw a proud sparkle, a different tilt to the head, and he was overwhelmed by her beauty.

Without speaking, he knelt beside her and took her hand in his, brushing it with his lips, and Eulalie shyly reached out to touch Robert's cheek. "Thank you, Robert, for saving the babies and me."

A look of contrition dulled his topaz eyes at her words of gratitude. He clasped her hand more fervently to his breast, but his words were harsh.

"I do not deserve any thanks. It was my fault that your life was put in danger. But I will make certain from now on, Eulalie, that you do not suffer for my selfishness."

Eulalie was puzzled at the ferocity of his voice. And at her startled glance, Robert used a gentler tone to continue. "Matthew and I will go out to see if we can find some food and water—and to look for the boat."

"How long will you be gone, Robert?"

"At least an hour, if not longer."

"You *will* be careful, won't you, Robert?"

He suddenly grinned at her. "Yes, Eulalie. You have no need to worry. And I will send Neijee up to keep you company. That should take your mind off anything else while I am gone."

Robert had no hopes of finding the boat intact. The storm had been too fierce. But it was a miracle that they had all survived. If they could find enough food and water to last the day, then all would be well. His message for help had been flashed to land, and within another day's time, the sea would be back to normal. Then the boat that had been promised could be launched upon the water from Charleston harbor.

As Matthew and Robert trudged along, Robert's mind was on Jason. Eulalie had not mentioned his name. It was almost as if she had been afraid to ask. Robert knew that Feena had lied to Eulalie about the child, for she had not been strong enough to be told the truth. There was no telling where Jason and Florilla had been taken. Robert knew that after he saw Eulalie and the twins safely into Charleston, he would begin his search for the missing child.

The old tabby house lay in ruins—a washed-out shell from the storm. Part of the roof had collapsed. Gazing at it, Robert knew he would never come again to the island. He would be content to leave the old house behind with its haunting memories.

Matthew and Robert walked into the ruins, carefully avoiding any shifting of timbers. And within an hour, they had completed their scavenger mission, taking what they could use and piling it high on the tabby steps—a ham, an empty basin, two wooden barrels, utensils from the kitchen, and bits of clothing. But the spring was still filled with brine, ruined from the seawater. Perhaps they would be luckier with the spring at the far end of the island, since it was on higher ground.

Leaving everything but the two wooden barrels, Robert and Matthew skirted the cove on their way to the spring.

The pier was gone, and the boat was nowhere in sight. Only the tops of the piles jutted from the water to indicate where the pier had once stood.

When they came upon the spring, Robert stooped down and cupped his hand to lift the water to his lips. He smiled as he tasted it. It was fresh. Matthew also knelt and dipped into the spring. With their thirst satisfied they filled the barrels with water to carry back to the lighthouse for the others.

Several trips later, the two men had carried everything from the tabby-house steps, and soon the air was filled with the aroma of ham being cooked on sticks over a small bonfire on the sand outside the lighthouse. Neijee stood beside Matthew, his dark eyes intent on the meat dripping its grease over the flames, causing the fire to shower out in a sudden crackling. And Robert was reminded of the time in the forest during his frantic search for Eulalie.

By late afternoon, Robert had seen the signal that a boat was on its way to rescue them from the island. With Matthew at his side, Robert stood on the beach and watched for the boat, his eyes shaded by his hand as he peered out to sea. He saw the slowly moving object from the distance and sent Matthew ahead to alert Feena and Eulalie at the lighthouse.

The small dinghy, tied to the boat's side, was loosened, and Arthur himself paddled it to the beach's edge beyond the piles of the pier. Robert waded into the water to draw the dinghy on to the beach.

"Robert, I've said it before," Arthur greeted the golden-haired man. "You're a lucky man. You know that, don't you? By all rights, you should be at the bottom of the sea."

Robert grinned. "It was a close call. You don't know how near we *all* came to it."

"Eulalie—how is she?" Arthur asked, his blue eyes trying to conceal his anxiety over the girl.

Robert's serious expression matched the severity of Arthur's. "She is quite weak. Understandable in the circumstances—with the twins. That's why I'm most anxious to get her into Charleston."

"Did you say—twins? You mean—"

"Twin daughters, Arthur. During the worst of the storm, Eulalie gave birth to twin daughters."

"My God!" Arthur was rendered speechless at Robert's confidence. He blinked at Robert and moved his mouth, but no further sound came.

The procession edged toward the cove—Neijee happily skipping alongside Matthew, Eulalie in Robert's arms, and Feena and Arthur each carrying one of the tiny babies.

Back and forth the dinghy went, until all were safely in the boat headed for Charleston harbor. Eulalie looked over Robert's shoulder to take one last look at the island, where the pleasant months past had suddenly turned into a nightmare. Then, her eyes closed, Eulalie laid her head against Robert's chest and silently grieved for Jason. Robert would tell her what had happened to the child when he thought she was strong enough to bear the news. Until then, she would have to wait and pray.

CHAPTER

43

CHARLESTON too was damaged by the storm. Many of the warehouses and sheds along the wharves had been leveled, and vessels in the harbor damaged. From Granville's bastion to Lloyd's wharf, the curtain line of solid wall had been beaten in, and a pilot boat rested in the yard next to the Governor's Bridge. Water was still in the streets everywhere, the creeks crisscrossing the city completely filled and overflowing.

But already, men were at work clearing the debris—the naval stores and timbers from the warehouses, the fallen chimneys, the tiles and slate that had been stripped from the roofs of the houses along the bay.

The townhouse on Tradd Street had been luckier, and Robert, seeing it from the carriage window, was glad that it was high enough off the ground to keep the water out.

Robert gathered Eulalie in his arms and carried her up the high steps, into the house, and down the hall to the master bedroom.

From that moment on, there was no idleness in the house. Robert issued commands right and left, seeing to water being heated, food shopped for, clothes attended to, and Eulalie, put to bed and ordered to stay there by

Robert, felt left out with the bedroom door closed between her and all the activity in the townhouse the next morning.

Feena brought water for Eulalie's bath, and a coarse white gown borrowed from some occupant in the house —a servant's perhaps. And as soon as Feena had helped her with her bath and dried her hair, the doctor, whom Eulalie had seen only briefly that first time in the townhouse when she had fainted, appeared again, staring at her with his narrowed eyes, taking in her wan face, her state of exhaustion. And then his attention turned to the tiny babies, now nestled in two of the drawers of the mahogany highboy, side by side on the floor.

Robert and the doctor discussed Eulalie as if she were not even there, and the two, without consulting her, made plans for a wet nurse to be brought in to feed the babies. And they paid no attention to Eulalie's protest.

Angry and upset, her dark eyes filled with tears. And when Robert returned alone, Eulalie faced him with quivering lips.

"I am planning to nurse the babies, Robert. I will not have a wet nurse brought in."

"You will do as I say, Eulalie. There is no need for you to squander the remaining strength you have, because of a stubborn whim."

"A stubborn whim? You call it a stubborn whim to want to care for my own daughters?"

"*Our* daughters, Eulalie. And I will see to it that my orders are obeyed. No longer will I be governed by your wishes, when you are the one who suffers from them. And the sooner the babies are taken to the nursery, the more rest you will be able to get."

"You're . . . you're going to let them be taken from me?"

Robert looked at Eulalie, her dark eyes pleading, but he set his jaw and his topaz eyes were hard as stone.

"They will remain here with you for the rest of the day, until Jetta comes from Midgard with the wet nurse. Arthur has already gone to get them. And when you are stronger, you may spend as much time in the nursery as you wish."

"It is happening again, isn't it?" The weak voice was distraught. "The twins are going to be taken from me, just as Jason was."

At the mention of Jason's name, Robert's face turned white. He took a step nearer Eulalie.

She looked up at him, and in a voice filled with dread, she whispered, "Feena was wrong, wasn't she, when she told me Jason was safe? Why have you not told me the truth? Robert, where is Jason?"

The man came and sat beside Eulalie, taking her hand in his. Troubled at her questions, he was not sure how he should answer. "You were not strong enough, Eulalie, to be told the truth," he began. "But I see that I can keep it from you no longer. Neijee said that the British took Jason away with Florilla and the servants. They are more than likely on one of the ships heading for port near St. Augustine." Seeing the stricken look on her features, he rushed on. "But don't worry, Eulalie. The British will not harm a child. And I promise you that I will not rest until I find him and bring him home to you."

He held her in his arms, and he felt the shudder of her body as her tears began to flow in earnest. Robert could do little to comfort her in her distress. He held her against his chest and stroked her long dark hair, at the same time wishing he could do more.

The crying of one of the babies brought Eulalie's attention back to them. It was the golden-haired one who was crying. Eulalie dried her tears while Robert stooped and picked up the flailing baby to bring to Eulalie. The baby stopped crying immediately as Eulalie put her to her breast.

"Have you decided on names for them yet?" Robert asked, hoping to divert Eulalie's attention from Jason. He sat on the side of the bed and watched mother and child.

"Only for the dark-haired one. She is so gentle and quiet. Maranta, I think, would be a good name for her. Do you agree, Robert?"

He gazed toward the smaller of the babies, who slept undisturbed by the initial crying of the other. His eyes softened and, turning back to Eulalie, he replied, "It is an appropriate name—the prayer plant in the garden. She already has the look of a little nun, with her angelic face, hasn't she?"

"Yes."

The child in her arms squirmed and grunted, and then settled down to suckle vigorously. Eulalie smiled and said, "This one is so like *you,* Robert, with her golden hair. And I suppose that she will eventually have the same-colored eyes too. They look as if they are changing already."

He leaned closer to see, but the baby had closed her eyes again.

"I would name her for you, Robert, except that I am sure you would prefer to have a son with your name instead."

Robert suddenly stood and walked toward the window. "There will be no more children, Eulalie. So it is not necessary to save any name for later on."

"No more children, Robert? But I thought you made it clear that you were starting a dynasty of Tabors. And what about your wish for a son named Ravenal?" Eulalie's voice, half-teasing, half-alarmed, taunted him, and she waited for his answer.

"I have changed my mind, Eulalie." Robert stood for some minutes before moving from the window and back towards the bed. "If you have finished nursing the child, I will call Feena to tend to her."

"Yes, Robert. I have finished."

He walked from the room, leaving a puzzled Eulalie. Why was Robert suddenly so distant, so cold? What had she said to cause such a chilled expression on his face?

Eulalie looked down at the sleeping child beside her. Had Jason looked like that too, at the same age? Again, Eulalie's heart was sad, thinking of her lost son.

When Feena came into the room, Neijee trailed along behind her. Fascinated by the twins, he sat on the floor and watched while Feena gave them their baths and settled them again into the drawers that served as make-shift beds.

At the noise downstairs, Eulalie said, "I wonder who that can be? Robert said that Jetta and—another servant would be coming from Midgard this afternoon, but it's much too early for them."

"Perhaps it is the seamstress that Monsieur Robert has sent for," Feena responded.

"But we don't need a seamstress, Feena."

Feena looked down at her own borrowed dress, lent to her by the cook, and the shoes that were much too big for her. "You think not, *ma petite?*" She then eyed the coarse cotton gown worn by Eulalie and continued, "Did you think Monsieur Robert would allow you and the babies to look like scarecrows in this town? Already, the servants next door have started their gossip about us, after seeing us arrive like poor refugees with not even a picayune to our names."

"I did not notice them," Eulalie said, with a sigh.

"Well, they noticed all of us, you can be sure."

Robert, seated in the small sitting room downstairs, heard the commotion at the front door. He pushed himself from the chair and walked to the threshold.

It was not the seamstress, but Jason and Florilla who stood in the open doorway. And when Jason spied Robert, he ran immediately toward him, while Robert, a wide grin on his face, halved the distance between them and in a few quick strides, he had Jason in his arms, swinging him through the air. The boy squealed with delight, and a vast relief was evident in the man's face as he realized his son was safe.

A tragic-looking Florilla stood aside, waiting for Robert to notice her. Finally, Robert did so, saying, "Florilla, how did you and Jason get here?"

"Oh, Robert, such a terrible thing happened on the island, right before the storm. The British came and . . . and took us back to the ship with them. It was a horrible experience with those common sailors. But at least the ship's captain was a gentleman. He apologized and planned to send us back, but then the storm came, and we had to wait. We have walked all the way from the bay. I had to find you and let you know what had happened."

"Then sit down, Florilla, and rest." He stared at her disheveled appearance and continued his questioning.

"What about the others? Are you and Jason the only ones the British released?"

Florilla looked woefully at Robert. "I am afraid so. The servants—Jimbo and Effie and the others—were transferred to another ship headed for the West Indies. We will probably never see them again. But aren't you going to ask about your wife?"

"My wife? What about my wife, Florilla?"

"Eulalie—Mrs. Tabor—hid somewhere on the island. She was not taken with us, and . . . and . . . " She looked toward Jason, and Robert, understanding that she did not want the child to hear what she had to tell, put him down and said, "Run upstairs, Jason. And look for . . . one of the servants."

"Eu-lie. Where is Eu-lie?" Jason demanded.

"I told you to run upstairs, Jason. I will talk with you later."

The child reluctantly obeyed his father and started slowly up the steps. "Eulalie," he called in a loud voice. "Eu-lie, where are you?"

"Poor little thing," Florilla said sympathetically when the child was out of sight. "He doesn't know that his mother is dead."

"What do you mean, Florilla?"

"I am afraid that your wife could not survive the storm, Robert." Her blue eyes filled with tears, and her chin trembled with grief.

He looked at the woman strangely, as if seeing her for the first time. "Perhaps she is not dead, Florilla. If she could have made it to the lighthouse—"

"Oh, but she couldn't do that . . . " Then Florilla stopped, as if she had said too much.

Impatient now with the woman before him, Robert said, "Why do you say that, Florilla? Do you know something I don't know?"

"No, Robert. I just assumed—in her condition—that she could not have made it by herself—from wherever she was hiding, all the way to the lighthouse."

"Let me put your mind at rest, Florilla. Eulalie is safe."

"But that's impossible. How could she be safe when—"

"I reached the island in time to save her."

Florilla sat up straight, her hands fluttering nervously to her hair. She had an unbelieving expression on her face, and a sudden tremor passed over her. "The house had not burned down?" she asked.

"No. There were a few pieces of charred furniture stacked up at the entrance. But that was all."

Already, Robert was walking out the door and toward the stairs. "Come with me, Florilla. And I will prove to you that Eulalie is very much alive."

Florilla, clasping her hands tightly together, followed. She made no effort to disguise the disappointed look in her eyes.

Before the two reached the doorway of the master bedroom, Florilla suddenly stopped and put her hand to her forehead. "Robert, if you don't mind, I will take your word that your wife is safe. It has been a difficult day, and I would prefer going to my room to rest. I can see Mrs. Tabor later."

"Of course, Florilla. If you are feeling ill, by all means go to your room."

Robert stood in the hallway, watching the woman hurry past him and toward her room. He frowned, recalling the look of fright in her eyes when he had mentioned that Eulalie was alive.

With his brow still wrinkled, he walked into the bedroom, but at the scene before him, his face cleared and a smile tugged at the corners of his mouth.

Spellbound, Jason and Neijee sat on the floor and watched the babies. Robert glanced at Eulalie and their eyes met and held. Warm and loving, Eulalie's eyes sparkled, and Robert, drawn to her, came to take his place beside her on the bed.

"You are happy, madame, with all your children around you?"

"All *our* children, Robert," she corrected him. "Yes, I am . . . quite happy."

"Florilla is here too," Robert said. "Luckily, she and Jason were sent back to shore by the ship's captain." Robert saw the glow die in her eyes at the mention of Florilla.

His own smile disappeared and in a serious tone he said, "Eulalie, I want you to tell me again everything you can remember about the morning you were locked in the spring room."

"But you have heard it all, Robert. There is nothing more to tell."

"Let me be the judge of that, Eulalie. You may have left out something very important. Now, start again, from the time you first got up that morning."

He sat by the bed and listened, while she relived those moments when she had first unlocked the bedroom door to go downstairs for water.

"And you called out loud enough for anyone in the kitchen to hear you?"

"Of course, Robert. I was frightened at being left in the dark. Naturally, I called out, as loudly as I could."

Still, Robert was not satisfied. But he had time to wait and to watch and to ponder. The immediate need was to see that Eulalie got her strength back as quickly as possible. And to make sure that her life was never put in jeopardy again by the birth of another child. He had come so close to losing her.

CHAPTER
44

ROBERT arranged Eulalie's life, closely guarding her and seeing that she was not disturbed by Jason or Neijee or the crying babies. Like an invalid, she was forced to remain in bed, forced to have her meals in the bedroom since Robert would not allow her to come downstairs.

Eulalie was not happy to have the babies taken from her and placed in the nursery. But she grudgingly admitted that Robert was right. She was getting stronger with the added rest. And it was not as if the twins had been taken completely from her. Jetta brought them into the bedroom each afternoon for several hours. It was the time of day that she looked forward to, to be surrounded by Jason and Neijee and the babies. She had named the golden-haired one Marigold, but already Eulalie had begun to call her by her French name—Souci. As soon as they became fretful, they were whisked back to the nursery by Jetta, along with Jason and Neijee.

Ten days after the babies had been born, Eulalie felt well enough to leave her bed. She walked about the room in the beautiful blue silk peignoir that matched the low-cut gown. It was much too revealing, but she had not been sufficiently strong to notice, much less protest, the clothes that the seamstress had made for her to replace the ones she had lost. Too late, Eulalie realized the mistake that had been made. Each dress hanging up, each article of clothing made for her, was designed to attract and please a man. The seamstress had evidently noted the strong virile specimen of a husband, and decided, since he was paying the bill, to please him and not Eulalie. And now Eulalie was saddled with clothes that would have been more appropriate for the fashionable salons of Paris than the quiet country life on a plantation.

Surprised to see her up, Robert walked into the bedroom and watched as Eulalie sat at the dressing table and brushed her hair. Muted with emotion, his topaz eyes took in the soft curves of her body, scarcely concealed by the material. He found himself taking the brush from Eulalie's hand, and he began the sensuous brushing of her wavy dark tresses.

It was even stronger this time, her feeling for the man who was her husband. She watched him in the mirror and saw the tender glow in his eyes. Was he beginning to care for her? Had she finally found a place in his heart after bearing his son and twin daughters? Could it possibly be that he had fallen in love with her after all?

Eulalie closed her eyes to hide the budding hope that had taken root in her heart. She had kept her Creole dreams to herself for so long—to be the wife of a strong man who would fight to the death for her honor, to be wanted and loved well by him. Her eyelids fluttered open when Robert's hands stopped, and she met his glance and blushed at her own thoughts. Robert, seeing the faint pink creep over her alabaster skin, was amused.

"And what has embarrassed you, my love, to make you blush like some virgin bride? Have my attentions caused you to remember another time, perhaps?" His voice purred in her ear, and as she turned her head, Eulalie's cheek grazed his.

She was immediately in his arms and her lips trembled under his demanding lips. Then his kisses ceased abruptly and she was carried back to bed.

"You almost make me forget my resolution, little witch," he said, his voice still thick with emotion.

She sat against the pillows and watched his back as he quickly disappeared through the doorway.

Robert—now so different from the arrogant man who had taken what he wanted without regard to her feelings. Robert—the only one who had ever caused her to blush and tremble at his touch. Eulalie rested and thought of her handsome, golden-haired husband. For the first time in her life, she began to feel like a woman, capable of stirring the fires of a man's passion. And was that not what Robert wanted? A woman capable of giving all her love to him, keeping nothing back from him?

A provocative smile hovered on her lips, and she sighed before snuggling down to sleep. The young girl was now a fading image, no longer a part of her being. And Eulalie hoped that the woman she was becoming would soon supplant the image of the wayward child she had been in Robert's mind.

Eulalie began to blossom under Robert's watchful care. And she did not mind that he turned the visitors away, not letting them see or tire her. She could recognize Arthur's and Hector's voices downstairs at various intervals, and she knew that some of the neighbors had left their cards at the door. But Robert, gentle and strict at the same time, had assured her that there was no hurry for her to repay visits or resume social life. He would make sure that she was entirely well. With Robert at her side, Eulalie would not be afraid. She would not even mind the barbs of the other women if she could be certain of Robert's love for her.

Robert continued to sleep on the cot adjacent to the window, so that Eulalie would not be disturbed in the larger bed. Soon, though, Eulalie knew that she again would be sleeping in Robert's arms, for he was not the type to wait overly long.

Eulalie grew stronger and more beautiful each day, and Robert did not demur when she began to spend more time downstairs. One afternoon, Eulalie sat in the downstairs sitting room and waited for the doctor, who had come to visit the twins. She heard Robert and the doctor walking down the steps from the nursery, and she put her needlework on the sofa beside her when they entered the room.

"Good afternoon, Mrs. Tabor," the doctor greeted her with his pleasant smile.

"Good afternoon, monsieur," she answered, returning his smile. "How did you find the twins?"

"In very good health," he answered. "I was worried at first with the dark-haired one, but she is progressing nicely. Of course, she will need more attention than the other for a while longer, but I see no reason why she should not soon catch up with the other in size."

"Thank you. I am glad to hear that," Eulalie said.

Aware of his scrutiny, she was calm, waiting for him to speak again. "You have made a miraculous recovery, have you not?" he asked, taking in her healthy glow, her eyes shining with happiness.

"There was nothing else I could do, with my husband ordering everyone to spoil me these past weeks."

The doctor laughed and turned to Robert. "A wise move, I should say, Mr. Tabor, considering the difference in your wife's appearance. Yes, a wise move," he repeated. "It is always hard on a man until his wife recovers completely from childbirth, but it looks as if your wife has done just that."

Robert nodded and began to see the man to the door. Eulalie stayed in the room, her face blushing at the doctor's obvious meaning. Had he voiced his thoughts in front of Eulalie so that she would know Robert did not have to treat her like a porcelain doll, or to remain sleeping on his cot alone?

Hurriedly, Eulalie walked up the stairs, aware of the nervous pulsating in her throat and the more rapid beating of her heart. And later, when she was dressed for dinner, she went downstairs to share the evening meal with Robert and Florilla.

Eulalie could not keep her eyes from Robert. She noticed his elegant dark waistcoat, his white frilled shirt whose cuffs showed below the sleeve of the coat, and the well-fitting trousers that clothed his muscular legs. His golden hair shone in the candlelight, and when he leaned over, Eulalie's hand involuntarily moved. She quickly brought her hand back to her lap, ashamed of the sudden urge to touch him.

His eyes bored into hers, and Robert asked, "Are you feeling well, Eulalie? You look as if you might be feverish."

"No, Robert," she assured him. "I feel fine."

"Then why have you not eaten your dinner?" He was now frowning at her and the plate that was still filled with food. She cast a guilty glance down at the food.

"We had a tea party this afternoon, Robert—Jason and Neijee and I. The cookies must have taken away my appetite."

He made no further remark about her lack of appetite, but Eulalie, seeing the frown still on his face, forced a few bites to her mouth before her plate was removed from the table.

Eulalie was not the only one who was nervous at the table. Every time Robert's attention turned to Florilla, her hands fluttered and her voice stammered in answer to his questions. She was not the same chattering person she had been before the British came to the island. Now she only talked when spoken to, and her voice was unsteady, as if she were afraid of something.

Eulalie glanced at Robert and then back at Florilla. Eulalie could not understand what had happened between them to cause Florilla to react in such a manner to Robert's attention. Usually, she welcomed it.

Later that night, Eulalie undressed and put on the sheer white gown trimmed with delicate lace and blue ribbons, along with its matching robe. She sat for a long time brushing her hair before the mirror, but Robert did not come into the bedroom. He had gone out immediately after dinner and had not returned.

A feeling of disappointment crept over Eulalie as she stood by the window and looked through the small opening of the curtains to the street below. Robert was not in sight.

Eulalie yawned and dropped the curtain back into place. Removing the robe that would only get in her way, she knelt beside the bed and began her evening prayers.

She had not finished when the door opened. But looking up and seeing her husband, Eulalie smiled and stood.

Robert's eyes narrowed, and the sudden look of distaste evident on his face caused her smile to fade. She had forgotten. Without the robe, the thin gown left nothing to the imagination, and now Eulalie blushed. Robert, watching her, had made her aware of her state of undress. He seemed to be repelled by it. Eulalie quickly slid into bed to hide herself under the covers.

"You do well to hide yourself from me, Eulalie," Robert uttered. "For if you had continued to stand there in the candlelight much longer, I might not have been responsible for my actions."

Fearfully, Eulalie peered at her husband and wondered why he was in such a rage. He acted as if he were being seduced by his own wife. And it was not to her liking, his attitude. Her puzzled expression annoyed Robert further.

With several long steps, he was at her side, gazing down at her. "Don't look at me with those dark, innocent eyes, Eulalie. You know very well what I mean. So if you would not have me forget the vow I made, then I suggest that you not flaunt yourself when I am in the room."

"Flaunt myself?" At his accusation, she was more enraged than Robert. "If you did not wish to see me clothed as I am, then you could have given orders to the seamstress for more modest nightgowns. Do you think I *enjoy* wearing what you ordered the woman to make? You act as if I put on this gown tonight to deliberately . . . to deliberately seduce you to my bed."

Robert chuckled at her anger and reached out to smooth a wayward strand of hair parted from the rest at the tossing of her head.

"You would never do that, would you, Eulalie? For you would be a proper wife who is not supposed to act as if she enjoys having her husband bed her. It is too bad, my pet, that you revealed the other side of your nature when I thought you a slave. I can never forget what you are capable of, even if you wish to pretend otherwise."

Eulalie, furious at him, turned her back to Robert. He patted her insolently on her *derrière* and walked toward his side of the room, to undress and go to sleep on the cot.

It did not help her to know that Robert had spoken the truth. She might deny it to him, but deep within, Eulalie knew that she actually enjoyed being in Robert's arms, being loved by him. Loved? He had never said he loved her, merely desired her. And to Eulalie, that was vastly different. But now it seemed that her husband no longer desired her. Even that was denied her as she slept alone in bed night after night.

The rapport between them, the solicitation for her welfare—all that was gone. Robert now looked at Eulalie with a constant frown, as if he hated her, and he stayed away from the townhouse more and more. And each night, he was late in retiring to bed.

But one night, Robert surprised Eulalie by coming upstairs earlier than usual. Eulalie was on her knees when Robert walked in. He made so much noise that she was unable to keep her mind on her prayers. She could feel Robert's eyes on her, feel his antagonism, as she finished and stood up.

"I suppose you are still praying for Jacques Binet?" he inquired.

Eulalie was wary at the sudden mention of the trapper's name. "Yes, Robert," she admitted, sitting on the bed to remove her slippers.

"Then, is it too much to ask of you that you practice your saintliness when I am not around?"

"I have tried to do so, Robert, but you are earlier than usual tonight."

"Then I must remember that—not to interrupt you by coming to bed too early."

"This is your bedroom, as well, Robert. I certainly do not wish to inconvenience you."

"Inconvenience me? You have inconvenienced me from the moment I set foot on my own plantation four years ago. Why should you so suddenly be concerned about it now?"

Eulalie bit her lip and remained silent. It was slowly turning into a nightmare again. From the moment the doctor had pronounced Eulalie well, the closeness she had shared with her husband had begun to deteriorate. And tonight, Eulalie felt the emptiness in her heart—and Robert's antagonism. But regardless of how he felt, regardless of everything that had happened, Eulalie could not forget that she loved him.

As Eulalie climbed into bed, she wiped a silent tear and turned her face from the candlelight so that Robert could not see her hurt. But she listened to his steps, and knew that he was coming toward her. What more did he want to say to wound her?

"Eulalie?" The voice was now devoid of anger.

Afraid to let him see her hurt, she kept her eyes closed and did not reply. But she could hear his breathing, could feel his hand as it tentatively touched her arm.

"I am sorry I said what I did to you just now. I am like a bear with a sore head these days, but it's unfair to take it out on you. I will try to watch my temper from now on, Eulalie."

His hand left her arm and began to brush her wavy hair from her face. His warm breath fell upon her ear as he whispered, "Tell me that you forgive me."

His voice, so contrite, caused her heart to act erratically. Her eyes slowly opened to reveal the tears glistening on her dark lashes. She sat up, looking at the apologetic man, and reaching out to touch him, she answered, "There is nothing to forgive, Robert. Let us both just forget any unpleasantness between us."

Robert took her hand and kissed it. "Thank you, Eulalie," he said, and then placed her hand under the covers and tucked the quilt about her before returning to the cot.

Robert was restless. Eulalie was conscious of his tossing and turning far into the night. And Eulalie, lying in the dark, felt a need to talk with the priest the next day.

Robert knew he had neglected Eulalie by going out each evening, and filling his days with his friends, discussing politics or racing his horses against them. And when he was home, he acted uncivil. But he was fighting his own need—his desire to take his wife in his arms and love her. He would have to behave better, as a husband—spending more time with Eulalie at home. Yet, it would be hard to keep his distance. There was now no excuse for keeping Arthur from seeing her, except his own jealousy—for that undesirable plague had once again reared its head, not only over Arthur, but over Jacques Binet. He had tried to drive it from his mind, but he had not succeeded.

The lighthouse had kept him busy enough before. But there was not even the necessity of using Tabor Island for surveillance of the British ships, now that the militia was actively guarding the harbor. And the lighthouse had not proved as effective as he had thought it would. The one time it was needed most, there had been a misunderstanding between the men that had caused it to be unmanned when the British came to the island.

Robert sat in the upstairs parlor, reading his newspaper. He was aware of Eulalie on the sofa, her grave expression causing him pain. She was more beautiful than she had ever been, with her hair pulled back in a sleek chignon, and her ruby velvet dress accenting the loveliness of her complexion.

Her sad, dark doe eyes watched him as she waited for him to finish the paper, so that she might discuss going home to Midgard. The malaria season was over, and the old plantation house had more room than the townhouse. Jason and Neijee needed more space in which to play. The garden at the back of the house was not suitable for a child used to the open spaces of an island or the vast fields and meadows and closed piazzas of the plantation.

Robert folded his paper and turned to Eulalie. "Did you wish to say something, Eulalie?"

"Yes, Robert. I was wondering when we could leave Charleston and go back to Midgard."

He looked at her for a long time before speaking. "There is no hurry, Eulalie. The overseer is doing well enough. There are no pressing problems. I thought we might stay on in Charleston until after the reception that Joseph has planned for Calhoun and the others before they return to Washington. After that, we might go back to

Midgard for a week before the legislature meets in Columbia."

"Do you expect us to go with you to Columbia?"

"You and Jason, yes. As to the twins, I will leave it up to you, whether to take them or let them stay with Jetta and their nurse at Midgard."

His answer was not to her liking. "I would rather stay at Midgard too, Robert, when you go to Columbia."

His topaz eyes turned stormy at her suggestion. "I'm afraid I can't let you do that, Eulalie. I want you in Columbia with me."

"But why, Robert? It's not as if—"

"You are my wife. That is reason enough." His voice was firm, and by the granite look on his face, Eulalie knew better than to argue with him.

CHAPTER

45

ROBERT attempted not to show his jealousy when Arthur began to spend more time calling on Eulalie. Yet it tried Robert's patience to watch his friend cast his lovesick eyes in Eulalie's direction. And he could not forget Arthur's name on Eulalie's lips even as she was bearing his own children. Remembering it and seeing the two together, it was all Robert could do not to forbid Arthur the house.

Finally, one late afternoon, he could stand it no longer. If they wanted to wallow in their loving glances, he did not have to be there to watch them. Robert stomped out of the house, leaving Eulalie and Arthur in the downstairs sitting room, chaperoned only by Jason and Neijee, quietly playing with their blocks in a corner of the room.

Eulalie, embarrassed at Robert's bad manners, got up to see Arthur to the door. Since Robert had promised to take her to the theater that evening, Eulalie was already dressed in the midnight-blue dress that Maggie had made for her. But this time, she wore the shimmering translucent silk robe over it. And in her hair she had pinned the golden nest of jeweled hummingbirds.

Arthur, acting as if he wanted to say something, hesitated at the door. "What is it, Arthur?" Eulalie asked. "Did you forget something?"

Arthur, slightly nervous, said, "You know that I am racing my best grays tomorrow?"

"Yes. Robert told me."

The blue-eyed man hesitated and then plunged on. "If I were fortunate enough to wear the colors of my favorite lady, then I know I would stand a chance of winning the race. Eulalie, it would mean much to me to wear something of yours—a scarf or an ornament pin."

His faced turned red. Arthur's words and actions touched her, and her hand flew to her hair, where she nervously fingered the nest of hummingbirds. On impulse, Eulalie removed the pin from her hair and, handing it to the man, she said, "Would this do, Arthur?"

He took it, touching her hand longer than necessary, and then hurriedly pressed the pin into his waistcoat pocket and left the townhouse.

Robert did not return for dinner. And afterward, when Eulalie and Florilla had finished eating alone, Eulalie went upstairs to remove her dress and put on a simpler one. Robert was not coming back that evening in time to take her to the theater.

Eulalie, unable to remain in the house, walked outside, and in the darkness she sat on the bench in the quietness of the garden, shadowed by the weeping cherry tree.

Sadness filled her heart. It was the time of the harvest moon, with the faint glow of yellow in the sky. The jasmine scent in the night air tugged at Eulalie's memory, reminding her of the time in the river house when the golden-haired giant who was her husband had first awakened her to love.

But she needed no moon, no cloying scent to prompt her or to tell her that nothing had changed from the first time she had met Robert. He was still the master, and she the slave, even more subject to his will because of her love for him—even more bound to him through the children of her flesh. She was a chattel to bear his children, a means by which he had inherited the land. And now that she had served her purpose, he had cast her aside.

The dark-haired girl twisted the heavy gold band on her finger. Even that symbol of a husband's devotion had been placed upon her hand by another, for Robert had not cared enough to do it himself.

Eulalie, overwhelmed by her sadness, made ready to flee from the heavy sweetness of the jasmine, but the movement at the edge of the garden stayed her.

It was Florilla, moving from the steps toward the carriage house, and as she walked, Florilla called softly to someone.

Curious, Eulalie remained on the bench. Suddenly, a tall, broad-shouldered, golden-haired giant of a man stepped from the carriage house, with his arms in a welcoming gesture to the woman. Florilla hastened down the path and ran into the man's arms before the two figures disappeared behind the carriage house.

Eulalie put her hand to her mouth to stifle the cry that threatened to expose her. But a small moan escaped, her heart breaking, now that she had seen with her own eyes what she had suspected and dreaded for so long. Robert and Florilla—how long had they been meeting in the garden late at night while Eulalie had kept her lonely vigil in the bedroom, waiting for Robert to return to her?

It was true, then—everything that Florilla had told her. Eulalie was the outsider, the unloved one. Despite having borne his children, despite everything that had occurred on the island, it was Florilla that Robert loved.

Running up the back stairs, Eulalie had only one concern—to reach the safety of the bedroom. What was she to do? She knew that she could no longer remain in the same house with Robert and Florilla. It would be too heartbreaking, now that there was no doubt how the two felt about each other.

The gold nuggets—they were still in the safe at Midgard. She would take Feena, Neijee and the children in the carriage, find some way of claiming the gold from the safe, and then leave the Carolina country.

There was no need to involve Julie and Desmond. Robert would be sure to look at Cedar Hill first, to find them. But where could she go? New Orleans—she would go to New Orleans and ask the sisters to help her find a position, either as a teacher or as a nurse. She did not care how hard she had to work, if only she could escape Robert and keep the children with her.

Having made her decision, Eulalie quietly undressed and climbed into bed. No tears came at her decision. She felt nothing but a numbness creep over her body, and a coldness envelop her heart.

She did not hear Robert's steps late that night, or hear his choked sigh while he held the candle in his unsteady hands to stare at his wife, before he moved to his own bed.

The next morning, Robert left early on foot for the livery stables where he had housed his chestnuts and phaeton. Matthew had brought them from Midgard two days previously, and had remained with them to care for them and get them ready for the race. And Robert, in his reckless mood, looked forward to the contest.

Eulalie waited until he had gone before getting out of bed. She knew Robert would be occupied with the race until late. That would assure her time to pack and leave. When he realized what had happened, it would be too late for Robert to follow, even if he wanted to do so.

She would take nothing that Robert had purchased for her. Florilla could have the new clothes, and the ones that Robert had bought from Maggie in Columbia. They were still like new, especially the ermine-trimmed cloak. Eulalie passed it by and retrieved the serviceable black cloak she had worn from the convent. It would be suitable to travel in. And taking the heavy gold band and the ruby ring from her hands, Eulalie placed them on the table beside the bed.

Feena was not happy with Eulalie's decision. "I think, *ma petite,* that you are making a big mistake. Monsieur Robert will never allow you to leave with the children."

Her words caused Eulalie to frown, but nothing Feena said could make Eulalie change her mind. Feena, seeing that Eulalie was adamant, finally gave in and helped her to pack. During their hurried preparation for the journey, Eulalie was relieved that Florilla did not disturb them.

In fact, Eulalie had not seen the fair-headed woman since the scene in the garden the evening before.

When they were ready, the family carriage was brought around to the front of the townhouse, and the two trunks strapped to the back. Soon Zilpah, the wet nurse, Feena, Neijee, Jason and the babies were all inside the carriage, waiting for the trip to commence.

The black manservant held the horses until Eulalie took over the reins. Shaking his head, the man watched the carriage move down the street and disappear from sight.

"Ain't right," he mumbled, "for de mistress to be drivin' those hosses herself." He scratched his head in a perplexed manner and then went into the house, still mumbling to himself.

Past the intersection the carriage traveled, past the orchards of the estates at the edge of the city. Then they were on the sandy road that pointed the way to Midgard.

Hidden by the black cloak, with its hood pulled low, Eulalie was not bothered with questionable glances. No one seemed to notice that it was a woman who guided the horses of the carriage, urging them on to leave the city behind.

They were in the country again and Eulalie slowed the carriage pace. The horses snorted and a steady breeze began to blow . . . .

Robert, with his chestnuts snorting impatiently for the impending race, brought the yellow-and-black phaeton up in line with the others. He made sure that the wheels did not touch either of the phaetons on his right and on his left.

Bets were still being made at the last minute, and curious bystanders had gathered at the point to see them off on the two-mile stretch ending at Hanging Oak.

The pistol fired and the excited horses dashed away, to the cheering of the crowd.

Robert pulled ahead immediately and then slowed his pace so that his horses would not become winded too soon. He looked to his left, and Arthur, who had also jockeyed for a position in the forefront, was coming up fast. They were almost side by side when Robert, glancing toward his friend with a smile on his lips, saw the pin fastened to Arthur's hat. He recognized it. It was the pin Eulalie had worn in her hair the evening before.

Intense anger caused Robert to tighten on the reins, and the surprised horses slowed enough for Arthur to pass Robert. Realizing what he had done, Robert loosened his tight grip. He touched the horses with his whip and spurred them on, for now Robert was determined to leave Arthur in a dry cloudburst of dust.

Just as determined not to eat Robert's dust, Arthur maintained his speed, recklessly matching Robert's. And the race, with ten opponents, fast adjusted into a race between only two men, each one determined to win, with both knowing that they were racing for more than the fat purse waiting for the winner.

Robert's face was taut, his tawny eyes were narrowed, while his horses' hooves made a steady rhythmic cadence upon the sandy road.

People clustered at various points along the race course cheered and shouted as they saw Robert and Arthur, side by side.

The muscles of the horses rippled in foamy sweat— the beautiful grays belonging to Arthur, the magnificent pair of chestnuts owned by Robert. The phaetons' wheels, well oiled, turned with a minimum of sound, and the faces of the two men were grave.

Now the swaying of the trees by the side of the road was the only other movement until a covey of birds, startled at the approach of the vehicles, took wing and flew from a nearby field.

One phaeton edged slightly in front of the other, to be overtaken by the second. Off and on, in a steady duel, the men continued, until the finish line, with its ribbon stretched across the road, became visible in the distance.

Nose to nose, neck to neck, wheel to wheel, the horses and vehicles went, until, in a sudden spurt of speed, Robert's horses pulled ahead, breaking the ribbon a split second before Arthur's. The men continued past the ribbon, gradually slowing their horses to a trot and then to a walking pace. The sand swirled about them, caking their wet horses, coating their phaetons, and settling on their coats.

"It was closer this time, Robert," Arthur said, still at his side. "One day, I will win, you know."

Robert glared at him and in a cold voice said, "I believe you have something that belongs to my wife."

Arthur smiled and removed the pin from his hat. He held it out for Robert, who leaned over quickly to take it. "You must thank Eulalie for letting me wear it," Arthur said. "As you saw, it brought me luck. I have never come this close to beating you before."

Robert wheeled his phaeton away from Arthur, and turning it from the race course, he headed back to town, instead of proceeding to the judges' stand to claim his prize. The spectators gaped at his sudden departure. Robert's hand reached inside his shirt to assure him of Eulalie's handkerchief that had remained hidden throughout the race.

Robert stalked into the townhouse. He was still covered with dust. His throat was raw and thirsty, but the jeweled pin burned in his pocket far worse than the dust in his throat. Robert mounted the stairs rapidly, shouting for Eulalie. She was not going to get away with it—this public humiliation of having another man wear her favors.

"Eulalie," he shouted again.

Sewell, the manservant, appeared at the sound of Robert's voice. "She's not heah, Mr. Robert," he advised him.

"Where is she, Sewell?" he asked impatiently.

"That I don't rightly know, suh. She took the chillun and Feena and the others in the fam'ly carriage, soon after you lef' this mawnin'."

Robert frowned and, looking at the servant, asked, "What else did she take with her, Sewell?"

"Two trunks. I helped her strap 'em to the carriage. But didn't seem right, her drivin' the hosses herself. Musta knowed where she was goin', though."

So she had left him, had she—probably to meet Arthur somewhere. What a fool he had been to leave them alone to make their plans. But Sewell said she was driving the carriage herself. If he had known she was leaving, Arthur would not have allowed her to do that.

Robert stripped the dusty clothes from his large frame and eased himself into the tub of water. He had to wait for his prize chestnuts to be rubbed down before he could use them again. But he had no hesitation about using them. He would start to look for Eulalie as soon as they were rested.

Where could Eulalie go without any money? She had none of her own, except the gold that her cousin, Julie, had given her, and that was locked away in the safe at Midgard. Midgard . . . Robert smiled to himself, and soon he was on his way toward the plantation. The phaeton was much faster than the unwieldy family coach. With that knowledge giving him satisfaction, Robert knew he would catch up with Eulalie sooner than she expected.

CHAPTER

46

THE carriage containing Eulalie, the children and Feena slowly wound its way up Biffers Road and then through the dark bog.

There was a chill in the air, and Eulalie glanced at the dark waters on each side of the road, with the gray moss swinging in the breeze. The sudden shriek of the God A'mighty bird pierced the air, and the horses were startled at the sound.

"Whoa, boys—steady," she called out, drawing the reins up short and soothing the horses until they had calmed down. Then they were out of the bog, into the sunshine. But the chill remained with Eulalie.

Eulalie trembled when she stopped in front of the house. The full impact of the bird's shriek had not hit her while she was so busy containing the horses. Now, it rushed over her, bringing with it the dread feeling that she had tried to forget. The last time she had heard the bird, Alistair Ashe was taking her to Charleston to leave her at the slave market. A bad omen. No, she would not let it affect her. Probably the horses had startled the bird. That was all.

Feena took charge of the retinue, seeing that the babies

were moved into the house. They went toward the nursery, for Maranta and Marigold were already crying with hunger. And soon Eulalie was the only one remaining downstairs.

The house was unusually silent. Bradley was nowhere in sight. Eulalie's steps echoed down the hallway, and like a sleepwalker, she pushed open the door to the drawing room. It was empty, save for her memories. The blue velvet chairs were standing in the same place. And the desk where she had signed the marriage contract with Robert gleamed with its beeswax shine.

Eulalie's eyes saw the empty hearth, and for a moment she imagined it filled with magnolia leaves and the bouquets of yellow jasmine. And the stool that she had embroidered for Papa Ravenal beside it—but that was gone, taken by the British when they had raided the plantation.

From the drawing room, Eulalie walked into the library, her eyes lingering on the window seat where she had sat quietly while Robert had gone over his accounts.

Eulalie brushed her hand across her eyes. What was she doing, reliving all the memories? She must forget—not remember the life with Robert. That was in the past, she thought bitterly. Now, he had Florilla—and Eulalie did not matter to him.

The painting on the wall behind Robert's desk was hanging awry. She reached out to touch it. But then she removed it from the wall to reveal the safe. Eulalie propped the painting against the desk and turned her attention to the safe. How could she get it open? She did not know how. But she must find a way to claim what was hers—the present that Robert had taken from her.

As her hand touched the door, it moved. Surprised, she grasped it and it swung open easily. How could that be? Had it been open all the time? But that was impossible. She knew that Robert kept it locked at all times.

Standing on tiptoe, she thrust her hand into the opening, to feel for the pouch of gold nuggets. Her hands touched papers and nothing else. Her gold was not there.

"So you have added safecracking to your other sins, I see."

The voice startled her, and Eulalie bumped her chin against the wall as she turned around. "R-Robert," she stammered. "How . . . how did you get here?"

"The same way you did, Eulalie. Up Biffers Road."

He walked closer and asked, "What are you looking for, Eulalie?" His eyes danced dangerously and Eulalie was suddenly afraid of him.

"The gold that is mine—nothing more."

"You did not have to break open the safe to get it," he remonstrated. "I told you that you could have it anytime you asked for it."

It was a charade, with Robert standing threateningly over her, laughing at her because the gold was not there. He had put it somewhere else. It made Eulalie furious and, forgetting her fright at seeing him, she turned on him, with her voice showing her anger.

"I don't believe you. You played a trick on me. You put it somewhere else, and all this time you've been waiting for me to fall into your trap. Well, I won't have it, Robert. The gold is mine, and I demand that you give it to me."

Robert reached toward her, and she fought against him, pummeling at his huge chest, until he gripped her hands and drew her against him, making any further movement impossible.

"What are you talking about, Eulalie?" he demanded. "I have not hidden your gold elsewhere."

"Yes, you have. It's not in the safe."

Cautiously he glanced at her and then at the wall safe. And with his hands forcing her to move with him, Robert walked to the safe and peered inside.

"How did you manage to find the key, Eulalie?"

"I didn't. The safe was open when I got here."

Robert freed Eulalie from his grasp and walked to the desk. She watched as he pulled out one of the lower drawers. His hand pressed a piece of wood underneath, and a hidden drawer suddenly sprang open. The drawer was empty.

"The key is gone. Someone else has evidently been at work here in my absence," Robert commented, seeing the empty drawer. He turned again to Eulalie, asking, "Where is Bradley?"

Defensively, Eulalie shrugged and answered, "I don't know. No one was in the house when we got here a few minutes ago."

The fight had gone out of Eulalie, and her knees were still weak. She walked to the window seat and sat down, while Robert went back to the safe.

"I will replace your gold, Eulalie," Robert vowed, "but first, you must tell me why you had to have it." His tones were deceptively smooth, and Eulalie's anger rushed over her again. She jumped from the window seat and faced Robert, with her hands clenched against her skirt.

"I am leaving you, Robert. I will not stay in the same house with you and Florilla. That is asking too much of me."

She should have known better than to admit her plans. Eulalie, swept off her feet, was crushed in Robert's arms, and he made no attempt to disguise his murderous glint.

"Leaving me? No, madame. You have run away from me for the last time. Arthur can cool his heels forever, for all I care. But you will not show up."

"Arthur? What has Arthur to do—"

He did not allow her to finish. His anger grew, and Eulalie pushed against him, at the tightening of his arms encircling her waist like a band of steel.

"The only place you are going is back to Charleston with me, in time for the reception tonight. You didn't think I would allow you to humiliate me publicly for the second time today, did you? You will be at my side to-night, Eulalie—even if I have to tie you to me."

"Robert, I can't breathe. Please—put me down."

His arms slowly relaxed and Eulalie's feet touched the floor. Her breath came in short gasps, and Robert's chest heaved in and out in his anger as they continued to glare at each other. The rebellious look in Eulalie's eyes matched Robert's dangerous gleam.

"Mr. Robert, Mr. Robert." Bradley's agitated voice sliced through the awkward silence of the library, and

Robert reluctantly turned his attention to the man rushing into the room.

"What it is, Bradley?" Robert asked, his voice normal, now that he no longer addressed Eulalie.

"Miss Florilla, suh. The big moccasin in the bog done got 'er. Me and Mr. Gil tried to stop 'er when she took the money from the safe—but it weren't no use. She run into Emma's Bog, tryin' to 'scape us, but the big cottonmouth was waitin' for 'er."

Robert rushed from the room with Bradley, leaving Eulalie behind. When she tried to follow, Robert said, "Stay here, Eulalie. I would rather you didn't see Florilla. She won't be a very pretty sight."

"But I might be able to help," Eulalie offered.

"No, there is nothing you can do."

Eulalie obeyed him and he continued walking with Bradley. She went to the window to watch. At that moment, she saw the overseer, Gil Jordan, walking up the circular drive. In his arms he carried Florilla, her dress dirty and wet from the waters in the bog.

Eulalie shuddered. Robert did not know, but she was well acquainted with the effects of the poison and what it could do to a person. She remembered the husky slave who had been bitten on the heel in the rice fields, and the sudden bloating of his body from the poison before anything could be done for him. And Eulalie knew that Robert was right. There was nothing she could do for Florilla.

The bird had shrieked its dreaded message. Emma's Bog had claimed another victim.

"Put her down on the grass, Gil," Robert said, taking off his waistcoat to make a pillow for the woman's head. Robert knelt beside Florilla, and his eyes stared in pity at the dying woman.

Florilla's lips parted, and her eyes fluttered open. "It seems . . . Eulalie has won, after all I did. You knew, didn't you, Robert?"

"That you were the ghost in the tabby house? Or that you locked Eulalie in the spring room and left her there to die?"

"Both," she admitted.

The muscle in Robert's jaw tightened. "I suspected as much, Florilla," he answered, "after you showed up with Jason at the townhouse."

"That was why I had to get away. And when Clem showed up again . . ." Florilla paused and licked her bloated lips. ". . . I knew it would be best to leave with him. I could never take you away from Eulalie." Florilla's voice became weaker, and Robert leaned over to hear her words. "But I needed the gold. I . . . almost made it too. If Clem hadn't left me to save himself . . ."

Her body gave one last shudder and then the woman's cornflower-blue eyes closed. Her hand still clutched the bag of gold nuggets belonging to Eulalie.

Robert stood and addressed his overseer, and Eulalie, still watching from the window, saw her unsmiling husband walk back to the house.

He had not wanted Eulalie to share his last moments with the woman he loved. What had she said to him? Had Florilla declared her love for him with her dying breath?

Subdued in the face of death, Eulalie listened for Robert's footsteps. He stood at the door, and in a strange voice he said, "Put on your nun's cloak, Eulalie. We are going back into Charleston."

She did as she was told. Leaving the children and Feena behind, she followed Robert to the phaeton, and they retraced the wheel marks along Biffers Road, through the dark bog, and onto the sandy road that pointed the way to the port city. No words were exchanged between them. Robert and Eulalie were both absorbed by their own thoughts.

Meanwhile, Feena, hearing what had happened, smiled to herself and hurried to her cabin along the long path to the rice fields. She opened the cupboard door and pulled out the doll, unwrapping the snakeskin from the wax image. She crumbled the skin over the logs in the open hearth and placed the wax image on top before lighting the fire.

The wax melted, and Feena watched while the doll disappeared, the blond hair and the wax giving off a singeing, tallow odor. Then she put out the fire and left the cabin.

The last time she would ever make black magic. There was now no need. Her *petite Lili* was safe from the evil woman.

CHAPTER
47

"YOU will get dressed at once, Eulalie," Robert said, climbing the stairs of the townhouse. "Since you are to be Joseph's official hostess, we cannot afford to keep him waiting."

Eulalie stopped and stared in disbelief at Robert. "That can't be true."

"I assure you that it is. But knowing how skittish you are about social functions, I neglected to tell you earlier, when it was decided."

He kept his hand on her arm and led her up the stairs to the bedroom. He was treating her as if she were a prisoner, not to be let out of his sight.

"Since you seem to have planned everything else, perhaps you will tell me what you have planned for me to wear," Eulalie said.

"Your dress is already waiting for you, across the bed. And if Sewell has followed my instructions, there will also be hot water for your bath."

Before Robert left the room, he glared down at his wife and said, "I will be in the other room. If you dare to run away while I am dressing, I vow I will break every bone in your body."

"You . . . you do not have to threaten me, Robert. I will be dressed and ready in time."

"See that you are," he said before closing the door.

Her eyes wandered to the bed where the ballgown lay. Of shimmering pale green, it was even lovelier than the dress she had tried on in Mrs. Windom's shop. But she did not stop to examine it. She hurried on to the old brass tub behind the screen, for she knew she must not waste time. Eulalie removed her dusty clothes and, sinking into the warm water, reached for the jasmine-scented soap.

How could Robert be so callous? The woman he loved was dead, and yet he was still planning to go to the reception as if nothing had happened. She did not understand her husband. Did he have no heart at all? Or was he hiding his grief well?

Eulalie stepped out of the water and dried herself with the towel that lay nearby. Barefooted, she walked across the room and selected undergarments that were part of the new wardrobe Robert had ordered. Silk stockings, dainty slippers to match the dress, and finally the ballgown itself, slipping over her head, and she was almost dressed. Unable to fasten the dress together in the back, Eulalie dashed to the dressing table to fix her hair, for she heard Robert's footsteps.

"You are ready, Eulalie?" he asked, coming into the room.

"Almost, Robert. I will need your help in getting my dress fastened, just as soon as I finish braiding my hair."

Eulalie quickly wound it around her head in a coronet, securing it with a plain pin. It was severe, and she wondered if Robert would be disappointed in the way she looked.

Before she turned from the mirror, Eulalie felt Robert's hands moving around her throat and fastening a clasp at the neck. Surprised, she stared into the mirror and saw the necklace—a strand of emeralds, with one magnificent emerald hanging as a pendant between her breasts. And then Robert deftly removed the plain pin from her hair and replaced it with the matching emerald clip.

"Robert, they are . . . beautiful," Eulalie said. "Did you buy them to go with the dress?" she asked.

"No, Eulalie. I have had them for some time. They belonged to my grandmother." He hesitated, and then in a voice tinged with a slight impatience, he said, "There is another piece—a bracelet—that I was foolish enough to part with, but I am now negotiating for its return."

Eulalie stood, and Robert's hands moved to fasten the hooks of her dress. He turned her around to face him, and the muscle in his jaw twitched. She could not tell if he were pleased with her appearance or not, for he said nothing.

Picking up the matching shawl from the bed, Robert finally said, "Come, Eulalie. It's late."

He was elegant in his formal evening clothes, and Eulalie, without meaning to, cast a surreptitious glance toward him while they walked down the stairs.

This time, Sewell was waiting at the phaeton to drive them, and Eulalie, handed up by Robert, moved to the edge of the seat to make room for her husband.

"Who will be at the reception?" Eulalie asked, her hands suddenly clasping her shawl to draw it around her.

"Many of the wives that you met in Columbia, since this is a political affair—and some of the landowners and merchants here in the city. And of course, Calhoun, Langdon and Cheves."

At the mention of Columbia, Eulalie looked up at Robert. "I . . . don't think I can go, Robert. I'm . . . afraid."

"You need be afraid of no one, Eulalie. As Joseph's hostess, you will be the most important woman there."

"But . . ." she still persisted.

"Are you going to be afraid because of the rumors Alistair Ashe spread? He's dead, Eulalie."

"But, Polly, his wife," Eulalie replied. "She's still spreading the same rumors. That day in Mrs. Windom's shop—" Eulalie put her hand to her mouth. She had never intended to tell Robert about it.

"So that was what made you leave the shop so hurriedly. I had wondered."

Suddenly he asked, "Eulalie, who was your grandfather?"

"Why, the Comte de Boisfeulet. But you knew that, Robert," she answered, puzzled that he should ask her such a question.

"Yes, I knew. But I think you need to be reminded, Eulalie, that you have more aristocratic blood in your little finger than almost the entire assembly tonight." Then his words were harsh. "Are you going to cower, just because someone has spread rumors about you?"

Eulalie lifted her chin. He had made her angry. So he thought she was going to be a coward, did he? Well, she would show him. Just wait. She would show him.

Eulalie held her head high as she walked with Robert across Colleton Square. The mansion, facing the Cooper River, was made of Carolina brick. The house stood tall, above the curving stone steps with four white columns across the open portico.

Up the steps Eulalie and Robert walked, and the door into the entry hall opened immediately. Inside stood Joseph Alston.

"I am happy to see you, my dear," he said, taking in Eulalie's green silk gown and the magnificent emeralds, enhanced by the glow of tapered candles in the chandeliers. "Thank you, Robert, for lending her to me." The dark-haired man's eyes twinkled as he faced Robert.

"It's only for the next few hours, Joseph. I trust you will remember that."

Joseph laughed and slapped the golden-haired giant on his back. Turning to Eulalie, Joseph explained, "We'll be in the garden for about an hour, my dear, and after the crowd disperses, we will come back into the house. A smaller group has been invited for supper and dancing later."

Eulalie nodded and walked between Joseph and her husband to the garden. They took their places near the gates, and at Joseph's signal, the servants opened the gates and the crowd filed in.

Robert stood at the side, his topaz eyes watching his wife, who now acted as if she were a princess, regally seeing to her duty. Graceful and beautiful, she stood, exchanging a few brief words with each one and then seeing that each person moved on down the line to where the three War Hawks stood—Calhoun, Langdon and Cheves, the giant of a man who was even taller than Robert.

"I am surprised that you have not already snatched her up to take her home."

Arthur's voice, low and amused, sounded in Robert's ear.

Robert laughed and said, "I do not mind if others look. That is harmless enough. Just so they know Eulalie is mine, and that I will never give her up."

He looked at Arthur, and the blond-haired man smiled. "I think you have made that clear, Robert, from your actions. No one would dare challenge you on that."

Arthur walked on, greeting Joseph Alston and then stopping before Eulalie. Robert frowned until Arthur moved on to speak with Calhoun and his wife, Floride.

On and on the people came, and Robert was content to watch Eulalie. Her eyes lit up when she saw Anna deLong and her husband, and then they became more sober as some of the women who had snubbed her in Columbia passed by. But Eulalie, gracious to all, did not falter or cringe, and Robert was proud of her for that.

In amusement, Robert saw Crowley and his wife, Maggie, who had owned the dress shop in Columbia. Crowley, with his hand possessively on Maggie's arm, seemed much aware of his own sartorial splendor. As they stopped in front of Eulalie, Maggie's expansive arms reached out to hug the diminutive Eulalie.

Every few minutes, Robert glanced toward the gates, while speaking to those around him. And then he saw them—Julie and Desmond.

Julie was walking—slowly and falteringly, but her steps would improve with time. It was the miracle that Desmond had prayed for.

"Julie," Eulalie said in surprise, when the beautiful dark-haired woman reached her. "I did not know you were to be here."

The two women embraced each other, and Eulalie,

all at once realizing that Julie was not in Desmond's arms but at his side, said in wonder, "You're . . . you're walking!"

Her dark-brown eyes glistened with tears, as Julie acknowledged the miracle.

"Not well, as you can see, Eulalie, but at least I am on my feet."

"This time next year, she will be able to dance all night, if she wants to," Desmond said, his loving glance falling on his dark-haired wife.

"But . . . but you didn't write me," Eulalie protested.

"When I knew we were coming, I decided not to write about it. I wanted to surprise you, my dear."

Desmond, with an anxious look at his wife, said, "You do not have to go through the rest of the line, Julie. I am sure you will be forgiven if you need to rest awhile now."

"You see, he still watches over me, Eulalie," Julie said. "And I must obey. But I will talk with you later, since we are staying for supper. Our son is with us, and I want you to see him."

On and on the crowds passed through the garden, which was now beginning to become chilly, until Joseph, his hand under Eulalie's elbow, guided her back to the house. The reception was over and the supper and ball could begin.

Hector had not returned from Flat Rock in time for the reception, and the only other person that Robert had hoped to see who was not present was Ebenezer Shaw, with his wife, Jessie. Robert supposed that Shaw was too new to the role of landowner and merchant to be at ease. But that would come with time. He must remember to tell Eulalie that he had made Shaw a partner at the mill.

Throughout supper, Eulalie listened and commented when she was called upon to do so. But it had been a long day, and the events had left her tired and sad—the trip to Midgard with the children, the forced return in Robert's phaeton, Florilla's accident. All these began to crowd in on her, but still, as hostess, she was obliged to dance nearly every dance.

Her anger at Robert had long since abated. But the

hurt was still there, for he had not come near her. He had vowed that he would not be humiliated publicly for the second time that day by Eulalie. But what of her? Was she to be humiliated by him? He had not bothered to claim one dance with his wife.

Eulalie wanted to go home. Her strength was ebbing and her sadness threatened to overwhelm her.

Robert, seeing Eulalie's face losing its vivacity and becoming paler by the minute, decided to wait no longer.

"Joseph, I have not complained once all evening," Robert began. "But now I wish this last dance with my wife before I take her home."

Joseph bowed to Eulalie and said, "If your mother had not turned down my cousin when he offered marriage, we would have been related, Eulalie. Then I could bid you good night with a cousinly kiss. But I suppose, with your husband looking on, this will have to do." He took her hand in his and looked into her brown eyes.

"Thank you, my dear, for standing in for my beloved Theo." He kissed her hand and then walked away.

The music was beginning, and Robert swept Eulalie onto the ballroom floor. The candles in the chandeliers burned low, and the rich green paper on the wall served as a suitable background for Eulalie in the shimmering, elegant dress and the family emeralds about her neck.

And Eulalie, her pride salvaged, remained in Robert's arms until he steered her toward the open door to the top of the stairs.

The servant at the door to the street handed her shawl to Robert and, putting it around her shoulders, Robert led Eulalie down the steps to the phaeton where Sewell waited.

CHAPTER

48

"YOU did well, Eulalie," Robert voiced when they were in the bedroom of the townhouse. "And I trust you were sufficiently aware of your success, for every woman present would gladly have traded her fondest dreams to be in your place of honor beside Joseph tonight." His words, spoken with a slight irony, incensed Eulalie.

She turned on him, and Robert was surprised at the angry spark in her brown eyes. "Dreams? What do you know of a woman's dreams, Robert? I grew up with the same dreams as every other young Creole girl. Yet, for me, they can never come true.

"Do you think a beautiful gown matters? Or jewels?" She touched the emerald between her breasts. "Or a chance to regain one's honor? All that means nothing if a woman's love is rejected."

A bleak look clouded Robert's eyes. "Arthur loves you, Eulalie. That is certain. But I will never give you up to him."

"Arthur? What are you talking about, Robert?"

"I will not allow Arthur to take you from me."

Incredulously, she looked at her husband. "Do you think it is . . . *Arthur* that I love?"

"Surely you cannot be speaking of that bastard lover of yours, Jacques Binet. It has to be Arthur."

Eulalie, now more exasperated than ever, gazed at Robert, and no longer caring to choose her words wisely, she answered, "Jacques Binet was never my lover except in your imagination, Robert. How could he be, when I was deathly ill from seasickness the entire trip to New Orleans? Every time he came near me, my head was in the pail."

"You do not expect me to believe that he never touched you?" He gazed at Eulalie with doubt and distaste in his tawny eyes.

"I don't care *what* you believe, Robert. But the man was never my lover. Oh, he tried to be, that first night he . . . bought me. But he was in a drunken stupor, and nothing happened."

Eulalie's face was flushed with anger, and her dark eyes dangerously alight. Robert saw this, but he kept on. "If it was not Arthur, or Jacques Binet, then who?"

He suddenly pulled her to him, trapping her in his arms, and his tawny eyes were ablaze. "Who is it that you love, Eulalie? I demand to know."

All attempts to hide behind her pride were gone. Flinging the words at him, she said, "Do you get some perverse pleasure in making me say it to your face? That despite your loving Florilla, despite your selling me as a slave, despite your highhanded ways and humiliation of me at every turn, and knowing you were forced into marrying me, it's *you* I love, and always will."

Her head drooped against his chest, and she fought the tears that were forming. His final humiliation of her— to make her say to him what she had been determined to keep from him.

The gentle kiss on her forehead confirmed his pity for her, and Eulalie pushed against him, struggling to get free. But he held her and would not let her go.

A soft voice whispered in her ear. "What ever possessed you to think that I . . . cared for Florilla?"

"I saw you in the garden with her, Robert. You kissed her and went on behind the carriage house with her."

"When was that, Eulalie?"

"The . . . the night you were to take me to the theater."

"Do you think I could ever love someone who tried to harm you? Who locked you in the tabby house and left you there to die?"

"But you planned to marry her, Robert, before I came from the convent and . . . and spoiled it all."

"*Marry* Florilla? How did you get such an idea, Eulalie?"

She was silent, and he repeated the question, more urgently the second time.

"She . . . told me, when we were at Cedar Hill."

Robert slapped his forehead with his hand. "I think Florilla must have done more damage than I ever thought possible. We will have to sift this out later. But I want you to know, Eulalie. I did not meet Florilla in the garden that night, and I never entertained the thought of marrying the woman. Have my actions been so deceiving that you never guessed what I was going through, thinking that you hated me and wanted to leave me . . . frantically trying to find some way of keeping you beside me?"

Robert, looking down at his wife, spoke to her tenderly. "From the moment I met you, I was like a man without a will. I loved you the first time I saw you in the slave nursery. And when I realized what I had done to you—my own wife—I was in hell, searching frantically for you. I could not believe my eyes when you appeared in your little nun's habit in *my* house. To be given a chance to make up for all the hurt I had caused you. Yet, I was determined not to touch you, thinking you had been the mistress of another man. And then even my damnable pride was stamped into the ground by one look of your seductive brown eyes. I could not keep my hands off you. My pride was broken. All I could think of was making love to you again. And I hated myself for having no better control over my desire. Just as now, I want to kiss you and continue to hold you in my arms." His voice, hoarse, was almost to the point of breaking. "And to make love to you again." His embrace tightened and his lips found hers.

Confused at his words, Eulalie did not respond. She turned her head and placed her hand against his lips.

What was Robert saying? That he had loved her from the first moment he had seen her? That was impossible. Eulalie looked up at Robert and shook her head. "But Sir George—you said you hated him because he was responsible for our marriage," Eulalie refuted.

He removed her hand from his lips and spoke. "No, Eulalie. I hated him because he took my ship from me—not because of our marriage."

Robert found her lips again, silencing her, and with his admission ringing in her ears, Eulalie responded to him. He loved her.

His hands slid to her throat and caressed the curve of her neck, before moving to the back of her dress and unfastening the hooks. The dress slid to the floor with her chemise, and Eulalie, wearing nothing but the emerald pendant, clung to her husband as he carried her to the bed.

He covered her face with kisses, and with desire in his eyes, he lifted his head and looked at her. Gently he removed the emerald clip and unwound her hair, and then removed the emerald pendant from her neck.

Eulalie's hands unbuttoned Robert's shirt—to feel his flesh next to hers—and Robert moaned at the meshing of their bodies. Then he came to his senses. Robert abruptly stopped. He stumbled from the bed and stood with his back to Eulalie. He began to button his shirt that she had unfastened.

"Robert?" Eulalie called, her head lifting from the pillow. "What is wrong?"

His rapid breathing was the only sound, until his strangled voice came to her. "I cannot make love to you. Not now, or ever again. I made a vow on the island."

Eulalie sat up, and slipping from the bed to walk to Robert, she put her hand on his arm. "Are you afraid to make love to me, Robert?"

His haunted topaz eyes looked into hers. "Yes," he whispered fiercely. Then he confessed in a more even voice, "I deliberately set out to make you pregnant, so that you could not leave me for Arthur. But because of my selfishness, you almost died. Eulalie, I could not bear to lose you again."

"I am not afraid, Robert, for you to love me," she said gently, leading him back to bed. "I am strong, and *want* to bear your children. Don't deny me, Robert."

"Eulalie!" His voice broke with emotion as he lifted her against his massive golden chest and lowered her to the bed.

Her hands reached around his neck, drawing him down to her. It had been so long since she had felt his flesh upon hers. Robert's hands caressed her body, and his kisses began their sensuous route from her mouth to her breasts and downward, beginning the exquisite torture that she had tried to put out of her mind.

The scar across his chest was a small imperfection of his otherwise perfect body—the outward mark of his search for her, and he was dearer to her because of it. Forgotten were all the hurts, all the misunderstandings. Only one thing mattered. Robert loved her. And because of it, she could show her love for him, willing him to love her with every ounce of his strength.

The bed protested, the candle flickered, and still their bodies enveloped each other, becoming one—without hesitation, without regret. Violent in its intensity, his loving brought back the time in the river house, when Robert had first initiated her into love's ecstasy.

Robert trembled and a shudder rippled through his body. The wave of desire mounted in Eulalie. No part of her body was exempt, her mouth, her breasts, her thighs. She felt release, and her moan matched her husband's.

"I . . . love you, Robert," she whispered, with his head now resting on her breast. And in answer, he took her mouth again, and between kisses, now gentle and without the violent passion of a few moments before, he murmured all the endearments he had stored in his mind for the one woman he had ever loved.

"Lili," he whispered, before falling asleep with Eulalie still in his arms.

He was already awake when she opened her eyes. Propped on one elbow, Robert stared down at her while he brushed aside the long wavy hair from her face. She sleepily met the triumphant gleam in his tawny topaz eyes, and then Eulalie promptly closed her eyes again.

"Wake up, Eulalie. We have many plans to make today," he said.

"Let us finish sleeping, Robert," she murmured, snuggling deeper into the pillow.

"No, Eulalie. You have slept long enough. It's past time to get up. And besides, I want to finish our conversation from last night. You said you had the same dreams as every other Creole girl in growing up. I am curious to know what they were, Eulalie."

"It is not important, Robert. I am no longer a young girl, but a . . . a matron with children. It is time for girlish dreams to be put aside."

"Tell me, Eulalie," he insisted. "I want to know."

He would not rest until she told him. Eulalie sighed. "They are mainly three, Robert," she informed him while sitting up. "The first, to be presented to society at the Théâtre d'Orléans in a Parisian gown—I was not correct when I said the gown didn't matter—and surrounded by suitors eager for her hand."

Robert frowned. "I will take you to the theater, Eulalie. But it will have to be here in Charleston, and not in New Orleans. And you may have your Parisian gown. But as for suitors, I'm afraid that part of your dream will have to go unrealized . . . And the next?" he prompted.

She hesitated before replying. Then in a low voice, she said, "To have men fight a duel over her."

Soberly, he nodded. "That has been fulfilled . . . and the third?"

Eulalie suddenly giggled. "A Creole honeymoon, complete with charivari."

"Charivari? What is that?" he asked cautiously.

"Creoles do not go away for their honeymoons, but instead remain together in a bedroom for five days and nights, without leaving it. And a servant slips food to them outside the door at various times during the day."

She hastily continued, "And that first night . . . their friends and well-wishers make a lot of noise under their bedroom window, with all manner of noisemakers—whistles, pots, pans and anything else. That's a charivari."

Robert laughed at her description. "And where would you like our Creole honeymoon to take place, Eulalie?"

"I told you, Robert. That is not necessary." Eulalie was suddenly shy.

"Oh, but I insist. Shall it be the river house, Eulalie?" His eyes were tender, and his voice soft in her ear.

"If you wish, Robert."

"And I think we can enlist Jason and Neijee to rattle a few pots and pans under the window," he added.

"Oh, Robert, you make it sound so . . . so senseless," she said, laughing.

"Dreams are never senseless, Eulalie. For I, too, have had my dreams."

"And yours, Robert?" Eulalie asked, her dark doe eyes now void of mirth, watching while she waited for his answer.

"Mine came true last night—when you hurled those words in my face—that you loved me." Teasingly, he said, "You have not changed your mind, have you, Eulalie?"

With her love for him making her eyes velvet soft, she replied, "No, Robert. I have not changed my mind . . ."

The harvest moon hung low over the river house, and Robert lay quietly, listening to the sounds of the river and the forest. In his arms, Eulalie slept, a strand of her long hair across his chest.

Just as the stag in the forest would leave his jasmine-scented bower, so too Robert would have to leave Midgard. The war with the British was worsening and the Indian uprising in the south could no longer be ignored.

Robert had not told Eulalie that he would be leaving to fight the Creeks as soon as he returned from Columbia. There was time for that later. For now, he was content with Eulalie beside him. His arms tightened around her and she stirred.

"Robert, I . . . love you," Eulalie whispered sleepily.

The yellow glow disappeared through the trees. The season of the mad moon was over. Yet, no season could limit Robert's love. No season would find his ardor lessened.

"Lili," he called to her and his lips found hers, while the jasmine scent surrounding the river house floated upward on wings of the gentle autumn breeze.

Romantic Fiction

If you like novels of passion and daring adventure that take you to the very heart of human drama, these are the books for you.

☐ AFTER—Anderson	Q2279	1.50
☐ THE DANCE OF LOVE—Dodson	23110-0	1.75
☐ A GIFT OF ONYX—Kettle	23206-9	1.50
☐ TARA'S HEALING—Giles	23012-0	1.50
☐ THE DEFIANT DESIRE—Klem	13741-4	1.75
☐ LOVE'S TRIUMPHANT HEART—Ashton	13771-6	1.75
☐ MAJORCA—Dodson	13740-6	1.75

Buy them at your local bookstores or use this handy coupon for ordering:

FAWCETT BOOKS GROUP, 1 Fawcett Place, P.O. Box 1014, Greenwich, Ct. 06830

Please send me the books I have checked above. Orders for less than 5 books must include 60¢ for the first book and 25¢ for each additional book to cover mailing and handling. Postage is FREE for orders of 5 books or more. Check or money order only. Please include sales tax.

Name_____
Address_____
City_____State/Zip_____

Books $_____
Postage _____
Sales Tax _____
Total $_____

Please allow 4 to 5 weeks for delivery. This offer expires 12/78

Dorothy Eden

*Ms. Eden's novels have enthralled millions of readers for
many years. Here is your chance to order any or all of her
bestselling titles direct by mail.*

☐	AN AFTERNOON WALK	23072-4	1.75
☐	DARKWATER	23153-4	1.75
☐	THE HOUSE ON HAY HILL	X2839	1.75
☐	LADY OF MALLOW	23167-4	1.75
☐	THE MARRIAGE CHEST	23032-5	1.50
☐	MELBURY SQUARE	22973-4	1.75
☐	THE MILLIONAIRE'S DAUGHTER	23186-0	1.95
☐	NEVER CALL IT LOVING	23143-7	1.95
☐	RAVENSCROFT	22998-X	1.50
☐	THE SHADOW WIFE	22802-9	1.50
☐	SIEGE IN THE SUN	Q2736	1.50
☐	SLEEP IN THE WOODS	23075-9	1.75
☐	SPEAK TO ME OF LOVE	22735-9	1.75
☐	THE TIME OF THE DRAGON	23059-7	1.95
☐	THE VINES OF YARRABEE	23184-4	1.95
☐	WAITING FOR WILLA	23187-9	1.50
☐	WINTERWOOD	23185-2	1.75

Buy them at your local bookstores or use this handy coupon for ordering:

FAWCETT BOOKS GROUP, 1 Fawcett Place, P.O. Box 1014, Greenwich, Ct.06830

Please send me the books I have checked above. Orders for less than 5
books must include 60¢ for the first book and 25¢ for each additional book to
cover mailing and handling. Postage is FREE for orders of 5 books or more.
Check or money order only. Please include sales tax.

Name_____   Books $_____
Address_____   Postage _____
City_____State/Zip_____   Sales Tax _____
                                          Total $_____

Please allow 4 to 5 weeks for delivery. This offer expires 12/78

Jean Plaidy

"Miss Plaidy is also, of course, Victoria Holt."—PUBLISHERS WEEKLY

☐	BEYOND THE BLUE MOUNTAINS	22773-1	1.95
☐	CAPTIVE QUEEN OF SCOTS	.23287-5	1.75
☐	THE CAPTIVE OF KENSINGTON PALACE	23413-4	1.75
☐	THE GOLDSMITH'S WIFE	22891-6	1.75
☐	HERE LIES OUR SOVEREIGN LORD	23256-5	1.75
☐	LIGHT ON LUCREZIA	23108-9	1.75
☐	MADONNA OF THE SEVEN HILLS	23026-0	1.75

Buy them at your local bookstores or use this handy coupon for ordering:

Mary Stewart

In 1960, Mary Stewart won the British Crime Writers Association Award, and in 1964 she won the Mystery Writers of America "Edgar" Award. Her bestselling novels continue to captivate her many readers.

☐	AIRS ABOVE THE GROUND	23077-5	1.75
☐	THE CRYSTAL CAVE	23315-4	1.95
☐	THE GABRIEL HOUNDS	22971-8	1.75
☐	THE HOLLOW HILLS	23316-2	1.95
☐	THE IVY TREE	23251-4	1.75
☐	MADAM, WILL YOU TALK?	23250-6	1.75
☐	THE MOON-SPINNERS	23073-2	1.75
☐	MY BROTHER MICHAEL	22974-2	1.75
☐	NINE COACHES WAITING	23121-6	1.75
☐	THIS ROUGH MAGIC	22846-0	1.75
☐	THUNDER ON THE RIGHT	23100-3	1.75
☐	WILDFIRE AT MIDNIGHT	23317-0	1.75

Buy them at your local bookstores or use this handy coupon for ordering:

FAWCETT BOOKS GROUP, 1 Fawcett Place, P.O. Box 1014, Greenwich, Ct.06830

Please send me the books I have checked above. Orders for less than 5 books must include 60¢ for the first book and 25¢ for each additional book to cover mailing and handling. Postage is FREE for orders of 5 books or more. Check or money order only. Please include sales tax.

Name_____

Address_____

City_____State/Zip_____

Books $_____
Postage _____
Sales Tax _____
Total $_____

Please allow 4 to 5 weeks for delivery. This offer expires 12/78